ECHOES FROM A FALLING BRIDGE

Also by Toni Morgan

Harvest the Wind
Lotus Blossom Unfurling
Queenie's Place
Two-Hearted Crossing
Patrimony

ECHOES
FROM A
FALLING BRIDGE

A Novel By

TONI MORGAN

Adelaide Books
New York / Lisbon
2018

Echoes from a Falling Bridge
a novel
by Toni Morgan

Copyright © 2018 By Toni Morgan

Published by Adelaide Books, New York / Lisbon
An imprint of the Istina Group DBA
adelaidebooks.org

Editor-in-Chief
Stevan V. Nikolic

For any information, please address Adelaide Books
at info@adelaidebooks.org

ISBN13: 978-0-9996451-2-3
ISBN10: 0-9996451-2-9

Printed in the United States of America

For the late Toshio Nibu, MD, and Nobuko Nibu.
Thank you.

Acknowledgements

Although the characters in this book are figments of my imagination, the richness of my years in Japan, my love of the people and their culture, led to this novel.

I am indebted to the many friends I made there, friends who took me into their homes and shared their knowledge of their country's culture. They took me to Hagi to see where pottery first came to Japan from Korea, to museums, shrines, and events. I will never forget their many kindnesses to me and my family. Anything I got wrong in this novel is on me, not them.

Most of all, I am indebted to the men and women who worked at the Iwakuni Pottery Factory. Every Thursday for over three years, they generously welcomed me into their lives and taught me how to throw pots—starting with what seemed like a million cups!

Toni Morgan

Contents

BOOK THREE: *Echoes from a Falling Bridge, 1997-1998*

BOOK ONE

Murder Comes to a Mountain Village

1997

1
THE SENSEI
Hirotaka

People called him *sensei*. Honored teacher. He'd been called it for so many years, he sometimes needed to remind himself he was still Hirotaka Katsuragawa. But he didn't think of names or titles. He ignored the beauty of the morning—the cloudless sky, the gold and red autumn leaves, the earthy aroma of harvested rice. Instead, as he made his slow way down the mountain track to the village of Nishimi and the pottery factory at its center, a journey he'd made countless times over the past sixty years, he pondered the desire for change that resided in the hearts of many young people—specifically in the heart of Kazuhiro Yoshida, Nishimi Pottery's current owner. He still contemplated this perplexity when he reached the factory.

Yoko Yoshida looked up from her position on one of two low tatami-covered packing platforms. The *sensei* found himself taken back to the first time he'd seen her. Just as now, she'd been kneeling on the packing platform. How young they'd been.

She squinted at him through the smoke from a cigarette hanging at the corner of her mouth. "*Ohayou gozaimasu,* sensei."

He grunted good morning in return, slipped out of his jacket and unhooked his glasses from behind his ears. He pulled a cloth from his pocket and polished the round lenses one at a time before returning the glasses to his face. He adjusted his black beret.

At last satisfied with his appearance, he turned to Yoko. "Where is Kazuhiro this morning?"

"Gone to the bank, sensei," she said, in the semi-hoarse voice of a habitual smoker. Nicotine had stained a faint yellowish moustache on her upper lip.

"How does it look for the loan he seeks?" The *sensei's* eyes never left hers as he waited for her to reply.

Yoko rose, shrugging. "He never tells me anything about money."

Beneath her seeming indifference, the sensei detected a flicker of resentment. "You're his mother. I thought he would confide in you."

Her mouth drew down. She shook her head. "No. *Gomenasai.* I can't help you." She squatted and returned to packing a teapot and two small cups into a partitioned wooden box, each item in its own nest of coiled wood shavings. Her movements were quick and efficient, belying her advanced years.

The sensei frowned, sure he'd seen anger in her eyes before she bent to her task. Then again, it may have simply been Yoko in one of her moods. More than likely the latter. He excused himself and left through the door at the back of the showroom.

Careful to grasp the handrail, worn smooth by the passage of time and hands, he stepped down to the production area of the factory, where the smell of damp earth greeted him. To his right, Sano, the factory's master potter, sat on a wooden platform opposite three other potters. To his left, an apprentice wedged a large lump of clay, preparing it for use by forcing out air bubbles. Another apprentice carried a long wooden plank loaded with newly thrown soba bowls to the drying room.

Little in the factory had changed since the first time the sensei had witnessed it, except that in 1940, most of the workers had been women. All the able-bodied village men had been conscripted and sent to fight the war in China, including Yoko Yoshida's husband.

Time had not changed the sensei's opinion of Takeda Yoshida. An evil man, he'd come home from the war seemingly intent on making life miserable for everyone in the village, perhaps no one more so than Yoko. Then one day he'd vanished. The police were called in, but because of Takeda's history of disappearing for days or weeks at a time, their efforts had been half-hearted. No one in the village had seen or heard from him in the years since.

With little effort, the sensei put thoughts of Takeda aside, and crossed the packed-earth floor to Sano's work station. Sano glanced up at his approach and lifted his foot from the wheel's pedal. It slowed and stopped.

"Sensei, did you hear? Kazuhiro has gone to the bank again."

"When do you think, he will find out if they will grant him a loan?"

Sano straightened, his round face looking serious. "Today, I hope. I need more money, or I will need to find work elsewhere."

"But Sano-san, you've worked here since you were a teenager, as your father and grandmother did before you.

Where would you go?" He left unsaid another important question: who would throw the large pots and platters he needed?

"I'm not sure what I'll do, but I've told Kazuhiro. My wife wants a child."

Everyone knew Sano's wife couldn't conceive and that the high cost of fertility treatments had drained most of the couple's resources. The sensei understood their desire for offspring—if they didn't have a child, there would be no one to pray for their souls when they died. Still....

He looked toward the wide-spread sliding doors at the far end of the factory. The opening framed Toshio Hara's farm. Often, he'd seen Toshio's son or daughter-in-law struggling to push a wheelbarrow up the steep path to the higher terraces or down the lane to the rice paddy. A shouted "hoi" or the bark of the dog chained in the yard sometimes drifted on the mountain air.

He returned his attention to Sano. "What is wrong with the way things are? With all the changes Kazuhiro plans, there will be too much activity and too many people getting in our way." He rubbed the back of his neck. "Maybe it is time for me to retire and tend to my chrysanthemums."

Sano shook his head. "You must not think that, sensei. With the improvements, Nishimi Pottery will become famous. Your fame will spread even farther than it already is. Wouldn't you like that?"

The sensei needed no time to consider Sano's question; everything Sano and Kazuhiro desired, he hoped would never transpire. He gave a slight shake of his head. "What am I to paint on today?"

"There are orders for three large platters and two vases. I've put them on the shelf in the drying room, near the door." Sano pressed his foot on the pedal. The electric wheel began turning and he bent once more to his work.

The sensei found the pieces Sano had directed him to and carried one of the leather-hard platters up the steps to the showroom. He set it on the cleared-off end of one of the packing platforms and arranged his brushes and pots of colored slip around it.

Just like the production area, little had changed here in the years since his first visit. What passed for the factory office—a filing cabinet and a battered desk—lay at one end of the space. In the showroom portion, rows of gleaming pottery were on shelves lining the walls, on the rough concrete floor and stacked in the centers of both packing platforms. The showroom and the office were the only places where Yoko and her assistant stayed ahead in the constant war they waged against clay dust.

He settled onto a low stool next to the packing platform, briefly turning his mind to the changes Kazuhiro and Sano sought. Nothing he could do or say would change the outcome. He sighed, picked up his brush and dipped it into a pot of slip.

A famous local battle scene seemed to leap onto the platter. The figure of a sixteenth century samurai, clad in helmet and full armor, dominated a background of mountain crags and peaks—the same crags and peaks visible from the road in front of the factory. Below the samurai's helmet rode a hawk-mask with a jutting beak and bristling mustache, designed to generate panic in the beholder. With a few strokes of the brush, the flowing tail of the samurai's horse emerged, its front hoofs pawing the air above rows of foot warriors clashing in the foreground.

He put down the brush. With the minimal lines of the classic *sumi-e* artist, he had created a complex scene. Kazuhiro would be pleased—the platter, after firing, would fetch a handsome profit for each of them.

The young woman who assisted Yoko interrupted his satisfied musings. "Time for break, *sensei*. You must stop now."

With a start, he realized he'd worked well into the afternoon.

The young woman dusted off a folding chair for him and set it close to the kerosene space heater. He settled, and she handed him a cup of tea. Yoko turned on the small television set atop the filing cabinet. On it, two young female contestants in school uniforms screamed and jumped in response to a game show host's questions.

Moments later, the door from the production area slid open and Sano and his co-workers filed into the office. Sano took one of the desk chairs while the other four arranged themselves on the nearest packing platform, careful to avoid the stacked boxes and pottery in the middle. The young woman passed around tea and bean-paste filled pastries.

When the bell above the outside door jangled, everyone turned expectant faces to it. Kazuhiro Yoshida entered. Like his father before him, Kazuhiro stood a head taller than most men. A handsome man, he sported a luxurious beard and a headful of thick black hair he routinely had curled at a shop in Sakayama.

He pulled out the remaining desk chair and sat. "Good. I've not missed tea time."

The young woman handed him a cup of tea and a pastry. He blew on the pale green liquid before taking a loud sip from the tiny cup cradled in his large hand. Everyone remained silent, waiting for him to speak.

A satisfied smile curled his lips. "We're going to be famous."

"You got the loan!" Sano leapt to his feet and snapped off the television.

"Not yet," Kazuhiro said into the transfixed silence. "They're still going through the paperwork, adding numbers, counting their profits. But soon, they told me, I will know —perhaps tomorrow or the day after."

"I've heard there may be some trouble at the bank."

Kazuhiro's brow furrowed and he glared at the *sensei*. "What do you mean? I haven't heard anything about any trouble. Have you, Sano-san?"

"No, nothing." Sano, too, frowned. "What is it, sensei? Has Akira said something?"

"As you know, my son is the head teller there."

Kazuhiro leaned forward. "Yes, yes. We know that. What does he say?"

With all eyes upon him, the sensei shifted on his seat, wetting his lips, unsure how much he could divulge of what Akira had hinted at. He swallowed his hesitancy and plunged on. "It is not for everyone to know, but my son says the bank is not being paid back for some of its loans."

Kazuhiro sat back in his chair, his initial frown of worry erased. "Well, they can't blame that on me. We will repay our loan. And with the interest they demand." He took another loud sip of tea, confidence once more sitting firmly on his wide, handsome face.

That evening, the sensei sat on the bench at the edge of his garden. The smell of wood smoke hung in the air, mingling with the rich clay soil at his feet and the aroma of ripening apple from the tree at the side of the house. Soon it would be too cold to sit outside, but for now he enjoyed the white blooms of chrysanthemums and asters glowing in the bright moonlight, the sounds of unknown animals scurrying through bushes, the call of a night bird.

A door slid open. Chieko stepped down from the wooden porch that stretched across the front of their house. Her feet sounded in the gravel pathway as she came toward him. "What are you doing sitting so long in the dark, husband?" At the sound of her voice the chirruping of a cricket stopped one second, two, before resuming.

The sensei considered how he should answer. "I am thinking of Akira bringing his family to live with us once more." The cricket fell silent again.

His wife moved closer, stopping in front of him. "Why would our son do that? They have their own place now. I don't want our daughter-in-law here complaining of one thing or another, watching television all day and leaving her things about the house. And what of Kotada? What of our grandson's schooling, his friends?"

"Our son may have no choice. I fear things are not going well at the bank."

"They are dissatisfied with his work?" She folded her arms across her bosom, the sleeves of her dark brown kimono fluttering her indignation. "I can't believe that."

"It is not Akira's work that is the problem, wife. It is the bank that is having trouble. Some companies are not repaying their loans." His frown deepened. "If the loans are not repaid, what people have deposited into the bank will be lost. There will be no money to loan anyone else."

"Husband, are you saying our money may be gone? What will we do?" Her eyes filling with fear, she clapped both hands to her mouth.

With no answer to his wife's questions, the sensei shook his head. In ways, the recent ballooning of property values and the blind belief in an economy that couldn't fail reminded him of the militarism that had swept the country in the thirties. He hoped there wouldn't be similar catastrophic results.

Those hopes, however, were in vain. Less than a week later, the words fairly leapt off the front page of the newspaper: SAKAYAMA BANK FAILS. More such announcements followed. For weeks, television reporters recounted the growing numbers of bank failures and consequent bankruptcies all around the country, while their cameras captured the bewildered, frightened faces of people who, for the first time in their lives, found themselves unemployed.

The sensei painted bamboo leaves on the inside of a large bowl. Nearby, Kazuhiro glowered at the television set, where another so-called expert decried the weakened economy and the plunging value of the yen. In Europe and America, the man claimed, stock markets had plummeted due to Japan's financial disaster. For reasons the sensei didn't understand, he felt a twinge of guilt, as though the problems in America and Europe were somehow his fault.

Kazuhiro stood and snapped off the television. "Already the orders from department stores are falling off." His voice throbbed with emotion. A muscle twitched in his cheek, visible despite his beard. "How can this have happened without warning, sensei? I had such wonderful plans for us—plans to make Nishimi Pottery famous. Now we'll be fortunate to stay in business."

Although he still had no desire for Kazuhiro's expansion plans to progress, the sensei couldn't help feeling sorry for this man who'd always exuded confidence. "You must have patience, Kazuhiro-san. The factory has stood in this place, in one form or another, for well over two hundred years— ever since your ancestors built it. It will survive. We will survive. And eventually the economy will right itself. You'll see."

Although his words contained assurance, the sensei, too, worried about what lay ahead. Of one thing, he felt certain. Without the factory, the village of Nishimi could not go on. For a time, in the fifties, sixties, and early seventies, Nishimi had grown and prospered. All the old pre-war houses, those two and three-room shacks, had been torn down and replaced with modern houses, houses with indoor plumbing and bay windows. But the building boom slowed then stopped as young people graduated from high school and moved on, either to university or to jobs in the city. Just as his son had done.

Of course, like Akira, others might lose their jobs and return to their parents' homes. But if they did, it would be temporary. As soon as the economy recovered, the young people would leave, and once again the village would be comprised of the pottery workers and old folks.

The country's economic problems weren't all the *sensei* worried about. At home, he listened to a growing catalog of complaints. He'd thought the anticipation of another grandchild to spoil would still Chieko's tongue. It had not. In fact, he'd begun to think his wife and daughter-in-law took pleasure in their quarrels. The single thing they both agreed upon, the need for additional space. They'd chosen his loft-studio as the most likely source.

On a cool October morning, Chieko held back the sleeve of her kimono while pouring his breakfast tea. "Husband, we are so crowded."

"I don't want to talk about it, wife. I need my studio." He broke off a piece of baked mackerel with his chopsticks. They both ignored the television blaring from the corner of the room. He pushed the fish into his mouth, taking only a moment to chew and swallow before breaking off another piece.

"But, husband, when the baby arrives, it will need to be with our son and daughter-in-law. Then what about Kotada? Our grandson needs a quiet place to study and to sleep." She knelt on a cushion at his side and rearranged various small dishes, sliding them around on the table to be within easy reach.

"Where am I to paint? Where am I to teach?" Although no longer many in number, he still had a few students who came by bus every Saturday from Sakayama.

"We could clear a place in this room."

"How am I to get any work done with you and our daughter-in-law always at each other?" Heat bathed his face. He pushed his tray away. "No more. I want to hear no more of giving up my space."

Moments later, as he climbed the steep steps from the kitchen to his studio, the shoji screen slid open behind him and his daughter-in-law, her voice muted, asked his wife what they should do next. He paused for Chieko's response, but a sudden blare of music from the television set drowned out her answer.

In the end, he would have to agree to her plans. He resumed climbing, his shoulders stiffening with resolve. Not yet, though. He was not ready to yield, not ready to give up his sanctum.

Snow came early, blanketing the roads, houses, and fields, melting as it landed on the water in the ponds and ditches. Then the water froze and the ditches and ponds, too, turned white. The sensei watched his son sweep snow off the graveled path leading from the house to the narrow road that connected them to the village. Only vine-covered remnants remained of the old earthen wall that once surrounded the Katsuragawa summer estate. They, too, were dotted with snow.

At least they were no longer snowbound every winter; several years before, the town had purchased a plow with a large blade that kept the roads clear, including the one leading to their house.

"I must put a straw overcoat on the pine tree," the sensei said, looking up at a sky packed with pendulous clouds. "Winter has arrived and I am not yet ready for it."

"I will do that for you, Father," said Akira.

"Good, good. And perhaps you can help me take up what remains of the asters and chrysanthemums as well. I think in the spring we will plant vegetables in their place."

In the cold, still air, the breath surrounding their words came out in puffs of white.

"Father, I am so sorry to be a burden on you and my mother. I will do whatever I can to help."

The sensei held up his gloved hand. It pained him to hear the humility in his son's voice.

Akira ignored the gesture and plunged on. "Every day I travel to the city, looking for work. Each day it is the same. There is nothing for me. You know we would not have considered Hiromi giving up her job at the telephone company to have another child had we known I would lose mine. But now that she is near term, it's too late to change our minds. Yet, at a time like this, how can we bring another child into the household? What are we to do?"

The sensei recalled Kazuhiro's bewildered face when he'd asked a similar question. The advice he would give his son must be the same. He rested his hand on his son's shoulder. "I don't know. Somehow, though, we'll find a way to manage. In the end, I believe we will all be the stronger for it."

Akira's mouth worked, but for several seconds he said nothing. Then he leaned the broom against the side of the house. "You are on your way to the village, Father. Come, I'll walk with you."

The sensei clasped his son's proffered arm. Together, they made their slow and careful way down the mountain.

2
SACHIKO
The Farmer's Wife

The sow grunted her greedy pleasure when Sachiko tipped the bucket's foul-smelling contents into its trough. She didn't stay to watch the creature devour its meal of rotting vegetables and table scraps. She had other chores to finish before going back to the farmhouse to clean up her husband's and her father-in-law's breakfast dishes.

The early morning sun pushed through cracks in the walls and through the open door, casting harsh streaks of light across scattered straw on the barn's dirt floor. Sachiko filled the emptied bucket with grain and swung it over a rail, placing it before the ox. While the ox ground his morning meal between his flat teeth, she took a pitchfork from its place on the wall and began the daily task of cleaning out the huge beast's stall. Although the placid animal needed little to calm it, she made soothing noises with her tongue as she pitched the soiled straw into a wheelbarrow. Once finished, she straightened and rubbed the small of her back, wincing when the child filling her womb moved in search of a more comfortable position.

The baby would come just as spring planting demanded her presence in the rice paddy alongside her husband and son. She couldn't worry about the bad timing, though. This child took precedence over everything else. She patted the bulge of her stomach, drew another deep breath, and spread clean straw over the floor of the stall.

Satisfied she'd thrown enough, she rocked the loaded wheelbarrow backward and forward until, with a final heave, she got it in motion, pushed it through the open door into the yard, dumping its contents onto the growing pile at the side of the barn.

In the spring, the dung would be used as fertilizer. That wouldn't be far off, judging from the melting patches of snow in the fields. Soon the ox's wintry respite, the long days when it did nothing but eat and shit, would be over.

With her arm, she brushed away strands of hair that had fallen into her eyes. She gazed across the narrow valley and up the mountain, to the back of the Nishimi pottery factory. Beyond it, but out of sight, lay her mother's store. After a moment or two, she pulled her eyes away, restored the wheelbarrow to its place in the barn and started toward the house.

The dog stood at the end of its chain, eyes hopeful. She patted its large head as she passed. In the small entry space, she slipped out of her padded jacket and kicked off her rubber barn boots. After stepping into indoor slippers, she went in search of her husband.

She found him sitting on the floor in his father's room, repairing a broken harness. Her father-in-law sat in the room's single chair, a month-old newspaper in his palsied hands, a heavy, dark green blanket draped across his narrow shoulders.

Her husband, a dumpling-faced man with wide-spaced, protruding teeth and his father's large ears, didn't look up.

"Remember, we're taking the sow to Sanyo's today." The pig about to come into heat, he'd negotiated with a local farmer to breed it to his boar.

"We'll be near Nishimi," she said. "I would like to visit my mother."

Her father-in-law made no effort to hide his feelings. "The kichiku? Hunh. You should stay away from that foreign demon."

Sachiko often thought Toshio Hara's contempt for her mother hid an unexplained fear. Whether he feared demons in general, or simply her mother, she had no idea. He always raved about something, often witches and evil genies. In the past year, he'd begun to talk of spirit people, whose black faces were painted white.

She refused to acknowledge him, and continued to address her husband. "May I?"

Intent on his work, Kensai ignored her question.

Toshio rattled the newspaper. "I don't expect my evening meal to be late."

The sow plodded up the steep track on short, stubby legs, with Sachiko on one side, her husband on the other. The farm, still visible behind them, appeared deserted but for the dog pacing back and forth at the end its chain. Kensai tapped the sow with his long stick, urging it to hurry, but Sachiko saw no discernable change in its pace.

She gazed at the rocky outcroppings above the track. The sticks they carried wouldn't hinder the animal were it to bolt, and she wondered if it could find a cave to hide in, what it would eat if it did. Not the fine slops she fed it every morning. Perhaps at some level the creature understood it would starve and that's what kept it from trying to escape.

They trudged on, passing the elementary school, built to replace the one crushed in an earthquake, yet still called new even though more than fifty years had passed. Their son had spent his days in the little two-roomed school before he graduated and moved on to high school. She and Kensai had also learned to read and write there.

The sun broke through the clouds. Sweat soon formed in Sachiko's armpits and in the hollow between her shoulder blades. The child pressed on her bladder. "I must relieve myself," she said when she could no longer bear the increased pressure. Kensai nodded his head. She ducked into a small stand of cedar at the side of the road, pulled down her trousers and squatted, using a tree to steady her awkward body. Steam rose from the frozen ground as the warm urine spread between her feet.

Their climb leveled off and they reached the lane leading to Sanyo's pig farm—the smell long before announcing its proximity. Clouds heavy with moisture moved in front of the sun, and the tops of the cedar and pine trees swayed in the wind. She worried it might snow before they began their homeward journey.

Kensai glanced upward as well. He frowned. "You may go on to the village and visit your mother for one hour. Don't forget my father's pipe tobacco. And don't be late," he called after her as she hurried along the track toward Nishimi, still a good twenty minutes away.

Throughout Sachiko's childhood, there had been unspoken tension between her mother and her grandparents.

Born and raised in America, Nobuko's very existence in their lives seemed to annoy Sachiko's grandparents, especially her grandmother.

Others, like Yoko Yoshida and Toshio Hara, were more vocal in their criticism. Her father-in-law had never recovered from his war experiences and being held as a prisoner of war in Australia. His hatred of all things Western bordered on lunacy. Yoko Yoshida's feelings were also irrational—she claimed Nobuko brought bad luck.

As a child, it had hurt that the woman she loved most in the world, her mother, was treated with such disrespect. Nobuko tried to explain, even justify it, but her explanation didn't fool Sachiko. She knew her mother resented it, too.

Despite that, she had many good memories of growing up in Nishimi. The village had been her playground, including the pottery factory, where she and Kazuhiro Yoshida, along with the other village children, played king-of-the-hill on the mound of broken pottery shards piled behind the factory.

As big a dare-devil as Sachiko, Yoko Yoshida's son had been her closest friend. In winter, she and Kazuhiro had sailed down the mountainside on make-shift sleds. In spring, they'd climbed higher than any of the other children, hunting for fiddle-necked ferns to bring home for their mothers to cook. In the summer, they explored. In the fall, they flew kites and dug up sweet potatoes, often making necklaces of the vines.

Although they separated when Sachiko went away to university and Kazuhiro stayed in the village, preparing to one day run the factory in place of his father, they had planned to eventually have the love-match marriage her parents had enjoyed. But as she passed in front of the pottery factory, she cast her eyes to the ground; Kazuhiro Yoshida no longer acknowledged the companion of his youth.

A smelly open sewer once ran through the village, but now Sachiko could breathe deeply as she walked past the gas station and the new post office, and approached her mother's store. A row of black umbrellas hung from pegs on its faded wood siding. The bus from Sakayama stopped in front, and in foul weather the umbrellas were a community service, to be used and then returned the following day. A long-standing custom—Sachiko couldn't remember a time the umbrellas hadn't hung there.

The moment she stepped in the door, the smell of vegetables, ripening fruit and kerosene carried her back to her childhood. Her grandparents had still been alive then. Her father, too. Long in frail health, her father died when she was ten. She still missed his quirky smile and teasing—when well enough, he took her with him to deliver mail or go on hikes. He loved to hike. After his death, followed soon after by the deaths of her grandparents, it had been only Sachiko and Nobuko.

As always, a cast-iron teapot simmered on top of the stove near the front of the store. On the wide-planked floor next to it, a basket of kittens slept.

"Mother?" Slipping out of her padded jacket, Sachiko looked to the door at the back of the store leading to her mother's living quarters. Perhaps Nobuko had stepped away for a moment. "Mother," she called out again.

"Sachiko? Is that you?"

"Yes. I've come for a short visit. Do you have time for tea?"

Nobuko stepped from behind a table stacked high with towels and linens. A tiny woman, less than five feet tall, she'd once stood ramrod straight, her ink-black hair falling like a sheet of rain to her shoulders. Now she walked with a slight stoop and her hair had turned iron gray. She wore it twisted into a bun. A faded scar ran from the corner of her right eye to her mouth. "I will always have time for tea with my daughter." Then she halted and frowned. "When is the child due?"

Sachiko's lips tightened. She picked up the kettle and poured hot water over tea leaves in the bottom of a burnished pottery teapot. "It is due in two months, Mother"

"Daughter, why would you do this? I gave you the medicine to prevent it from happening again." They spoke in English, as always had been their custom when they were alone.

Sachiko tore the cellophane wrapper off a package of pink teacakes. "But I didn't miscarry this time, Mother." She didn't try to soften the hint of defiance her words contained. "This child is going to be born strong and healthy, not like the others. I am hoping for a girl."

Nobuko drew closer. "Then you're crazy. What kind of life will she have? The two of them, your husband and father -in-law, will work her like an ox, just as they do you—both too cheap to buy a tractor or a truck, a telephone, even, anything to make life a little easier. When she's old enough, for a mere few acres of land they'll marry your precious daughter off to some farmer who'll work her as hard as they work you."

Sachiko's shoulders slumped; her mother's words contained too much truth. Still, she couldn't be sorry. She wanted this baby with her whole heart.

After a moment, her mother's face softened and she changed the subject. "How does my grandson do?"

"Hayoto does well, Mother," she said, always happy to speak of her son. "His last report card held high marks."

"Excellent. Next time you visit, perhaps you'll bring him. It has been too long since I've seen him."

They sat in the two chairs kept next to the stove, sipped their tea, and ate the little cakes. Her mother reached for the teapot and refilled their cups. She told Sachiko about the sensei's son moving his family back to Nishimi when the bank where he worked closed. "His wife is expecting a baby, too. A girl they say, due any day now."

Sachiko ran her hand over her dome-shaped stomach; any other time she would have been jealous to hear of another woman's successful pregnancy.

"What is Akira going to do?"

"He goes to the city on the bus most mornings, looking quite fine in his suit, carrying a briefcase, but his mother tells me that every time he goes for an interview he finds ten other people applying for the same position." Her mother leaned back in her chair. "Chieko says her husband believes the economy won't recover for some time, maybe years."

The sensei's son had been something of a loner when they were children, seldom taking part in their games. Sachiko had never been sure if he'd stayed on the sideline because of shyness, or because he felt superior to the village children due to his father's noble birth.

"I'm sorry to hear about him losing his job. I hope he finds something soon." She glanced down at the basket of kittens. "How old are they?"

Her mother raised an eyebrow. "I'm not sure. Their mama kept them hidden too well. Only yesterday evening did she bring them out for my approval."

"And where is the proud mama now?" Sachiko asked, smiling at the image her mother's words evoked.

"Hunting, no doubt. Apparently, she's decided they are safe with me." Her mother's eyes twinkled. "Little does she know, but her babies will soon be gone. When they are ready to be weaned, I will be searching for people to take them off my hands."

"Perhaps I'll take one to keep the mice from the tatami mats."

"Good," her mother said. "The *sensei's* wife is having one, too. With a baby sister coming, she thinks it would be beneficial for her grandson to have an animal to care for."

Sachiko would like to have remained by the warmth of the fire, but she stood and reached for her jacket. "I must leave now."

Her mother stood. "I suppose the old man wants his usual container of pipe tobacco."

"Yes, please."

"Let me make up a package for you." While Sachiko donned her jacket, her mother gathered together the tobacco and other items. "I've included some candy and a new shirt for Hayoto. Also a few pretty tea towels for you," she said, wrapping everything in brown paper and tying it with string.

Sachiko took the package. "Thank you, Mother."

"Have him get word to me when the baby arrives."

"I will."

That night the pains began, gently at first, swelling, ebbing, swelling. Gradually, the waves became higher and harder— Sachiko felt like a black weight pulled her down, down. She thrashed on the futon, fighting to keep her screams turned inward, and still the pressure and pain grew. Toward morning, her water broke in a bloody gush, followed by a pathetic blue-tinged scrap of mewling humanity. By the following evening, the baby girl she'd carried below her heart for seven months lay beneath the ground.

3
KAZUHIRO
The Pottery Factory

The shop where Kazuhiro had his hair cut and curled, his beard trimmed, appeared less busy than normal.

"Business has fallen off since the Sakayama bank failed," said the young girl as she worked shampoo into his hair. "So many people are out of work now." She rinsed away the soap and used the towel she'd earlier draped around his neck to begin drying his hair. "Those who still have jobs are being more careful with their money."

Fools, Kazuhiro thought, scowling. They should know that now, more than ever, one must keep up appearances.

The girl went on chattering as she trimmed his hair and beard. He observed her every move in the mirror, lifting his chin, turning his head to the left and the right whenever she paused. When both were done to his satisfaction, she took away the sheet that covered him and he stood. "Put it on my account."

The girl looked embarrassed. "Yoshida-san, I'm sorry. We are no longer accepting credit."

"That's ridiculous." He thrust out his chest. "I've always paid my bills. Are you suggesting I can't be trusted?"

The girl flushed. "No, nothing like that, Yoshida-san. It is the new policy for everyone."

"Well, you can make another new policy. I'm not paying you today. Send the bill to my house as you normally do, and my wife will take care of it as she always does."

Sudden tears trembled on the girl's lower lashes. "I am sorry. I must speak to my manager."

"Get him then." Kazuhiro crossed his arms and tapped his foot while she trotted to the back of the salon and disappeared behind a door. She reappeared a moment later with a middle-aged man wiping his mouth on a napkin.

The man bowed. "Yoshida-san, it is good to see you again. Please accept my apologies for this woman's ignorance. We will be happy to add this to your bill. In these times of hardship, we particularly value long-time customers such as you."

Satisfied with the degree of the man's subservience and his correct analysis of the situation, Kazuhiro nodded. "I certainly hope so." Before leaving the shop, he glanced at the girl his mouth curved down on one side, expressing his disdain.

Once out on the sidewalk, his self-assurance dissipated like fog in sunshine. Keeping up appearances might be vital, but something must change soon. Orders continued to fall off, while expenses remained. He felt confident the economy would come around soon. It had to. In the meantime, he still needed to pay the gas bill for the kiln, the phone bill, electric bill, and all the other bills piled on his desk. Not to mention wages.

A lucky thing the sensei didn't receive a wage, instead shared in the profit of his work when it sold. But, fewer and fewer of those expensive pieces were selling. The sensei had already cut back on the hours he came to the factory each week, and Kazuhiro couldn't remember the last time a request had come for one of his large, impressive works.

He paced down the sidewalk, his hands thrust deep in his pockets, brushing past several other pedestrians, ignoring the horns and bells of the pushcart vendors peddling ices and other treats—such things were for children and tourists. He paid no attention to the man who stood outside the chicken restaurant, loudly extolling the day's menu. He even managed to ignore the savory scent of garlic and soy sauce delivered through the restaurant's open door.

Soon he would need to speak with his wife, a task he dreaded. Unlike the household finances, the factory, including its operation and expenses, were not in Eriko's realm. Though that had not kept her from offering her opinion, including encouraging him to expand.

So far, he'd been able to keep the factory's financial problems from her. When she learned how bad things had become, she'd no doubt blame it on him, telling him he should have managed better. Maybe she was right.

He idly kicked at a scrawny cat streaking out from between two buildings. What would Takeda have done if this crisis had occurred in his time? Kazuhiro brushed aside the fact that it had been Yoko, not Takeda, who'd managed to keep the factory going through the great depression of the thirties; his father had been away fighting in China and then New Guinea. In fact, his mother had successfully operated the factory for over a decade, from the mid-thirties until the Emperor's surrender in 1945 ended the years of war.

Things were different in those days, though. They'd used wood-fueled kilns; Yoko had only to hire someone to go out in the woods and cut it down. Labor had been cheap as well, unlike today when everyone demanded higher wages. He scowled, thinking of Sano's latest request.

The ka-chinging from a pachinko parlor broke into his brooding thoughts. He stopped pacing and peered through the open door into the parlor's smoky interior. The machines' colorful lights flashed. He hesitated then went inside. As good a place as any to kill time while he waited for the man he'd come to meet.

Near midnight, Kazuhiro stepped out of a cab in front of his house. A blue glow came from the living room window. One of his sons must be watching television—Eiichi, no doubt. The rest of the house appeared wrapped in a cloak of darkness.

He'd never liked the house, little more than two prefabricated boxes stacked one atop the other, each box about fifteen feet wide, thirty feet long and twelve feet high. Eriko had insisted they buy it. "I'm proud to be a modern Japanese woman. This house will reflect that. You can save your ancient traditions for the pottery factory," she'd said.

She'd made all the arrangements to buy it eight years earlier, including borrowing much of the money from her wealthy cousin. Located in Sakayama's northern suburbs, she hadn't cared it took him an additional thirty-five minutes to drive to the factory every morning.

He slid open the door and went inside. Fourteen-year-old Eiichi sprawled on the sofa in front of the television set, the sound turned low. The boy didn't bother looking up.

Kazuhiro frowned. "Where is Yoshi?"

Still without looking at him, Eiichi jerked his head toward the ceiling to indicate his younger brother's whereabouts.

In the kitchen, Kazuhiro found a covered bowl of leftover curry in the refrigerator. He slid the bowl into the microwave and pushed the reheat button. A few minutes later he joined his son on the couch.

Besides the large, western-style furniture, the detritus of two boys and two adults filled the small room. An uncluttered space, the only one in the room, lay in front of the window where Eriko's *samisen* resided. His wife, the 'modern Japanese woman,' devoted her time to the ancient instrument of geisha and kabuki, an irony he no longer thought much about. He assumed the money she earned teaching the instrument to four other middle-aged women offset what she spent traveling to Hiroshima and Kyoto for concerts and private lessons.

"Who's playing?"

"Brazil and Portugal."

As he ate, Kazuhiro watched the television screen, but his mind fell far distant from the soccer game being played out in front of him. He thought instead about his meeting that afternoon and what he'd committed to.

"Husband?"

He looked up as Eriko limped into the room. Dressed for bed, she'd already disposed of the special shoe that balanced her shortened left leg with the right.

"It is late. Where have you been?"

"Arranging for the money I need to enlarge the factory."

"What?" Eyebrows drawn together, Eriko's face mirror- ed her consternation. "Eiichi, turn off the television and go to bed."

"The game isn't over yet."

"You heard your mother."

Eiichi remained in his seat. "Why can't the two of you go upstairs? I was here first."

Without pausing to think, Kazuhiro slapped Eiichi and felt only a moment of guilt when the force of his blow caused his son's head to snap back.

Eiichi surged to his feet and glowered at him before brushing past Eriko and stalking to the stairs.

Kazuhiro scowled after him. "He needs discipline. Why do you let him talk to you like that?"

"He wouldn't behave that way if you were home more," Eriko countered. An old argument, and neither of them spoke with spirit. She limped farther into the room and turned off the television set. "What did you mean about borrowing money for the factory? The bank is gone. Who would loan you money at a time like this?"

He gave her a name.

Eriko's face paled as her hand rose to cover her mouth. "The yakuza?" She whispered the word as though afraid to say it aloud. "Are you mad? You know what they do to people who don't pay them back on time."

"It won't be for long. As soon as this crisis is over and the bank reopens, I will get a proper loan and repay them." Although he spoke with confidence, his wife's words filled him with foreboding. His head throbbed.

Eriko's widened eyes searched his face. "What have you done? They'll kill you. They'll kill me. Even the boys won't be safe."

"Don't say that, wife. I have everything under control. When the economy is restored, which will happen soon, the factory will be larger, more productive than ever. I will have no problem getting a loan from the bank." He furtively wiped his sweaty palms on the sides of his trousers.

"And in the meantime, husband? What about in the meantime?"

4
THE SENSEI
Hirotaka

Although spring arrived late, creeping in on silent feet, birds now twittered in the late afternoon sunshine, and insects whined in the weeds along the side of the road. After a long day at the factory, the sensei looked forward to a steamy soak in the ofuro. The gods willing, his new granddaughter would settle down early, and there would be no quarrels between Chieko and Hiromi waiting to be resolved. Either his wife and daughter-in-law had made peace, or they'd found a way to settle their differences without involving him.

He would be thankful for this small blessing, because he already had enough on his mind. Kazuhiro had arrived that morning, bursting with excitement—the scheme to expand the factory back in place and larger than ever. Besides a bigger kiln and stations for three new electric pottery wheels, Kazuhiro now planned an outdoor garden to attract the busloads of vacationers who traveled to the mountains around Nishimi each year, to view the cherry blossoms in the spring, and the colorful foliage in the fall.

"Think of it, *sensei*," Kazuhiro had said that afternoon. "We'll have a garden with a waterfall. There'll be tables and chairs set around it. And music. Maybe I'll hire a woman to play the *koto*, like at that famous restaurant in Kyoto."

For a moment, he silently savored the vision his words created. "We'll serve tea and cakes from our own cups and platters. The more famous we become, the more tourists will flock to us."

Tension had filled the *sensei's* body at Kazuhiro's enthusiastic words. He'd looked up from the crane he painted on the side of a short cylindrical vase, trying to keep the alarm he felt from showing on his face. The plans were growing grander by the minute. "Are you sure you want strangers milling all over the factory?" he asked. "They will be certain to get in the way and break things."

Kazuhiro had scoffed at his objections. "They'll spend money, sensei. They'll spend money on our wares."

Trying to look unconcerned, the *sensei* had dipped his brush in the slip and painted another line in the crane's outspread wing. "So, who will make the tea, serve the cakes? Your mother has enough to do, running the showroom and the apprentices." As efficiently as she'd once run the entire factory, he might have added.

Kazuhiro responded that many people in the village would be willing to do the job, and he'd been right; everyone looked for a little extra money these days.

Sano, delighted, couldn't stop talking about the plans. "I told you, sensei. It's only a matter of time before we're all rich and famous. Nishimi will benefit, too. Food vendors and souvenir stands will spring up along the streets. Maybe even an inn."

To clear his thoughts of Kazuhiro's and Sano's grand and unwelcome schemes, the sensei stopped his climb to gaze back the way he'd come. Still-empty paddies and newly plowed fields alternated with stands of evergreens. The blossoms of the cherry trees edged the dark pine and cedar like fine lace. He waited for the peace that always came over him when he took in this view. When it did, he drew in his breath, let it out on a long sigh and continued his homeward journey.

Chieko greeted him at the door. She wore a sturdy cotton yukata, this one of steel gray with a brown and yellow obi. His wife disliked the western-style trousers and dresses most women, including their daughter-in-law, now wore. A vision of his slim mother in a luminous silk *kimono* of silvery gray appeared before him. He blinked and the vision disappeared.

"There is good news today, husband," his wife said.

He stuffed his beret into his jacket pocket. "Oh?"

Chieko helped him off with the jacket. "I will let Akira tell you."

"I will bathe first, wife."

She nodded. "The ofuro is ready for you."

Later, while Chieko and Hiromi remained in the kitchen preparing the family's evening meal, the two men, each clad in navy blue and white robes, sipped tea. The *sensei* would have preferred sitting on the bench in his garden, what remained of it, but the evenings were still too cool.

"Your mother says there is good news."

Akira's face lit up. "I ran into Toyo on the street today, Father. The bank's senior loan officer. He had outstanding news."

"What did he tell you?"

"Two things," said Akira. "The government insurance company is speeding up the return of everyone's money—you and my mother should have yours by the end of the month. Also, another bank is in the process of buying our bank and will soon re-open it. The government is helping with the negotiations."

Akira stopped talking and lifted his cup to his mouth—as if to prolong anticipation for the rest of his news. But he couldn't contain his excitement, and set the cup down without taking a sip. "Toyo is quite certain we will have our old jobs back."

"That is excellent news. When is all this to take place?"

"Toyo didn't know the exact date, but he said he heard it would be soon, perhaps in a few weeks."

The sensei enjoyed seeing the optimism on his son's face, an emotion he hadn't witnessed there for several months. "I wonder if that means an end to our economic problems. Kazuhiro is convinced all will be well by the time summer is here. He told me as much today, which is why he has undertaken this project of enlarging and modernizing the factory." The sensei shifted position on the cushion. "I fear his thinking may be over-optimistic and he may regret the hastiness of his decision. What is your opinion?"

The optimism on Akira's face faded. "Father, I have no idea. I am hopeful I'll soon have my job back, but when I think of all my failed attempts to find work, I cannot believe the end of this calamity is in sight. I'm afraid it will be a long time before our economy is once again sound."

The sensei nodded. "That is my belief as well."

The clatter of hurrying feet sounded in the gravel path outside the house, followed by a quickly opened and closed door. A moment later, the sensei's grandson burst into the room, still wearing his school jacket, and carrying his book bag.

"Father, my teacher is taking three students to the Peace Park in Hiroshima, and he said I may be one if it is all right with you and my mother." The boy stood before Akira, eyes pleading. "It will be, won't it?"

Akira gave his son a benevolent smile. "When will you go, Ko-chan? And how will you get there?"

"Saturday by train. And we'll stay in a hotel. There will be students from all over the prefecture. Please say I may go."

Chieko and Hiromi entered the room carrying trays holding a variety of small dishes, bowls, and utensils. They set the trays on the floor and began to lay the table.

Kotada turned to Hiromi. His voice keyed with excitement. "Did you hear, Mother? I may go to Hiroshima on Saturday with my teacher and two other students."

Chieko glanced up from setting a dish of pickled ginger on the table. "Why would you go to Hiroshima, Ko-chan?"

"To visit the Peace Park, Grandmother," Kotada said.

Chieko nodded her approval of the outing. "It has been many years since I last visited Hiroshima. I wonder how much it has changed."

Kotada returned his gleaming eyes to his mother. "My teacher says you and Father must agree before I can go. Please say yes."

Hiromi paused before answering. "What does your father say?"

Kotada turned to his father, the question on his face.

"I haven't said anything yet," Akira answered. "But if it is all right with you, I suppose I would have no objection."

"But husband, do you think we can afford the extra expense right now?"

Akira took a sip of his cooled tea. "Hiroshima isn't that far away, and our son will be gone for only one night. It shouldn't cost too much."

"But, still...."

Akira set down his cup. He hesitated, then turned to Kotada, his face stiff. "Your mother is right, Ko-chan. Even a small amount is more than we can afford right now."

Kotada's lower lip trembled. "I can't go?"

"Not this time," said Akira. "I'm sorry."

The boy hung his head, but made no further complaint.

Chieko picked up a tray. "Come along, Ko-chan. Let your father and grandfather talk. You need to put your school things away before we eat."

That night as Chieko lay next to him, her gentle snores as soothing as the sound of the cicadas outside their window in summer, the sensei thought about his conversation with Akira. He wondered if Japan would ever again have cradle-to-grave employment, a concept workers had grown accustomed to when Japan's giant electronics firms and auto plants came into being in the fifties.

He chuckled, thinking of his father. Had he lived, how pleased his father would be to see he'd been right about technology being Japan's future. Of course, his father wouldn't have been surprised—he'd never doubted his opinions on that or any other subject.

He resettled onto his side. He took pride in the way Kotada had accepted his parents' decision; not an easy thing for a young boy, disappointment, especially a boy who, up until a short time before, had most of his wishes granted. Maybe this difficult time would be good for him, would teach him he couldn't always have what he wanted. Still, perhaps a way could be found for the boy to make the trip to Hiroshima.

His mind then took another turn. Where had Kazuhiro found the money to enlarge the factory? Perhaps his wife had made the arrangements. Everyone knew Eriko had a rich relative. But the man couldn't be so foolish as to underwrite Kazuhiro's expensive dream at this risky time, could he?

The answer to that question must have been yes, because two weeks later, six dark-skinned Vietnamese arrived at the factory in a battered van and an old truck filled with equipment and supplies. The men scrambled out of the vehicles and unloaded the equipment.

The sounds of hammering and sawing soon filled the air, along with the foreigners' incessant yammering. They sounded like a flock of shrieking birds, their sing-song voices so unlike the calm monotone of the more civilized Japanese tongue. Unable to close his ears to the cacophony, the sensei gave thanks he now came to the factory only one or two days a week.

Not long after the foreigners arrived, the sensei witnessed another disturbing scene, this time between Kazuhiro and a man who wore his long hair pulled back in a ponytail. Despite the day's warmth, the man wore a long-sleeved shirt and jacket.

Kazuhiro had been giving directions to the foreman of the building crew on how to raise a roof beam—Vietnamese did not build in accordance with Japanese tradition.

Kazuhiro's voice filled with agitation and it grew louder the longer the discussion continued. When the ponytailed man arrived, Kazuhiro broke off the argument and rushed to the ponytailed man's side.

The stranger walked with an exaggerated swagger. That he had no appreciation for Japan's ancient art form became apparent by the disdain he showed when Kazuhiro pointed to the rows of completed pottery.

Although the sensei returned to his painting project, from the corner of his eye, he kept track of Kazuhiro and the stranger. When the two men left the showroom, heading toward the construction site, the sensei put down his brush and turned to Yoko. "Who is he?"

Yoko shrugged without looking up, and the sensei picked up his brush again. But his puzzlement at Kazuhiro deference remained. The stranger looked like a gangster, his long sleeves hiding the tattoos that gangsters were known to have on their arms and torsos. But, what interest could the yakuza have in a pottery factory?

After the ponytail man left, Kazuhiro got in his car and drove away, not returning to the factory until late in the afternoon. The moment he walked in the door, the sensei saw clearly that something bothered him. Without a word of greeting, Kazuhiro slumped into his desk chair, where, until closing time, he did nothing but stare into space.

5
SACHIKO
The Farmer's Wife

Sachiko, in water several inches above her ankles, took a small rice seedling from the tray hanging from her neck. She shoved the plant into the mud at her feet, tamped it in place with her heel, and moved on. Mind blank, she gouged hole after hole in the mud, filling each with a seedling. In her wake, the young plants stood erect, their tapered leaves dancing in the light breeze.

She took little notice of the quiet beauty surrounding her, the rugged mountains above, the floor of the narrow valley below, the sun shimmering on the rippling water surrounding her—such a sight as she used to take pleasure in. She didn't notice the passing of time either, though along with Kensai and Hayoto, she'd been at her task since early morning.

Sachiko had noticed very little since the loss of her tiny daughter. In the two months since, day had followed joyless day. Her son had tried to cheer her. Even Kensai, less gruff than usual. But nothing anyone said or did could bring her the solace she yearned for. At thirty-nine, the child had been her last chance. There would be no more babies.

An insect buzzed near her ear and several more skimmed along the water. Hammers banging and the whine of electric saws rolled down the mountain from the pottery factory. She had grown accustomed to the noise. It somehow soothed her, had become part of her mourning.

Kensai stood and threw a scornful look at the back of the factory. "That damned Kazuhiro. Always lording it over us, just as Takeda did before him."

Hayoto straightened from planting a seedling. "At school, I heard there will be a garden and a waterfall. They say after it is complete, Mr. Yoshida expects hundreds, maybe thousands of tourists to visit the factory every year."

Kensai grunted. "Ridiculous. Does he think no one has seen waterfalls and gardens before?" His rhetorical question received no answer. When another hour passed, he called for a break. "Go back to the house and see to your grandfather," he said to Hayoto. "You will need to help him to the toilet. See if he needs anything else."

Sachiko waded out of the rice paddy and dried her feet on the grass verge. "You can give him his lunch," she said. "It's on a tray in the kitchen." Once, Sachiko enjoyed nothing more than gazing at her son's handsome face. Now, she didn't look up as she spoke.

After Hayoto left, she got the meal from the basket she'd brought that morning and handed Kensai a sticky rice ball wrapped in dried seaweed. She set the box with the rest of his lunch on the ground next to him.

"I'd like to show him gardens and waterfalls," he muttered before shoving the rice ball into his mouth and reaching for another.

Food couldn't fill Sachiko's emptiness. She lay in the grass that covered the dike surrounding the paddy and closed her eyes. Insects buzzed. The sun warmed her face.

Far off, as if through a wall of gauze, she heard shouting. She sat as it grew louder. Hayoto, galloped down the lane toward them. Kensai leapt to his feet. Then she, too, grasped Hayoto's shouted words.

"He's dead. My grandfather is dead."

Sachiko's father-in-law sat slumped in the chair, his eyes wide and staring, his mouth hanging open. Kensai gently closed his father's eyes. Together, they got the old man stretched out on a futon where they stripped away his soiled clothes. Sachiko fetched a bowl of water, soap and cloths and began washing him; Kensai took Hayoto outside to build a casket.

She washed Toshio's stringy hair first then his face, neck, and ears, working her way down his wrinkled body to his feet. His skin, dry and sere, looked like she imagined a desert animal's skin must look. When finished cleaning the body, she would stuff bits of cotton into all its orifices.

While she performed this final service to her dead father -in-law, she tried to keep her mind from roaming. No bad thoughts should enter her head at this sacred time. But she couldn't keep the memory of Toshio's hatefulness at bay.

She recalled the day she'd come to the farm as a bride. The farmhouse—so large, especially when compared to the confined space behind the store—contained several rooms aside from the kitchen, each with high ceilings and rafters. She believed she could be content there, prepared to do everything possible to make her new husband and father-in-law happy.

From that first day, however, Toshio had done all he could to turn Kensai away from her, poisoning his son's mind with accusations and mad mutterings about witches. He often railed about Nobuko, claiming Sachiko's mother should have been driven from Nishimi years before.

She had thought Hayoto's birth would soften Toshio toward her, but it didn't. Although careful to hide his feelings from Kensai, the old man resented her son. "He comes from tainted blood," he whispered to her, shortly after Hayoto's birth. "He will bring you no joy."

Hayoto had been frightened of his grandfather and avoided the old man whenever possible, but Sachiko couldn't avoid him. She'd needed to help him dress in the mornings, take him to the toilet, feed him. He had repaid her by calling her worthless. "Why can't you produce another son?" he'd asked the day following her baby daughter's death. "Nothing but a scrawny female who couldn't last twenty-four hours."

Finished with the soapy water, she threw it into the yard.

Her dead father-in-law would have to do without the traditional white kimono, leggings, and sandals. Tight-lipped, Sachiko went to a small tonsu containing his things and pulled out the uniform he'd worn home from the war, the war that had taken his health and whatever humanity she supposed he must once have possessed. In the kitchen, she found a white rag to make a headband. While she drew a triangle with soot in the center of the rag, the sound of hammering came from the direction of the barn.

Although they had no spare money for him to pay the toll across the River of Three Hells, Sachiko took a few pieces of candy from the box her mother had sent to Hayoto, also a twist of tobacco, wrapping everything in old newspaper. They would place these gifts in the coffin for her father-in-law to enjoy in the afterlife.

Kensai sat up with his father's body that night. Sachiko awakened often, each time hearing her husband's mumbling voice coming from the adjacent room. The next morning, she prepared breakfast. After they ate, Kensai and Hayoto harnessed the ox and put the empty casket in the wagon. The three of them carried Toshio's body outside and laid it the waiting casket.

The temple's roof soared above the trees, visible well before they turned up the lane. Unlike the neighboring Shinto shrine, the Buddhist temple had grandeur. Painted red, it had sweeping curved eaves trimmed in gold. Next to a line of waving flags, a long flight of stairs led to ornate doors. Off to one side, in a grove of cedar trees, lay a meditation garden, composed of rock and sand. Years before, after her beloved papa had died, Sachiko had taken her American uncle to see it.

Kensai pulled the ox to a stop in front of the stairs.

Twenty minutes later, Sachiko followed Kensai and Hayoto into a small room, where Toshio's open coffin had been placed on wooden legs. A low table in front of the coffin held an urn where incense burned. Positioned in front of the table, a red silk cushion.

The rows of cushions filling the rest of the room remained empty. Sachiko had no expectations anyone would join them other than her mother, who arrived out of breath.

"I had to take care of a customer before I could close the store," Nobuko whispered after bowing and expressing appropriate regrets to Kensai for his loss.

They sat and the priest came in. Without speaking to the four mourners, the priest began to read the sutra. Partway through, with a nod of his head, he gave the signal to begin offering incense.

Kensai rose and went to honor his father. He walked to the low table in front of Toshio's casket and folded his short frame onto the red cushion, briefly bowed his head over folded hands, and then added a pinch of incense to the urn. After Kensai, Sachiko rose. She went through the same motions as Kensai, but with no sorrow in her heart. Then Hayoto moved to the red silk cushion, followed by Nobuko. Like her, she doubted either had regrets about Toshio's passing.

The priest paused, and Sachiko looked over her shoulder to see the sensei move with determination down the aisle. He paid respect to the dead by wearing formal black and white striped hakama. Over the wide-legged pants he wore a black kimono with his family crest embroidered in white on its back. His family sword swung at his side. She hadn't seen him dressed so formally since her father's funeral. Before her father died, the sensei often came to their home for a game of chess or simply to talk—on rare occasions he and her father shared stories about New Guinea. A humble man, she found it easy to forget the sensei's noble birth. She'd heard this humility was not always so. She'd heard that in his youth the sensei had been quite arrogant, haughty, even.

When he reached the table with the urn, the sensei sat and bowed his head. He offered incense in the same manner the others had done, but when he stood, he took a roll of paper from his waistband and placed it in the open casket. A poem he'd written? He turned and made a low bow to Kensai. Body stiff, Kensai returned it. Then the sensei left the room, leaving Sachiko to wonder why he'd come—the few times she'd heard Toshio speak of the sensei, it had been with disdain.

The priest finished chanting. With no guests to thank or to place flowers in the casket, no telegrams from far-flung family members to read, and no pallbearers to carry the casket to a hearse for Toshio's final journey, Sachiko stood with her husband and son as the priest disappeared through the same door as the sensei. With her mother in their wake, they carried the casket out of the temple, down the steps, and loaded it back on the wagon.

"You must save essential bones to put in his burial urn. Large bones will survive the fire. And remember, the Adam's apple is most important. You must not forget the Adam's apple."

Sachiko nodded. "Yes, I know, Mother." It never failed to surprise her how traditional Nobuko had become over the years. After saying goodbye, she hurriedly followed Kensai and Hayoto and the casket-filled wagon down the lane.

The gods were angry. How else to explain their losses? With this non-traditional burial of the family patriarch— and no remorse at his loss, at least on her part—the gods would become angrier still.

The noise of construction at the pottery factory had not abated during the funeral. Even as the priest chanted the sutra, the sounds of distant hammering and the whine of saws had entered her ears. Now, the clamor of hammer and saw followed them down the mountainside, not like a funeral dirge, but as evidence of life, life Sachiko felt no part of. She doubted she ever would again. She wept not for her father-in-law, but for her infant daughter.

To build the funeral pyre, they tore down a shed that had once been used to store vegetables. Kensai threw on an armful of clean straw. Both the wood and the straw were dry and caught fire on a single match. Her husband led the ox toward the fire, bringing the casket closer. The ox rolled its eyes and threw its head, but came forward without further protest.

Sachiko and Hayoto on one side, Kensai on the other, they pulled the casket from the back of the wagon and heaved it onto the fire. The burning boards collapsed around the casket. After a moment, the casket, too, burst into flame. Soon, a black pall rose above it.

"Here are the chopsticks the priest gave us to pick the bones," she said hours later, when the fire had consumed the casket and most of its contents. "And here is the funeral urn my mother gave us." They began their gruesome task of fishing bits of Toshio's bones from the ashes.

When they finished, they buried the urn next to the tiny grave that had only a small stone to mark its existence. Perhaps in death, her father-in-law would show mercy to his granddaughter's young spirit.

The next day, under a warm sun, hammer and saw echoing above them, they finished planting the rice.

6
KAZUHIRO
The Pottery Factory

Everyone had left the factory for the night. Kazuhiro paced through the new construction, examining walls, floors, and ceilings. The kiln he'd ordered remained crated because the gas line had yet to be installed. Part of the freshly-poured concrete floor needed to be torn up first. The three new pottery wheels were in place, but the wiring remained only half complete, rendering the wheels useless. He kicked an uneven door jamb. It should have been finished weeks ago, but one thing after another had gone wrong, costing him a fortune. Pulling at his beard, he muttered contempt for foreigners' incompetence.

Footsteps and low voices came from the showroom. He left the construction site and hurried toward the sound. This time Ponytail had a companion, a small, wiry man wearing a light blue suit and a tan fedora hat.

"Your Vietnamese workers aren't worth shit," Kazuhiro said without preamble to the two men. "It's going to cost me half-again as much as it should, just to correct all their mistakes."

Ponytail shrugged, pulled out a cigarette and lit it. Only then did Kazuhiro notice the missing end of the man's left little finger. He swallowed, staring at it. Everyone knew the yakuza maintained order within its ranks by cutting off the tips of fingers.

Ponytail wasted no time. "We've come for our payment."

"Why should I have to pay you when the work you promised isn't getting done?" Although his words sounded defiant, Kazuhiro's hands were clammy and a cold sweat broke out on his back.

The newcomer answered. "That's not our problem. You came to us proposing we invest in your business. We offered you terms and you agreed to them. Now we're here to collect."

"I borrowed the money and agreed to your terms, yes, but you're not living up to your end of the bargain. The workers you provided are no good."

"Then hire someone else."

"I have no more money. It's all gone to pay those damned Vietnamese and they haven't done the job."

The newcomer showed no sympathy. "Like I said, that's your problem. Right now, the only thing we're interested in is getting our payment. We want it, now."

"What if I tell you I don't have it?"

"I don't recommend you do that."

The newspapers often contained graphic descriptions of the 'or else' behind the man's words. The tiny bit of bravado Kazuhiro had been holding onto collapsed. Without saying anything more, he handed over an envelope containing the money.

"That's better." Ponytail opened the envelope and counted the bills. He nodded. "We'll see you next month."

Kazuhiro knees buckled and he fell into the chair at his desk. He buried his face in his hands, dimly hearing car doors slam, an engine start up. The new bank refused to lend him what he needed. Factory orders hadn't improved. If anything, they'd fallen off more. He'd let two apprentices go. The money he just gave to the men had come from a special account Eriko had set up for Eiichi's and Yoshi's future schooling. He didn't want to think what she would say when she found it gone. Worse, he didn't know where he'd get the money when the next installment came due.

Kazuhiro alternated between hovering and scowling, and pacing and scowling, while the workers guided the new kiln into position—a job that had taken twice the time it should have. At last, it rested on the metal plates that would secure it to the concrete floor.

Ten days had passed since Ponytail and his companion had come for their money, and Kazuhiro did his best to forget them. The new kiln should be operational by the end of the week and a large order had arrived that morning from a restaurant in Sakayama. The future already looked brighter. He'd been right to think the country's economic problems would soon be righted.

Rubbing his hands together in anticipation, he smiled at the sensei's grandson, observing the operation from the open doorway. "So, you are interested in construction?" When Kotada nodded, Kazuhiro invited him into the room to get a closer look.

The boy remained by the door. "Grandfather said I must stay out of the way."

"You won't be in the way. The workers have gone outside for a smoke break." Kazuhiro placed a hand on the boy's thin shoulder and guided him to the kiln, stepping over the tracks that ran into its maw. He stroked the kiln's side. "It's the finest I could find. And it's twice as big as our old kiln, so we'll be able to produce twice the work."

The boy peered inside.

"Maybe someday you'll become an apprentice and work here. Would you like that, Ko-chan?" Kazuhiro smiled expectantly.

"I'm going to be an architect," the boy said.

Kazuhiro's eyes widened, taken aback by the matter-of-fact tone. He thought of his own sons. Nothing but soccer and baseball interested Eiichi, five years Kotada's senior. Who knew what would become of his youngest son; whenever he saw Yoshi, the boy's nose was buried in a book.

Not that he saw either of his sons much, especially now, when he avoided their mother. Eriko hadn't discovered the missing money, but she soon would.

"They're coming back," he told the boy as the workers straggled into the room. "You'd better go see your grandfather."

There'd been a time when both Eiichi and Yoshi had come to the factory whenever they had a school holiday. They'd played king-of-the-hill on the mountain of shards behind the factory, just as he had done as a boy. Just as all the village children had done for generations, despite their parents' warnings of injuries. He'd taken them hunting for fiddle-neck ferns as well. Sachiko Abi, now Sachiko Hara, briefly flitted through his mind before he dismissed all thoughts of her.

As his sons grew older they offered excuses why they couldn't come to the factory with him. They were too busy studying, doctor's appointments, a movie with a friend. Always something. Who would carry on after him? If neither Eiichi nor Yoshi wanted to be involved with the factory, which at this point appeared likely, Eriko would no doubt sell it to some stranger when he died.

"Kazuhiro-san?" Sano's voice interrupted his bleak thoughts.

"Yes?"

"I need you to come and look at something. I'm concerned with the installation of the new wheels."

What now? Kazuhiro thought, bracing for more bad news.

"I am worried about the third wheels' placement. No one will want to sit with his back to the kami," the master potter said, referring to a small shrine in the otherwise vacant lot adjacent to the factory.

At one time, Kazuhiro had considered buying the property and expanding the factory in that direction, but he'd been afraid such a move would cause affront, both to the god and to the villagers who tended the little shrine. He rubbed his forehead with the tips of his fingers, trying to ease the tension forming there. He should have thought of this himself.

"Why didn't you say something earlier? Never mind. Maybe we can get the villagers to move the shrine."

"Where?"

Even moving it ten feet could create havoc in the village. The shrine had been there for decades, long before the rebuilding that had followed the years after the war.

Things had been constructed in relation to the shrine's location.

Kazuhiro heaved an exasperated sigh. "We'll need to move the wheel." Good thing it could be reassembled somewhere else, so long as it had adequate wiring—yet another thing for him to worry about.

Yoko called from the office. "Kazuhiro, telephone."

"I'm coming." He turned back to Sano. "See if you can figure out where to put it." At Sano's nod, he went to answer the phone.

"Eiichi has been suspended from school for bullying." Eriko blurted out the words before he could finish saying hello. "You must come home and deal with him."

"What do you mean, bullying?"

"They say he and another boy beat up two younger boys," Eriko said. "One of them got a bloody nose."

"Boys are always fighting." He shrugged. "Why should our son be suspended because of that?"

"Husband, they were little boys—younger even than Yoshi."

"Ah." He closed his eyes as the stone lodged in his stomach grew heavier. "Okay, I will deal with him when I come home."

"I want you to come home now, husband."

His wife's demanding voice grew louder. He opened his eyes and pulled the phone away from his ear, frowning at it. More of Eriko's words spilled into the room. He looked at his mother who stared back at him. The young woman assistant pretended to be engrossed in dusting a shelf. He turned back to the phone. "I said I'll see to him when I get home, wife." He hung up before she could reply.

Yoko told the young woman to leave, then faced Kazuhiro. "Eiichi is in trouble?"

"He's been suspended from school for bullying."

She shook her head. "Something's wrong with that boy. I've known for years. It must come from his mother's side of the family."

He wondered how she could forget the bully she'd married, his father, but didn't ask. "I'd better go home and see what I can do."

At one o'clock in the morning, the cab driver let Kazuhiro out. His house stood dark, foreboding and silent. He fumbled opening the front door, kicked off his shoes and tiptoed up the stairs, holding tight to the bannister to keep from falling backward. As soon as he slid open the bedroom door, a light snapped on.

"Where have you been? Your mother said you left the factory soon after I called. I thought you were in an accident."

"Shut up, wife."

Eriko let out a small shriek. She rolled to face the wall, her breathing coming in uneven gasps. He pulled off his clothes and sank down next to her on the futon, quickly falling into a dreamless sleep.

He dragged himself awake the next morning. The hands on his watch showed nearly nine o'clock. No sign of Eriko. He got up and splashed cold water on his face and beard, then searched for some aspirin to ease the pounding in his head. Once dressed, he went downstairs. Eiichi sat at the table eating his breakfast and reading a sports magazine.

"Where's your mother?"

"Gone to teach her samisen class."

Insolence filled the boy's voice, but Kazuhiro chose to ignore it. "And your brother?"

"In school, of course."

"Don't get smart with me. How long are you out?"

"A week."

"Good. That will give you time to do some things for me at the factory."

"I'm not going to the factory." Eiichi gave a defiant shake of his head.

Kazuhiro remained unmoved. "Finish whatever it is you're eating and let's go."

"I have other things to do," Eiichi said, shifting his approach. "I'm supposed to do all sorts of homework while I'm off."

The whining in his son's voice struck Kazuhiro's ears like fingernails on a blackboard. "You can do whatever you need to do at night," he said. "Hurry up. I'm already late."

Eiichi stood, his chin thrust out. "I'm not going."

"You are." Kazuhiro stared at his man-boy son with narrowed eyes. Although a brawl with Eiichi might have lightened the tension in his shoulders, he felt relief when his son reconsidered and dropped to his chair. "Finish your breakfast," he said. "I need to find my car."

After a series of phone calls, he discovered he'd left the car at the first bar he'd visited the afternoon before.

Eiichi remained silent and sulking in the taxi ride to the car and on the drive to Nishimi, but Kazuhiro ignored him.

As soon as they arrived, he put his son to work cleaning out a pug mill.

"I'll be back in a couple of hours," he told Yoko. "I need to meet someone."

7
THE SENSEI
Hirotaka

A fan propped near the open window in the sensei's attic studio rotated back and forth through the muggy air. The work he did at the pottery factory followed the traditional sumi-e style, but oils were his preference. They were also the preference of the Sakayama gallery that had represented him for years. He pulled a handkerchief from his pocket and dabbed sweat from his forehead, still intent upon the scene he painted.

It came from memory, two children flying kites: Kazuhiro Yoshida and his childhood friend, Sachiko Abi. Kazuhiro wore a yellow shirt, Sachiko a red jacket, her long black hair blowing around her face. He dipped the tip of his brush into a daub of titanium white and cadmium yellow and added several small highlights to the autumn-colored maple trees in the background.

He took a step back, careful not to tread on any of Kotada's possessions, scattered over the floor in this space he and his grandson shared. His head tilted to one side, he wondered if Kazuhiro and Sachiko would recognize their long-ago selves. They'd been so young and happy. Their high -pitched laughter still rang in his ears. The two had been inseparable from the time they were children until they were teenagers. Even well into their twenties, despite Sachiko going off to university and working in Sakayama while Kazuhiro remained behind.

He had always expected they would make a love-match marriage one day. Things had not turned out that way, though. Sachiko had married Kensai Hara, a poor farmer, an event no one would have predicted. A few months later, Kazuhiro had married a well-connected woman from Sakayama. A matchmaker arranged the marriage, an event occurring less often in recent years. Now the childhood companions didn't speak. Something lay behind the abrupt severing of their friendship, but he had never discovered what.

From the kitchen below came the soft murmurs of Chieko, talking to their infant granddaughter. Things were going much smoother now Hiromi had returned to her job at the telephone company. If only Akira could find employment. The job his son had counted on had been given to an employee of the acquiring bank. It had been a terrible blow to Akira's pride and his spirit. He feared his son spent more time than he should in bars. He suspected, too, that Chieko unwittingly supported this by slipping Akira extra money from time to time. He would speak with her. It would not be good if word got around; people might consider their son unreliable.

Lost in his thoughts, he started at the sound of the door sliding open with a bang, followed by Kotada's shout. Chieko screamed. His granddaughter wailed. He set his brush down and as quickly as his aging limbs permitted, climbed down the steep steps to the kitchen.

"What's wrong?" He looked from one horror-filled face to the other. The baby, still in Chieko's arms, wailed louder. He turned to his grandson. "Kotada, tell me. What has happened?"

"It's Mr. Yoshida. Grandfather, it's…he's…he's dead!"

The sensei frowned. "How do you know this? Are you certain it's Kazuhiro Yoshida? What makes you think he's dead? Perhaps he's only fallen and hurt himself."

Kotada shook his head with energy. "No! He's dead! Grandfather, someone cut off his head!"

Chieko howled, clutching the protesting baby closer.

With an unsteady hand, the sensei gripped the edge of a counter to keep from falling. Seconds passed before he could speak. "Did you see anyone? Could someone else have been nearby?" He took a deep breath. "We must contact the police. I will go to the factory to break the news to Yoko and make the call from there." He put his shaking hand on his grandson's shoulder. "You must stop crying Ko-chan and tell me where you found him."

Kotada gulped back tears. "The garden near the temple. I was following my kitten hunting a mouse."

Chieko continued to sob, but quieter now, rocking and shushing the crying baby.

"Stay with your grandmother," the sensei said, his voice hoarse as he tried to absorb the full portent of his grandson's words. "Stay with your grandmother," he said again. "I will return as soon as possible." He drew another deep breath and straightened his shoulders.

Akira and Hiromi arrived home as the sun slid behind the mountains and its light began to fade from the sky.

"Police cars are blocking the way near the temple. What has happened?" Akira asked as soon as they entered the house.

Hiromi didn't wait for an answer. "We asked a policeman, but he wouldn't tell us anything."

"You must brace yourselves." Then, as simply as possible, the sensei explained.

"Where is he? Where is my son?" Hiromi cried out the moment he finished speaking.

Akira echoed her, his voice rough.

"He's in the garden," the sensei said. "A young policewoman is talking with him. You can go see him in a moment, but first you must calm yourselves."

Two hours later, most of the police had gone, including the young woman who'd spent the afternoon with Kotada. His grandson had fallen asleep in his parents' room, cuddling his kitten. The shoji screens were left open so they would know if he woke. Once or twice Kotada whimpered in his sleep. When he did, the kitten moved closer, butting its head into the boy's chest.

While the women stayed near the sleeping child, the sensei slid open the outside door and he and Akira stepped into the balmy night air. Their shoes made crunching noises on the gravel pathway as he led the way to his bench at the edge of the garden.

"Who would do such a terrible thing? And then, to place his head on that rock for our Ko-chan to find." Akira's voice held suppressed fury. "What sickness would drive a person to do that?"

"It looked as if a samurai had slain him." Kazuhiro's eyes had been closed, his curled hair and thick beard, the man's great pride, looked untouched. The sensei shuddered at the memory.

"I can't understand why someone would want to harm Kazuhiro. I never liked him. He used to call me 'rabbit'." Akira's mouth twisted. "But to kill him, and in such a brutal way. It just doesn't make sense."

"I know. I've been trying all afternoon to come up with a reason. Had it been his father...well, I could give you several names of people who wished Takeda Yoshida ill. I would even need to include myself on that list. But Kazuhiro? As you said—it makes no sense."

Even as the words passed his lips, the sensei knew their untruthfulness. He'd tried to avoid thinking about it, but each time he managed to forget that day three months before, the memory of the ponytailed man strutting through the pottery factory once more injected itself into his thoughts. At the time, he'd thought the man looked like yakuza. He'd dismissed the idea as foolish and nonsensical. Now....

"Father, you're pale. Are you all right?"

The sensei forced aside thoughts of mobsters. "We've been so concerned about Kazuhiro we haven't even considered his family." He'd met Kazuhiro's high-strung wife only a few times, but easily recalled her reedy, demanding voice, her haughty manners. How could she cope with the terrible details of Kazuhiro's murder? And the boys...what would they do without a father's hand to guide them?

"I can imagine their shock," Akira said. "But there is something else to think about. With Kazuhiro gone, what will happen to the factory? Who will run it?"

Later that night, with the house quiet and everyone asleep, the sensei lay in the dark and considered his son's question about who would take over the running of the factory. Kazuhiro's sons, fourteen and ten, were too young and Eriko had no experience. Surely Yoko was too old to carry such a burden again.

Then he considered the other question Akira had raised. Who would want Kazuhiro Yoshida dead? And just as puzzling, why?

BOOK TWO

What Came Before
1939-1945

1
TOSHIO
Farmer – Soldier

Toshio stared without recognition at the woman shaking his shoulder and hovering over him. Covered with sweat, his heart thudding, he forgot for the moment he was home and on his own futon.

"Husband? What is wrong?"

The dream again. Back in Nanking, rolling bodies into a mass grave—old people, young people, boys and girls, their bodies broken and bleeding. One cried out. Others began to cry out as well. Soon they all moaned and wept. One by one, the bodies rose from the pit, and blood dripping from their gaping wounds, they chased him until he woke.

"It is nothing, wife. Go to sleep."

Several times in the night he had used her, hoping to erase the memory, thinking maybe he'd be too exhausted for the dream. But fucking hadn't worked any better than marching through heat, mud, and slime until he reeled. He felt his wife shift and lie back on the futon. Before long her even breathing whispered in his ear. He closed his eyes and tried to force his mind blank, but memories of the past two years refused to be pushed aside.

Toshio squinted in the late August sunshine. "Someone is coming."

His father, next to him in the rice paddy, straightened. His mother, two rows over, shaded her eyes and looked as well. Never had Toshio seen someone, other than one of his parents returning from a rare trip to the village, turn up the path leading to their farm.

"It is Mr. Abi," his father said.

Mud sucking at their feet, his parents waded out of the paddy to greet the Nishimi postmaster. Toshio remained standing in the knee-deep water; the ripening rice surrounding him waved in the breeze like golden beads on strings. At eighteen, he didn't need to see the red postcard Mr. Abi carried to know he'd been conscripted.

His mother knew, too; stone-faced she handed Mr. Abi a cup of water from a jug.

"Can't he wait, at least until after harvest?" his father asked. "It will soon be ready." He waved his arm to indicate the ripening rice.

"The card says he must report for training in two weeks," Mr. Abi said, batting at a swarm of gnats. He handed back the empty cup. "I must go. I have two more call-ups to deliver."

Three months later, Toshio arrived in China in time to take part in the battle for Shanghai. Shanghai fell quickly and there'd been mass celebrations, with barrel upon barrel of sake. He'd felt invincible. They'd all felt invincible. After Shanghai, they pushed through the Yangtze River valley, virtually unopposed, and Toshio was again glad to be part of such glorious success.

Then they reached Nanking.

He never imagined there could be so much blood. For nearly six weeks, the streets ran red with it. Women, young and old, were raped repeatedly before they were killed and their bodies mutilated. Men were beaten and tortured then made to kneel so their heads could be cut off, sending streaming gouts of blood into the air. Worst of all were the babies, ripped from their mothers' arms and impaled on the ends of bayonets. Their pathetic, agonized cries filled Toshio's ears. He prayed for the carnage and the tortured screaming to stop, but both went on until he wanted to smash his own skull against a wall. After six long weeks, the nightmare of death finally ended.

"Did you hear?" another soldier said when they were alone, scrubbing pots, behind the mess tent. "A man in the next platoon—he attended a missionary school and can read English—found an English-language newspaper that calls what happened 'the massacre of Nanking.'"

Toshio grunted. The killing over now, he saw no reason to talk about it.

"The newspaper claims 300,000 civilians were killed," his companion said. "Our government denies it."

The great number caught Toshio's attention. "So many...I didn't know." He shook his head, but his eyes remained on the pot he washed; the higher-ups frowned on gossip in the lower ranks.

Despite the English-speaking soldier's cleverness in keeping it hidden from superiors, the newspaper was found.

Toshio and another man were told to dig a short trench. Neither of them dared ask the purpose of the trench. The pale winter sun shone weakly through bared tree branches. Even so, breaking up the near-frozen ground soon had them sweating.

Finally, a sergeant peered in the trench and nodded. "Deep enough."

The company fell into formation, and the English-speaking soldier was dragged forward. The company commander and five other officers stood to one side while the soldier's platoon leader, Lieutenant Shunsuki Katsuragawa, only recently assigned to the regiment, strode forward. He drew his sword and solemnly poured water on it from a long -handled bamboo cup.

Toshio frowned, recognizing the ritual from when Chinese prisoners were executed. Surely, they wouldn't execute a Japanese soldier. He drew a deep breath. His frown deepened as what was about to happen became obvious. Head back and shoulders squared, he stared straight ahead and tried to blot out all sound. He couldn't.

The English-speaking soldier whimpered. The lieutenant took a determined step forward, lifted his sword and brought it swiftly down on the soldier's bowed neck. The head landed with a thud on the ground and blood spewed onto soldiers in the front ranks. The smell filled Toshio's nostrils. The lieutenant kicked the head into the trench and the two who'd held their comrade on his knees threw the body in after it.

The company commander strolled away with the other officers, all laughing and talking, as though satisfied justice had been served.

The breath Toshio had been holding went out of him. Blood pounded in his temples, and he swallowed the bile rising in his throat. A drop of splattered blood slid down his left cheek; he itched to scrub it away. Instead, along with his fellow soldiers, he remained braced at attention, his clenched fists at his sides. Before being dismissed, they were threatened with similar deaths if they talked to anyone about what happened in Nanking. They were not to speak of it even among themselves.

No one talked, but the sounds of water trickling over a naked sword and the thud that followed rang in Toshio's ears. And every night, for two long years, bloody bodies chased him.

A mouse scurried across a beam above his head; bits of straw rained down on the light quilt covering him. Outside, a rooster crowed. With relief Toshio saw daylight creeping into the room—daylight meant respite from the dream. This daylight also meant his return to duty; his two-week-long home leave up. He swallowed to ease the pain forming in the back of his throat.

His wife slept on. Five years his senior, she had been nearly past marriageable age when he asked the matchmaker to approach her parents. With three other daughters to feed, her parents had been happy to agree. They had married only days before Toshio first went to China. His mother called her a good worker.

He prodded her arm. "Are my things packed?"

She nodded. Though her eyes remained closed, she waved her hand toward the wall where his duffle-bag leaned.

At breakfast, his mother said little, merely knelt on a worn cushion, and watched him eat. His wife moved back and forth from the kitchen, placing more food on the table until finally he told her to stop.

The sun was only partway to its zenith and the day still cool when Toshio arrived in the village of Nishimi. Takeda Yoshida waited outside the pottery factory. Conscripted six months before him, Takeda had recently been promoted to the rank of corporal. They were not friends. Many times, Toshio had witnessed Takeda's acts of barbarism, especially in Nanking where the man seemed to take special delight in torturing women. He felt nothing but sympathy for Takeda's skinny wife and two daughters.

"You're late," Takeda said.

Not true, but Toshio didn't bother to deny it.

Takeda wouldn't let it go. "Did you need to hump your woman one more time? Stuff her with a brat to make sure she stays in line?" He gave an ugly laugh, but receiving no response, he picked up his pack. "Okay, let's go."

Toshio slung his duffle bag onto his shoulders once more and they set off. Takeda, who dwarfed most men, continued unsuccessfully to bait him. Toshio took grim satisfaction when the man finally gave up. Normally, Takeda never stopped, especially if he sensed a weakness in his intended victim.

They reached the train station in Sakayama in mid-afternoon. On the platform, a young woman scanned the waiting crowd, an anxious look on her face. A middle-aged woman approached her and the young woman set down her suitcase. They bowed. The young woman picked up her suitcase and they both disappeared into the station, the middle-aged woman speaking all the while.

Something about the young woman, in her wrinkled navy-blue skirt and white blouse, seemed out of place. Japanese, but for some reason, Toshio thought her a foreigner. He shrugged and boarded the train for Hiroshima.

When first called up, he'd been anxious, frightened even, about what lay ahead. He'd felt the prick of excitement, too, wondering if he had what it took to be a soldier, what war would be like, if there'd be women. Everything had been new to him then, including traveling on a train. He'd come to hate trains, especially this one, taking him through field after field, village after village, farther and farther from home, closer and closer to the battlefields of China.

Night had fallen. They marched toward Japanese-controlled Manchuria, or Manchukuo as it had been renamed, through an area mostly held by the enemy. Almost without thinking, Toshio reached beneath his tunic and touched the soft white fabric and red stitching of the thousand-stitch belt sewn for him by his mother and his wife. Wrapped double around his waist, the spirit of the belt would ward off bullets.

Single-file, they made their way along a narrow path through what recently had been a battlefield. Tanks had churned up the ground, making walking difficult. Although no one spoke, the total silence of one hundred-fifty men passing through the dark was not possible. A twig snapped.

Fabric rubbed against fabric. A rifle butt clinked against a canteen. Someone slipped and uttered a whispered curse.

When they were finally given a signal to take a ten-minute rest, Toshio collapsed beneath a broken and leafless tree, his rifle cradled in his lap. Silhouetted above him, the tree looked like a creature from the netherworld. Through its branches, the stars in the night sky shone bright. Many were the same constellations he saw from home—only a few obliterated by random clouds.

He thought again of his home leave. His wife and his mother wept the morning he left. His father merely grunted, but Toshio knew the grunt hid a heavy heart. A gentle man, seldom had Toshio felt the wrath of his father's fists. He tried to picture the three of them, wife, mother, father, but already their faces had faded.

He rose as the line began to move. They were still several hours from their destination. A cloud slid across the moon. Far off, shots. Without warning, a burst of light overhead, accompanied by the rattling noise of gunfire, this time closer at hand. Someone cried out.

Toshio dove for cover. The *shosh-shosh-shosh* of an artillery shell passing overhead sounded like blood through an artery. Seconds later, a thudding explosion. The earth shook and bits of dirt pelted his helmet. More explosions, more dirt clods falling to the earth like great chunks of hail. He was about to die. He choked back a sob and felt once again for the thousand-stitch belt.

The death Toshio had expected, perhaps some part of him had hoped for, didn't come. Instead, his unit rejoined the regiment, encamped alongside a river. Intent on cleaning his rifle, he frowned when handed a thin and flimsy envelope. He turned the envelope over and stiffened when he saw the postmark. Nishimi. Neither his parents nor his wife could read or write; Mr. Abi must have written for them.

His hands shook when he tore open the envelope and took out the single onionskin page. He caught his breath and his eyes widened. Not the bad news he'd feared. His wife was with child. For the first time in over two years he had something to live for. He read on. A boy, his wife felt sure, due in the spring.

A slight furrow formed between his brows. A fortuitous time for birthing, but also the time for planting; his parents would be short-handed. Well, they would need to get along as best they could. His frown disappeared as he carefully refolded the letter and placed it in his tunic pocket. A boy, his son, would be worth any temporary struggle.

Toshio slung his pack onto his shoulder and picked up his rifle. Now on a plain to the north of Nanking, rest period was over. Dead bodies of Chinese lay piled like cordwood or floating in the rivers and streams where they accumulated and formed into dams, needing to be kicked loose so water could flow freely. The Chinese either didn't know or didn't care about the necessity of tending to their dead.

Whenever possible, when a Japanese soldier died, he was cremated, his ashes bagged, tagged, and sent to the homeland for burial. Toshio had helped perform this rite several times. To leave them lying where they fell, as the

Chinese did, would bring great dishonor to ancestors and descendants alike. Because of the untended bodies, the air smelled putrid, the place rank with disease.

Lieutenant Shunsuki Katsuragawa—the one who'd executed the soldier for having a foreign newspaper—fell sick first. From a noble family and a recent university graduate, the lieutenant had been unused to marching fifteen or more hours at a stretch. Within two days, he succumbed to the disease. Soon, men were falling like flies at the end of summer. Even the two medics attached to their unit fell ill and soon died.

They strung a rope perimeter around a grove of trees where the sick lay quarantined. The ailing men promised to stay within the groves confines, but the regiment's commander decided guards were necessary to ensure they remained separated from the rest of the camp.

Assigned that duty, Toshio couldn't shut out the cries of sick and thirsty men. He took to filling his helmet with water, tying it to the end of a long tree branch, and passing it over to whomever could take it. Few were well enough. Nor were there many to take the rice he passed over in the same manner.

They remained encamped for several days. He assumed they were waiting for more medics to come and tend the sick. No one came.

"Get your gear together," his sergeant said. "We're moving out."

"What about the men in the grove? Are we just going to leave them?" He got only a shrug in reply. He gathered his gear. "Hang on," he called out one last time. "A medic is coming."

What a lie. No one would come. Unable to do anything more, he vowed to pray for their souls so they would not become nameless wanderers in the afterlife.

They marched north. Summer passed. Toshio's platoon separated from the regiment and moved into the mountains. At least the cooler temperatures meant no more cholera. Recently promoted to corporal, he led four others on an advance patrol with orders to locate a contingent of Chiang Kai-shek's army.

The afternoon of their second day searching, a monsoon -like rain started. It bucketed down in torrents and wiped out all traces of their quarry. Reluctant to admit defeat, Toshio urged his men to persevere. Finally, faced with no let -up in the heavy winds and rain, he held up his hand. "There's no point in going on. We'll never find them in this."

Although his men offered no complaint, they looked at him from the corners of their eyes, and he knew they were thinking of what Captain Sagura would say when they returned to camp with no information on where the enemy lay hidden. They had good reason to wonder. Captain Sagura didn't suffer fools—he would likely take away Toshio's new corporal's stripes. Or worse. Toshio rubbed the back of his neck.

They scrabbled over rocks and scree, loosened by the relentless rain. On the third day, like a faucet turned off, the rain stopped and the sun broke through the clouds. Toward evening, they reached the spot where they'd left the others.

Toshio frowned. No sign of a sentry. His earlier concerns over Captain Sagura and his response turned to alarm. He shoved chest-high underbrush aside and came to an abrupt halt. Pots with dried and burnt rice, tipped over onto the remains of several s fires, scattered equipment, and sodden bedding—all lay strewn amongst the long shadows cast by the setting sun.

There were no bodies. His comrades weren't dead. But neither had they come back and claimed their gear. Had the enemy he and his men been chasing doubled back? He kicked one of the burnt pots.

The last of the weak sunlight disappeared. "What shall we do?" one of his men asked, staring into the growing darkness.

"In the morning, we'll head down the mountain, back the way we came. Maybe we'll come across them."

Even to his own ears, the words sounded hollow. Their comrades must have been captured. Even if they weren't, the chances were nearly non-existent of finding them in China's vastness.

When they reached the plains two days later, nearly out of food, they approached a small village. Toshio planned to surprise the villagers and take what they needed at gunpoint. They were too late. All the villagers were dead. Japanese troops were ransacking every house, taking whatever they found fit to eat or use. Takeda Yoshida was in charge.

"Well, look what's turned up," Takeda said, a snigger in his voice. "And where the hell have you been? Major Tamayama is pissed that you and Captain Sagura couldn't find those bloody Chink troops and do your job. Where is Sagura, anyway?"

"I don't know. I hoped he and the rest of the platoon might have rejoined the regiment."

A private approached. "We're done clearing the huts, Sergeant Yoshida."

"Well, finish the job," said Takeda. "You know our new orders—burn all, seize all, kill all." The private gave a quick bow before trotting off to where the other men were clustered. Takeda stood with his feet spread and his fists on his hips, watching as his men split up. Soon, the entire village blazed.

A young boy burst out the door of one of the hovels.

"Grab him," Takeda yelled.

With nowhere to run the boy couldn't avoid capture. His eyes wild with fear, two men dragged him to Takeda.

"Look, the piece of dung has pissed his pants," Takeda said.

Though clearly terrified, the boy struggled to stand. Takeda swept out a foot and the boy crumpled to the ground. Takeda laughed and unbuttoned the front of his trousers. "You like piss, shithead? Here's more." Still laughing, he finished relieving himself and rebuttoned. Then, with no warning, his demeanor changed. He shouted. "Who is the son of a whore who missed finding him?"

A soldier little older than the Chinese boy reluctantly came forward. Toshio had often witnessed the hulking Takeda challenge the unwary to arm wrestling or other feats to prove his superior strength. The young soldier would be no match for the man's heavy fists.

Meeting no resistance, Takeda lost interest. He kicked the bleeding and beaten young soldier aside.

"What should we do with him?" another soldier asked, pointing to the Chinese boy still on the ground.

"Shoot him," Takeda said. "Then toss his body on the heap with the other villagers. Let this be a lesson to the rest of the mongrels in this dung-filled country."

Toshio picked up his pack and walked away, his lips curled in a contempt he didn't try to hide. It was one thing to fight a war for the Emperor, killing the enemy when necessary, but quite another to enjoy it.

When they reached the regiment's encampment that evening, Major Tamayama ordered Toshio to him. "Where is Captain Sagura?" he asked, the moment Toshio entered the command tent. A small man with darting eyes and a shaved head, the major stood behind a small campaign desk of polished teak. He wore a spotless uniform, and carried a riding crop tucked under his left arm.

Toshio saluted. "I don't know, sir."

Major Tamayama ignored the salute. "What do you mean, you don't know?" The words fired from his mouth like bullets. At the same time, the crop smashed down on the desk.

Toshio blinked at the sound, swallowed, and explained what he and his men had found. "I don't know if they were killed, captured or got away."

"They are dead. If they'd gotten away, they'd be here," the major said, slapping his palm with the riding crop and glaring at Toshio, as if daring him to deny it. "They wouldn't have allowed themselves to be taken. For a soldier, there can be no greater shame than capture by the enemy."

2
YOKO
The Pottery Factory

Yoko stared at the backs of the two men headed down the mountain toward Sakayama—the farmer-soldier from across the valley, and Takeda Yoshida, her despised husband. Gone, at last, and with any luck, he wouldn't be back. She didn't need him grabbing her, throwing her to the ground and mounting her, even when their daughters were within hearing. And if not rutting like a pig, he shouted and complained, or beat her or the children for some infraction. Both girls were terrified of him.

"Good riddance," she muttered when the men disappeared around a bend. She went back inside the factory, putting thoughts of Takeda aside. She had too many other things to worry about, like who she could hire to replace the apprentice she'd lost. It would need to be another woman. The only young men who hadn't been conscripted were those doing what the government called necessary work—building airplanes or working in munition factories. Even boys were called up the moment they finished secondary school, unless they had some sort of special deferment.

Well, she didn't care if they all got sent to China, just so they didn't take old Mori or Ishihara. Those two had worked at the factory for decades and between them knew every aspect of pottery making. Those two she needed. The rest of them could go to whatever devil had spawned them.

Once at her desk, she picked up the order that had arrived that morning from the noble Katsuragawa family. It would be for the servants at the main house in Sakayama, not fine ware for the family's use, but a large order, nonetheless. She'd heard the Katsuragawa family would again be spending much of July, including the week of Obon, at their summer estate near Nishimi. Only the two youngest sons would be with them this time. The oldest son now served in China. An officer, perhaps he'd give her husband the kick the dog deserved.

For the most part, Yoko liked Obon, when the spirits of dead ancestors were believed to visit their loved ones. Although skeptical of the spirits' return from the afterlife, she always found the bonfires, lit at the doorway to every house, a pleasant sight. There would be plenty to eat and drink, too.

Whenever the Katsuragawa family came to stay in their Nishimi residence, Obon or not, Nishimi became livelier; a special energy filled the air, an energy that dissipated when the family returned to their palatial estate in Sakayama.

Yoko looked up from packing a short, cylindrical vase in a wooden box to see a young man with a broad chest and long arms standing in the factory's doorway. She quickly rose to her feet and bobbed her head. "*Konnichiwa*, sir."

The young man, whom she recognized as the youngest Katsuragawa son, returned her greeting. "Good afternoon.

I am Hirotaka Katsuragawa," he said with a slight bow. "I haven't been in a pottery works before. Please show me what you do here."

Despite the 'please' affixed to the request, being a Katsuragawa, she didn't doubt he expected her instant acquiescence.

"It would be my pleasure, sempai." She stepped down from the platform and indicated he should follow. They went through the door at the back of the showroom, down three steps, onto the packed earth factory floor.

Asai, her most skilled potter, whose upper arms strained the sleeves of the shortened yukata she wore over pants gathered at the ankles, sat on a platform opposite three equally burly female potters. The paraphernalia of their work surrounded each: a jug of water to lubricate hands, bits of leather to smooth edges, and assorted tools for molding and scraping. The faint whirr of pottery wheels turning and the occasional slap of hands on clay were all that disturbed the quiet.

"What are they doing?" the young man asked, pointing to two girl apprentices, each working with a large, gray lump of clay.

"They are forcing out air bubbles, preparing the clay for the potters. If an air pocket is in the clay, there will be a thin spot in the side of the vessel and the wall will be uneven or collapse. Or the thing will split open when it's fired."

He nodded and she followed him to the wedging bench where the two young women worked. While he studied their movements, Yoko covertly examined him. Despite his broad chest and long arms, he stood no more than two inches taller than her. The seriousness in his intense gaze belied his young age, which she calculated to be nineteen or twenty.

When the Katsuragawa sons were young, they'd played and run with the village children. But when the older two grew to be teenagers, their father put a stop to any interaction between the village and his family. One of the Katsuragawa maids was from Nishimi, however, so everyone in the village knew what went on in the Katsuragawa household, including the rift existing between the father and this, his youngest son.

She cast another glance at him, wondering what lay behind his sudden interest in pottery making. The controlled expression on his face told her nothing. With a slight jerk of his chin, he indicated they should move on.

Yoko nodded toward the potters at their wheels. "They are throwing rice bowls for your family. Or, I should say, for your family's servants." She picked up a leather-hard bowl and held it out to him. "Notice how it is incised near the rim with your family's crest."

He held the bowl with both hands, turning it over, examining its shape from every direction before returning it. "Very nice," he said. "I suppose the structure visible from the road is your kiln. May I see it?"

She led the way through the wide doors at the rear of the factory and down the hill toward the kiln, surprised she still held his attention, surprised he hadn't been satisfied with a brief look around the factory floor. Mori, supervising the loading of the kiln, nodded to them as they moved down the slope toward the oven at the bottom of the long, tunnel-shaped kiln.

"When all the chambers are filled, the oven here at the base is stacked with wood and the fire started. That's Mori's job." She waved her hand in the old man's direction.

Hirotaka knelt and peered into a partially filled chamber. "Since it is being loaded, I assume you'll be firing soon." He rose and brushed dried grass from the knees of his trousers.

"We begin in three days."

"I would like to see it."

She bowed. "You would be most welcome."

A slight breeze stirred the early morning air. Everyone from the factory and many from the village gathered on the hillside next to the kiln. Yoko, too, waited with anticipation. A mystical quality always surrounded the lighting. Breath was held. No words were spoken aloud, though silent prayers for a successful firing were doubtless sent to the kiln-kami as Ishihara struck a match and held it to the bundle of sticks in Mori's hand.

When the bundle caught, Mori thrust it into the oven. A moment passed, then two, before flames shot up and the fire took off, devouring the neat stack of wood Mori had earlier placed there. He shoved in more wood. As the fire grew, it leaped over the fire wall into the first chamber. Mori shouted orders. "Open the first stoking windows and prepare to throw in wood...Now."

Wood repeatedly thrown on the fire, it continued to build, leaping from chamber to chamber. Finally, black smoke poured out of the chimney at the top end of the kiln, accompanied by satisfied grunts and murmurs from those watching.

Yoko stood on the perimeter. Even though she ran the factory in her husband's absence, custom decreed women couldn't be within fifteen feet of the lit kiln—her presence could cause offense to the kiln-kami. Although she resented such ignorant beliefs, disregarding them would result in unnecessary turmoil, especially with old Ishihara.

Hirotaka Katsuragawa stood beside her. Earlier, when she'd looked up and seen him once again standing in the doorway, she'd been only mildly surprised. This one wasn't like the father. This was an altogether different Katsuragawa. For a moment, she'd wondered if the father knew the whereabouts of his son and how he would react if he did. But she'd thrust that disquieting thought aside. She had too much on her mind to worry about potentially frayed relationships within the Katsuragawa household.

Old men and teenaged boys, recruited from the village or nearby farms and arranged on both sides of the kiln, continued to throw wood through the stoking windows on Mori's command.

"It will be early tomorrow morning before the fire is right," Yoko said. "We need a bed of coals to maintain a steady heat at exactly the right temperature." A slag heap of failures nearly two hundred years in the making—bowls fused to plates, vessels twisted and warped from too much heat or split open like an over-ripe melon from too rapid cooling—grew on the hillside behind them.

Throughout the morning, the young man's keen eyes darted from one person to another, taking in everything.

Shortly after noon, without a word to her, he approached Mori. "Let me throw in some wood."

Mori turned to her, the question on his face. She nodded, not daring to say no to a noble Katsuragawa, no matter how different he might be from his father.

"You must be careful not to knock anything from the shelves," Mori told him. "Listen to Ishihara—he will show you the proper angle to throw it. And the wood must be thrown at the same time as the person across the kiln from you. Watch Ishihara closely, then you may try."

Yoko held her breath, but she need not have. Nothing dislodged from the shelves within the chamber. Hirotaka threw the wood at the precise angle Ishihara demonstrated, as he did with all the wood that followed.

Finally, two and one-half days after Mori first lit the fire, two and one-half days of continual tending, coals bright and steady throughout all five chambers, the firing was complete.

Mori straightened and with the back of his arm, he wiped sweat from his forehead. "It is done."

The stoking windows were quickly closed and plugged and the unused wood pushed away from the kiln. Hirotaka Katsuragawa sank down on a nearby rock. Yoko studied his weary face. Surprisingly, he had stayed with the firing from start to finish, sleeping only in brief snatches. The rest of the time he'd worked tirelessly hauling and throwing wood. Suddenly, he tensed. She followed his gaze up the slope to the open doors at the back of the factory where, hands on hips, his father stood.

The young man rose from the rock and gathered the jacket he'd earlier discarded. He turned to Mori and made a formal bow from the waist then slowly walked up the hill toward his father.

Father and son were of equal height, though the son appeared deeper in the chest. They stared at one another for what seemed like a full minute, a minute in which neither of them spoke or looked away. Finally, the son dropped his eyes and lowered his head in a brief bow. The two then turned and stepped back inside the factory, disappearing from Yoko's view.

Each time someone came through the door of the factory Yoko tensed, the hair on her neck lifting. Each time, she expected a stranger with a missive voiding the Katsuragawa order. She'd relax when it turned out to be an apprentice or one of her daughters or Mr. Abi with the mail, only to tense again when someone else came through the door. Three days passed without receiving the dreaded word. Finally convinced they were to be spared, she gave a quick prayer of thanks the very profitable order would stand.

With boxes of pottery from the cooled and emptied kiln stacked on the two packing platforms, Yoko and Mori sorted through them. Mori, as usual, prattled. Yoko interrupted his stream of talk—something about an American woman, a gaijin, coming to stay with him and his family the week following Obon.

"The Katsuragawa family should be pleased with the quality. I want their order ready to ship down the mountain with the mail cart in two days." He nodded. Satisfied, she handed him a rice bowl. "See how distinctive their family crest looks. With any luck, we may get additional orders from them."

"And through them, some of the other noble families," said Mori.

"Let us hope so, assuming there are any noble families left after this war. I hear the second Katsuragawa son is anticipating call-up soon."

3
NOBUKO
The Gaijin

No trains connected the city of Sakayama, where Nobuko Ito had lived with her aunt's family for the past eleven months, to the village of Nishimi, where the cousin of her father and aunt lived. Arrangements had been made for her to travel up the mountain by farm cart. She dropped her suitcase onto a pile of empty burlap bags in back and clambered over the cart's spoked wheel to sit next to the farmer. Old and stooped, his face as wrinkled as a walnut, the old man mumbled a brief greeting and slapped the reins. The huge ox, it's feet the size of pie tins, shambled forward, pulling the lurching cart along with it. Nobuko clung to the edge of the bench for support, and waved goodbye to her aunt.

Before long, they left the last traces of Sakayama behind and, with only a slight shift in the ox's rippling shoulders, began a twisting and turning climb.

Nobuko welcomed the farmer's on-going silence—it left her free to enjoy the sound of birds singing, the whine of insects in the weeds bordering the track, and the ox's plodding feet striking stone. She shifted on the hard, wooden bench and adjusted her hat to keep the warm July sun off her face.

Men and women, all wearing loose-fitting clothing and conical straw hats, worked in the rice paddies and terraced fields of millet and wheat on the mountain's flank, which steadily became steeper. Interspersed were stands of cedar and rocky outcroppings. It looked nothing like home—the fields and flooded paddies were miniscule compared to the acres of flat fields and orchards in California's Central Valley. But those differences charmed her. She felt like Gulliver traveling in a miniaturized country; every bend revealed a new and exciting vista.

Her delight came to an abrupt halt late in the afternoon, when they entered the village of Nishimi. Nothing she had imagined on the long and winding trip up the mountain came close to the reality of the unpainted shacks, most too small to contain more than two or three rooms. A noxious smell rose from a ditch that appeared to run the length of the village. Mosquitoes teemed in the air above it.

Barely wide enough for the ox and cart, half-a-dozen short strides would carry her across the narrow main street. Her back and shoulders rigid, she sat in frozen silence as the ox and cart lumbered past shadowed doorways, where women and a few old men stared out at her. Children and two mangy-looking dogs darted out of the ox's path. A young boy ran ahead, gleefully shouting, "It's the gaijin. She's come. The foreign American is here."

Unlike in Sakayama, they passed no shop displaying lengths of embroidered silk draped over polished wooden racks, or one with ink stones, brushes, and other calligraphy materials in the window. And none with little pots of fragrant and exotic teas and spices. Nor were there any street vendors, pushing their carts and ringing their bells, offering treats like roasted chestnuts, frozen ices, or skewers of teriyaki. Nobuko saw only what looked to be a general store, with dishware, clothes, and some foodstuffs arranged in baskets outside its door.

Ahead, on the left, stood a large rambling building with a strange-looking structure flowing down the hillside behind it. Stacks of dusty pots and dishes were piled on benches across the front of the building and under an open shed at one side—no doubt the pottery factory where her father's cousin worked. A thin woman wearing a dark blue *yukata*, her hair confined by a kerchief and her brows drawn into a fierce-looking frown, stepped from its open door. Long after the cart had passed, Nobuko felt the woman's eyes boring into her back.

At the edge of the village, the farmer pulled the ox to a stop in front of a house somewhat bigger than its neighbors. Several people, whom she assumed were her father's cousin and his family, were lined up in front of the house, smiling and bowing. "Welcome, welcome," the man said.

Holding her breath, Nobuko climbed from the cart, adjusted her wrinkled skirt and blouse with trembling hands, and responded with a bow of her own. The farmer handed down her suitcase to two children who, together and with muffled giggles, half-dragged and half-carried it into the house.

After profuse thanks were rendered to the farmer, he and his cart rumbled away.

"I am Mori," the man said. He had iron gray hair. Deep lines bracketed his mouth and fanned out from eyes that held both sympathy and wisdom in their depths. "This is my wife and my daughter-in-law." He indicated the two women at his side.

Nobuko bobbed her head to the two women and drew another shaky breath.

"Come," Mori said. "We will go inside."

Still unnerved by what she'd witnessed of the town and the hostile-seeming eyes of the woman in front of the pottery factory, Nobuko's heart quaked as she followed the family into the house. At least the awful odor of the ditch didn't follow.

Mrs. Mori, whose shoe-button eyes sparkled her good humor, showed her where to put her things—in a room she would share with the Mori grandchildren. "They are bit untidy, I'm afraid, but they are excited to have you. We all are."

The room's large tonsu would hold futons and bedding, and there were several baskets containing clothes and toys—those that didn't litter the tatami-covered floor. There obviously would be no more room here than in her aunt's cramped house in Sakayama. But Nobuko didn't think she'd mind. She wouldn't be in Nishimi long—a couple of weeks at most. And the warmth of the Moris' welcome would be enough to make her brief stay enjoyable.

"Our son is with the Army in China," Mr. Mori told her, once she had freshened and distributed the small gifts she'd brought—puzzles for the children, scarves for Mrs. Mori and her daughter-in-law, a book for Mr. Mori. "He came home on leave several months ago, but we've heard little from him since his return to duty."

His daughter-in-law lowered her head, hiding the pain

that flared in her eyes. Mrs. Mori patted the younger woman's hand.

At dinner, Nobuko told them about her family and the farm where she grew up. "It's not actually ours," she said. "Immigrants are not allowed to own property in California, and my brother, who, like me, was born in America and therefore a citizen, is still too young. The man who owns the property has promised to sell it to Mako when he turns eighteen, but that's still two years off. Until then, my parents can only lease it."

Mr. Mori nodded. "Farmers must lease their fields here in Japan, as well—most of the land is owned by just a few noble families. What do your parents' grow? Rice and millet, like we do here?"

"Mostly fruit—apricots and strawberries. But some vegetables, too. We sell to a local cannery, where they make jams and jellies, but we also have a produce stand." At their frowns, she explained how their stand, located at the end of their lane, opened in spring and summer. "People from town often drive out into the country, especially on weekends." She smiled then, thinking of how she and her brother had bickered or played endless jokes on one another during those long summer days—anything to relieve the boredom of waiting for someone to stop and buy something. At least their mother kept them supplied with plenty of lemonade.

Mr. Mori's eyes crinkled at the corners. "I think you must miss it—your family's farm."

Nobuko blinked sudden tears from her eyes. "I do." She pressed her lips together then turned a wobbly smile to Mrs.

Mori. "Thank you for this delicious dinner. At my aunt's, we sometimes have chicken, but pork is rarely available."

"It is the war," Mr. Mori said. "Everything must go to our soldiers in China."

"As it should," said Mrs. Mori.

Her daughter-in-law murmured agreement.

Whispers. A muffled giggle. Nobuko jerked awake. Morning seeped through a narrow window, casting streaks of sunlight on the *tatami* mats. She stretched and looked around.

Jiro and Myoko stared at her. Myoko giggled. Jiro jabbed his sister with his elbow.

Wiping sleep from her eyes, Nobuko grinned at the children. "Is it time to get up?"

Myoko, her straight black hair pulled into two short pigtails and somehow still in place after a night's sleep, answered. "We must go to school."

"Where is it?" Traveling through the village the day before, Nobuko hadn't seen anything that looked like a school. "Must you walk far?"

Jiro lifted his chin, a proud expression on his face. "Four kilometers." At ten, much more direct than his eight-year-old sister.

Nobuko pushed into a sitting position and wrapped her arms around her knees. "That is a good distance. Would you like me to walk with you?"

Eyes twinkling, Myoko nodded her head, and Nobuko sensed that, for this child, laughter never lurked far away. Jiro shrugged.

After a rapidly eaten breakfast of rice balls and miso soup, and an admonition from the children's mother to hurry as the rest of the village children had already left, they set off, Jiro in a white shirt and black shorts, Myoko wearing a black kimono with a yellow, scarf-like obi tied around her waist.

Like a curious sparrow, the little girl skipped and hopped at Nobuko's side, keeping up a steady stream of questions. "What is it like in Sakayama? What are my cousins like? Are they nice? How old are they?"

Nobuko answered the little girl's questions, but when she tried to tell about life in California, Myoko gaped, unable to comprehend the idea of a land across the sea. At Nobuko's declaration that some Americans had yellow and even red hair, the little girl burst into unbelieving peals of laughter.

The school, an unpainted wooden building very like the houses in Nishimi, though larger, was set in a clearing at the bottom of a rock-faced cliff. A group of twenty or so students, clad in uniforms identical to Jiro's and Myoko's, were already lining up in front of the door. Jiro said some of them lived on outlying farms. Through a gap in the trees, Nobuko had earlier caught glimpses of several such farms, clinging like limpets to the side of the mountain.

"I'll see you when you get home from school," she called after the children. A moment later, the school door opened and the children and their classmates filed inside.

After a final wave, Nobuko began retracing her steps. She looked forward to getting to know the children. Jiro so serious, and Myoko—what a little imp. Their mother, quiet, no doubt worried for her husband. Nobuko wondered if she'd ever have a husband, and what it would feel like if he had to go off to war.

Cedar trees marched up the mountain along much of the dirt track between the village and the school, even narrower than the one she'd traveled the previous day in the jouncing and swaying cart. It surprised her to find so few proper roads in Japan. She pictured Fresno's wide tree-lined streets, and imagined the looks of awed wonder on the faces of Mr. and Mrs. Mori if they were plopped down there. She laughed aloud, clapping her hands together in sudden delight.

She breathed in the air, fragrant with the earthy odors of musky-smelling fungi, sweeping cedar boughs, pine pitch. The craggy rocks and stands of trees reminded her of the summer her father drove the family to Yosemite for a rare vacation. Thinking about it made her miss them more than ever—even her bratty brother.

For a moment, she pictured them as she last saw them, standing on the dock in San Francisco, their arms raised in farewell. Despite the August heat, her father had worn his black wool suit, normally reserved for the most formal occasions. Mako, fifteen and already a head taller, stood next to him, trying to appear nonchalant, his stubbornly straight hair parted in the middle and slicked down. Mama stood in front, wearing the flowered navy blue dress and yellow straw hat she'd worn with pride to Nobuko's recent graduation from Fresno Junior College. They'd looked so small, almost as if their importance to her had already begun to diminish.

When a loud horn sounded and the ship began to ease away from the pier, she'd felt a sudden and desperate panic. "I'll write," she shouted as the gap between her and her family widened. Seagulls screamed overhead. Her father cupped a hand to his ear. She pretended to write in the air. "Every day," she called again.

It felt like forever since she'd seen them. She took a steadying breath and walked on, once again vowing to remember every detail of each member of her family.

A large rock about fifty yards above the track caught her attention. She stopped, eyes narrowed, her head cocked to one side. Did it quiver? And the birds that had been chirping and flitting from tree branch to tree branch—where had they gone? Apprehension crawled up her spine. A strange feeling filled the air—as though the clock of nature had stopped, waiting for something momentous to happen.

Craaack!

The loud, echoing boom reverberated all around her. The rock split into two, one half crashing over bushes and sticks, coming straight toward her. She screamed and leapt aside as it thundered past.

An earthquake!

Rocks skittered in every direction. She dodged and jumped. A tree, still upright, its roots encased in a mound of dirt, slid across the track. The ground in front of her heaved and rolled like the ocean. The entire mountain shifted.

The school. The children…must reach the children.

She ran down the track, back the way she'd come. She tripped and fell…a tooth drove deep into her lip. Resisting the urge to curl into a ball, she scrambled to her feet. Running and stumbling. Running. Her breath came in loud, wheezing gasps. Heart pounding…head ready to explode… fear tasted sour in her mouth.

Must get the children.

The violent dipping and swaying faded, but still, she ran, ran until she reached the clearing. Her eyes went wide with horror. The cliff had broken off. Where the school had been, a massive pile of rock and debris.

She shouted, hoping the children were running down the mountain to safety. Only the echo of her voice answered her frantic call. She rushed to the heap of broken granite and began to claw and push at it.

Time expanded and contracted. She didn't know if hours or minutes passed before others came. Together, they rolled and pried the huge chunks of rock away, only to reveal another just as large. At last they reached the remains of the school. Nobuko held her breath as a piece of wall got raised and dragged aside. A man lifted a broken body from the debris beneath it. Then another, and another. Jiro next. Though dirt covered the little boy's thin face, she saw no sign of external injuries. Her voice trembled. "Is he alive?"

The man, a farmer by his dress, shook his head.

Myoko's body soon lay next to her brother's. Nobuko knelt between them. Her tears went unchecked as she stroked their small faces. How could God have let this terrible thing happen?

Distant shouting heralded another group of people, the Moris and their daughter-in-law among them, rushing down the mountain track from the direction of Nishimi.

The children's mother screamed when she saw Myoko and Jiro stretched out on the bare ground. She ran to them and threw herself across their prone bodies. "No, no!" she cried.

The Mori knelt by their daughter-in-law and their grandchildren, their lined, stricken faces reflecting their pain and shock.

The sun sank behind the mountain as the last small body was raised from the rubble. There were no survivors.

With visible effort and despite Nobuko's feeble protests, Mrs. Mori pulled herself together enough to clean and dress Nobuko's wounds. In her mad dash, she'd been hit by several rocks, one hard enough to leave a gash on her cheek that extended from below her right eye to just above her lip.

Mrs. Mori's hands shook as she worked on it. "Nobuko -san, I fear this one will leave a scar."

Nobuko closed her eyes. How could she care about a slight disfigurement when compared to the Moris' loss and the losses suffered by so many families that day? Only as she thought this did she realize she might have been killed as well. She started to shiver and couldn't stop. Later, in her room, the room she'd shared the night before with two inquisitive children, she cried herself to sleep.

For days, keening wails came from every household in the village. Several times Nobuko tried to say something to the Moris and their daughter-in-law, something to ease their suffering, but her own short and sheltered life failed to give her the necessary words to bring comfort in the face of such unimaginable loss. Even so, she inhaled their grief with every breath. Their pain lay like a heavy stone on her heart.

Funeral services were held at the nearby Buddhist temple. The flower-adorned caskets of the children were arranged across the front of the temple's vast central room. Despite the day's heat, Nobuko felt chilled. Whenever she looked at the row of small coffins, she saw instead the line of broken bodies on rough, twig-strewn ground. She couldn't get from her mind the images of Myoko's bright eyes and Jiro's serious ones staring at her the morning after her arrival in Nishimi.

One after another, villagers knelt before each casket, paying respect with bowed heads and incense. The Katsuragawa family, whom Nobuko was told were important local landowners and had a summer estate nearby, attended the services. Despite their grief, their tears and swollen eyes, the parents of the dead children greeted the family with deference. The priest also treated the family with great respect, his bows nearly as deep as the villagers'.

Not wanting to intrude and still feeling like an outsider, Nobuko kept to herself during the long afternoon. She stayed close to Mr. and Mrs. Mori and their daughter-in-law, however, ready to offer whatever support she could. If only this were all a terrible nightmare, and she would wake up to those giggles, to those bright eyes staring at her. If only.

The day following the funeral, a priest from the Shinto shrine came through the village. At each door, he left the traditional gifts of sake, salt, and rice, to appease the gods and ask their benediction.

After his visit, Nobuko told Mr. and Mrs. Mori she should return to her aunt's home in Sakayama. "This is a private time, for you and for the others whose children were lost. I am an outsider."

Neither wanted to hear of Nobuko's departure. "Our shared grief has made you part of this village," each insisted. "You must stay."

Despite rumbling aftershocks that set everyone on edge, bit by bit, the immediate pain of loss released itself and a subdued life in Nishimi resumed. The Abi's store opened once more, its floor cleared of broken glass and other wreckage, its shelves restocked and organized. Though their faces were sad, housewives came every day to shop. Children, too young to have been in school, once more played in the street.

The pottery factory, where pots, vases, and platters were thrown to the ground and smashed, also had been cleared and reopened. But it operated without Yoko Yoshida, the woman who ran it in her husband's absence—like the Mori's son and many other village men, Takeda Yoshida fought with the Army in China. Nobuko felt sure it had been Yoko Yoshida she'd seen outside the factory the day she arrived in Nishimi. She'd also seen her at the funeral, but the woman had soon disappeared.

"Yoko lost both her daughters in the earthquake—she is too overcome to attend to factory business, at least for the present," Mr. Mori said. Compassion filled his eyes.

The Moris' daughter-in-law announced she wished to go to her parents' home to await the eventual return of her husband. "When the war ends, perhaps we will come back," she said, her voice wavering.

Whenever Nobuko brought up the idea of returning to Sakayama, Mrs. Mori's eyes glittered with tears. "Please stay. Our house would be so empty with you, too, gone."

Perhaps she should stay, Nobuko thought. Her aunt didn't need her. In fact, with three children and a husband to care for and feed, Nobuko had probably been more a burden to her aunt than anything else.

What would her parents think, though? Her trip to Japan had been arranged between her father and his sister when Nobuko turned eight. For years, her parents had saved for the trip, talked about it. As a young girl, three years in the country of her ancestors had sounded like an adventure. The morning she stepped off the packed Inland Sea steamer in Hiroshima, though, she'd been terrified.

Everything had swirled around her. Charcoal-powered cars belched gray smoke as they putt-putted past the corner where she stood, waiting for a chance to cross the cobbled street. A streetcar, its bell clanging, blue fire spitting from the crisscross of wires above it, stopped in front of her to let off a flow of passengers—students in uniform, kimono-clad women carrying shopping bags, men in Western-style suits. Intent on their own business, they brushed past her, one after another muttering *sumimasen,* excuse me. With a clang and a hiss, the streetcar's doors slammed shut, and it continued down the street.

Moments later, a wiry, barefoot man in a loincloth, pulling a large man in a rickshaw, paused in front of her to wipe his forehead with one tanned arm before resuming his journey. Bicycles streamed past, hundreds of them. Fish mongers and other vendors shouted their wares, adding to the cacophony.

When a break in traffic finally came, Nobuko stepped from the sidewalk to dash across the street, but from nowhere came a man on a bicycle. He wore a tall chef's hat, and two squawking chickens were perched on the bicycle's handlebars. She sprang out of the way just in time to avoid being struck. When another brief lull in traffic appeared, she drew a quick breath and darted forward, this time making it all the way across.

Heavy suitcase in hand, she hurried along the wooden sidewalk, following the directions her aunt had sent, trying to keep her fears at bay. What if she missed the bi-weekly train from Hiroshima to Sakayama? What if she did or said something to bring shame to herself and her family? What if she couldn't understand people or they couldn't understand her?

For the most part, her fears had proved groundless. Her aunt had met her at the train station in Sakayama and immediately made her welcome. She'd eventually even grown to enjoy the bustle of Sakayama—though happy to find it much smaller and without Hiroshima's frantic, impersonal rush.

At times, though, she still felt homesick for her family and friends. Thankfully, nothing like the first mind-numbing weeks. The many classes arranged by her aunt and meant to teach her centuries-old skills and customs, had served only to remind her of her foreignness. This despite, for the first time in her life, she looked like everyone around her.

The homesickness usually came over her in a crowd. With a start, she realized she hadn't experienced those miserable feelings, not even once, since she'd come to Nishimi. The villagers, who'd at first looked at her with wariness, now accepted her—many even treating her as a heroine. The Moris needed her.

When she wrote her aunt of her decision to stay in Nishimi, the letter she received in reply seemed to be one of relief. "Auntie says the food shortages in Sakayama are growing worse," she said to Mrs. Mori.

Her parents were harder to convince. What about all your lessons, they wanted to know. She allayed at least some of their fears. She explained that, every day, Mrs. Mori spent time teaching her flower arranging and cooking, and that Mr. Mori had introduced her to an old gentleman who'd recently retired and moved back to Nishimi.

He used to live in Sakayama, where he taught tea ceremony, she wrote. *I'm sure he is only taking me on as a courtesy to Mr. Mori, but it is very pleasant to sit with him and learn this ancient art form. Also, to listen to his gossip about people long gone from this world. Like a popular geisha who once demanded he come to Kyoto and prepare her for a visit from a special guest—one of the Imperial family as it turned out. As for my comportment lessons, all I can tell you is I'm doing my best to behave in an appropriate manner, no matter what the occasion. I think, I hope, you would be proud of me.*

4
HIROTAKA
Art Student

Hirotaka paced through the grounds of his family's Sakayama estate, passing fishponds filled with his father's black and orange koi, stone lanterns tucked into moss covered rockeries, and a thatched pavilion where, in warm weather, his father served tea to his guests. An ancient bronze water vessel, meant for washing hands before entering the pavilion, stood on a tree stump near the steps. As a child, the vessel's dragonhead-spigot had fascinated him. Passed down through the Katsuragawa family, eldest son to eldest son, it would one day go to Hirotaka's brother, Shunsuki.

Something more immediate lay on Hirotaka's mind, however, and the beauty of his surroundings was so familiar it barely registered. He could only think about how to convince his father that two sons with degrees from the University of Tokyo were enough. His father must be made to understand that his youngest son was simply not suited to a life of banking, industry, or engineering.

His father claimed the future would belong to Japan only when the old ways, the study of art and literature, were put aside. New fields of study must be explored, he told Shunsuki, Kinya and Hirotaka. His brothers dutifully obeyed. Shunsuki had graduated with a degree in business and Kinya would soon follow with one in engineering.

Hirotaka much preferred art, Western or Asian, modern or traditional. His mother understood, although her advocacy on his behalf so far had yielded little.

Despite his father professing to be an enlightened man, an adherent of modern ideas, those ideas didn't include the emancipation of women, certainly not his wife's. Nor did they include allowing Hirotaka to attend the school of his choice, in the field of his choice.

"We are living in an age of machines. Art will have little value in Japan's future," his father said during one of their final discussions on the matter. They'd been in his father's book-lined study. His father stopped pacing to stare out the window at the cherry tree, covered in spring blossoms. Seconds ticked by. Turning, he spoke again, this time in a slightly softer tone. "To succeed, my son, you must understand the new technologies. I shouldn't need to tell you this. You're a young man. You should know this truth in your soul."

Neck rigid, Hirotaka fingered the mahogany base of a large world globe with shaking fingers. He pressed his lips together to keep from speaking out while his father outlined the course of study he would take; he'd promised his mother he would not get into another argument with his father.

Finally, he could contain himself no longer. "I'm sorry, Father. But this is my life being charted, and I don't want to follow in Shunsuki's or Kinya's footsteps. I don't want to study engineering or business. And I'm not interested in new technologies." His heart pounded in his ears. His fingertips felt numb. It seemed he was pleading for his very existance.

"If I'm to study something modern, let it be the art of Henri Matisse, Pablo Picasso, or Salvadore Dali even."

His father threw back his head and glared, red blotches appearing on his cheeks. "I'm not going to discuss this with you any further. Come back to me when you've regained your good senses."

In the days that followed, Hirotaka's thoughts churned. He couldn't eat, no matter what his old nurse or his mother tempted him with. Sleep abandoned him. But try as he might, he could find no way to escape the obligation of every son to obey his father. In the fall, he enrolled at the University of Tokyo, where, for two years, he'd dutifully studied economics.

His recent experience at the Nishimi pottery factory showed more than ever where his heart truly lay. The morning they'd finished firing the kiln and he'd looked up to see his father coldly observing the scene, he'd felt sick. His father hadn't delivered the stern lecture Hirotaka expected, though, because the earthquake that destroyed the Nishimi school drew all his father's attention.

With his parents, Hirotaka traveled up the mountain to attend the funeral services of the nearly two-dozen children and their teacher. He paid condolences to Mr. and Mrs. Mori and their daughter-in-law, and tried to do the same with Yoko Yoshida, but she barely glanced at him, appearing to be in a state of insensibility. Later, his father was kept busy assessing the damage the earthquake had done to the family's many tenant-run farms in the area.

He rolled his head and shoulders, trying to loosen the tension there. Although a month had passed without receiving a lecture, he knew he'd again managed to earn his father's displeasure.

He stopped pacing and stared at an ancient pine tree, pruned and trained for over one-hundred years to twist and bend close to the ground. Forced into a life he didn't want, Hirotaka felt his soul would one day become as tortured and misshapen as the tree's gnarled trunk. At times, he thought he could feel the burgeoning of despair in his chest, as if his heart had already begun to contort.

Several minutes passed before he tore his eyes away from the tree and continued along the graveled path, over another bridge, to a bamboo-shaded stone bench. Shoulders slumped, he sat, picked up a pebble from the path and tossed it into the water, watching the ripples widened and spread.

The year before, his brother, Shunsuki, had been called into the Army. As soon as Shunsuki completed his officers' training course, he'd been sent to China. Their mother had wept for days. Now, war had broken out in Europe.

"At least the West will be too busy to interfere with Japan's activities in China and Southeast Asia," his father said at hearing the news.

His father's indifference to the plight of the Poles and the French troubled but didn't surprise Hirotaka; he and his father held widely dissimilar views on most things to do with foreign affairs. For one, his father remained convinced Japan had an historical imperative to exercise its power where it wished, specifically, in China and Southeast Asia. He didn't argue with his father, but neither did he agree. Already Japan experienced shortages caused by embargoes—enacted against them by bigger, richer, and more powerful nations.

He sighed and tossed another pebble into the water. If the war in China didn't end soon, his brother, Kinya, would be called to join Shunsuki.

Footsteps sounded. His mother, wearing a kimono the same autumn colors as the maple trees she passed beneath, walked toward him on the path. She smiled when she saw him watching her. On the bridge, she stopped and took a linen square filled with bread crumbs from the sleeve of her kimono. She cast the crumbs to the koi, circling in the water below.

"Father won't like that," Hirotaka chided, a smile in his voice. "You know how he admonishes us about feeding them anything but the special food he orders."

His mother didn't reply. Instead, she brushed her hands together and came to sit beside him on the bench. "Kinya will be next to go."

"I know." They both gazed over the water. It went unsaid that eventually he would follow Kinya. "Mother, isn't there some way you can make Father see I must study art. I don't want to study economics anymore. I can't. Please make him see that."

"I will try, Hiro-chan," she said, using his childhood name. "That is all I can promise."

He bowed deeply. "Thank you, Mother." He couldn't trust himself to say more.

She never told him how she accomplished it, but with his father's reluctantly given blessing, instead of going back to Tokyo when the time came to return to school, Hirotaka, newly enrolled in the Kyoto City School of Painting, boarded a train for Hiroshima and Kyoto.

He'd hoped both parents would see him off, but his father claimed to have an important meeting. His mother stood alone on the platform when the train began to move. He lowered the window and leaned out, waving until the train rounded a bend and he could no longer see her.

It didn't take long to settle into a routine at his new school. When he wasn't painting, or studying, he drank sake or beer with other students, often with forced gayety. Like Hirotaka, each knew that soon he, too, would be called into the Army and facing the rigors of China.

One afternoon, Hirotaka received a sobering letter from his mother. The news it contained didn't surprise him. Just as they'd predicted, Kinya had been called up.

Your brother has been chosen to fly airplanes. When his training is complete, I fear he will go to China, just as Shunsuki. Your father insists the China Incident will soon end. I pray he is right, but fear otherwise. Hirotaka, my son, have you thought of what we discussed? If you volunteered to go to Manchukuo and settle—they still claim to need pioneers to subjugate the native Manchurians, and, of course, we need the coal and iron from that region—if you did that, perhaps you'd not have to join the army.

Agricultural goods, too, Hirotaka thought as he folded the letter and slid it into his pocket. He'd been a young teenager in 1931, when Japan took Manchuria. With his country's exploding population, there'd been no lack of volunteers to settle Manchuria's vast and untapped frontiers. He'd read that the settlers were forced to build walls around their villages to protect themselves from bandits, who each day picked a new place to plunder. Soldiers were sent to chase the bandits down, like the cavalry in the American old west. Eventually, Manchuria, or Manchukuo as they now called it, became stable.

As he left the administration building, where student post boxes lined one wall, Hirotaka thought of how, at fifteen or sixteen, the prospect of such an adventure as his mother suggested would have appealed to him. Now, though, much as he'd like to assuage her worries about his future safety, he could no longer picture himself as a Manchukuo settler.

He held the lapels of his jacket together in the chilly fall air and headed toward his dormitory, his thoughts returning to his brothers. It had always seemed as though a wide gulf lay between him and Shunsuki. With five years' difference in their ages, they'd had little in common. His father had frequently admonished Hirotaka to study as hard as Shunsuki, or remonstrated with him for behaving in a thoughtless manner, unlike the always dutiful Shunsuki.

Happy-go-lucky Kinya, on the other hand, had been the brother he had looked to whenever he had a problem. Kinya, who'd so often put himself between Hirotaka and their father's ire, had been the one to lift Hirotaka's spirits when he'd been so miserable at the University of Tokyo.

When he reached his dormitory room, he sank down onto a cushion and lowered his head into his hands. His throat constricted as he thought of his carefree brother, who would soon be on his way to fight and maybe die in a war that wouldn't end.

The door to Hirotaka's room slid open and a friend entered. It had been several weeks since his mother's letter, but Hirotaka still brooded.

"What are you reading so studiously?" Tomiko grabbed the book from Hirotaka's hands and read the title with eyebrows raised: "From Monet to Van Gogh. Why do you waste time reading about European artists? You should be reading about ours."

"I do read about Japanese artists. Korean and Chinese, too." He held out his hand for the book, snapping his fingers with impatience.

Tomiko handed it back to him. "Are you coming to the meeting of the Patriotic Students' Alliance? It starts in twenty minutes."

New to their campus, the Alliance had been popular on other campuses for nearly a year. Hirotaka had gone to a meeting in Tokyo. "I don't think so. I have too much home-work."

"Forget studying. You want to be at the meeting. We need to let the world know we're going to save the East Indies from their Dutch masters."

"I thought it was supposed to be secret."

"You're not going to tell anyone."

"But you just said we need to let the world know." Although he didn't doubt the seriousness of the subject, he couldn't resist needling his fervent friend.

"You know what I mean. When the time is right, we'll do it and then the world will know. Those of us in the Patriotic Students' Alliance will go first, prepared to take over leadership." Tomiko's face grew red with the strength of his conviction. "You're my friend. I want to make sure you're with us. When we finish in China, it will be a better country. The same will be so in the East Indies. It is our duty to our Asian brothers to show them the way—not the Americans, the British or the Dutch."

Hirotaka had heard such altruistic sentiments before, from Tomiko, other students and for far longer, from his father. Militarism had been sweeping the country for months. Newspapers venerated Hitler and talked about a brave new world. How anyone could think Japan stood a chance against such formidable adversaries as the United States and all Great Britain, Hirotaka didn't know. Not even with Germany at its side. Even more, he couldn't fathom how Tomiko and the others in the Patriotic Students' Alliance were so eager to be groomed for such a war.

He said nothing, however. Voicing opposition to the swelling ranks of so-called 'patriots' would be pure folly. Not to mention bringing the wrath of his father upon him.

"Sorry. I really do need to study."

Tomiko shrugged. "Okay, I'm leaving. But I'm not giving up on you. One day you'll see I'm right."

After he left, Hirotaka resumed reading, but soon closed the book and set it aside. He couldn't keep at bay depressing thoughts of his brothers: one already in China, the other soon on his way. Would he have time to finish school before being called to follow? It didn't seem likely.

Life at the Kyoto School of Painting wasn't all politics and war talk, though. Eager to learn everything his instructors could teach him while he still had time, Hirotaka wished he could stay awake and alert twenty-four hours a day.

One morning in class, Professor Yoshimura came to stand behind him as he added highlights to the dragonhead spigot on the side of a large bronze vessel, resting on a tree stump. Sunlight, filtered through the graceful, viridian green fronds of a nearby fern, glowed on the vessel's dark, rounded sides. In the background, the orange, yellow and red leaves of a maple tree shaded the thatched roof of a tea pavilion. An arched bridge spanned a small pond. Although Japanese in subject matter, he painted in the style of Monet.

"Hirotaka-san, I believe you should enter this painting in a contest."

Hirotaka knew the work to be his best to date, but hadn't given any thought to entering it in a contest. For one thing, many considered western-style painting degenerate.

"I have the information in my office," Professor Yoshimura said as he began moving to the next student. "If you will join me there this afternoon at two o'clock, I will discuss it with you."

When he reached the professor's office, Hirotaka's hands shook and he needed to take several calming breaths before knocking on the door.

Professor Yoshimura's office also served as his studio. An easel stood in front of a large window. Paintings were stacked on the floor and leaned against the walls, a small desk wedged into one corner.

"Sit," Professor Yoshimura said.

Hirotaka spotted a cushion near a stack of paintings. He folded his legs and sat.

"You are a fan of impressionism—American as well as French."

Hirotaka nodded.

"You realize Western-style art of any kind, even that of Claude Monet, is out of favor in Japan?"

Hirotaka flushed, fearing the mention of a contest had been a ruse, and that he'd been brought to the professor's office only to be criticized.

"Yes, sensei."

Professor Yoshimura shrugged. "Well, the contest is in Paris. I'm not sure how you will get it there, given the state of the world today, but I think you should enter your painting."

A spurt of pleasure infused Hirotaka and he struggled to keep it in check. Instinctively, he started to protest, deny his work worthy of such high praise.

The professor brushed his weak objections aside. "I have a friend who owns a gallery in Osaka. Perhaps he can help you with shipping." He wrote down an address and handed it to Hirotaka along with an entry form and information about the contest.

The day after he took his painting to the gallery in Osaka, getting assurances from the gallery owner it would be in Paris in time for the contest, Hirotaka received a message to report to the dean's office at once.

"I'm very sorry to convey this news," the dean said when Hirotaka presented himself. "Your brother, Lieutenant Shunsuki Katsuragawa, whose service to his country and his Emperor has been most honorable, is dead."

5
YOKO
The Pottery Factory

Like a terrier on a rat, the earthquake had gripped and shaken the mountain. When it stopped, all Yoko's concerns about the pottery factory, about future orders from the Katsuragawa family, about everything, were obliterated. Her daughters were dead. Nothing else mattered.

She closed her mind to the pain and suffering of others. She had only contempt for the priest who came to bless the village and root out the evil spirits responsible for the horror of that day. Both Mori and Ishihara tried to talk to her, but she closed her ears to their weak explanations of why this terrible thing had happened.

Summer ended. Fall worked its way into winter, and still her grief remained as raw as the day the earthquake struck. No one understood. Out of the degradation, the pain, and the humiliation her husband routinely inflicted upon her had come her daughters, her beautiful daughters. Now they were gone. She refused to go to the factory each day and pretend her grief had run its course, refused to smile, to give assurances that everything she cared for had not been destroyed, crushed in a single calamitous, cataclysmic event that changed everything in her world.

The door to her house slid open and Ishihara sidled inside. "Yoko-san?"

"What do you want?" She tipped her head and drained the sake in her cup. Sake had become her only solace. When its warmth blossomed in her stomach and spread though her body, she could forget the pain of her loss, at least for a time. She refilled the cup.

"We have received an exceptional order," Ishihara said. "It is from the Katsuragawa family. They want us to do a special set of dishes to honor their second son, who is going into the Kwantung Army as a pilot."

She paid him no heed. The problems in Manchukuo and China were not her concern. Why should she care if another Katsuragawa son went to fight? They were nothing to her.

"Yoko-san, did you hear what I said? It's another order from the Katsuragawa family. It is what we had hoped would happen."

"Yes, I heard you. Do whatever you want about it."

Without uttering another word, Ishihara withdrew, careful as he slid the door closed behind him.

She picked up the sake bottle and emptied it into her cup. From the time the Katsuragawa's first order had arrived, she should have known better than to talk of future orders. Everyone knew that when one spoke of tomorrow's matters, the rats in the ceiling laughed. They must have yelped in glee at her confident words.

Ishihara came to see her again, this time with Mori.

"We have completed the new order from the Katsura-gawa family," Ishihara said.

"We have also completed orders from various restaurants and department stores," said Mori.

She grunted, but said nothing.

Mori tried again. "We are concerned, Yoko-san. We feel it is time for you to return to the factory once more, return to living."

"You must get hold of yourself, Yoko-san," Ishihara added. "Your daughters would not want you to isolate yourself in this way."

Yoko's lips pulled back in a grimace as she resisted the urge to snap and snarl, throw her head back and howl at their ignorance. "Don't talk about my daughters. You know nothing about what they would or would not have wanted."

"You are right, Yoko-san. We do not know what your daughters would have wanted." Mori blinked several times before venturing further. "But you cannot continue as you are. You haven't eaten properly in months. Sake is draining away your health." He paused, then continued. "If life is so painful you do not wish to go on, you should end it. End it now and be done with it."

She stared at him.

Mori stared back. He spoke again, his voice stronger. "You heard what I said. It is not a shameful thing. If it is what you wish, Ishihara and I will understand. We will run the factory until your husband returns."

Her nostrils flared, her eyes narrowed. "Get out. Get out and leave me alone, both of you."

The two old men hastened to leave. At the sound of the door sliding shut, Yoko's shoulders sagged. She took another drink of sake, searching for blessed oblivion.

Not even in her deepest despair had Yoko thought of ending her life, yet she couldn't rid herself of Mori's words. *Do it*, a voice in her head said. Thoughts of putting an end to her anguish became seductive. That she could make all the pain disappear, join her daughters in the afterlife, lulled her to sleep at night like a mother's soft voice.

She did nothing about the voice, however, and as the weeks passed, it came less often. Then one morning she noted with surprise that the snow had gone and the cherry trees were in blossom, the long winter over.

Yoko followed Mori down the short flight of stairs, on a tour of the factory she had ignored for so many months.

She scowled when she saw the gaijin. "What is she doing here?"

The gaijin, carrying a block of clay to the wedging platform, didn't glance in their direction, but Yoko knew well enough what she looked like behind the cascade of black hair that shielded her face and hid eyes that calmly watched from below slanted brows.

"We've lost another apprentice," Mori said. "This one to a munitions plant near Hiroshima. Nobuko wants to be useful."

"Get rid of her. She's bad luck."

Mori looked at her, confusion written on his usually placid features. "What do you mean, she is bad luck?"

"How do we know she didn't bring the earthquake? We've never had as bad a one before she came."

"That's crazy talk." Anger shook Mori's voice. "Nobuko nearly killed herself running back down the mountain, trying to get your daughters, my grandchildren out of that pile of rubble. You didn't see her hands. And look at the scar she carries on her cheek. She'll be disfigured the rest of her life."

"I don't care. Get rid of her. Find someone else to do the work." She turned her back to him.

The gaijin didn't make a scene after Mori spoke to her, merely walked up the stairs and out the door.

Yoko pinned her arms across her stomach, steeling herself against an unexpected stab of guilt. When the door slid shut, she dropped her arms and raised her chin. She couldn't have endured seeing the woman each day, a constant reminder of all she'd lost.

Soon, she was working from early morning until long after sunset. Her words were often sharper than she meant, her tone harsher, but she didn't take them back. At night, she fell onto her futon, too tired to think, and sank into an exhausted slumber. In the morning, still tired, she fumbled into her clothes. After forcing down a bit of breakfast, she went back to the factory to begin another day.

"Have you written to your husband yet? Have you told him what happened?"

She looked up to see Ishihara standing by her desk. He'd been nagging her to write Takeda since she returned to work. Each time, she'd refused. "Why should I? He cared nothing for them."

"But he should be told," Ishihara said.

"I don't even know where he is now. He's never written. I doubt he gets mail."

"Write," said Ishihara.

As much as anything to stop Ishihara's nagging, Yoko sent her husband a letter with only the briefest of details, and got an answer equally brief: *"Don't worry, I still have the equipment to make more. The next one better be a son."*

6
HIROTAKA
Art Student

A wreath of white flowers hung on the door. Servants wept openly. Hirotaka's mother, dressed in funereal white, received him as soon as he arrived home.

"I knew something like this would happen," she said in a dull voice. "I knew it the minute the Emperor called him to serve."

A short time later, warmly dressed in fur-lined jackets and boots, they walked in the garden. Hirotaka recalled the day, only months before, when he'd pleaded for her help. It seemed like an eon had passed since then.

"I know our religion teaches us that death is a part of life, that nothing is permanent," his mother said. "But I can't accept that he is gone from us. I cannot." She buried her face in her hands.

Hirotaka searched for words to bring her comfort. "I would do anything to make it not true, Mother." Even as he said them, he knew his words were not enough.

His mother tried to stifle her sobs. "Though he hides it, your father is devastated. I don't know how to ease his grief."

"It is natural that he would be," Hirotaka said, his voice roughened by emotion. "Father has long loved Shunsuki best."

His mother quickly turned back to him, tears pooled in her eyes. She placed her hand on his chest. "No, you must not say that. Your father loves all his sons equally."

"I don't begrudge Shunsuki the love Father had for him. He worked hard to make our father proud." He tried not to mind how well his brother had succeeded where he had failed.

His mother's hand dropped from his chest to his arm. "You are all good sons. I mean that. You are not to think your father loves you or Kinya any less than he loved Shunsuki."

"Mother, it's okay."

She shook her head, denying his claim, but didn't try to convince him further.

After a moment, he took her hand and looped her arm through his. They walked on. "Have you heard from Kinya yet? Does he know?"

"I don't think so. Your father has tried to get word to him, but Kinya is in Manchukuo and it has been difficult to reach him."

"Knowing my father, if Kinya can be reached, no matter how difficult, he will receive my father's message."

They stopped in the middle of the bridge to gaze at the fat koi swirling in the water below. "One thing greatly troubles me." His mother's knuckles were white where she gripped the railing of the bridge. "I worry that the rituals necessary for your brother's safe journey into the afterlife were not performed."

"I'm sure his fellow soldiers did everything possible."

"But if they *couldn't*, is it too late to do those things now?"

"I would have you rest easy, Mother. I will go to the temple and ask your question of a priest."

A servant approached and bowed.

"Yes, Kazuko," his mother said.

"Your honored husband wishes to see both of you. He is in his office."

His father, who had always seemed ageless and all-powerful, sat cross-legged on a cushion behind his desk, a letter open before him. The fatigue now showing on his father's face struck Hirotaka hard. It appeared the years had caught up, evident in the deepening of the lines bracketing his father's mouth, the weariness reflected in his eyes, the gray threaded through his hair.

"Our son is receiving a great honor." A flush of pride suffused his father's sunken cheeks. "Shunsuki is to be enshrined at the Yasukumi Jinja in Tokyo. Only the bravest soldiers are so honored."

Hirotaka wondered how dying of cholera could be considered an act of bravery, but quickly pushed the thought aside as unworthy. "What of my brother Kinya?"

"He will meet us there," his father said.

"You've spoken with our son?" his mother asked, her face brightening.

"How would I talk to him when he's on the Manchukuo-Russian border? A messenger delivered the news." His father spoke the words with unusual abruptness, and in a tone of voice he generally reserved for underlings.

His mother dropped her head.

It came as no surprise to Hirotaka that his father knew Kinya's exact whereabouts. His father's many high connections in the government would doubtless have kept him apprised.

Despite fuel shortages, a lieutenant and an Army sedan met Hirotaka and his parents at the train station. Even in the damp and cold, Tokyo's streets were congested with bicycles, carts, and people; it took nearly two hours to reach their destination, a western-style hotel in the Chiyoda district, only blocks from the shrine.

Kinya waited for them in the hotel lobby, erect in his uniform, his hand on the hilt of the sword at his side. Hirotaka barely recognized his formerly carefree brother. When Kinya turned his shaved head, spotting them, he hurried across the lobby, the heels of his boots striking a rapid tattoo against the marble floor. The links on his scabbard clinked as he bowed stiffly from the waist, first to their father, then to their mother and finally to Hirotaka.

Straightening, Kinya turned to the young lieutenant escort. "I've already checked my parents and brother into our hotel rooms."

"Very well." The lieutenant gave a respectful bow. "I will return for you in the morning. Please be ready at ten o'clock." He saluted, turned smartly on his heel, and left.

While his mother rested and his father remained closeted with Kinya, Hirotaka spent the afternoon alone, wandering the crowded streets. His thoughts fell to growing up in the shadows of his two older brothers, one so dutiful, the other so confident. He returned to the hotel in time to share a subdued evening meal with his family. After dinner, his father and Kinya once more retreated to his father's room.

"Will you excuse me if I take leave of you as well, Hirotaka-san?" his mother said as soon as his father and

Kinya left the table. "I've barely slept since we received word of Shunsuki's death. Now I find it hard to stay awake."

With nothing to do, Hirotaka retired to his room. He hoped for a knock on the door signaling Kinya, finally free to talk. The knock never came and after a while he gave up and went to bed.

At the shrine the next day, people talked about Shunsuki being a military god. "His kami will be greatly honored when he reaches the afterlife," proclaimed a well-known general. He and the other officials—government and Army alike—treated the entire Katsuragawa family with deference.

Other soldiers were recognized as well. Judging by the awe-struck faces of their families, many were simple country folks. Though nothing like the extraordinary respect shown to his family, the government still treated them with such high regard that Hirotaka wondered if some might almost be grateful to their sons for having died and brought them this distinction. Ashamed, he swallowed and looked down, wishing he were somewhere, anywhere else.

After a banquet held in Shunsuki's honor and attended by representatives of all the noble families including an envoy of the Emperor, the brothers escaped. In the hotel's nearly empty bar, they drank beer and shared memories of their dead brother.

"I never understood his passion for yabusame," Hirotaka said, referring to the ancient sport of equestrian archery. Shunsuki had spent countless hours on horseback preparing for contests.

"It's the sport of samurai, and you know how he always wanted to follow the way of Bushido," Kinya said. "The religious aspect would have added to his dedication."

"I wonder if he ever got to ride horses in China."

His brother chuckled. "I doubt he had time for pleasure riding."

Hirotaka stiffened, suspecting Kinya thought him naïve. "I'm sure he must have been an excellent officer. I admire him for that."

"I must leave first thing tomorrow, you know."

Hirotaka's stiffness dissolved as quickly as it had arrived. "Our parents will not want to see you leave so soon. Especially our mother—she's having a difficult time."

"I know. But we're on a tight schedule. My fellow officers need me."

A middle-aged woman in a navy-blue kimono brought them each another beer and took away their empty glasses. Both brothers nodded thanks.

"What's it really like out there?" Hirotaka asked.

Kinya, grimacing, took a swallow of beer and wiped the foam from his lips with the back of his hand. "Cold as hell, now that winter has set in. The wind blows straight down from the North Pole. There are few buildings. The men have dug trenches and dugouts where we sleep and eat. We're on three-day shifts. For three days, I sit in my airplane, ready to scramble on three minutes' notice. My crew brings me everything I need, but it's so cold, you can't imagine. Frostbite is common—I know pilots who've lost toes or fingers."

Hirotaka's eyes flew to Kinya's hands. His brother laughed and held them up, wiggling his fingers. "All there. Toes, too." Kinya's smile faded. "When our three days in the planes are done, we move to three days in the ready room. It's warmer than the cockpit, at least, and there's someone to talk with. After that, we stand down for three days—but with nothing to do in that godforsaken place, I'd almost prefer sitting in my airplane."

Hirotaka fingered a drop of beer that had rolled down the side of his glass onto the table. His cheeks tingled, thinking of his and his friends' petty complaints about their living conditions at school. Then he grew angry at the waste of it all. "But why are you even there? I thought the non-aggression treaty with Russia meant we could concentrate our forces elsewhere."

"The Russians can't be trusted," Kinya said with a shrug. "If we show any weakness, they will sweep into Manchukuo and take it."

They continued drinking and talking until the bar closed. By then they were both weary after the emotion-filled day, and more than a little drunk.

"Try not to anger our father," Kinya said as they made their way through the lobby and up the stairs to their rooms. "You know Shunsuki was his favorite."

A slight smile curved Hirotaka's lips. He nodded. "I know."

The following day the family rose early. After their morning meal, Kinya bade them each farewell. Their mother put on a brave front to say goodbye, but as soon as Kinya left, her face collapsed into now-familiar sad lines. His father suggested she begin packing. "It will help keep your mind off our son."

Before they were due to leave for the train station, Hirotaka answered a summons to his father's room. His father, seated on a cushion in front of a short-legged table writing a letter, didn't look up. While his father continued to write, Hirotaka regarded the bared winter bones of an enclosed garden, visible through the window. He felt cold and hollow.

His father set his pen aside. "What do you plan to do when you return to school?" Still without looking at him, his father folded the letter and slid it into an envelope.

"What do you mean, Father?" The empty feeling in his stomach hardened.

At last his father looked up. He waved Hirotaka to the cushion opposite him before answering. "I expect you to begin showing some patriotism. You have been playing games long enough. I know you've made friends with a reporter from that liberal magazine, *Chûô Korôn*. They may not come right out and say they oppose the war in China, but their views are well-known."

"Father, are you speaking of Koji Wata? If you are, your news source is wrong. We are not friends. He merely asked some of us our opinion about the dean of our school." His stomach twisted. He felt like a knife had been thrust into it.

His father scowled. "It makes no difference. The people who run the magazine are known left-wing, communist sympathizers. You should have nothing to do with him."

"But Father—"

"There are no 'buts' Hirotaka. You bring shame on your family when you disregard our wishes and befriend those beneath your station. You must show true patriotism, as your brother Shunsuki died doing and as your brother Kinya does now. I have held my tongue on this in deference to your mother, but, I will remain silent no longer. In view of

Shunsuki's great sacrifice, I insist you begin behaving in a manner that befits your illustrious lineage."

"I will take what you say to heart, Father." Hirotaka lowered his head. His cheeks burned. His throat thickened and he struggled to get the words out. "I am sorry if I have brought you shame."

"You have not brought me shame, my son. But nor have you brought me pride. I expect that to change."

Hirotaka stood. He lifted his chin and drew his shoulders back. "Yes, Father."

Once back at school, Hirotaka went in search of Tomiko.

"I heard about your brother," his friend said. "You must be very proud of his service to the Emperor."

"Yes." Hirotaka's voice sounded harsher than he meant. "But I sought you out to let you know I am ready to join the Patriotic Students Alliance."

Tomiko beamed. "Excellent. Our leader is eager to meet you."

Determined to please his father and demonstrate his love for his country, Hirotaka attended weekly meetings of the Alliance. He went to lectures and rallies and took part in quasi-military exercises.

A sham, though, his performance a lie. He felt sure there had to be others who believed as he did, that Japan was about to make a colossal mistake. He wished he had the courage to speak out, but knew such defiance would be as futile as throwing grains of rice into a raging storm. He bit his tongue and carried on the pretense his father demanded.

When word came from Paris that his painting had won first place in its division, he folded the letter and put it aside.

7
NOBUKO
The Gaijin

Nobuko thumbed through a two-month old issue of *Life* magazine her mother had sent. She paused at a picture of an itinerant worker in an apple orchard. After studying it a moment, she rose from her cushion and wandered to the window, the magazine still in her hand. Instead of seeing the Mori's small garden, her mind drifted to an early memory.

Just turned three, she squatted on the sun-dappled ground in the orchard, picking up fallen fruit and putting it into a wicker basket. Her mother, on a ladder with an infant Mako strapped to her back, was nearly lost among the branches of a tree. Only her papa's legs were visible among the branches of an adjacent tree. From a distance came the rumbling sound of the neighbor's tractor.

"Nobuko-chan, be careful of the bees," her mother said,

Nobuko looked up as her mother reached for a golden apricot.

She blinked. The remembered scene dissolved, and the Moris' garden reappeared.

Mrs. Mori's voice sounded behind her. "Although it is a poor excuse for tea, let us have a cup."

Glad of the diversion, Nobuko set down the magazine. "I'll get the cups."

With her bright, shoe-button eyes and quirky smile, Mrs. Mori sometimes seemed more like a mother than Nobuko's own. Her mother, always so busy, had little time for Nobuko's girlish chatter, especially about people and places she didn't know. Nobuko flushed and pressed her lips together, ashamed of such disloyal thoughts. Her struggles to be understood when she first came to Japan had given her a much greater appreciation for what her mother must have endured upon arriving in America. Likely still endured.

Mrs. Mori passed her a steaming cup. "Dozo, Nobuko-san. Please drink."

She took a tentative sip, but the pale liquid burned her lip and she set the cup down. "Why is it that I never see men and women together unless they're married?" She'd noticed this in Sakayama. At first, she'd thought the cause to be the many young men away, fighting in China, but soon realized it was more than that.

"Men and women must not be alone together—not unless a priest has blessed their union." Mrs. Mori gave a slight shake of her head.

Nobuko didn't consider herself unduly forward. Still, she had a hard time accepting a taboo on something as innocent as an unmarried man and woman meeting, going for a walk, or simply passing the time of day.

"There are other things that seem strange to me. For instance, I know bowing is considered the proper way to greet someone, but Auntie told me it would cause a scandal if a man and woman were to shake hands."

Mrs. Mori pulled in her chubby chin, peering at Nobuko from beneath lowered brows. "Nobuko-san, you must realize this is not America. There are rules and you must obey them or people will consider you…" She paused for a moment, in search of the right words. "They will consider you an improper person."

"I understand there are rules. What I don't understand is why they must be so restrictive. Like shaking hands… what could be more innocent?"

Mr. Abi came down with the flu, and Nobuko offered to help in the store until he recovered. Mrs. Abi rejected her offer at first, but eager for something to occupy her time, Nobuko persisted until the older woman agreed.

One morning, while wrapping Mrs. Tanaka's purchases in brown paper and tying it with string, the bell above the door jingled and a young man she'd never seen before entered. Conscious of his eyes on her, Nobuko counted out the appropriate change, bowed and spoke the words Mrs. Abi insisted be given to each customer. "Thank you, Tanaka -san. Your patronage of this humble store is appreciated."

Nose twitching, tiny, mouse-like Mrs. Tanaka returned the bow before hastening to the door. The young man held it open and nodded a greeting as she passed. Mrs. Tanaka bobbed her head and scurried past him. Nobuko could almost visualize a long thin tail trailing from beneath the skirt of the woman's sturdy brown kimono. The young man would soon be the subject of gossip up and down Nishimi's narrow streets.

He wasn't there to shop, of that Nobuko felt certain. She didn't know quite how to address him. She wondered if the rules of men and women applied, if she should keep her eyes downcast. She did not. "May I help you?" She looked straight into warm brown eyes, magnified by thick lenses.

"Miss Ito, thank you for helping my parents."

Ah, the scholarly Masato, son of Mr. and Mrs. Abi. When Mrs. Mori had told her about him, the only child ever to leave the village for university studies, she'd spoken with such pride, he could have been her own son.

Taller than Nobuko by several inches, and whip thin, his unabashed gaze disconcerted her. She started to offer her hand, but then recalled her conversation with Mrs. Mori; a handshake would be inappropriate. Cheeks throbbing, she bowed her head. "I am happy to be of service."

In the two weeks that followed, Nobuko spent several hours each day helping in the store, while Mrs. Abi stayed close to her ailing husband. When not off delivering mail, Masato worked in the store with her. One afternoon, with no customers to wait on, the two cleaned and rearranged shelves.

"During school breaks, I stay in the dormitory. Or sometimes with a friend who lives in Tokyo," Masato said, moving aside several cans of mandarin oranges and fruit cocktail.

Nobuko swiped her dust rag across the empty space. "Why is that?" She enjoyed Masato's wry and lively sense of humor—he could mimic Mrs. Tanaka to nose-twitching perfection. Some of the other villagers, too, including Mrs. Mori. Even knowing she shouldn't, Nobuko laughed.

Just as often, though, Masato's humor turned inward, on himself. Nobuko found his ease and informality, something no doubt acquired from university life in Tokyo, a welcome change from the rigidity of country customs and manners.

He moved the cans back to their place on the shelf. "I wanted to avoid the expense of the trip home. But when my mother wrote that my father had fallen ill, I felt I must come." He stopped and turned to her. "I should have come home sooner."

Nobuko's eyes flew to his. "Masato-san, I am sorry. I didn't realize your father was so ill."

"That's not what I meant."

He looked straight at her, holding her gaze for several seconds. She couldn't mistake his meaning; no one had flirted with her since her arrival in Japan two years before. A flush crept across her cheeks. She lowered her eyes and fumbled with a box of laundry soap.

Mrs. Abi called from the doorway to their living quarters, saving Nobuko the need to reply. Masato went to see what his mother wanted. Although unable to make out the woman's words, Nobuko couldn't mistake the scolding tone. Still flustered, when Masato returned to help straighten the shelves, she pointed out the cooling weather and the likelihood that it would soon snow.

The next afternoon, Masato told her he needed to return to Tokyo and school. "I'll be graduating at the end of this term. I'll be back." He spoke the words as though making her a promise. In the days that followed, whenever she reflected on that moment and those words, she got a fluttery feeling in her stomach.

Brows drawn together, Nobuko reread her parents' letter telling her she must return home as soon as possible. *"Go to*

the consulate and get your travel papers and passport in order," her father wrote. *"We've deposited the money for your ship passage in your postal account."*

Nobuko pictured him at the kitchen table, where he did all his bookwork, and her mother worriedly looking on as he wrote. "I'm afraid something may have happened to one of them or to my brother," she told Mr. and Mrs. Mori. "I must leave right away."

She wrote at once to her aunt, who replied that Nobuko should stay with them while getting her travel papers. *"You'll need to go to Hiroshima for that. But your uncle says you first must get travel authorization from the police. He will arrange it."*

The same old farmer, this time carting his last load of yams to market, took her down the mountain. Freezing fog spread across the narrow track. Huddled under a heavy quilt, Nobuko felt as though she rode in a boat being towed through a white stream. Above her, low-hanging clouds obscured the tops of the cedar trees. Sterling beads of moisture clung to the bared branches of the cherry trees. On the mountain's lower flanks, the millet and rice had been harvested and the tilled, empty fields looked like brown corduroy. The bleak landscape mirrored her emotions.

Once again at her aunt's house, Nobuko understood the reason for her parents' demand that she come home nearly a year earlier than planned. Diplomatic relations between the US and Japan had deteriorated; war might be coming between the country of her birth and the country she'd come to love.

On the twenty-seventh day of November, well-muffled

against the cold, Nobuko carried her suitcase up the gangplank of the *Osaka Maru*, scheduled to dock in San Francisco on the fifteenth of December. *"Just in time for Christmas,"* she told her family in the cable she'd sent them.

Piles of luggage littered the wet deck despite an unrelenting icy drizzle. She paced along the railing with other passengers while they waited to be told what to do. An hour passed. Finally, they were instructed to take their luggage below and find their cabins. Nobuko discovered she shared space with three middle-aged women, the somber trio nothing like the chattering group of girls she'd sailed with to Japan.

She quickly stowed her things and returned to the deck. The rain had stopped, but the wind whipped the water in the harbor into small, white-crested waves. Arms crossed and shoulders hunched for warmth, Nobuko watched the *Osaka Maru* being prepared for departure. A lifetime seemed to have passed since that warm summer day she left San Francisco, the pier crowded with friends and relatives waving goodbye. This day, only dockworkers were there to see them off.

Her leave-taking of Mr. and Mrs. Mori, knowing she would never see them again, never again enjoy Mrs. Mori's lively chatter, Mr. Mori's kindness, had wrenched her heart. It had been difficult saying good-bye to her aunt and cousins, too, though she had to confess, she wouldn't miss her uncle—a man filled with self-importance because of his job with the city government.

And then there was Masato. She'd wanted to write to him, let him know about her return to America, but she couldn't bring herself to ask his mother for his address. And though she hated to think of it, if war did come between Japan and the United States, Masato would be conscripted—they would be on opposite sides.

She'd swallowed her tears a thousand times on the way down the mountain. Now, as she stood at the rail and the ship slowly slipped away from the dock, she had no tears left to gather on her lashes and slide down her cheeks.

The weather warmed and Nobuko supposed they must be nearing Hawaii. She wondered if they'd stop there. When the ship stopped in Hawaii on the way to Japan, she'd enjoyed the band playing Hawaiian music when they left, and the Hawaiian girls dancing barefoot on the dock. What a festive time that had been. How different from now, when dread of what could happen in the months ahead, lay cradled like an egg in her belly.

She found a vacant deckchair at the rear of the ship and settled into it. Her eyes closed. Lulled by the sound of the ship plowing through the water, the tensions of the past several weeks began to melt away. Her thoughts went to her waiting family. She pictured them just as they'd looked that long-ago day, as if they'd never left the pier.

"Look!"

Startled, she opened her eyes and sat upright. She peered around, unsure what she should be seeing.

"The wake. Look at it," the young woman sitting next to her said, this time her voice a fraction lower.

Nobuko stared at their foamy and slightly effervescent trail in the sea, shaped like a giant U. "Do you think someone has fallen overboard?"

They both jumped to their feet and rushed to the rail, but could see nothing that looked like a rescue underway.

Crew members ignored all questions. They scurried about their duties with a concentrated focus Nobuko hadn't witnessed in them before. Throughout the day, small groups of passengers gathered to speculate on what had transpired.

"Maybe there's someone on board that must be returned to Japan, a criminal or a spy," one man said in a low voice, glancing around the group as though searching for the guilty party.

Others thought something might be wrong with the ship. "Perhaps there is a problem with the engine," a woman suggested.

Another passenger dismissed that idea, saying there were places to stop for repairs if that were the case. Nobuko agreed. Why turn around when they could continue to Hawaii?

That evening, the captain made an announcement that put all puzzlement to rest: "Japan has attacked the Americans in their heart, Pearl Harbor. Japan and America are at war. The *Osaka Maru* returns to Japan."

Nobuko's fractured thoughts refused to give her respite or solace. Would she be forced to remain in Japan? If she had to stay, would she be treated like an enemy, put in jail, or a prison camp? If not, where would she live? What would she use for money? She'd spent nearly every cent she had on gifts to take home. And her parents—they would be frantic. Would she be allowed to contact them?

The ship followed a zigzag course. The old man who mopped the hall outside her cabin told her it was to avoid being struck by a torpedo; she became more terrified than ever. Like the other women in her cabin, she took to sleeping in her clothes, even shoes and a coat, ready to don a life-preserver at a moment's notice. Abandon-ship drills were held every morning and afternoon. She should have gotten her papers sooner.

The *Osaka Maru* sailed back into Kobe's harbor in a cold spit of rain. The line of passengers waiting to disembark stretched to the back of the ship. Most were quiet, many were tearful, and some needed physical support as they shuffled forward like prisoners going to their execution.

Wet and cold, Nobuko shivered. Her trembling increased the closer she drew to the gangway. The *Kempeitai*, the feared military police, stood waiting on the pier. They grabbed a man she had spoken with in the ship's lounge only days before.

"My wife and I are from Iowa. We came to Japan to run a missionary school," he'd told her. "I'm just glad she and the children left on an earlier ship."

Nobuko gasped when the police shoved and marched the man to a waiting Army truck. They quickly loaded him into the back, where several other Occidentals from the ship already huddled.

The police allowed anyone of obvious Japanese descent to disembark without being questioned. Still, by the time she reached the bottom of the gangway, blood thundered in Nobuko's ears, at her temples. She hesitated. A man pushed past her, almost knocking her off-balance. Her shaking fingers tightened around the handle of her suitcase. She drew a deep breath, straightened her shoulders, and stepped once again onto Japanese soil.

8
TOSHIO
Farmer - Soldier

He had a son. Kensai. That news was the only bright spot of Toshio's year. He'd earned another home leave, but just before his departure, all leaves were cancelled. No one said why. Instead of cradling his infant son in his arms, he spent spring, summer and fall first slogging through mud, and then dust, as they chased Chiang's or the communists' armies back and forth across the plains.

Why didn't the bloody Chinese give up? The "Three All" tactics—seize all, burn all, kill all—should have brought an end to their resistance. Instead of demoralizing them, it had done the opposite, moving them to become wise in their use of force: hiding behind the moon, sneaking up at night and attacking when Toshio and his fellow soldiers were exhausted from long or difficult marches, and then disappearing as if into the air.

When enemy soldiers came into their hands, a rare occurrence, they faced extreme torture. They would not break, however, preferring to die first. Such valor might be commendable, but remembering Major Tamayama's words, Toshio understood the shame of capture overshadowed the bravery the Chinese soldiers displayed. "As prisoners, they are beneath our contempt," he told his men.

Little broke the monotony of marching from one place to another, often for a third and fourth time. It all seemed pointless.

Then, in the fall, as leaves swirled and snow threatened in the north, they received the welcome order to head south, to Canton Province, an area that had long been in Japanese control.

Three weeks later, striding into the outskirts of the conquered city of Canton, surrounded by his regiment, Toshio passed countless bombed-out and ruined buildings. Only a few civilians were on the streets, and when he and his fellow soldiers went by, they quickly turned their heads or ducked into alleyways. Despite the broken buildings and the city's frightened inhabitants, the warm, soft breeze off the nearby South China Sea brought Toshio an unaccustomed sense of wellbeing.

Their second night in Canton, his company received permission to visit the brothels designated for Japanese use. After a short rickshaw ride to the part of the city where the brothels were located, Toshio made his way to a dimly lit alley where a red light bloomed above a door. Inside, the air reeked of cigarette smoke and the smell of sweat and sex.

Through the haze, he saw the women were Korean and Chinese. Most naked, or nearly so. Their dulled gazes told him they existed in another world, one of drugs or alcohol, perhaps both. His only interest their bodies, he didn't care where the women's minds were. He hadn't been with a woman in months, unless he counted the girl he found cowering in a barn. But at only twelve or thirteen, not yet a woman.

He took the first one he came to. A Korean, she was big-boned, though very thin, and her dished face looked like she'd been hit with a shovel. He grabbed her arm and jerked his head. She led him up a flight of stairs and down a narrow hallway lined with doors, indicating an open one at the end.

She flopped on the bed and closed her eyes, giving no indication of her awareness of him or her surroundings. Not bothering to kick off his boots, he pulled down his trousers and threw himself on top of her, plunging into her. His manhood went limp.

Ashamed, he slapped the woman and yelled at her. "Drunken slut! Why do you just lie there?" The woman stared at him, her face and eyes blank. He hit her with his fist and she cried out. He hit her again. His manhood began to stir. Hard and throbbing once more, he felt he could ride her for hours. Instead, he spilled his seed in moments.

He climbed off the woman and pulled up his trousers. "Cow," he threw at her as he slammed out of the room. He stomped down the hall and the stairs, yelling obscenities at the man behind the counter and the other women. "That slut cheated me," he shouted. "What pleasure is there in fucking when the woman lies like an empty sack?"

The man gazed back at him with barely concealed contempt. A few women stared incuriously while the others remained indifferent in their stupors.

Toshio shoved out the door and into the fetid, urine-soaked alley. At its end, he turned onto a street lined with bars, tattoo parlors, tobacconists, and apothecaries. He followed the gaily-lit street several blocks bumping shoulders with other Japanese soldiers, who all seemed to be either drinking or already drunk. Many had a laughing, heavily made-up woman in tow.

He brushed past them, and roughly shoved aside street urchins grabbing at his sleeve. Cries of "Good fucking this place," or "I have sister," or "You maybe like boy instead? I take you good spot, many boys," followed him.

When the brothel and the source of his shame were sufficiently behind him, Toshio entered one of the bars. He elbowed his way through the crowd to the back of the room, where he found a table and ordered a beer from a scantily-clad young girl. He took a slurping gulp.

A woman in a stained silk dress with a side slit to her waist asked him to buy her a whiskey. He snarled at her. "Get away. Leave me alone." She laughed and sauntered to another table. "Stupid sow," he muttered, and drank the remaining beer straight down before ordering another.

The jeering face of Takeda Yoshida loomed over him the following morning. Takeda had been gone from the regiment for over a week. Toshio had hoped the man's absence might be permanent.

"It's happened," Takeda crowed. "I knew it was only a matter of time."

"What are you talking about?" Toshio pushed himself into a sitting position and winced.

"Japan attacked Pearl Harbor."

"So?" Toshio didn't want to admit he had no idea where or even what Pearl Harbor was.

"Hawaii, dumb shit. Pearl Harbor, Hawaii. We're at war with America."

The distant thumping of artillery fire and the drone of heavy bombers flying overhead wormed their way into Toshio's aching head. As he would soon learn, war had been declared not only with America, but Great Britain, as well. The Battle of Hong Kong had already begun.

"Get moving," Takeda said, prodding him with a foot. "We're heading south."

Like Toshio, most of the men in the regiment were battle-hardened veterans. The British soldiers they met on the march to Hong Kong were no match for them. His bayonet fixed to the end of his rifle, he led the men in his squad, shooting or stabbing anyone foolish enough to get in their way.

They swept through settlement after settlement, town after town. Civilians, Chinese and Europeans alike, huddled inside their houses. Shops were shuttered.

Toshio felt no remorse for those who fell before him. The man who'd carefully conveyed food and water to cholera victims, the man who'd been outraged at a young soldier's beheading merely because he had an English-language newspaper in his possession, was gone.

A cold, hard numbness possessed him. That feeling stayed with him when, days later, they entered Hong Kong.

The moon glowed bright. On the pitted runway of Kai-Tak Airport, the skeletal remains of a torpedo-reconnaissance plane loomed above Toshio's head. Beyond the hulk of the destroyed airplane, flames burned unchecked on Devil's Peak, casting a glow over its south flank. They'd been fighting for over a week.

"What's wrong with these crazy British? Don't they know when they've lost?"

For reasons Toshio failed to understand, Takeda Yoshida seemed to stick to him like a flea to a dog. He shrugged in response. His only interests were eating and getting an hour of sleep. He'd built a makeshift fire under the plane's wing, where he continued to squat and stir rice boiling in a pot. Once cooked, he didn't wait for it to cool, but ate with his fingers, shaking and blowing on them between bites.

From the near distance came the pop-pop-pop of rifles, and farther away, the thump of heavy artillery. Japanese artillery had been pounding Hong Kong Island's north shore ever since the British had, for the second time, turned down demands for their surrender.

A young private trotted up and bobbed his head. "Lieutenant Toto wants you."

"Me or him," said Takeda.

"He wants all NCOs," said the private. "He's over by what's left of the tower."

Toshio wiped his fingers on his trousers. He left his pack and the cooking gear, grabbed his rifle, and headed for the tower at a brisk jog.

"What's the rush," panted Takeda, a few steps behind. Toshio ignored him.

Lieutenant Toto studied a map. Several others were already gathered around him. Toshio approached and saluted. The lieutenant spread the map on the ground. They all squatted around it.

"Tonight, at midnight, we begin the advance on Hong Kong Island. Although they've purposely destroyed their harbor facilities, we will cross by boat to here and here," the lieutenant said, pointing to two spots on the map.

At the appointed hour, in complete darkness, the boat bumped against the shore. Toshio clambered out first, followed closely by twenty others. They swarmed up the bank, pitted from a barrage of artillery fire, and scrambled around destroyed buildings and up-ended machinery. "Spread out," Lieutenant Toto whispered. "And remember, no prisoners."

Shortly before dawn, Toshio led his squad of five through the doors of the British field hospital at St. Stephen's College. Amidst pleas for mercy and screams of retribution, they went from bed to bed, systematically killing the injured soldiers with their bayonets. The medical staff came next. A young doctor, hands clasped together as if in prayer, knelt on the floor and pled for his life. Without pause, Toshio plunged his bayonet into the man's chest. After wiping the blade on the doctor's white coat, he calmly exited the building.

That afternoon, he stood at attention outside the Peninsula Hong Kong Hotel, where headquarters had been established. Under a flag as white as his hair, the governor of Hong Kong, his face grim and back erect, officially surrendered.

Hong Kong now under Japanese control, Toshio's regiment headed northeast. He sat on a bench in the back of a truck, wedged together with twenty-five weary soldiers. The truck pitched from side to side along a rough and winding road, cut into the side of a mountain. The mountain on the left, a thousand-foot drop on the right, the driver couldn't avoid huge pot holes, or rocks that had fallen onto the narrow road. From time to time someone protested the rough ride by pounding on the roof of the cab. A pointless gesture; their truck formed part of a long line of trucks, each churning up dust until the air filled with it. At least they were riding this time, not marching.

Perhaps there would be another attempt to take Changsha. Toshio didn't care. He'd barely noted the bombed-out remains of several towns they'd rumbled past the day before. He'd grown immune to the loss of life such wreckage represented. After Nanking and Hong Kong, all cities were the same to him; human life had no value. Pointless to think otherwise.

He'd given up the dream of going home. Twice his enlistment had been extended. Now at war with America and Britain, he saw no end to the fighting and killing. He felt sure he would die somewhere in this forsaken wilderness and that his soul would wander for eternity. He no longer feared death. He only hoped his son might someday pray for his soul. He tried not to dwell on thoughts of his son; he doubted he'd ever see the boy. Better not to think at all. Better to simply follow orders and do as he was told.

Despite the heaving and lurching and the sheer drop-off next to the road, Toshio nodded in and out of sleep. The truck hit an even larger pot hole, jerking him awake, as four airplanes flew over—bombers, heading back toward Canton. Japanese. He didn't need to look up to identify them; he could tell by the sound of their engines. And he didn't bother to wonder where they'd dropped their bombs. He'd find out soon enough.

Men huddled around small fires, boiling rice for their morning meal. No one spoke and most heads were lowered. A thin layer of clouds covered the dawn sky. His rice bubbling, Toshio stared at a crane poised in the shallows of the river they were camped next to. His eyes on the large bird, patiently waiting for a fish to swim near, he glumly contemplated the disaster of the last six days.

Major Tamayama had paced before a group of officers and NCOs, his shaved skull gleaming in the weak sunlight. "We are to inflict as much damage on the Chinese as possible, striking an additional blow to the Allied Forces following the defeat of the British in Hong Kong."

From the hill where they'd gathered, Toshio stared down at the walled city of Changsha, wondering how these orders were to be carried out. The Chinese had formed a line of resistance around the city and set up ambush parties. They'd evacuated the town except for their own troops and a handful of civilians.

The major continued talking and pacing. "The river protects the western side of the town, putting it out of easy reach. Instead, two platoons will attack the northern wall of the city, two will attack the east, and two more will hit from the south."

Toshio's platoon was assigned to the latter group. For two days, they laid siege. On the third day, the town under heavy bombardment from the north, he and his men finally breached the southern rampart. Others made it in as well. Once inside, however, they met another, stronger line of resistance set up near the center of the city.

After many hours of fighting street-to-street and hand-to-hand, the enemy refusing to give an inch, Toshio sensed a slight shift in momentum, sensed the Chinese beginning to fall back. The momentum shifted more. Then, just as it appeared fate would let them win, renewed resistance arrived in the form of fresh Chinese troops—two entire columns swept down from the surrounding hills.

Out-numbered, out-maneuvered and their supply lines cut off, the Japanese fought their way out of the city, over the walls or through gates. But like cats outside a mouse hole, the Chinese waited for them. Their eventual escape had been ignominious and costly. Toshio alone lost three of his small cadre of men.

The crane spread its wings and lifted into the air, beads of water dripping from its talons. At the same time, a loud pop sounded and Toshio's rice pail exploded. A second later, what felt like a great sledge hammer hit him in the chest and knocked him into the fire. Rapid popping sounded. Men screamed. Toshio rolled onto the dirt. Slowly lifting his left hand, he reached inside his tunic to finger the thousand-stitch belt.

Toshio opened his eyes. Swimming above him was the face of a man with grizzled hair and a wispy moustache. The man stared at him through wire-rimmed glasses.

"Where am I?" Toshio said, his voice a whispered croak.

"You are awake," the man said.

"Where am I?" This time the words were clearer.

"You are in a field hospital."

"What happened?"

"You were shot near the Sinchiang River following another unsuccessful battle for Changsha. You're lucky you didn't die while the litter bearers carried you to an aid station, or later, when they brought you here."

All Toshio remembered was floating for what seemed like an eternity, followed by stillness, and then what felt like the weight of a huge boulder pressing on his chest.

The man went on. "You've been here for three weeks. You've had pneumonia. You still have it, although you are improving. When you are well enough, if you get well enough, you will be sent back to Japan. Recovery will take time; we cannot afford to keep your bed occupied that long."

"I'm going home?" The words were the best Toshio had heard in a very long time. He closed his eyes and a weak smile tugged at the corners of his mouth.

"Do not sound so eager to shirk your duty," the man said. "You and the others failed your Emperor at Changsha, bringing additional embarrassment to our nation with cowardly retreat. As soon as you are recovered, you'll rejoin your regiment. Perhaps then you can redeem yourself."

But in the meantime, he was going home. The image of a white crane, lifting into the sky, soaring, imprinted itself on his closed eyelids.

Thoughts of the farm and his new son drove Toshio's recovery. He received little attention and little to eat—a thin broth made from rice and an occasional piece of fish. No meat. Often left in his own filth, when his temperature flared, he had to beg for water. Despite all that, he began slowly to recover.

Then one day, in a pouring rain, he watched from his litter as goods were loaded and passengers were herded up the narrow gangplank of a Yangtze River steamer. A poncho had been thrown over his head and shoulders to keep at least part of him dry. Another hour passed before he and seven other patients were carried aboard and set down beneath a make-shift awning. Chinese peasants, along with bundles of clothing and household goods, occupied the rest of the rain-slicked deck.

When the laden craft, engines throbbing, finally edged away from the pier and into the current, Toshio believed he saw the vague outline of a crane flying through the drizzle.

They steamed first to Nanking and then on to Shanghai, reversing the course of what seemed like a thousand years before. From Shanghai, they sailed for Japan and home.

9
NOBUKO
The Gaijin

Though faint with relief the military police hadn't taken her, all the way back to Sakayama Nobuko agonized about her future. Drained, by the time she reached her aunt's house she wanted only to fall onto her futon and sleep for twelve hours straight.

Her uncle, officious as always, scowled and barred the way to the room she'd shared with her cousin, Mimi. Beyond him, her aunt hovered.

"Please, let us talk tomorrow, Uncle," Nobuko said, fighting to keep her voice calm, fighting to not show her near-paralyzing fears of a future she had no control over. "I'll be able to think better once I've slept."

He stared at her. "You are no longer a guest in this house. Now you must work."

Nobuko darted a look over his shoulder to her aunt. Cheeks flushed, her aunt ducked her head.

Her uncle lifted his chin and crossed his arms high on his chest. "The maid has been sent away. You will take her place, including sleeping on her futon in the space next to the kitchen." His right foot tapping the tatami mat-covered floor, he ticked off Nobuko's new duties. "You will do the mopping and cleaning. You will do the cooking. You will do the family's laundry. And you will do it all to my satisfaction or suffer the consequences. In return, you will have food and a place to sleep. Do you understand?"

Her shattered mind unable to conjure options, Nobuko nodded.

"Good." Her uncle gave a quick jerk of his head. "Now you may retire from my sight."

She picked up her suitcase. Eyes averted, her throat so thick she felt she might choke, she hurried past him and her aunt. Once in her new sleeping quarters, little more than a lean-to attached to the kitchen, tears flowed unchecked. Despite them, Nobuko managed to pull a thin, lumpy futon from the tonsu, the room's single piece of furniture. The futon covered most of the floor in the frigid, closet-sized room.

Once again, she didn't bother to undress. Under the heavy quilt, her last coherent thought before falling into an exhausted sleep, at least the little room offered some privacy.

In the days and weeks that followed, Nobuko often worried about the displaced maid, regretting that she'd made little attempt to befriend the unsmiling woman. Besides feeling somehow responsible for what had happened to her, the maid's situation made the tenuousness of her own circumstances all the clearer.

"I hope she has a family to take her in," she said to Mimi, who often kept her company when Nobuko's uncle was out of the house.

Mimi shook her head. "I think she's an orphan. At least

I never heard her speak of a family—and she'd been with us since I was a child."

Nobuko's shoulders slumped at Mimi's words. At least she could be grateful that the work her uncle assigned made her too tired to think when she fell into bed each night, kept her from wondering what the future held and how worried her parents must be. She didn't want to think of them waiting on the dock for a ship that never arrived. Nor did she want to think of them walking away, her father's comforting arm across her mother's shoulders, her mother crying, their bleak trip back to Fresno and the farm. So long as it kept those images at bay, she didn't mind the work.

What she *did* mind was her uncle's gloating as first Guam fell, then Wake, Manila, Hong Kong, and Rangoon. Singapore went down along with Ballan in the Philippines and Mandalay in Burma. Finally, Corregidor fell, the last resistance in the Philippines. "Within six months of the attack on Pearl Harbor, the American and British empires in Asia are crushed," he crowed.

Although Nobuko didn't reply, she couldn't help wondering what had happened to the two most powerful nations in the world.

In the marketplace, she overheard two women talking in hushed tones about American airplanes dropping bombs on Tokyo. She dismissed what they said as gossip and, perhaps, even fear-mongering. If such a thing had occurred, wouldn't it have been in the newspapers? Her uncle surely would have commented on it.

Dear Nobuko-san. We are so sorry to hear you were unable to safely return to your parents' home. We would be most pleased

for you to return to Nishimi. You will always be welcome here.

Nobuko dropped the Mori's letter into her lap. How she longed to see them. And tiny, mouse-like Mrs. Tanaka. The other villagers, too. Mr. Abi. Even sour Mrs. Abi. She broached the subject of returning to Nishimi, but her aunt's eyes widened with alarm.

"You cannot. Your uncle will never allow it."

Sure enough, that evening her uncle called her to him. "I believe you think you can wander around this country as you please." He glared at her, his mouth drawn into a purse of dislike. "You are crazy to think you have such liberty now. Don't you understand you are a citizen of our sworn enemy? The secret police know you are with my family. That alone protects you. The moment you leave this house, they will be notified you are a fugitive. They will hunt you down and imprison you along with those idiot villagers."

The muscles in Nobuko's jaw tightened. He had no right to talk to her that way. Nor speak so disdainfully of Mr. and Mrs. Mori and the others. But with no other recourse, she bowed and sped to her room. She prepared for bed—donning a sleeping robe and pulling out her futon—blinking back angry tears the whole while. If only her parents had written earlier. If only she'd never come to Japan in the first place. She sniffed again and closed her eyes.

It had been mid-summer and the thermometer pushed above one-hundred-ten degrees. They were never supposed to swim in the irrigation ditches. 'The dirt banks are too fragile.' 'You are sure to drown.' 'You couldn't climb the steep banks.' Their elders

and common wisdom asserted these and other disastrous fates. But teenage boys rarely paid heed to either their elders or common sense, so while Nobuko and her girlfriends spread blankets and put out picnic lunches, the boys shucked their jeans and jumped in.

Nobuko eased her cotton blouse away from the sticky skin between her shoulder blades, and looked longingly at the cool, rapidly flowing water.

Mako called out from the bank. "C'mon in, chicken. The water's great."

His challenge too much, she told the boys to turn their backs, stepped out of her skirt and threw off her blouse. In bra and panties, she ran up the incline, down the bank and into the water. It felt wonderful. Before long the other girls were jumping in, and laughing and splashing as well.

Her father and the neighbor found them. Mako received a flogging with her father's razor strop for not guarding his sister's modesty. Nobuko spent the rest of the summer restricted to her room or working in the fields. There were no more picnics.

After a restless night, Nobuko woke with a stiff neck and an ache at the base of her skull. Why didn't Papa tell Auntie of my disgraceful behavior? If Auntie had known me to be so wicked and depraved, she never would have invited me to Japan. I would be home right now and in my own bed instead of on this lumpy futon. She thumped the *futon* with her fist.

But then, unbidden, came thoughts of Masato Abi. He wasn't handsome, not in the typical way, but funny and kind and thoughtful. She wished she'd had the chance to get to know him better.

While they'd worked together in his family's store, he'd confided in her. "I felt so lonely when I first left the village and went to Tokyo to study. Cut off from everything I knew. Then I made friends with some other students—most, like me, from remote villages."

Understanding how he'd felt, she told him about growing up a Nisei, a first-generation Japanese-American, in California's hot, dry Central Valley. "I always felt different because of the shape of my eyes and the color of my skin. And yet, when I came to Japan, I felt like an outsider here, too."

She wondered if Masato ever thought of her now. If he did, he probably imagined her back in California. As she would be, if she'd taken an earlier ship. She also wondered if Masato had been conscripted. If not, doubtless he would be soon. But she didn't want to think of him in uniform, going off to war. She especially didn't want to think of him going to war with her own country.

She roused herself and dressed, knowing it useless to languish on her futon fantasizing about 'what ifs'. Her cousins soon joined her in the kitchen. Only Mimi would look her in the eye and call her by name. The boys, Takanori and Sadaoka, took cues from their father, at best treating her as a servant.

Sadaoka, now seventeen, poked at the two slivers of eel on his plate and sniffed. "This has gone bad."

"You should know better than serve us rotten fish," said fifteen-year-old Takanori, following his older brother's lead.

Sadaoka smirked. "Have you eaten the good fish yourself? Father is going to be very angry with you."

Nobuko's lips tightened. Although he lacked a scraggly goatee, Sadaoka even looked like his father. Just like his father, too, in the way he strutted around like a little tin-pot general. In no mood for his antics, she glowered at him.

Mimi, as always, tried to calm the waters. "You know how hard it is to get food now. I'm sure Nobuko hasn't served us bad fish on purpose.

Sadaoka sniffed again. "And I'm certain that's exactly what she's done."

The argument was in full sway when Nobuko's uncle called for his breakfast. "You'd better serve him something other than eel," whispered Mimi.

Everything now in short supply, Nobuko's eyes flew around the room until she spotted a small jar of pickled ginger. Ladling miso soup into a cup and then scooping a bit of rice into a bowl, she gnawed on her lower lip. Then she lifted her chin. Like everyone else going without, he'd just have to be satisfied. She picked up the tray bearing the soup, the rice, the ginger and what must pass for his morning tea, and carried it to the next room. Her uncle sat in front of a low table. She knelt, set the tray on the table and arranged the few dishes in front of him.

He frowned. "What is this? Where is my breakfast? Where is my fish?"

"There is nothing else, Uncle."

"What are you doing with the money my wife gives you to shop for food? Are you hoarding it? Sadaoka! Go to this woman's room and search it."

"Uncle! I have done no such thing. How could you suggest it?"

Her aunt came into the room. She looked from one to the other. "What is wrong, husband?"

"Look! This is what she has served me for breakfast, nothing but a paltry bit of rice and soup. She is stealing from us."

"What happened to the eel you bought yesterday, Nobuko?"

"It has gone bad, Auntie. I didn't feel it wise to serve my uncle tainted fish."

"I found nothing, Father," Sadaoka called from the kitchen. "She must have hidden it too well."

"No doubt." Her uncle nodded, his eyes narrowed. "But I will find it. She is to stay out of her room until I return home this evening. Do you hear me, wife? Do not let this woman out of your sight. She's a thief."

That evening, as her uncle tore apart her small room, Nobuko clenched her teeth together until the muscles in her jaw flicked with tension. Her eyes narrowed even more when he reached his hand into the pockets of her clothes. He opened the tonsu and removed the futon then got down on his hands and knees to peer inside the chest. With a grunt, he opened her empty suitcase, turned it upside-down and shook it. He even checked the seams.

When he found nothing, neither hidden yen nor contraband food, he made no apologies. He merely told his wife to exercise better control over her niece. "From now on, you go with her to do the shopping. See she doesn't cheat us again." He left the little room, her aunt trailing behind him like a puppy.

Nobuko's fists opened and closed. How she would have liked to strangle the man—always gloating, always reminding her she had a roof over her head on his sufferance; just because of his job in the city government, a job he claimed to be so important. Probably nothing more than a clerk, she thought. Too angry to settle, but with nowhere else to go, she prepared for bed. Hours passed before she fell asleep.

Nobuko sighed and wrung her wet rag into a bucket of dirty water. She'd had no appetite for weeks and knew she'd lost weight. Rising from the stone floor of the entry hall, her head spun. She staggered and reached a hand out to brace herself, but found nothing to hold on to. She fell to the floor, knocking over the bucket.

Her aunt came running. "Nobuko? What was that noise? You didn't break anything, did you? Your uncle will be angry if something is broken."

Nobuko couldn't answer. The damp floor felt cool against her hot cheek.

"What happened? Did you stumble? Are you hurt?"

Nobuko tried to push upright, but her head started spinning again and she lay down on the cool stone once more. "I'm just so tired, Auntie."

Her aunt took hold of her arm to help her rise. "You're burning hot! I can feel the heat right through the sleeve of your kimono. Why didn't you tell me you were ill? Never mind. Let's get you to your futon. As soon as he returns from school, I will send Takanori for the doctor."

Nobuko drifted in and out of sleep, alternately burning with fever or shaking with chill. One time, whether morning or night she couldn't tell, she roused enough to know she lay on her futon in the little room next to the kitchen. Mimi knelt beside her, bathing her face, combing back her hair. "Have I been sick?" The words came out a whisper.

"You have been ill for several days, Nobuko-san. The doctor has come twice."

"Oh." She closed her eyes. When next she opened them, her aunt held a cup to her mouth. "Drink this. You will feel better." It tasted foul and Nobuko tried to turn her head away, but her aunt insisted. She went back to sleep. Every time she woke, either her aunt or Mimi sat beside her. She wanted to tell them how much she appreciated their kindness, but lacked the energy.

Several days passed before the fever receded and Nobuko could sit up without help and without her head aching and spinning.

"The doctor said you must eat if you are to regain your strength."

She pushed at the rice in her bowl. "I'm sorry, Auntie. I can't eat any more. Maybe my stomach has shrunk."

"You've eaten only a few bites. You can't be full."

Food held no appeal. She gave up and put down her chopsticks. "I'm sorry."

"I should have seen you weren't eating enough—no doubt for my family's benefit."

"No, Auntie," Nobuko said with a weak smile. "I promise you I had no altruistic motives—I just wasn't hungry and I'm not now. Save the rest for my cousin—you know Takanori always claims he is starving. Maybe I'll be able to eat more tomorrow."

Her aunt sighed, but rose and took away the bowl and chopsticks.

"Tomorrow I'll be able to resume my chores. You've waited on me long enough."

When Nobuko entered the kitchen the next morning, however, her aunt already stood at the counter, preparing the morning meal. "It will be skimpy with so little to choose from," her aunt said.

By the end of the week, Nobuko felt her old self. "Because of your youth," her aunt said. They worked side-by -side in the house, developing a closeness missing from their earlier relationship. "You're just like your father. I remember he had flu once, too, but our mother couldn't keep him in bed for long."

"My brother and I often fought growing up. Did you and my father get along?"

"He is older than me by about ten years. He used to tease me, calling me tomboy because I liked to play sports."

Nobuko found it difficult to imagine her portly aunt as a young girl, an active, athletic one. "What kind of sports did you play, Auntie?"

"I liked tennis very much. I was captain of my school team."

"Really? I like tennis, too. At home, I often played with my girlfriends or my brother."

"Takanori plays. Perhaps he would offer you a game."

Nobuko doubted that would happen. Things were better since her illness—not quite so much hostility toward her from Takanori at least, though there'd been no change from Sadaoka. Somehow, though, she didn't see herself playing tennis with her youngest cousin. Even if his mother convinced him, his older brother would put a stop to it. And if Sadaoka didn't, her uncle would.

She had expected her uncle to comment about the expense of the doctor and her missed chores, but to her surprise, he made no reference to either. Perhaps he'd softened. And with the easy relationship she now enjoyed with her aunt, Nobuko felt almost happy. Considering what was going on in the world, and considering she didn't have any idea what might be happening with her family in California. At eighteen, her brother surely would have been called into the Army—how would her parents manage the farm without him; another thing she must worry about.

One day, Nobuko's uncle brought home a radio, an expense few families could afford. He gathered everyone around and with reverent hands placed the machine atop a small chest then plugged it in. "None of you is to touch this." He glared at each in turn. "Do you understand?" They all nodded and he returned his gaze to the radio—a brown, rectangular-shaped affair with three knobs across its top. He twisted one of the knobs. Static sounded. He twisted another knob and the static grew louder. He turned it off. "Never mind—the war news isn't until later."

That evening, after she had cleared his tray and washed the dishes, her uncle called for Nobuko. Thinking she'd forgotten something, she wiped her hands on a towel and hurried to him. He sat cross-legged on a cushion in front of the radio. "Kneel." He pointed to a spot a few feet away. "You will listen." Every night thereafter, at precisely seven o'clock, her uncle called in a preemptory voice and demanded she kneel and listen to the war news. Whenever she heard *The Battleship March*, the anthem that preceded the nightly reports, Nobuko braced for yet another Allied defeat.

One evening, though, *The Battleship March* didn't herald such a loss. Instead, in a somber voice, the announcer spoke of a place called Changsha. "Six months ago, after a lengthy and hard-fought battle, our Army failed once again to take the city. General Sato, responsible for this shameful defeat, has now been relieved."

Nobuko stole a glance at her uncle. His mouth pulled down, his brows drawn together in a frown—she didn't wait to be dismissed, but rose and slipped from the room. Had she dared, she would have given a cheer. Changsha. She had no idea where it might be, but knew she'd never forget it. Japan's failure to take it, the first positive thing she'd heard since the attack on Pearl Harbor.

10
YOKO
The Pottery Factory

With a box of soba bowls in her arms, Yoko struggled to open the door to the Abi's store. A moment later, she heaved the heavy box onto the counter.

Mrs. Abi's usual frown gave way to a begrudging smile. "These are just in time—my shelves are looking sparse. If the fighting doesn't end soon, I won't have anything to sell."

"At least we'll be able to keep you supplied with dishware," Yoko said, breathing hard.

Mrs. Abi counted out money to pay for the order. The bell above the door jingled and a rosy-cheeked Mrs. Mori entered, snow glistening on the scarf wrapped around her head and shoulders.

Yoko quickly gathered up the coins and notes from the counter. She didn't want to get dragged into a conversation.

Mrs. Mori stood firm, barring her way. "How are you getting along, Yoko-san?" Concern shone in the old woman's eyes.

Each day of the past eighteen months, Yoko had wept for her daughters. She missed their laughter and gay chatter. She often woke in the night, listening for their quiet breathing. Sometimes she thought she heard them giggling. *Oh, Mother, we've played such a good joke on you.* Although reluctant always to share her feelings, even with someone who'd known her since childhood, Yoko answered truthfully. "Looking backward is painful. Looking forward is no easier."

"I know." Mrs. Mori patted her arm. "Since the earthquake, since we lost our grandchildren and our daughter-in-law moved back to her parents' home, I tell my husband we must take happiness wherever we find it."

Yoko managed to refrain from jerking her arm away from the woman, always a fountain of meaningless platitudes.

Mrs. Mori leaned closer. "You must do the same. Come, we'll go to the temple and we'll both feel better."

Yoko had avoided the Buddhist temple since the first anniversary of her daughters' deaths. She'd only gone then at the insistence of Mori and Ishihara, and because tradition demanded it. Even so, priests and temples held no answers for her.

"I have too much work to do," she said, drawing her brown wool scarf close to her chin. "Besides, the path is probably filled with snow." It had been snowing off and on for several weeks with a constant wind piling the snow into deep drifts.

"No, no. I went there yesterday and two young priests were out clearing all the pathways."

"Still, there is much I must do today." Before Mrs. Mori could say more, Yoko ducked around her and out the door.

Her head lowered against the wind, she trudged through the snow and thought about the year that had drawn to a close several months before. The factory had done well, but its success brought her little comfort.

She knew, however, even without Mrs. Mori dutifully noting it, life went on. She also knew she had to keep the factory going for the sake of the villagers.

"Yoko-san," said Mori, the moment she walked in the door. "I can't find the order from Toda's Department Store. We need the dimensions for the serving bowls they want."

"I thought that order had been completed."

"All but the serving bowls."

"The request should be in the file."

"I looked. It isn't there."

She sighed, knowing she tended to put off filing paperwork. "I'll find it."

The factory stayed barely above freezing throughout the winter. Wind whipped in around the sliding doors at the back of the production area, regardless of the wadded-up newspapers pressed into the crevices around the doorframe. The showroom and office weren't a great deal warmer. Yoko's feet were numb with cold. She wiggled her toes inside her felt boots as she searched through the piles of papers on her desk. I must do a better job keeping track of invoices, she cautioned herself.

The door burst open and the fire in the stove jumped as a blast of frigid air mixed with snow blew in.

At first, Yoko thought a stranger had arrived. Then the man, bundled from head to toe, unwound the thick wool muffler from around his neck and face. Her body stiffened when she recognized the heartless eyes of the man she'd believed, or at least hoped, she'd been rid of. Her husband.

"What are you doing here?"

Takeda Yoshida took off his thickly padded jacket, scattering snow over the papers on the desk. He ignored her question as he held his hands to the fire. "Where's Mori?"

The muscles in Yoko's jaws tightened, but she forced her voice to remain indifferent. "In the drying room, last I saw."

"Get him. Ishihara, too."

That night, Takeda stayed at the factory talking with the two old men. He grunted when Yoko set a pot of soup on the desk along with three bowls. "Go home," he said after she had served them. "Warm my bed for me."

Her back rigid with resentment at being shut out of their man talk, Yoko returned home and forced down some food. She should have stayed and listened. She'd run the factory for nearly six years; there shouldn't be anything she couldn't hear.

Takeda hadn't bothered to mention their daughters, either—not that she had any desire to discuss their deaths with him. She thrashed on the futon, rolling from one side to the other. Unable to settle, she got up and paced the room several times before returning to her bed. Midnight passed before Takeda finally came home, removed his clothes, and fell upon her.

In the morning, she rose bruised and sore, too upset to eat. If anything, her husband's behavior in bed had grown worse. Muttering oaths and curses, she tramped through newly accumulated snow the short distance to the factory.

Mori and Ishihara waited for her. "Where is Takeda?" Ishihara asked.

Yoko, unhappy with both men, answered with a toss of her head. "Snoring like a pig, last I saw him." Why didn't you have more spine last night, she wanted to demand. Why didn't you insist I stay? Rustling about removing her coat and outdoor boots, she pretended to ignore them. She would not lower herself to ask what they'd talked about in her absence.

"Takeda told us how the war with America is going," Mori volunteered.

"Hunh! What is the difference between war with China and war with America?"

"He believes the factory can make hand grenades," Ishihara said.

"Hand grenades? What nonsense is this?"

"Ceramic hand grenades have been around for hundreds of years. They work. And with no steel to spare, the idea is something to think about," Mori said.

"And what makes any of you think, even if we wanted to, even if the government ordered us to do it, a pottery factory such as ours can make them?" She looked from one to the other, not attempting to hide her scorn. "They would no doubt require a different kind of clay, different techniques. I doubt we could get our kiln hot enough to fire them. Everything would be completely different."

"I think we could learn," Mori said, a touch of optimism in his voice. "Maybe Ishihara and I should visit some ceramic factories in Kyushu. There we can learn what we need to do differently."

Ishihara seconded his co-worker, siting the importance of doing whatever they could to advance the war effort. "America is a big country. They have vast resources while we have few. If we are not united behind our Emperor, our country could fail."

Yoko remained unimpressed. War was men's work and she wanted no part of it. "What am I supposed to do while the two of you are gone? Who will run the production? Who will manage the kiln? Who will tell the apprentices what to do?"

But they had answers to all her questions. "Asai is young, but she can take charge of production and handle the apprentices. We can schedule our visit between firings," said Mori. "It won't happen for a while, anyway."

"Takeda will notify us when the time is right," Ishihara said, giving a quick nod of approval.

So, they had it all worked out. Behind her back, they had done this. She had counted on Mori and Ishihara to look out for her interests. They'd been like elder brothers to her. Now, they'd joined with her dog of a husband. Why should she be surprised? They were men—naturally they would band together. Well, damn them all. If they wanted to run a hand grenade factory, let them.

Takeda stayed another night. Yoko felt his eyes following her as she made their evening meal and cleaned up afterward. More than half-way through a bottle of sake, Takeda let slip that he'd been sent to deliver important papers to an Army command at the naval base near Hiroshima. "The major will have me killed if he finds out I added this side-trip to Nishimi," he said, half into his *sake* cup.

Yoko's eyebrows went up. "He doesn't know you've come here?"

"What?"

"That major, the one who sent you, he doesn't know where you are?"

Takeda gave a sharp growl. "What are you talking about? Shut up and go to bed, woman. I'll deal with you later."

When he finally stumbled into their sleeping area, he threw himself on her. She grunted with the impact of his weight and steeled herself for another assault, but in moments his drunken snores sang loudly in her ear.

So, the Army didn't know he'd come to Nishimi. She pushed her husband's lax body away and began to plan. She would lay in wait on the road to Sakayama, kill him and hide the body in the woods. No one would know. When he didn't show up, they'd think he ran away or fell off the ship and drowned.

She passed an hour in pleasant reverie before finally falling asleep. She woke the next morning to find Takeda gone.

News came slowly to Nishimi. The winter's heavy snows made the roads nearly impassable. No one had a shortwave radio. They'd long ago been banned. Mori's son had given him an old radio, but its age and the poor reception in Nishimi made it of little use. Not until spring, when the roads were cleared, did Yoko and the rest of the villagers learn their country was at war not only with China and the United States, but also with England, Australia, the Netherlands, and several other countries. Most had only a vague notion where those countries were located.

"Who is left to fight?" Ishihara wanted to know.

"Masato Abi, for one," Mori answered. A swarm of orders had arrived in the recent mails and the two men were sorting through them.

"Have his parents heard from him?" asked Ishihara.

Yoko sat at her desk, listening to the discussion with half an ear. She'd been furious when Takeda slipped away, disgusted she'd been unable to carry out her plan to kill him. And she still hadn't forgiven Mori and Ishihara for allying themselves with her enemy.

"His father said there were three letters from him," Mori said.

"Don't you two have anything better to do than gossip?"

"What is wrong, Yoko-san? You've been on edge for weeks." Only someone like Mori, who'd been at the factory longer than she had, would dare to address her when she was clearly in such a black mood. "Is it something we've done?"

Though tempted to tell them the truth, tell them they were no better than that damned cur, Takeda, she held her tongue. "Nothing. Never mind. Just get on with what you're doing and don't talk so much."

"Yes, Yoko-san," they said, exchanging a look.

She grunted and returned to her paperwork.

They needed chemicals for making glazes; their normal supplier had written that he could only send half her order. She scowled at Ishihara. "When will you be able to dig more clay? We're almost out." The rectangular blocks of milled clay, wrapped in wet burlap, had filled the storeroom in the fall. They were down to less than two rows.

"In a few days, now that it has grown warmer and the ground is thawing."

"Who will you take to dig?"

They had to rely entirely on women, even for the hard work of digging clay. They'd be firing the kiln the following week. She'd get some argument from Ishihara—Mori, as well—when the two realized most of their help would come from women. Unskilled women at that; housewives for the most part. It could no longer be avoided.

"We have several strong apprentices," Ishihara said. "They'll manage."

Although Ishihara was right, the women managed to dig the clay, just as Yoko predicted, an argument ensued when it came time to fire the kiln.

Ishihara stood in front of her desk, his shoulders back, his wrinkled face flushed with emotion. "There are some men still left in the village. I will show them how to throw the wood at the correct angle."

Yoko mustered as much patience as she could find. "Ishihara-san, the only men left in the village, in the whole countryside for that matter, are old and feeble. And even if we used them, there aren't enough. We must forego ancient traditions until the war is over. The kiln-kami will understand."

The old man frowned and shook his head. "No, Yoko-san. We do not dare. We have no idea how he will retaliate for such an insult."

She slammed the desk drawer closed. "Train the women how to do the job, Ishihara-san."

He did so, but not without flashing hostile looks in her direction. When they opened the kiln, and found no more than the usual number of cracked or warped pieces, the old man fell silent for a full minute. Then he muttered it meant nothing. "The kiln-kami won't seek retribution in such an obvious manner as breaking a few pots."

Where to find the necessary chemicals for the factory's customary deep red glazes remained a problem.

"We could do more with tactile decoration," Mori told Yoko following another futile search.

She gave the old man a distracted look. "What are you talking about?"

"Incising, marbling, inlay—we can use paddles with patterns on them to shape the pots after they're thrown. It may take longer, but it will add the visual interest we have traditionally gotten from color." She stared at him, now intrigued. Mori, warming to the subject, went on. "And we can burnish. There's enough iron in our clay—it will burnish well."

"Why haven't we done any of this before?"

"Chemicals are faster. Whenever I brought up the idea to your husband, he reminded me this is a production factory where speed is important."

"Well, until the government turns us into a hand grenade factory, we'll do it your way."

Over the following weeks, Yoko took growing pleasure in the idea, a solution to the glaze problem and at the same time something of which her husband didn't approve.

With little further intrusion from the outside world, spring passed into summer. But as July approached, Yoko braced herself for *Obon*, the second since her daughters' deaths. Though prepared to follow the custom of gathering their favorite foods and toys, she'd do it for appearance only. Not for a second did she believe her daughters would return to her in spirit form.

But even if they did, it would bring her no comfort. She didn't want their spirits, she wanted *them.* She wanted to see her girls chasing butterflies and flying kites with the other village children. She wanted to see them bending over their homework, the youngest chewing on the end of her writing brush. She wanted to smooth the hair from her older daughter's eyes once more, tie a ribbon on a pigtail, find an errant shoe. She wanted *them* back.

No matter how much she resisted it, though, *Obon* came. And when it passed, she felt as empty and angry as she'd been before it arrived. Then Mori managed to make her life even more intolerable.

As she flipped through the morning mail, sorting it into piles, he stepped into the office. "Yoko-san, I have news. Do you remember Nobuko Ito?"

Fool. How could she forget the woman who brought so much misery to the village? "What about her?"

"I believe she is coming to stay with us again. She is back with her aunt in Sakayama, but her uncle has been called to serve in the Navy and her aunt must move to a smaller house. There will be no room for Nobuko."

The last thing Yoko wanted, the *gaijin* showing up again. "I thought she went back to America. Isn't that why she left here in the first place?"

"Yes." Mori sighed and shook his head. "Sadly, her ship turned back after the attack on Pearl Harbor."

"It is as I said before, bad fortune follows that woman. She must have been born under an evil star."

A red flush crept over Mori's lined cheeks. "I'm sorry you think that, Yoko-san." His fingers twitched. "My wife and I feel she is the daughter we never had. With our daughter-in-law moved back to her parents and our grandchildren gone, Nobuko will bring life into our home."

Yoko gave him a scornful look. He'd obviously gone soft in the head. She'd fire him if she could, if he wasn't necessary to the smooth running of the factory.

"Mark what I say, Mori-san. If you allow that woman to return, she will bring misfortune with her."

11

TOSHIO
Farmer - Soldier

After two weeks in the dispensary at Kure Naval Base, a doctor told Toshio they needed his bed for a more seriously ill patient. "Go home to complete your recovery," he said. Toshio didn't hesitate to obey.

His breath coming in tortured gasps, he slipped and fell on a melting patch of ice, landing hard on one elbow. He'd fallen more than once over the past few hours, each time pushing erect and setting off up the mountain once again. This time, he lingered a moment, willing his breathing to even out. The sound of a clanging bell floating on the cold air made him look over his shoulder to see a welcome sight: an ox pulling a large cart. He struggled to his feet and moved to the side of the narrow road, waiting for it to come abreast.

The driver huddled under a faded quilt, leaving only keen black eyes and a pair of gnarled hands holding the reins visible. The apparition reached up and pulled the quilt aside. The maze of wrinkles that made up the old man's face cracked open in a wide grin, revealing a gap of several missing teeth. "On your way to Nishimi?"

"Seven kilometers beyond, to my family's farm."

"I can take you as far as Nishimi. Get in. You look about done for."

Toshio stepped up on the wheel hub then clambered onto the seat. As soon as he settled, the old man made a clucking noise and the ox plodded forward. Toshio paid little attention to the stream of talk from the old man, until he nodded toward the back of his wagon. "Lots of mail for Nishimi—didn't see any call-up cards though. Guess there's no one left to call up."

Toshio's eyes shut at the old man's words. He found himself once again in the rice paddy with his parents on a late autumn morning, the sun beating down and the rice almost ready to harvest. He felt the warm water lapping against his legs, the mud beneath his toes. He shuddered, remembering the sight of the red call-up card in Mr. Abi's hand. He swallowed hard and opened his eyes once more, focusing on the road ahead. He would not think of that day or the thousand days that followed. Only home. Nothing else mattered.

Finally, Nishimi appeared in the distance—its tumbled shacks clustered together as though seeking warmth. Toshio's breathing quickened. Almost there.

The old man flicked the reins and clucked once more to the ox, but the huge beast's pace didn't alter. "I'll stay at the store tonight," the old man said. "The government pays for my lodging and Mrs. Abi throws in a meal—not that any meal amounts to much these days. Maybe you should ask her if you can stay, too. There's plenty of room on the floor in front of the stove."

For too long Toshio had dreamed of the farm, his parents and wife, and of seeing his new son. "Thank you," he said to Mrs. Abi when they arrived at the store and she offered him a meal and a warm place to sleep. "But I will continue."

The three-quarter moon spread its glow across the thatched roof of the house, the barn, and over the barren fields, dotted with patches of snow. Toshio stopped at the foot of the lane to gaze at the welcome sight. He'd begun to fear home a myth, something his fevered brain had made up. He drew a shaky breath and stumbled forward.

No one expected him; the windows were dark. He thrust the door open, flooding the room with light from the moon and stars. His mother, more bent than ever, sat up screeching, clutching a blanket to her thin chest. His father scrambled to his feet and reached for the handle of a broken pick. His wife bolted upright on her futon and screamed. His son began to cry. Not an auspicious beginning.

"Hold on! It's me, Toshio!"

His father dropped the pick handle and lit a candle.

The women's frightened screams turned to happy laughter and a flurry of questions.

Toshio ignored them all and went to examine his son. The child sat in a makeshift crib, his thumb in his mouth, big tears still making their way down his cheeks.

Lips parted, Toshio reached trembling hands for his son. The boy pulled his thumb from his mouth and let out a howl. He didn't stop crying until his mother picked him up and put him to her breast.

Before long, Toshio's father pinched out the candle. "Enough. It is time for all of us to be asleep."

Toshio's wife took him by the hand, leading him through the darkness to their futon. His son, sated, had fallen back asleep, emitting an occasional little hiccuping sigh. With his wife's help, Toshio took off his clothes and collapsed onto the futon. He closed his eyes. "I'm too tired for fucking," he told her. "Tomorrow night will be soon enough. Go to sleep."

The next night hadn't worked either. Once again, Toshio's manhood deserted him. He tried and fumbled, but like the night in the whorehouse in Canton, his efforts went unrewarded. Finally, in frustration, he used his fist. His wife cried out. He quickly put his hand over her mouth then hit her again. She struggled to get free. His manhood responded. He held her down until he satisfied himself.

The next morning, the recrimination in his wife's eyes and the dismay on his parents' faces made him grimace and turn away. Self-loathing flooded through him; he couldn't bring himself to touch his wife again.

Trying to make friends with his son brought him no joy, either. The child appeared terrified of him, crying for his mother or grandmother the moment Toshio came near. He turned accusing eyes on his wife. "Why haven't you taught him better? He's too old for all this sniveling."

Toshio's mother glanced up from her task of patching a worn spot in the sleeve of his uniform tunic, but quickly lowered her head to her work.

His wife made no reply as she took the little boy into her arms. The child clung to her, burying his face in her neck. She bounced him on her hip and whispered in his ear until his tears turned to giggles. Once again, Toshio reached for his son, but the child stiffened and refused to let go of his mother.

Unable to bear another day surrounded by the comfort he'd dreamed of but which remained beyond his grasp, shame filling him, Toshio packed his few things and left. He could not report for duty early. He'd been ordered home for thirty days. If he turned up before the designated time, he'd be punished. He found a room in a rundown inn.

For the twenty days remaining of his leave, he mostly slept, waking only to eat a bit of rice or millet, sometimes a limp turnip or piece of yam. On the thirtieth day, he presented himself at the Military Affairs office in Hiroshima.

"You are to report to Kure Naval Base for further assignment," a clerk said, after glancing at Toshio's papers.

Toshio's jaws tightened when he discovered Takeda Yoshida sitting on a bench, also waiting for the bus to Kure. The stars once designating Takeda's rank of sergeant had been removed from his collar. Bits of thread still clung there.

"What did you do?"

Takeda glared and turned away.

"Cheating at cards? Stealing? Either would be like you."

"Shut up, farmer."

"That's Corporal Hara to you, Private."

"Fuck you, *Corporal.*"

Toshio clenched his teeth and his fists against the man's disrespect, but with Takeda's huge bulk, he could do nothing more. He supposed it pointless to hope they would be assigned to different units.

12
HIROTAKA
Art Student

For months, everyone Hirotaka met brimmed with certainty of Japan's ultimate glory. Instead of being euphoric, like his countrymen, Hirotaka felt only astonishment as victory after victory fell to Japan.

He kept reliving the fateful minutes in the school cafeteria, when, without warning, the opening bars of *The Battleship March* had come over the loudspeaker and Hideki Tojô began to speak.

"Japan is now at war with America," the Prime Minister bluntly announced.

Everyone, including Hirotaka, dropped their chopsticks and stared at one another as Tojô went on to tell of the assault launched on Pearl Harbor, concluding with words Hirotaka would never forget: "I am resolved to dedicate myself, body and soul, to the country, and to set at ease the august mind of our sovereign. And I believe that every one of you, my fellow countrymen, will not care for your life but gladly share in the honor to make of yourself His Majesty's humble shield."

When the Prime Minister's voice faded, the room erupted, everyone talking at once. Hirotaka stumbled from the cafeteria and headed for a spot where he could be alone.

Thoughts tumbled through his mind as he hurried toward a stand of pine trees, ignoring the bitter wind furiously whipping at the thin sleeves of his shirt. When he reached the trees, he sank onto a bench. His head down, he closed his eyes and tried to put order to what he'd just heard.

Even though war with America had been drawing closer by the day, he had clung to the hope that somehow it wouldn't happen, hope that somehow the Emperor would wrest control from the generals and admirals and pull the country back from the brink. It hadn't happened. Instead, his country had committed national suicide.

Four months later, he still thought that. Even with Japan's early triumphs, he didn't see how his small country could achieve the kind of success the admirals and generals insisted would be theirs. Could such a thing be possible against the combined power of most of the western world? Surely not.

On the way to a meeting of the Patriotic Students Alliance, Hirotaka's lips tightened as his friend, Tomiko, spoke in a pride-filled voice. "The Alliance shares in every one of Japan's military successes. Aren't you glad now you joined?"

Although Hirotaka gave a brief nod, his thoughts churned. He didn't know how much longer he could keep up the charade of pretending approval of something he thought a grave mistake. But if he spoke out, stood up for his own beliefs, he'd be arrested—achieving nothing and destroying his parents in the process. Still, he took neither pleasure nor pride in his actions.

Although late in the spring, a wintry mix of snow and freezing rain made walking difficult. Both young men kept their heads lowered against the buffeting wind.

"I'm thinking of joining the Navy," Tomiko said.

Hirotaka stopped in mid-stride. "But, we only have one more year of school. Why don't you wait until you graduate?" The wind whipped at the ends of the gray silk scarf wrapped around his neck and seemed to rip the words out of his mouth.

Tomiko continued walking, but he looked back over his shoulder. "With a degree in art? What good is such a degree in what is sure to be a new world?"

Hirotaka hurried his steps to catch up. "Now you sound like my father."

Tomiko shrugged. "Your father has good sense. Anyway our student deferments won't be good much longer. I've already talked to them. I will be an ensign as soon as I've completed my training."

"It sounds as if you've already made up your mind."

"Yes."

His friend's departure from school prompted many more. Although he resisted, in the end, Hirotaka felt he had no choice. *I'm coming home*, he wrote his parents. *If I'm to join the Army, I'd rather it be a regiment from our prefecture.*

Saying goodbye to his mother proved even more difficult than Hirotaka had imagined. She received him in her room, head bowed and kneeling on a cushion the shade of ripe persimmons. "First Shunsuki then Kinya and now you, my youngest. Shunsuki is gone. Kinya may be dead at this very moment. How would I know?" She sighed. "Now I am to give you, my youngest son, to the Emperor. It is too much. He asks too much."

The sad resignation in her voice tore at Hirotaka. "I'm sorry, Mother. I don't want to go any more than you want to send me."

"You could have finished school. Who knows what might happen in that time."

He reached across the space between them and took her hand. "Mother, it's true we have won many victories…but you must not entertain false hopes. America and the Allies are concentrating on Europe right now, but things are bound to change. They are sure to refocus. I believe we will be in this war for a very long time. I would not have been allowed to finish school. It is as well to do the joining on my terms." He gazed at her, willing her to accept what neither of them could change.

His mother pulled her hand free. "I suppose you're right." She dabbed at her tears with a silk square she took from the sleeve of her green and silver kimono. "Have you spoken with your father?"

"Only for a moment," Hirotaka said, glad of the change of subject. "He had someone in his office."

"A nasty little man with a goatee and glasses?"

"That's a good description of the man I saw. Father didn't look happy."

"The man is from the city government. They are complaining your father hasn't given enough to the war effort."

Hirotaka stared, unable to imagine anyone having the nerve to accuse his father of not doing his patriotic duty. "You can't be serious. How does he dare?"

"I'm very serious. Everyone is asked to give more money. They are also asking for metal. The man says your father must give up the bronzes passed down from his ancestors, including the dragon vessel by the tea pavilion."

Hirotaka detected a faint gleam of anticipation in his mother's eye and smiled, thinking she, too, would like to see the battle sure to unfold between the man and his father on that topic. The fact that the battle would be waged over ancient art pieces only added to his keenness.

When he could finally pay his filial respects, Hirotaka found his father sitting cross-legged on a cushion, eyes closed in meditation. He stepped back, about to withdraw.

"Come in," his father said, his eyes still closed. "Sit beside me for a while."

Hirotaka lowered himself onto another cushion, closed his eyes, took a deep breath, and willed his body to relax. He'd practiced meditation since his teens and soon floated freely. Time passed. When he came back to awareness, he found his father watching him intently. It distressed Hirotaka to see how age rested even more heavily on his father's sloping shoulders and lined face.

"Your stay with us is to be brief. I understand you must leave for Army training tomorrow."

Hirotaka nodded.

"I approve your decision. It is better to enlist than wait to be called. As a Katsuragawa, it is your duty to show others the way."

For a moment, Hirotaka couldn't speak. When he did, he forced his words to remain neutral. "I'm glad you approve, Father."

Nine officer-candidates boarded the bus. Though still dark when they pulled away from the Military-Affairs office in Hiroshima, Hirotaka could still make out the words on the banner hanging above the door: *Congratulations on Being Called to the Colors.*

The sky began to lighten. He gazed out the bus window at the many small islands, limned by the sun's early morning glow. The islands seemed to float on the Inland Sea, while the sea itself shimmered in shades of gold and orange. Beyond it spread the vastness of the Pacific Ocean.

He wished he could enjoy the beauty before him. Instead, his heart beat wildly in anticipation and dread of what lay ahead. He glanced at the other officer-candidates and saw, like him, all had withdrawn into cocoons of silence.

Hirotaka had known the training would be grueling. Friends who had gone before him had filled his ears with all the horrors awaiting him. He'd heard about the diabolical sergeants and how he'd be awakened before dawn and marched everywhere. He knew about the mind-numbing and endless exercises and drills, their purpose to tear him down to zero before building him back as the Army wished him to be. He knew what to expect.

What he hadn't known was how long three months could be. Three months of physical and mental torture. Three months of ridicule, of learning not to think for himself. By the time his training was complete, he had become exactly what the Army and the Emperor wanted: a robot, ready to follow any superior's order without question and without hesitation. Hard as he might try, he couldn't put into words how that fact made him feel.

Most of his friends had long before been conscripted or enlisted, but the few left or home on leave held a party to celebrate his commission. They drank until they were thrown out of the geisha house then found a darkened inn, roused the proprietor, and drank more. His father held a reception for his business acquaintances and to celebrate Hirotaka's commission. Hirotaka became very drunk at that party, also. In fact, he spent most of the five days of his leave drunk.

He arrived at the Military-Affairs Office feeling as though ten men with taiko drums were practicing inside his skull. His stomach near open rebellion, he swallowed hard and stood to attention. The officer-in-charge, a thin man with stooped shoulders, who looked as though he may once have been an accountant, showed no mercy for his obvious condition.

"You are to report to Kure Naval Base this afternoon at fifteen hundred hours," the man barked. "You will be accompanied by two men being transferred to your new company."

Hirotaka felt too miserable to worry about where to meet the two, or how they would get to Kure, some forty or fifty kilometers from Hiroshima. He saluted and left the captain's office, rushing for the door leading outside. Maybe fresh air would revive him.

"Lieutenant Katsuragawa?"

Two men, both several years his senior, one a good eight inches taller than the other, stood braced before him. Their faces were devoid of expression, but their eyes were like those of feral cats. Still afraid he might embarrass himself by being sick, Hirotaka forced down the gorge rising in his throat. "Yes."

"I am Corporal Hara," said the smaller man, whose ears stood out from his shaved head like handles on a jug. "This is Private Yoshida."

Briefly, Hirotaka thought of the woman at the Nishimi pottery factory. Yoko Yoshida. Nishimi and pottery were light years behind him now. He nodded, wincing when the hammering inside his head intensified.

"The bus for Kure leaves in thirty minutes, sir."

He nodded again, this time with more care. He reached for the duffle bag he'd left near the door.

"Private. Get the lieutenant's gear."

13
NOBUKO
The Gaijin

Nobuko kept her eyes on the pot she scrubbed, unable to avoid hearing her uncle's raised voice. "It's that damned Katsuragawa's fault!"

"Husband, everyone will hear you," Nobuko's aunt said.

Her uncle made no effort to subdue his voice. "I know he is behind this. All because he is unwilling to give up his bronze water vessel for tea ceremony, and other things he claims have belonged to his family for centuries. I don't care how old or important he thinks his family is, doesn't he know their lineage means nothing if Japan fails to win this war? It is his duty to surrender every scrap of metal he owns, just as it has been my duty to see he does."

Nobuko rinsed the pot in a bucket of heated water and handed it to her cousin Mimi to dry. Mimi's eyes widened as her father continued to rail.

The red conscription card had arrived the day before. Nobuko knew it boded ill when the postman handed it to her with his eyes lowered. She quickly took it to her aunt, who cried out. "My son! They are calling my son into service when he has not yet finished school. How can they do this?"

But it was not Sadaoka the Army wanted. It was Sadaoka's father.

Nobuko reached for another pot, wondering if the rich and powerful Katsuragawa her uncle yelled about might be the one with the summer estate near Nishimi. If so, she wished she could give the man her thanks. For her aunt's and cousins' sakes, she hated to think of her uncle fighting in some faraway place, but it would be a relief to have him out of the house. Besides, at fifty-three, surely the Army would not send him into combat. A desk job more likely.

Whenever Nobuko and her aunt went to the market, it seemed more people contested over less. Women waved yen notes, scrabbling and grabbing for the merest amounts of rice or millet. Pork and beef were unheard of, chicken nearly so. Her aunt claimed there'd been no real tea in the house for well over a year. A short time after her uncle's abrupt departure, money became more difficult to come by as well. To help, Nobuko earned a few yen a week teaching conversational English to a retired professor who lived nearby. One day he met her at his door.

"I am sorry. You are a good tutor, Nobuko-san. But I can no longer afford to pay you for your kind instruction."

She'd been expecting it, surprised the old man had held on to her so long, surprised he'd even hired her in the first place—most likely out of kindness. Still, it came as a blow.

Her aunt delivered a blow even more devastating. "With my husband called to serve, we can no longer afford this house."

About to remove her coat and unwind the scarf from around her head and neck, Nobuko stopped. "Where will we go, Auntie?"

"My husband's sister has invited the children and me to live with her."

Nobuko waited for the invitation to include her.

Her aunt's lips trembled. "I'm so sorry, Nobuko-san. There won't be room for you. Even with her children raised and her husband dead these many years, my husband's sister says the house is too small for anyone else."

For a moment, Nobuko only cocked her head to one side, unable to grasp her aunt's words. But as they penetrated, she froze inside. Despite her uncle, this house had been a sanctuary, an oasis of safety. The muscles in her arms jerked with tension.

"What about me, Auntie? Where am I to go?"

Her aunt closed her eyes and shook her head.

"It's not fair," Mimi said that evening. "We can't just leave our cousin like that, Mama. Why can't we all stay here?"

Nobuko's aunt again shook her head, but to Nobuko's surprise, Takanori echoed Mimi's sentiments. Sadaoka, however, looked up from his homework and claimed they owed Nobuko nothing. "She always acts so high and mighty with her American ways. Let her find her own place to live."

Nobuko felt sure Sadaoka's acne, even more livid than usual, was symptomatic of the anger that churned inside him. Before she could say anything, he gave her a look filled with so much hatred, it felt like a physical blow. He laughed, but without humor. "We'll no doubt see you begging in the street before long."

For days, unable to eat or sleep, Nobuko thought about the future and Sadaoka's dire prediction. She often found herself staring at a familiar object without seeing it. As frightened as she'd been on the *Osaka Maru*, after it turned around at sea and made its zigzag way back to Japan, her lips quivered. Her aunt, either in tears or packing, helped little.

Maybe Sadaoka was right. Maybe, like the fired maid, she would end up begging on the streets. Only the day before, in the marketplace, a woman with pleading eyes and wearing a tattered kimono, held out her hand. Although she had none to spare, Nobuko dropped two yen into the woman's outstretched hand. Now she shuddered, thinking that woman could be her.

She briefly considered Nishimi, but her uncle's earlier threats about the police unnerved her. Even if Mr. and Mrs. Mori still wanted her to come to them, she might not be allowed to go.

If only she had someone to talk with, someone who might understand her fears, tell her what to do, someone like Masato Abi. She caught her breath on a sob. Masato wouldn't be interested in helping her—to him, she would be the enemy.

"Write to Mr. and Mrs. Mori," Mimi said.

Nobuko shook her head. "I don't want to get them into trouble with the police."

"They're the only ones who can help now. You have to write to them."

In the end, with no other option presenting itself, Nobuko wrote.

Just like the first time, Mr. and Mrs. Mori stood outside their door, waiting to greet Nobuko.

"You are so thin and wan," Mrs. Mori exclaimed, shaking her head. "But I will feed you up until you are plump as a chicken ready to be plucked." She then threw her hands to her face, appearing torn between tears and laughter.

Mr. Mori kept smiling, bowing, and saying, "Welcome, welcome."

Nobuko felt as if she'd come home. When all the tears were dried, hers as well as Mrs. Mori's, they showed her to her old room.

Mr. Mori carried her suitcase. "What do you have in here? It is much heavier than when you left."

She smiled. "It's a surprise." They were too polite to inquire further, but she knew by the many glances they gave the suitcase they were curious to know what she had brought them. "I'll show you." She knelt on the floor and opened the suitcase, pushed aside her worn clothes, and lifted out her uncle's radio.

"Ohh," said Mrs. Mori as Mr. Mori took the radio from Nobuko's hands and examined it.

"My aunt insisted I bring it." It had been a significant act of defiance on her aunt's part. Nobuko could only imagine her uncle's anger when he returned and found it missing. On the other hand, she felt justified in accepting his precious radio after finding out he'd lied to her. She could have come to Nishimi at any time since the *Osaka Maru* returned her to Japan.

Mr. Mori handed back the radio. "It is very fine, Nobuko-san."

"Shall we try it out?"

Mr. Mori sucked air between his teeth and cocked his head before shaking it. "I'm not sure it will perform, Nobuko -san. We are high up in the mountains."

"Oh," she said. She hadn't thought about a problem with reception.

"But we can try," Mrs. Mori said, clasping her hands together, a smile lighting her face.

It took a great deal of trying. At first, the electricity didn't work, and when it did work, static obliterating everything.

"I'm afraid it's no use, Mori-san," she said with a sigh.

"I've heard of something that might make the reception better," Mr. Mori said, not yet ready to give up. He strung a fine wire through a window and into a tree, moving it this way and that, until they could understand the announcer's words and recognize the music when it played.

Mrs. Mori swayed to the sound. "It's magical. I have never heard anything so fine. Thank you, Nobuko-san. I will write your aunt and thank her as well."

The radio soon became part of Nishimi daily life. So long as the electricity flowed through the wires, every evening the villagers crowded into the Mori's house to hear the news—women of all ages, old men, including Nobuko's tea ceremony teacher, Mr. Nakamura, who'd resumed instructing her in the art, and a scattering of teenagers too young for conscription. Laughing and gossiping, they waited for Mr. Mori to lift his hand for silence, an indication the broadcast was about to begin.

To her surprise, Nobuko discovered she no longer hated hearing the opening bars of *The Battleship March*. Instead, she found herself sharing with the villagers the ups, the downs of battle, as they worried or rejoiced for the safety of their sons and husbands. With no political mantra or ideology besides love of country, the villagers thought only of how their loved ones fared as the war moved from China to Burma, from the Philippines to the Solomon Islands, from the Marshalls to Java.

The one person who refused to come and listen to the broadcast was Yoko Yoshida. Whenever Nobuko came face-to-face with her, Yoko averted her eyes and refused to speak.

On her way to the village store one morning, Nobuko spotted Mr. Mori, directing activity around the kiln on the hill behind the pottery factory—he'd said they would be firing it in a few days.

The hot, dry weather made plumes of dust swirl with every footstep. Nobuko gave an exuberant little hop. With upturned face bathed in sunshine, she gazed from one mountain-filled horizon to the other. Only a few wisps of clouds interrupted the azure sky. She drew in a deep breath, grateful to Mrs. Mori for giving her the excuse to be out of the house on such a fine day. She barely even noticed the smell of the ditch running alongside the road.

The one thing bringing down her good spirits, the wide-legged pants called mompei she wore. Gathered at the ankles by a band of elastic stitched into their hems, many women wore them these days, especially country women. For some reason, one Nobuko failed to understand, the pants were considered patriotic.

Mrs. Mori had surprised her with a dreadful gray pair. "It is not good to appear different," she'd said when handing them to Nobuko.

Nobuko looked down now and sighed. She might not be plump as a chicken ready for plucking, but at least she wasn't the scrawny thing that arrived in Nishimi two months before. Food in Nishimi, though also growing scarce, was still more plentiful than it had been in Sakayama.

She opened the door of the Abi store, the bell jingling. She caught her breath. Masato stood behind the counter. She ducked back outside, unwilling to go in with Masato there, not wearing the awful mompei. But, Mrs. Mori expected her tofu. Nobuko wiped her palms on her pant legs, raised her chin and opened the door once more. In the cool and dim, she pretended surprise. "Oh, you're here. How is school?"

Masato smiled, a hint of amusement in his eyes. "I've graduated."

"Mrs. Mori needs a block of tofu." She tried to ignore the way she felt in his presence. On the outside, butterflies danced on her skin; inside, her stomach did a handstand.

Masato rolled up his sleeve and reached into a barrel containing water and tofu and brought out a jiggling white block. "Is this enough?"

"Yes."

Masato wrapped the tofu and handed it to her. "Thank you, Nobuko-san."

Tongue-tied and unable to think, Nobuko dropped the money Mrs. Mori had given her onto the counter and turned to leave. Masato's next words brought her up short.

"I've been conscripted. In ten days, I must leave to begin my training."

"Oh!" She nearly strangled on the word as her heart gave a sudden thump. She clutched the wrapped tofu to her chest, and rushed out of the store.

She ran all the way to the Moris' house, where she spent the afternoon pacing her small room, blinking away tears, or dropping onto a cushion and burying her face in her hands. All she could think about was Masato leaving Nishimi, going to war. With her country.

The evening of the second day of Nobuko's self-imposed confinement to the house, Mr. Mori asked her to sit with him. This surprised her. After the war news ended and the villagers left, he generally enjoyed an hour of solitude before retiring.

"Of course, Mori-san." Puzzled despite her misery, she sank to her knees on the cushion next to him. She felt even more mystified when Mrs. Mori left the room and slid the door closed behind her.

After a long silence, a silence in which Nobuko began to wonder if Mr. Mori remembered her presence, he cleared his throat and spoke. "You are not my daughter, Nobuko-san. And yet, I feel that I am your father, at least until you can be re-united with your own."

"Thank you, Mori-san. You and Mrs. Mori are very good to me."

"As your Japan father, I must speak to you of something very difficult."

She offered a tentative smile. "And what is that, Mori-san?"

"I understand you saw Masato Abi yesterday afternoon."

Her bewilderment increased. "I went to the store to buy tofu for Mrs. Mori."

"Masato is a fine young man," Mr. Mori said. "The village is very proud of him."

"He told me he's been conscripted." She nearly choked, saying aloud the word she'd repeated in her mind a hundred, no, a thousand times.

"That is so. He must leave in little more than a week's time."

"Mr. and Mrs. Abi must be worried." At that moment, she wished herself somewhere, anywhere else—preferably a place where no one would hear her howls.

Mr. Mori shifted, looking more uncomfortable. "It is their son's duty to serve the Emperor."

Duty. Always it came to that hateful word. "Yes." She stared at a spot on the tatami mat, lips drawn tight.

"Masato wishes to marry you before he leaves."

Her head sprang up. "What?"

"Mr. and Mrs. Abi do not favor the match, but they want their son to be happy. They know there is a chance he may not live through the war, and they wish his last days in Nishimi to be joyful ones. Therefore, they have agreed."

Ringing sounded in her ears. "What about me? Don't I have any say?"

"It is your choice, of course, Nobuko-san. Masato is a fine man and would make you a fine husband. But his life is in a precarious place right now. And the war we fight is with your country."

"Yes." In an instant, her shoulders sagged, her outrage drained away. "My own brother may be joining the U.S.

Army or Navy at this very moment." She swallowed, trying to ease the tight band of tension forming around her throat.

Mr. Mori nodded and she saw by the pain reflected in his eyes that he understood. "Perhaps you should give the idea some thought," he said. "If you really were my daughter, I would not force you to marry Masato, even though I know he would make you a good husband. But, you are not my daughter, and this is a difficult time. Many young men and women are marrying prior to the men going to war. I'm not sure this is a good thing."

The night hot and her small room nearly airless, Nobuko lay sweating on her futon, trying to make sense of Masato's proposal. What should she do? She couldn't deny her attraction. Maybe he was the one her heart searched for, longed for. But she couldn't commit to something as important as marriage without first consulting her parents. And yet, the world was different now and her parents an ocean away, the circumstances far from anything they could have imagined when they sent her to Japan to learn the culture of her ancestors.

The lack of parental consent was but part of Nobuko's worries. If she married Masato, Japan would become her permanent home. Nishimi. Did she want her life to be so limited, so constrained by the customs of country people?

The moon shone in her window. She glanced at her wristwatch, tilting it to see the dial. After midnight. She rolled onto her side and her scattered thoughts returned to Masato. She liked so much about him. Even though they hadn't spent a great deal of time together, she'd never felt such kinship with a man—like an invisible bond stretched between them. Still....

She rose the next morning dry-eyed and groggy from lack of sleep, yet keyed up and jittery. Mr. Mori had already left for the factory. In the kitchen, Mrs. Mori smiled but said nothing as she ladled miso soup into a bowl.

Setting the soup on the table, Mrs. Mori gestured for Nobuko to sit. "Dozo. Please eat." The motherly woman then knelt on the cushion opposite her, settling in for a chat. "Will you accept his offer?"

Nobuko drew a shaky breath. "I think so. Yes."

Mrs. Mori clapped her hands. "I will tell my husband right away, so that he can pass the word to Mr. and Mrs. Abi. Then we will need to make arrangements with the priests for the ceremony."

Nobuko's heart raced. All the questions she'd struggled with the night before came rushing back. Then she thought of Masato and a sudden calm came over her. She'd made the right decision.

But that decision proved meaningless. Her status in Japan too ambiguous for local authorities to deal with, she was denied permission to marry.

Nobuko saw Masato only once before he left for officer's training. Mrs. Mori insisted she accompany her to the store to buy supplies for their evening meal.

Masato, tidying a shelf when they entered, straightened to face them. Cheeks hot and flushed, Nobuko kept her eyes on the wide-planked floor at her feet. Mrs. Mori stood at her side and Mrs. Abi waited behind the counter. Nobuko sensed their eyes on her, and her cheeks reddened more. Although she couldn't bring herself to speak, there was much she wanted to say. Things like 'be careful' and 'come back safe' and 'I love you.' She could say none of those things with his mother and Mrs. Mori watching and listening.

And then he was gone and it was too late to say anything.

14
TOSHIO
Farmer - Soldier

The night they left Kure Naval Base, Toshio stood at the rail of the troopship, a converted freighter and one of a large convoy under the escort of six warships. Because of the blackout, only stars and a pale moon illuminated the receding shoreline. Throughout the long night, the convoy slipped past the dark silhouettes of island after island in the Inland Sea. Just before dawn, they crept through the Bungo Straits and into the Pacific Ocean.

The farther south they sailed, the hotter and steamier Toshio's sleeping compartment grew. The air in the compartment reeked of sweat and vomit. Water constantly dripped down the walls. He often lay on his narrow cot and listened to unfamiliar sounds coming from the bowels of the ship.

Every ten or fifteen minutes they changed course to avoid possible torpedoes. At any moment, he expected one to slam into them. He'd never learned to swim. He pictured the ship cracking open like an egg, his body slipping out and slowly sinking to the bottom of the sea.

Ordered onto the crowded deck each morning, he and his platoon were led in exercise by either Lieutenant Katsuragawa or Lieutenant Abi—to keep up their stamina, they claimed. To keep up morale, many played at quoits or card games. Toshio ignored invitations to join in. One afternoon, brooding over his miserable home leave, he leaned against a bulkhead in the shadows and stared vacantly out to sea.

Takeda Yoshida sidled up behind him. "Did you manage to stuff your woman with another brat?"

"Shut up."

"What's wrong with you, farmer? Does the first one look like someone else? Her brother or maybe her father, does it—"

Toshio spun around. Despite Takeda's size, he swung and hit the bigger man squarely on the nose. The satisfying crunch of cartilage rang in his ears.

Takeda cursed and threw his hand to his face. When he pulled it away and saw blood pooled in his palm, he howled. "Miserable son of a whore."

Toshio quickly ducked out of Takeda's reach, but not before throwing another jab; never had he hated another man as he hated Takeda Yoshida. He prepared to take yet another swing when a hand fell on his shoulder.

"What's going on?" said Lieutenant Abi.

Though the lieutenant lacked Takeda's size, his voice carried the weight of authority. Toshio unclenched his fists and dropped them to his side. Takeda backed away as well, using his shirtsleeve to wipe blood trailing from his nose.

"Private, go below," Lieutenant Abi ordered.

Takeda lumbered off, throwing a sullen glance over his shoulder at both the lieutenant and Toshio.

Lieutenant Abi turned his attention to Toshio. "You are setting a bad example for your men."

With difficulty, Toshio held his temper in check. Even as a boy Masato Abi had held himself superior to everyone else in and around Nishimi, just because his parents owned the only store in the village. "Sorry, Lieutenant," he muttered through taut lips. "It won't happen again."

"See that it doesn't. We'll meet the enemy soon enough. Save your fighting for then."

Several mornings later, while a pink and golden glow washed the eastern sky, their troopship and another, along with one warship, broke off from the rest of the convoy. They'd passed the Philippines. Toshio had overheard a crew member say so two days before. He stood at the rail and watched the other ships steam away, idly wondering where the ship he rode on headed and where the other ships were going. He wouldn't bother to ask Lieutenant Abi or Lieutenant Katsuragawa. Even if they knew, he doubted they'd tell him. He didn't care anyway.

Monotonous day followed monotonous day. On a sweltering afternoon, in hopes of finding a breeze, Toshio went up on deck, already crowded with winches, lifeboats, stores, and other men in search of a break from the oppressive heat. No breeze stirred and the sun beat down with relentless intensity.

About to go back below, Toshio glanced at the horizon. At first, he saw only a narrow strip of beach beneath dark, rain-filled clouds, rugged peaks poking above them. The ship appeared to be heading toward whatever it was. He moved to the forward rail. Before long, others joined him. Although mostly obscured by clouds, the bit of land grew bigger as their ship neared.

"Do you think it's an island or a peninsula?" asked the man next to him.

Toshio shrugged.

An hour later, in a torrential rainstorm, they disembarked near a town called Finschhafen, on the northern coast of New Guinea. They waited on the dock for over an hour, shuffling from side to side, their gear at their feet, their shoulders hunched against rain that came straight down.

"The fucking shit doesn't even cool things off," a young private fumed.

Finally, Lieutenant Katsuragawa formed up Toshio's platoon. With rifles and duffle bags on their shoulders, boots squishing with every step, they marched from the still-crowded dock to the headquarters compound, a former church mission five kilometers away. Once there, Toshio and his newly assigned six-man squad crowded into the back of one of several canvas-covered trucks, and stowed their gear at their feet.

After some back-and-forth between the driver and an officer Toshio didn't recognize, the truck started up and headed out. Through the rear flaps, he noted two other trucks pull out of the compound after them. Rain splattering on the truck's canvas top reminded him of the day he'd been driven from the hospital to the dock in Nanchang for the beginning of his trip home. Home. He scowled; he would not think of home. He had no home. Only the Army.

They traveled over a partially-cleared road, filled with washouts and sinkholes they needed to skirt, before arriving at an airfield still under construction. Graders, dump trucks and other behemoth machines moved slowly through the deluge.

"Corporal Hara, how can anyone work in this shit?" one of his men asked, hollering to be heard over the noise of the truck, the rain, and the machinery. Toshio didn't bother to answer.

When their truck finally pulled to a stop, he and his men jumped down. Mud squelched under their feet. Toshio directed the men to unload their equipment, pitch tents and set up camp. "We've got orders to guard the airfield's perimeter while it's being finished." They stared at the muddy ground and the rain, but did as they were told.

The sound of the rain beating down every night nearly drove Toshio mad, and each morning he woke to rivulets of water running through his tent. Everywhere he went, water sluiced between his feet and under the soles of his boots, carrying the earth with it. He wondered how the island remained, why it hadn't simply washed away into the sea.

Occasionally, the sun broke through the low-lying clouds. Then it wasn't merely hot, but steaming hot. To make things worse, an assortment of flying and stinging insects made going without a shirt impossible. With his years of fighting across China, from the plains to the mountains, from north to south, he'd thought himself prepared for anything. Nothing could have prepared him for New Guinea.

They weren't allowed to go into Finschhafen. They hadn't been paid since before leaving Kure, and few had much, if any, money left. There were no comfort women and nothing to spend money on anyway; their only pastime was gambling. They gambled with an assortment of things, like cigarettes or shoelaces, and they gambled on everything, from slug races to whether the next plane to fly high overhead, above the clouds, would be American, Australian, or Japanese. The planes were distinguishable by the sounds of their engines. Toshio once saw two men bet a week of the other man's duty on who could lace his boots faster. Fights frequently broke out. They gambled on the outcome of those, too.

Throughout July and August and into September the rain continued. "On the other side of the mountains, they say it's dry half of the year, but that it's so hot it's like a green desert," said a corporal who drove one of the construction battalion's huge trucks. A farmer, too, but from farther north, near Nagoya.

The two were huddled in Toshio's tent, playing cards, and drinking a powerful native brew they'd traded for rations. Although rain pounded on the canvas above them, Toshio no longer noticed—he'd become inured to the sound. He wished he had a decent cigarette. No one had real tobacco any more. Recently he'd taken up smoking ginger leaves.

The tent flaps parted and Takeda Yoshida stuck his head inside. "Colonel Ogawa wants you."

Toshio crawled out of the tent and stood swaying for several seconds, the rough alcohol gone to his head.

Takeda gave an unpleasant chuckle. "He's in the command tent. Better make it quick, farmer. You know his reputation."

Everyone knew Ogawa's reputation and everyone was right to fear him; the colonel carried a club he used to punish men for the least infraction.

Toshio hurried through the rain toward the command tent, bent his head and ducked inside. Lieutenants Katsuragawa and Abi, plus three non-coms were already there, crowded around a table, looking down at a map. A lantern hung from a pole above their heads, shedding light on the map and casting eerie shadows into the corners of the tent. Toshio wiped his face and saluted.

"You're late," barked Colonel Ogawa, ignoring the salute.

Toshio braced, expecting the club. That damned Takeda had purposely delayed delivering the message. "Colonel, sir, my apologies. I came as soon as I was informed you requested my presence." The colonel scowled, but did nothing more.

Toshio had no time to contemplate retribution on Takeda. "A convoy of LSTs has been spotted heading toward Finschhafen," Lieutenant Katsuragawa said. "Our part of New Guinea is no longer to be ignored."

The first plane dove from the clouds, its machine guns spitting out hot, rapid death. Anti-aircraft guns roared to life. Everyone in the open scattered and dove for cover. More planes followed. Toshio took refuge beneath a large crane. A moment later, someone piled in after him. The two peered out as a fierce wave of bullets swept across the runway, sending bits of crushed gravel and concrete flying.

A sharp sting as a small rock hit Toshio's cheek. Anti-aircraft fire rattled the air.

"I should have fled into the jungle with the rest," the other man shouted.

Although some had made their way to the airfield, Toshio had heard many in Finschhafen had turned tail and run into the jungle rather than stand their ground and fight the Australians. He grunted. "Then you would have been a coward, like them."

The other man shook his head. "You have no idea what we faced. The gaijins may be fewer in number, but their weaponry is superior. We didn't have a chance."

Toshio's lips turned down. "That's no excuse."

Darkness descended, ending the air attack. Toshio scrambled from beneath the crane, eager to put distance between him and his cowardly companion. The rain didn't slacken.

Once again called to the command tent, Toshio entered to find a breathless runner standing in front of Colonel Ogawa. Rain dripped from the runner's clothes and boots to puddle on the wooden floor. "The enemy is coming fast," he said. "Nothing is stopping them."

The field telephone on Colonel Ogawa's desk rang. He answered. When he hung up, he glared at each of the NCOs and officers. "There is no rescue coming—from either the air or the sea. We are ordered to abandon the airfield."

15
NOBUKO
The Gaijin

Desperate to take her mind off Masato's departure, missing her parents and worried about her brother, Nobuko volunteered to give English lessons to anyone interested. It surprised her when some took her up on her offer. Two were high school students, whom she taught after school on Saturdays, and the rest were housewives, friends of Mrs. Mori.

"It is so kind of you to teach us, Nobuko-san," said Mrs. Mori.

Nobuko smiled and bowed to the five nodding women who knelt in a semi-circle in front of her. "It is my pleasure," she said, happy she could repay the kindness so many had shown her.

She first tried formal instruction. The women, however, were more interested in hearing about America and about her mother, who'd been what people called a picture bride. "My father had already immigrated to California. A matchmaker in Japan, with the help of a photograph, arranged their marriage."

She went on to tell them stories of her childhood and schooling, about her family's farm. And, being as honest as she could, she told them of the difficulties faced by Japanese women in America, both for immigrants like her mother, and for those like her, who were born in America.

In exchange, she learned the customs of her adopted village, along with all the gossip. She heard the horror stories of Yoko Yoshida's husband, a man they all feared.

"He is sly as a weasel," one woman warned.

"Though a very handsome one," another woman said before putting her hand to her mouth to stifle a giggle. Above her hand, her dark eyes danced with merriment.

"It is well-known if a weasel cuts across your path, he will bewitch you if you don't throw a rock at him," Mrs. Mori added with a knowing look to the other women. "When Takeda Yoshida returns from the war, you must always remember to carry a stone in your pocket."

The women laughed, but Nobuko felt a momentary twinge, reminded of something her mother used to say, something about being careful not to step on a sleeping tiger's tail.

Nobuko also learned about the old and noble Katsuragawa family, whose large estate lay less than two kilometers up the mountain. The women explained how the family used the estate during the summer to escape the heat of Sakayama. They told her how the oldest son died of cholera in China. Also, about how the mother had to plead with the father to allow the youngest son to study art.

"But now he has enlisted in the Army," a woman said.

"The father is very powerful, with many connections high in the government," said another. Five heads nodded solemn agreement.

Nobuko nodded, too, more certain than ever this was the Katsuragawa responsible for her uncle's conscription, or so her uncle claimed.

"I remember the sons," said the first woman. "When they were young, they used to play with the village children, but when they grew older, their father didn't allow it."

"The youngest son once worked with my husband, helping to fire the kiln," said Mrs. Mori. "My husband was very impressed with the young man's industry." The look of satisfaction on her face gave evidence that Mrs. Mori felt a great honor had been conferred upon her husband.

"Are there just the two sons?" Nobuko asked.

Mrs. Mori shook her head. "No, there is also a middle son. In Manchukuo for a while, but now I believe he is on an aircraft carrier in the Pacific. He is a pilot."

"No daughters?"

"Only sons," the women said.

After the women left, Nobuko decided to visit the Katsuragawa estate and see if it lived up to their admiring descriptions. Following Mrs. Mori's directions, she took the narrow lane leading up the mountain from Nishimi. The lane, nothing but two deep ruts with a hump of weeds between them, just wide enough for an ox-driven cart.

She passed the Buddhist temple, set back in the trees, the gold and red trim on its sweeping eaves gleaming in the dappled sunlight. In a grove of trees next to the temple lay a rock garden, tended by the priests. She'd visited the garden several times, taking pleasure in the tranquility it offered. On the left side of the lane, beyond the equally large but less ornate Shinto shrine, were paddies planted with rice and lotus.

Before long, she came to the estate. To her disappointment, she found the thick earthen wall surrounding it too high to see over. She rang the bell next to the covered wooden gate. No one answered. She gave it a gentle push, the gate refused to budge. From the width of the thatched roof, partially visible above the walls, she envisioned the house's enormous size. Since she'd been told the family lived in Sakayama most of the year, she assumed the place to be deserted.

She walked around the walls, shoving aside brush and vines, looking for a way in or a spot where she could view the grounds. Near the back, she came to a small gate with a broken latch. She opened it and stepped into a breathtaking garden. A large pond beckoned. Flickers of orange slipped through the pond's green depths. The only sounds she heard were the twitters of birds in the trees outside the wall.

The gardens surrounded a house a dozen times or more the size of the Mori's, which itself was larger than most of the houses in Nishimi. Besides the main house, there were several smaller buildings. Peering in windows, she discovered two were storage sheds. One looked like it might have been a stable. An ornate saddle hung on one wall, though she spotted no sign of a horse or any other animal.

Another building, set some ways off, appeared to be a small house. About to approach it, a shouted "hoi" stopped her in her tracks. An old man came toward her, a dead rabbit, strung by its back feet, slung over his shoulder. The gravel on the path crunched beneath his feet. "Who are you and what are you doing here? This is private property. You are trespassing."

Nobuko bowed deep and apologized for her brazenness in invading the estate. "My manners were overcome by my curiosity for what lay behind these walls. It is magnificent." She raised her head, but kept her eyes lowered.

"You must be the gaijin living with Mori," the man said, his voice gruff. "Since you are obviously ill-brought up, your trespass will be excused this one time."

Nobuko lowered her head once more. "Thank you. You are most generous to excuse my rude behavior." She straightened. "Would you show me more of this splendid estate?"

The next two hours were spent with the old man, Haiashi, the estate's caretaker. Seated on a stone bench beside the pond, she learned all about the strictness of the senior Katsuragawa and the kindness of his wife. Haiashi told her, too, about the many pranks the sons played as children, hiding from their parents, or climbing too high in trees. Also, the troubles the middle and youngest had gotten into when they were older, most often over their courses of study.

"The youngest one follows after his mother. He likes art and poetry." Haiashi shook his head. "Such rows he and his father had. The middle one—before he joined the Army—had little time for serious study. He preferred listening to his jazz records. His father hated them." The oldest son, the one who'd died in China, had been the equestrian. "Everyone knew Shunsuki to be his father's favorite. His death broke the old man's heart. Although he could not bear to keep his son's horses, he did keep his saddle."

Just as she rose, about to leave, Nobuko learned the youngest son, who had enlisted a few months before, was in the same regiment as Masato Abi. "Where are they, do you know?"

Haiashi shrugged. "Somewhere in the Pacific."

16
TOSHIO
Farmer - Soldier

Forty-seven days had passed since the Australians attacked the airbase, driving the Japanese into the jungle. Even though hundreds, maybe thousands, were on the trail with him, Toshio felt isolated in his misery, as insignificant as an ant in the long, silent line of half-starved men plodding the muddy path along the lip of a deep gorge.

Far below, a river snaked around huge boulders and in and out of dense growth. The ceaseless rain ran from the short brim of his cap, down his face and into his mouth. Despite the rain, the enervating heat lay like a sopping cotton blanket, sapping his strength. Every indrawn breath was laden with the scent of decay. Insects burrowed their snouts into his skin and sucked his blood. He tripped on a half-buried root and cursed. "We should have stayed and faced the enemy," he muttered under his breath. "Better to be killed there than slink away like cowards."

The line halted when a runner appeared. "A suspension bridge is a day's march ahead. Everyone must hurry and cross, before it is blown up," he said, hands on knees, panting. "When it is destroyed, the enemy cannot follow." Even as he spoke, a spurt of distant gunfire sounded behind them. The man straightened and nodded before heading down the line to continue delivering his message.

For the first time in weeks, Toshio allowed himself a twinge of hope, which stayed with him throughout the day.

When darkness fell, it closed in quickly. He kept his eyes fixed on the white square sewn to the back of the tunic on the man ahead of him. They all had the squares. Still, in the utter blackness of the jungle night, a few feet away and the white square disappeared. Whenever he lost sight of it bobbing in front of him, Toshio panicked. He imagined stepping off the rim of the gorge, into the void.

The sky lightened. Toshio's boots were heavy and caked with mud. He yearned for sleep, but stumbled on, focusing on the bridge. Hours passed, the rain increased, almost drowning out the sound of gunfire behind them. Eyes on the ground in front of him, Toshio decided the bridge was one more of the Army's false rumors. There is no purpose to this existence, anyway, no reason there should be a bridge. We will march until we are dead and no one will care.

"Look," someone called out. "There it is."

Toshio's head snapped up. His heart beat faster and he quickened his pace, trying to shoulder past men in front of him. They pushed forward as well.

Then he saw it, a series of wooden planks held together by rope and suspended by cables. Men were already crossing. Their line extended over the swaying bridge and up the trail beyond, until it disappeared into the jungle on the opposite side of the gorge.

Toshio shoved forward with renewed energy, jostling shoulders, pushing aside those slowed by exhaustion or illness. The gorge had necked down to about fifteen meters, narrow enough to make out the figures on the opposite bank, who were preparing the charges that would take down the bridge.

He drew close enough to distinguish the faces of the men on the other side. Lieutenant Katsuragawa, for one. Another, Takeda Yoshida. Their eyes met. Toshio cursed. Why was that whoreson always in his way? He pushed aside his anger, unable to restrain his eagerness to cross the bridge and thwart the enemy closing on their heels.

A loud boom rang out, sending shock waves racing through the sodden air. Toshio struggled to remain on his feet. He felt he'd been punched in the chest by a giant, who then used an auger to puncture his eardrums.

Slowly at first, then gaining speed, the bridge dipped and fell. Men were on the span as it started to go down. Others, unaware or disbelieving, ran onto it, perhaps thinking they still had time to cross. Screaming, they spiraled toward the river and rocks far below.

Toshio stared at the void where the bridge had been just moments before. Bits of blasted rock were attached to the dangling cables' ends, which swung and twisted about, bouncing off the side of the gorge below him. His cracked lips parted as the cables finally came to a rest. With unblinking eyes fixed on the cables, he waited for them to swing back up, reattach themselves to the other side.

When they didn't, he lifted his head and looked across the chasm. The men on the other side had resumed climbing until, one by one, the jungle swallowed them. Takeda Yoshida brought up the rear. He stopped and looked back one last time. Again, their eyes locked. Takeda threw back his head in a kind of brazen acknowledgment then turned and he, too, disappeared into the jungle.

Toshio had no will to move. He wished he'd been on the bridge when it went down, could almost feel his body spinning through space, the air rushing past his face. At last he turned away, hunched his shoulders against the rain, and followed the others. Maybe there'd be another bridge.

17
HIROTAKA
Art Student

Colonel Ogawa, a stern man with little tolerance for ineptitude, had instructed Hirotaka to destroy the bridge after the last man safely crossed. But the ragged line of weary men plodding along the opposite rim of the gorge appeared endless.

Enemy rifle and machine gun fire drew ever closer. How did the enemy still have weapons that fired? His own, and his men's, were so rusted and corroded, the triggers often failed. Many were discarded. On the rare occasion one of their weapons did function correctly, the return fire from the Americans or the Australians overwhelmed them.

"The charges are set," Private Yoshida informed him.

Hirotaka looked once again at the straggling men on the other side of the gorge, mentally urging them to hurry. "Our orders are to wait until everyone has crossed," he said. As he spoke, he tried to ignore the cramping in his guts. The dysentery he'd suffered since arriving on New Guinea hadn't left him.

Private Yoshida scowled. "It will take hours before they've all crossed."

Hirotaka drew a calming breath. Ever since the first day at the Military Affairs Office in Hiroshima, Takeda Yoshida had gotten on his nerves. "Wait," he said.

Another spasm gripped his intestines and he gritted his teeth against the discomfort. He went into the bushes beside the path and squatted as the paroxysms passed through him. With so little to eat now, he mostly passed only mucus.

An explosion rocked him, nearly knocking him to the ground. He scrambled to his feet, struggling to pull up his trousers, and rushed back to the trail. Eyes wide, he stared in horrified disbelief as the bridge dipped and broke apart, sending at least twenty men spinning downward, screaming. Not until the last body struck the rocks at the bottom of the gorge could he tear his gaze away. At last he looked up and across the chasm. Corporal Hara, his mouth a grim slash, stared at the now empty gap between them.

"It was an accident."

Hirotaka whirled at the sound of Takeda Yoshida's voice. Something, maybe the sly look on the man's face, made him doubt he spoke the truth. Certain Yoshida had set the charges to go off early, Hirotaka's eyes narrowed. He could not prove his suspicions, however. The deed was done, the bridge gone.

Without a word, he started up the trail. With a final glance over his shoulder, he saw that most of the men on the other side of the gorge had begun to move again along its rim. Only Corporal Hara remained, staring into the void. Hirotaka grimaced then ducked his head and escaped into the jungle. Perhaps they would find another way to cross.

After the bridge, the trail grew steeper, the vines denser, and the muddy trail even slicker. Without pause, Hirotaka stepped over a yellow snake with a flat, black head. If only it would stop raining, he thought. Ahead, next to the trail, he saw what appeared to be a discarded uniform. The uniform moved. It contained a man.

When Hirotaka drew abreast, the man struggled to a sitting position and bared his chest. He pointed to Hirotaka's rifle. Hirotaka understood the man's unspoken request, but couldn't bring himself to lift the weapon and deliver a final gift of mercy. From then on, he avoided looking at men who fell out of line.

Instead, he plodded on, ever upward, mind as empty as he could make, stopping only when the cramping in his guts caused him to step off the track. Others needed to step out of line, too. Private Yoshida alone appeared healthy. Hirotaka shook his head in disgust; the man must thrive on everyone else's misery.

Eventually they reached the topmost ridge and started down the western slope. The rain stopped and the jungle became less dense. At the same time, the heat intensified. Worse, they hadn't escaped their enemies. The destruction of the bridge had accomplished nothing; there were Americans and Australians on this side of the island as well.

They broke into small groups, crossing and re-crossing the intertwining paths, avoiding an enemy that also moved through the jungle in small groups, hunting them. The chain -of-command evaporated. Hirotaka felt avoiding capture and staying alive, for himself and his men, his only mission.

Bone weary, they'd had no fresh water and nothing but grubs and leaves to eat in days. In the canopy above their heads, colorful chattering birds and small primates flew or sprang, mocking them. From somewhere close came the boom of a frog Hirotaka knew to be no larger than his thumb. A year ago, he would have wanted to capture everything in paint, especially the luminous green air. Now even the idea of setting brush to canvas exhausted him.

He'd prodded the men to get them up and moving that morning. Resigned, they fell into line and trudged behind him along the overgrown path, too tired and hungry to complain.

Vines slapped against him. An ugly-looking insect burrowed into the flaking skin on his stomach, bared because the buttons on his tunic had come off and he'd had no thread or needle to sew them back on. With detached curiosity, he watched the insect's slow progress, before pulling it free and tossing it aside. His lips were dry and caked. As they did every morning, his intestines twisted and heaved in unrelenting cramps. Lost in his own wretchedness, he slogged on, placing one tired foot in front of the other.

As if they'd dropped from an overhanging tree, three black men appeared on the path in front of him. They were naked but for woven armlets they wore around their biceps, and cod pieces, made of twisted grass, that covered their genitalia. Feathers bristled in their bushy, tightly curled hair. Each held a spear in one hand, raised and pointed at the small band of exhausted soldiers. Hirotaka dropped his rusted rifle and extended his hands, palms up. His men followed suit.

The natives, their faces twisted into fierce contortions, refused to lower their spears. Instead, they circled behind the small band of soldiers, gesturing for them to pick up their rifles and continue along the path. They followed it for several kilometers until stopped by one of the natives. The man used his spear to nudge them onto a second path, nearly hidden by the jungle growth.

Images of what could be awaiting them flashed through Hirotaka's mind. He'd heard there were cannibals in New Guinea.

When they emerged into a clearing, men, women, and children of all ages, stared, silent, as he and his men wearily filed by. They passed several platforms set on tall polls and covered in twigs and grass, before finally reaching a man Hirotaka assumed to be the village leader. The man sat on the ground in front of a tree. The three native men stepped back, but kept their spears pointed at Hirotaka and his men.

Several long moments passed. Hirotaka and the man stared at one another. When it became apparent they weren't to be killed, at least not immediately, Hirotaka gathered his courage and, using sign language, asked for food and water.

The man gestured toward two bare-chested women wearing short grass skirts and necklaces of bone. He spoke a few words. The women left and a short time later returned carrying gourds of sweet water. After Hirotaka and his men drank their fill, the village leader indicated they were to sit.

The women reappeared with two large wooden bowls containing a paste-like mixture. Hirotaka's men looked from him to the purplish-gray mass. Equally puzzled, he shrugged. The village leader barked an order and one of the women brought him a bowl. The man stuck two fingers into the mess and brought it to his mouth. After swallowing, he passed the bowl to Hirotaka.

It tasted strange, though not as revolting as Hirotaka had feared. At least it would fill the void in his stomach.

He took another scoop, nodded, and passed the bowl to his men. The bowl and its mate soon emptied.

They stayed in the village for three days, sleeping next to the villagers on the raised platforms, eating food they didn't recognize and drinking a strange brew with the village men, including the three who'd captured them and now appeared to be their best friends.

Hirotaka knew they must leave the village. They were soldiers and pursued by a relentless enemy. He was their leader, responsible not only for his men, but to his commanders, wherever they might be. He had a duty. The brief rest, with food and water, had been beneficial not only physically, but mentally and emotionally as well. He and his men repeatedly bowed their thanks and waved reluctant goodbyes to the headman and the villagers. They left by the same path they'd entered.

From time-to-time, they met other natives, some equally friendly and helpful—like taking them up or down a muddy river in their shallow-bottomed boats—some less so. Sometimes they were invited to stay in a village. Just like the first time, they would stay for a day or two, sleeping in hammocks strung in trees or on raised platforms, often eating and drinking more than their stomachs could easily digest, but they never stayed long; the enemy continued to press.

Whenever one of his men raised the question of cannibals, Hirotaka shrugged. "Maybe they're on one of the other islands."

At night, when the Americans were near, Hirotaka sometimes caught a whiff of coffee. While he and his men had only what they could kill, dig up or beg from villagers, the enemy drank coffee. They often came to piles of empty food cans, but whatever had clung to the insides of the cans when they were discarded, had been scoured out by insects and rodents. He fantasized what they might once have held.

Hirotaka believed a year had passed since he'd come to New Guinea. Twenty-three years old and he felt as though he'd lived his entire life in the jungle. Between the dysentery and malaria, much of it he didn't remember. Perhaps that was just as well.

One thing he couldn't forget, however, Toshio Hara's face after the bridge fell. Awake or asleep, that face, which to him embodied all those who'd been sacrificed and left behind that day, hovered on the edge of his conscience. He cried out to it in his recurring delirium, begging forgiveness for his failure to ensure the bridge remained in place until everyone had crossed. But his cries did no good, and the tortured face remained with him.

Infrequently, he and Takeda Yoshida crossed paths. Each time they met, Private Yoshida was full of false flattery and sly innuendos, and each time Hirotaka was once again reminded of Corporal Hara and the destroyed bridge.

He hadn't seen the man for several months and thought perhaps Yoshida, too, had finally succumbed to malaria or one of the other diseases running rampant. But one day, as he and his men moved along a narrow path bordering another river, they rounded a bend and came face-to-face with a small cadre of fellow Japanese. Among them, one whose tall, broad frame Hirotaka couldn't forget. Despite his frayed and ragged clothing, Private Yoshida looked healthy and reasonably well-fed.

"Lieutenant Katsuragawa, sir. It is excellent to see you once again. Also, to see you in good health." They had all long since given up saluting.

Hirotaka merely nodded, eyeing Private Yoshida with utter disdain.

For a few minutes both groups mingled. Keeping their voices low, they exchanged news. As usual, they soon separated.

To Hirotaka's dismay, Private Yoshida remained. "I know of a place not far from here where we can dig wild taro roots—all we can eat," he said when those he'd been with had disappeared down the trail.

Constantly hungry, Hirotaka's men became excited. Reluctantly, Hirotaka agreed to see the taro patch. It took them nearly two hours to make their way through the jungle to the spot Yoshida kept claiming lay just ahead. Finally, they came to a cleared space.

"This belongs to one of the native villages," Hirotaka said. "It has been well-tended."

"Maybe so," Private Yoshida said, ignoring his previous statement the taro grew wild. "But they are not here."

"Still, we should ask, not just take it. The natives have as hard a time as we do finding adequate food. Many have been very generous to us."

Outnumbering Hirotaka and driven by hunger, his men fell on the little patch, digging up roots with no care to what they destroyed. Taking no time to rid the roots of the dirt clinging to them, the men hacked and cut and crammed piece after piece into their mouths. Hirotaka's own gnawing hunger finally became too much to bear. Soon he too used his bayonet to dig up the starchy root.

A shout rang out and Hirotaka's head snapped up. Angry natives, bristling with spears, bows and arrows, surrounded them. Ashamed of the weakness that had driven him to take part in the orgy of eating, he rose and stepped toward the native group's leader. Bowing deeply and using a combination of gestures and the handful of words he knew of their language, he offered apologies for himself and for his men.

The leader's face remained unmoved. The other natives muttered and made threatening gestures.

They were trapped. Knowing he had only one option, Hirotaka knelt and held out his rusted bayonet. He, an educated man, a man who'd read the teachings of both Buddha and Confucius as well as Shakespeare, who'd studied the lives of great warriors and philosophers, of civilizations large and small, surrendering to a tribe of uneducated natives. He shuddered as he imagined the shame his father would feel if ever he heard what his son had done.

It worked. The leader took the proffered bayonet, turned it over in his hands several times, tested its edge on his thumb. In exchange, he handed Hirotaka a stone-tipped spear.

Hirotaka straightened, unsure what would happen next. Despite what he thought were grumblings from the rest of the natives, the leader gestured for them to leave.

"Let us go before they change their minds," Hirotaka told his men.

On their way to the trail they'd earlier left, Yoshida began to laugh. "Having a full stomach is worth being caught by a bunch of ignorant natives."

Hirotaka's lips flattened in disgust. "They will never help us again."

"There are other villages," Yoshida said with a shrug, and Hirotaka was once again repulsed by the man's indifference to others.

Once back to the trail, they set up a makeshift camp and settled in for the night. When they rose the following morning, Hirotaka discovered that Takeda Yoshida had slipped away.

★

Many nights Hirotaka dreamed of his past life, the life he'd lived before the jungles of New Guinea claimed him. He pictured his mother strolling through the gardens of their Sakayama home, his favorite place to imagine her. His father? His father always sat at his desk, writing letters, answering mail, or reading. He tried to imagine Shunsuki, still alive, riding his favorite horse. And his brother, Kinya—he saw Kinya seated, eyes closed, listening to Duke Ellington or Ella Fitzgerald. Kinya, much to their father's despair, was crazy about jazz.

Hirotaka also liked to think of the entire family at their summer estate in Nishimi. He'd loved the time they spent there. They always went during school breaks, so for him, their stays had been lighthearted, and untroubled by homework. He recalled old Haiashi, the estate's caretaker. Countless times Haiashi had taken him and his brothers hunting in the forests surrounding the estate. He'd taught them how to snare rabbits and track deer. Hirotaka tried to remember if they'd ever properly thanked the old man.

Not only Haiashi. The villagers revered them and did everything to make their visits more enjoyable. And yet, it seemed his family had done little to help the villagers. He didn't think he'd ever felt so alive, so much a part of the world around him, as the time he spent at the Nishimi pottery factory helping Mori and Ishihara fire the kiln.

Despite the revulsion that Takeda Yoshida produced in him, despite his complete distrust of the man whose family owned the pottery factory, the village's sole employer, Hirotaka decided that if he survived the war, if ever he was fortunate enough to return to his homeland, he would go back to Nishimi. Not as a noble Katsuragawa, but as a part of the village.

18
YOKO
The Pottery Factory

Yoko laughed aloud at the news—from the wife of her second cousin, who appeared to take great pleasure in seeing she received it. Her scoundrel husband had been arrested in a brothel in Sakayama and thrown into the brig.

He'd been in Nishimi first, carrying on in his usual barbaric way. When not plaguing her, he huddled with Mori and Ishihara, no doubt talking about ceramic hand grenades. Although still fuming that she'd once again been left out of their discussions, she had no problem admitting it was the idea's source she hated most.

She cursed to learn the Army hadn't kept him in jail, but instead assigned him to a new unit, the same one as Hirotaka Katsuragawa, Masato Abi and that farmer-solder, Toshio Hara. Too bad she hadn't managed to carry out her plan to kill Takeda and hide his body.

She sat on the edge of the packing platform, wiping each piece of newly fired ware, and examining it for defects. At least the factory continued to do well, though most of the orders they received these days were for utilitarian things needing little in the way of decoration. The shortages of electrical power, kerosene, and labor did frustrate her. Food, too, worse now that the government rationed rice. Rice. It grew all around them. Why should she have to register for a staple of Nishimi area farms? She shook her head and reached for a storage jar.

Mori, helping sort, cleared his throat. "You should come to our house tonight, Yoko-san. Most of our village men, including my son and your husband, have been in New Guinea for months. Maybe we will hear of victory there."

"Hunh…I don't even know where New Guinea is. I have enough to do just keeping this place running. I don't need to worry about the war, too."

Since the Ito woman brought the radio to Nishimi, Mori had often invited Yoko to hear the latest war news with the other villagers. Each time, she refused. Although she couldn't speak her thoughts aloud, she didn't care about the war—not so long as it kept Takeda far away from Nishimi.

Besides that, she couldn't bring herself to look on the gaijin without feeling anger. Sometimes, when unbidden thoughts of her dead daughters came to her, she would grow faint, the room would spin. Other times, she wanted to scream her agony to the world. All of it, every bit, the gaijin woman's fault. She had no right to come back to Nishimi and expect to be treated as anything but the enemy. Yet everyone fawned on her. Mori and his wife, even superstitious Ishihara sang her praises. Yoko had even heard several housewives—who obviously had little else to do— were now taking English lessons from the woman.

Disgusted with weak-minded people, she picked up a platter, carefully running her fingers along the top before flipping it over to examine the bottom.

She wiped sweat from her forehead and reached for the next platter in the stack. Muggy, even for August, clouds had rolled in that morning, and by mid-afternoon, thunder rumbled in the darkened sky.

Ishihara set down another box of newly-fired pottery from the kiln. "The last one." He took off his cap and wiped raindrops from his face just as lightning flashed and a loud clap of thunder rattled a window. "That was close."

Mori looked up from the pot he examined. "Too close."

Yoko glanced at him. "You think we'd better go to the shrine and pray lightning doesn't strike the factory?"

Mori grunted."I don't suppose it would change anything. If it's going to strike us, it will—whether we are bowing low at the shrine or here doing our work."

"So, you are a fatalist? I didn't know that about you, Mori-san."

Ishihara gave them each an angry look. "You are both irreverent when you speak in such a way. The gods won't forget your blasphemy."

Yoko raised her eyebrows and stared at Ishihara a moment, then shrugged. "You may be right, Ishihara-san. But I think my soul is already doomed to wander in the afterlife." She picked up an octopus pot and frowned at a thinning in its wall. "This one we'd better set aside. It will break the minute it's thrown into the sea."

The door slid open with a bang, and a young teenage boy ran into the room, breathing hard, beads of moisture on his forehead and cheeks. "Fire! There is a fire! Lightning has struck the Katsuragawa estate. Everyone is needed." Yoko gaped at the boy, but before she could say anything, he turned and ran out, again shouting, "I have to alert others!"

Yoko rushed to the door at the back of the room and shouted down to the potters and their apprentices. "There's a fire. They need our help."

In a knot, Yoko and her workers sped up the narrow track to the Katsuragawa estate, the two old men, Mori and Ishihara, lagging a few paces behind the women. Above them, fire licked into the sky. Out of breath from the rapid climb, Yoko hastened through the open wooden gate. A line of women, old men, young teenagers and even children passed buckets, filled with water from the nearby Koi pond, to the woman at the front of the line.

The woman threw a bucketful and staggered backward, as tongues of flame leaped at her. Yoko sprang forward and took the woman's pail. In the twenty minutes that followed, she threw bucket after bucket of water, but her puny efforts and those of the others had no effect on the flames. The wind-whipped, roaring inferno, which started in the thick thatch of the roof, was too widespread.

Mrs. Mori panted in Yoko's ear. "If only the men of the village were still here. What good are women and children and a few old men?"

Yoko gave a distracted nod.

The Ito woman, the gaijin, sprang up everywhere, helping at one side of the house, then the other, urging everyone to work faster and harder. When the fire leaped from the house to the roof of the stable, she ran inside and staggered out again with an ornate saddle. "It belonged to Shunsuki. I'm sure his father will want it," the woman said. Moments later, the stable's thatched roof collapsed in a shower of fire and sparks.

The winds died and rain began to fall, lightly at first, then in a near deluge. Too late. The fire had consumed the large house, leaving only one wall standing. The stable and storage buildings were reduced to rubble.

The smell of wet ashes filled Yoko's nostrils. Set off by itself, Haiashi's house remained untouched. She glanced around, but didn't see the caretaker anywhere.

"He was here," said a woman. "When we first came, he gave us all directions." The circle of women and old men looked to one another, but no one had an answer.

"I think I saw him go inside," a young boy said, nodding to the burnt remains of the house.

Ishihara and Mori found the old caretaker's body beneath a large, partially burned timber. The same boy who'd come to the factory with news of the fire ran to fetch a priest.

Mrs. Mori wiped rain from her round face. "Poor Haiashi. He served the Katsuragawa family for so long. They will be deeply saddened."

Yoko wondered if the old man had gone into the blazing house on purpose. When it became evident the fire would win, perhaps he decided he couldn't face his employer with the news. For his sake, she hoped death had arrived without delay.

"Only a week ago, Nobuko visited with him," Mrs. Mori said. Tears mingled with the rain on her cheeks. "Haiashi took great pride in the estate and his long association with such an important family. Nobuko was very impressed."

Several others bobbed their heads in approval, but Yoko had heard enough about the gaijin and her exploits. With the fire out, she saw no point in remaining. Nodding to the others, she hurried from the compound, passing Haiashi's empty house on the way.

The wind started up again, whipping at her wet clothes. It blew her hair into her face, stinging her cheeks; at some point, she'd lost her kerchief. She pushed her hair back with one hand and with the other clutched her jacket to her chest.

Other villagers soon caught up to her. In the gathering darkness, grim-faced and dirty, they made their way down the mountain. Yoko turned to a woman walking beside her. She shouted to be heard above the noise of the wind and rain.

"Did you hear Mrs. Mori say the gaijin went to see him? It is just as I told Mori and Ishihara. That woman brings bad luck. Mori scoffed at my fears, but first the earthquake that killed our children, now this fire. Each time she was there. What more proof do we need?"

19
NOBUKO
The Gaijin

For days Mrs. Mori seemed distracted, talking too much at times and at other times distant and silent. Her confusing behavior had Nobuko on edge as well. After lunch, preparing to return to the factory, Mr. Mori gave his wife a stern look. "You must tell her."

When the door slid closed behind him, Nobuko frowned. "Tell me what?"

"I'm sorry, Nobuko-san." Mrs. Mori looked away, pressing her lips together.

"Sorry? For what, Mori-san?"

"They aren't coming."

Nobuko's frown deepened. "Who isn't coming?"

Mrs. Mori looked even more uncomfortable. "The women, they aren't coming for the English lesson."

"Why not? Have they tired of the lessons? Or have I done something to upset them?" Nobuko hoped neither to be the case. She'd grown to feel close to the women, who often brought an origami flower or a tidbit of food to express their thanks.

"You are not to get angry."

"I'm not angry. I just don't understand." What was Mrs. Mori getting at?

"They believe you bring bad luck to the village," Mrs. Mori blurted.

Nobuko almost laughed in relief. "The women think I bring bad luck?" The idea was too ludicrous to be serious.

But Mrs. Mori's face remained grave. "The earthquake, the fire at the Katsuragawa estate."

Nobuko's fingers found the rough scar on her cheek, and her smile died on her lips. "They blame those terrible things on me?"

"I'm afraid they do, Nobuko-san."

Nobuko picked up a cushion and clasped it to her chest. "I suppose, since their mothers are in the group, the high school students won't be coming either. And what about my tea ceremony lessons? Has Mr. Nakamura joined with the others?"

Lips trembling, Mrs. Mori nodded.

"What can I do to make them see how crazy their fears are?"

"I don't know." Mrs. Mori dropped her head. "I've told them it is more likely the swallows didn't return to their old nests under the eaves of the Katsuragawa's house. In the year when swallows do not return, it is known that there will be a fire in that place." She lifted her head, a pained look on her face. "They were unconvinced. They said if the swallows hadn't returned, old Haiashi would have known."

Yoko Yoshida started the rumors. Nobuko didn't doubt it. She understood Yoko found her a painful reminder of her daughters' deaths, but she hadn't thought the woman would turn everyone against her. Sorrow welled in her chest and throat. How swiftly she had gone from feeling a part of the village to being an outsider, a gaijin, once again.

She drew a shaky breath. "I need to think what I must do."

Mrs. Mori shook her head once more. "There is nothing you can do, Nobuko-san."

"Do you and Mr. Mori think I am unlucky, too?" She rubbed the ends of her fingers together, afraid what the answer might be.

"No. No, of course not." Mrs. Mori turned and walked a few steps away then returned. Her face, always easy to read, filled with even more distress. "We know you had nothing to do with either catastrophe. But…" She dropped her eyes to her clasped hands.

"But?"

Still looking down, Mrs. Mori shook her head. "No, it is nothing."

Nobuko's heart raced. Her throat tightened more. "It must be something."

Mrs. Mori lifted her eyes once more, an unspoken plea for understanding in them. "It is just that my husband must work at Yoko's factory."

Shaken, Nobuko took a step back. Superstition she could deal with, but with Mr. and Mrs. Mori's livelihood being threatened, that changed everything. The pain at the back of her throat grew and she swallowed, hard. "Forgive me, Mori-san. I didn't know. I will go for a walk and think. We can talk more when I return."

"A good idea." Mrs. Mori's face brightened. "You are not to worry, Nobuko-san. Things will work out."

Mrs. Mori sounded so much like her mother that homesickness washed over Nobuko. Don't worry. Everything will work out. How often her mother had given that same bit of advice: to her father, when money was tight or the crops threatened; to Mako, when he worried about a test or an important baseball game; even to Nobuko, when unable to decide about her future.

Though the uncertainty of how she would manage filled her with panic, that night Nobuko told Mr. and Mrs. Mori her decision. "There is only one thing I can do, and that is leave. I will go back to Sakayama."

Mr. Mori's gentle eyes were filled with questions. "What would you do in Sakayama? Where would you live?"

Mrs. Mori echoed his concern. "You can't live with your aunt; there is no room."

Nobuko took a deep breath, hoping to slow the rapid beating of her heart. "I believe I can find a place. Someone should be willing to rent me a room. Perhaps the professor I used to tutor."

Mr. Mori's brows furrowed. "But Nobuko-san, where would you get the money to pay the rent?"

"That part I'm not so sure of, but I am young and healthy. I know I can find something—especially now that my Japanese is fluent. Perhaps there is need for a translator."

"You would be willing to do that? You might be called upon to work against your own country."

"I hadn't thought of that." Nobuko's shoulders slumped. Between her thumb and index finger, she folded the corner of the cushion she sat on. "I'll need to think of something else. Maybe I could teach English at a school." Even as she said this, she knew it would need to be a very enlightened school to offer English instruction now.

Mr. and Mrs. Mori exchanged a quick glance. "There is something you might consider," Mr. Mori said.

"Yes?" At this point, Nobuko would consider anything.

"You were raised on a farm so you know about growing things. You know how difficult the work is. And you know how lonely it is at times."

Nobuko thought of the long hours her mother spent working in the fields with her father, and nodded.

"There is a farmer and his wife, Mr. and Mrs. Hara, who require help," Mr. Mori said. "Like many of the village's sons and husbands, their only son, Toshio, is in New Guinea. The couple is quite old. Two months ago, their daughter-in-law, who helped in the fields, died. She left a young son." He paused and studied Nobuko a moment. "Their requirement for help coincides with your requirement for a place to live. It is fortuitous, do you not think?"

"Won't the villagers have turned them against me?"

Mr. Mori, his head tilted, shrugged. "Maybe that is so, but their need is great. And their farm is some distance from the village. They are seldom here. Perhaps they have not heard the rumors."

Nobuko walked to the farm the following day and presented herself to Mr. and Mrs. Hara. They were doubtful that a gaijin, especially one so young and slight, could be of much help to them, but with the rice nearly ready to harvest, they had no choice.

That first harvest was brutal. Even now, a year later, Nobuko shuddered to think of it.

"I'm going to drain the paddy today," Mr. Hara had said to her the morning after she'd arrived. "Tomorrow, I will need your help setting up poles."

A few days later, when the poles had been erected and were strung with cords, Nobuko and the Haras waded into the mud of the emptied rice paddy. The mud pulled at Nobuko's feet with each step. In less than an hour, the muscles in her calves and thighs quivered with exhaustion, but Mr. and Mrs. Hara, her seniors by forty years or more, appeared unfazed by the effort.

That night, sore and tired, Nobuko hobbled to her futon. The next morning, she woke aching and stiff, thinking the Haras had been right to doubt her. She thrust that thought aside and straightened her aching shoulders. She would persevere, prove them wrong.

It took several days of working together, to bundle all the rice into sheaves and hang the sheaves on the stretched cords. When they had dried, Nobuko and Mrs. Hara separated the rice from the chaff. With round flat baskets, they repeatedly threw the rice into the air and caught it in the baskets, until all the chaff had blown away. After separating the rice and carefully measuring it with a small, square wooden box, they poured it into jute bags.

By the end of the week, the muscles in Nobuko's back screamed so loud, it took supreme effort to keep from crying out.

A milder than normal winter followed the harvest, but snow soon cut the farm off from the village, barring Nobuko from visiting Mr. and Mrs. Mori. She missed them, but she kept busy in the house and barn. In the spring, she helped fill the rice paddy with water, diverted from one of many creeks, then she and the Haras planted young rice seedlings in the mud.

All summer she and the Haras worked, repairing the banks surrounding the paddy when needed and getting rid of weeds in the paddy, keeping watch as the beads of rice matured and turned golden.

The rice needed constant attention. Also, a field of millet on the upper terrace, along with small plots of oats and hay. A large garden lay near the house.

The late summer sun warm on her back, Nobuko hoed between rows of sweet potato vines. The smell of turned soil reminded her of home. For a moment or two, she wondered if her parents might be likewise occupied, but she didn't dwell on that thought, as she might once have done. Her mind also skittered away from any speculation of where her brother might be—fighting with the Army, but where, she didn't want to think about.

She pushed a vine aside and scraped at a weed. Mornings had grown cold. The first frost would come within the next few weeks, and with it the time to dig up the sweet potatoes. Most would go to the government, but some they would take to the Abi's store in Nishimi. The rest she and Mrs. Hara would wrap in straw and store in a wooden barrel to save for winter.

Poor Mrs. Hara. Her back so bent from years of stooped labor and poor diet, she had to look up to see the path in front of her. Two rows over, with every thrust of the hoe, her head bobbed at the end of her scrawny neck—and yet she kept a steady pace.

Mr. Hara, not quite as stooped, worked in the rice paddy on the terrace below, preparing once again to drain it. Although Nobuko didn't look forward to the harvest, she did look forward to a supreme sense of satisfaction when they finished the job. Besides, after working all summer building muscles, this year she wouldn't be so sore and exhausted.

Like the sweet potatoes, most of the rice would be commandeered by the government and shipped to the front. They would be allowed to retain only the amount their combined rice rations allowed. Nobuko saw no evidence that the government taking most of their crops angered Mr. and Mrs. Hara. They seemed to take it as a matter of course. She didn't understand their lack of resentment. They weren't that patriotic. For the most part, in fact, they acted as if the war didn't exist. Their son never wrote to them, and Nobuko rarely heard his name mentioned.

She straightened and put her hand to the small of her back. From beneath the brim of her straw hat her gaze traversed the narrow valley and up the mountain to the back of the pottery factory. Figures moved around the kiln. She smiled, sure she recognized the figure of Mr. Mori among them.

Her smile fell away as she recalled her last visit to Nishimi. She'd needed to go to the post office in the Abi's store to re-register for rice rations. She'd stood at the counter and filled out the papers. "I hope this will be the last time I need to do this," she said, smiling and handing Mrs. Abi the completed paperwork.

Mrs. Abi gave a curt nod in reply, but didn't take the papers, instead indicated by tapping her finger they were to be placed on the counter.

After leaving the store, Nobuko turned toward Mr. and Mrs. Mori's house. She hesitated a moment, then dismissed the idea that a brief visit from her would cause the villagers to turn against them.

Her spirits, already low, plunged deeper at the sight of her dear friends. Mrs. Mori's once bright eyes were red-rimmed with fatigue, and a network of lines adorned the skin of her once plump cheeks. Mr. Mori had grown so thin his belt wrapped nearly twice around his waist. She comforted herself that their aging might be natural and only more apparent to her because she no longer saw them every day. That thought was quickly dispelled.

"We haven't heard from our son in many months," Mrs. Mori said, her voice catching on a sob. "No one in the village has heard from a loved one serving on New Guinea. Everyone fears they must be dead."

Despite her determination not to think of him, an image of Masato flashed in Nobuko's mind, and she thought she understood Mrs. Abi's animosity and recriminatory glares. If Masato had chosen someone else to marry, there might now be a grandchild to give Mr. and Mrs. Abi comfort.

More than ever, she wished she'd been able to talk to Masato before he left. But even if he were still alive, which now appeared doubtful, it was unlikely she'd have the chance to tell him how she felt. She'd likely never see him again—as soon as the war ended she would return to America. She wiped her eyes with the back of her hand. How she longed to see her family's faces, hear their voices.

"Nobuko."

Recalled from her troubled thoughts and memories, Nobuko turned to see Kensai trotting toward her between the rows of sweet potatoes. She thought the little boy the best part of her move to the Hara's farm. A delightful child, full of fun and curiosity. The fact that he was the homeliest child she'd ever seen didn't bother her a bit. His big ears and crooked, gap-toothed grin held their own charm.

"Nobuko-san, look what I found." He held out a grubby fist.

"What is it?" She put down the hoe and knelt beside him.

Kensai opened his hand to reveal a lifeless butterfly. He frowned then threw the butterfly into the air. It fell to the ground.

He scowled. "It won't fly."

"You can't catch butterflies in your hand, Ken-chan. They're too delicate. We need to let them fly free."

"But I want to catch them, Nobuko-san."

"Why don't you help me weed instead? Look, your grandmother is far ahead now. Let's hurry and catch up. There, see that weed?" She pointed to the ground by the fallen butterfly. "Can you pull that up for me?"

Nobuko had lived with the Haras several months before learning what had happened to Kensai's mother: a precarious pregnancy and a miscarriage from which she never recovered. "We had someone in the village write to our son, telling him what happened, but we never heard back. Even before, she'd lost her will to live," old Mrs. Hara said.

At first, Kensai often woke in the night, crying or screaming, but over time his fretful nights eased. Although she had little experience with young children, Nobuko believed he now acted like any other well-loved four-year-old. She tightened her grip on the hoe and returned to work. After a brief struggle with the weed, Kensai set off after another butterfly.

Although the harvest did seem easier and took less time, Nobuko had little opportunity to feel gratified. Winter moved in, the worst winter of her life. Heavy snows piled up by the middle of September. At Mr. Hara's instruction, she strung ropes between the house and the barn so that she could find her way to the outbuilding to feed the ox.

She had little to feed the animal, though. Few oats and even less hay. Not because of poor planning on Mr. Hara's part, but because the government had dictated the amount of land he could use to grow what he needed. Like everything else on the farm, the poor creature grew so thin Nobuko could nearly get her fingers around his ribs. It came as no surprise when one morning she found him on his knees.

"We will need to kill him," she told the Haras. "He won't last through the day and we can use the meat."

Mr. Hara nodded in solemn agreement. "Even in death, he will be of service."

They ate the tough, stringy meat with relish.

"No more, Ken-chan," Mrs. Hara said to her grandson, whose face was covered in grease and bits of meat. "You will make yourself sick."

What they couldn't eat, they wrapped in the hide and packed away in a barrel Nobuko and Mr. Hara rolled outside, where it would quickly freeze. That night she awakened to strange noises. At first, she attributed it to the wind, but in moments knew something else caused the ruckus. She slid open the door and peered out. A pack of wild dogs ripped through the tipped barrel.

"Shoo! Get out!" she shouted, waving the skirt of her sleeping robe. Intent on their treasure, the dogs ignored her.

She whirled around and darted back inside, sliding the door shut. She scanned the room, searching for anything to use as a weapon.

"What's happening?" Mr. Hara asked, his voice hoarse with sleep.

"Wild dogs are eating our meat! I need something to drive them off." She snatched the quilt from her futon and handed it to him. "Wave it at them. I'll try to find something that will make a racket or to hit them with. Wait for me."

By flapping the quilt and banging on a pot with a large spoon, they succeeded in driving the dogs away, but little remained of the store of meat meant to see them through the rest of the winter. "We should have moved the barrel into the barn," Nobuko said, her voice weary. The barn had seemed so far away.

Over the following days, they ate what little meat Nobuko could salvage. Then she made soup from rice and the remaining bones, watering it down to make it stretch. She scoured the barn and storage area for any over-looked remnant of rice or sweet potatoes, anything to add to their meager supplies, anything that would fill the cavernous hollow in their stomachs.

Nobuko's throat ached when Kensai cried from hunger. She rubbed his back and tried to distract him with songs and stories, which helped for a while, but soon the little boy began crying again. The old couple became more fragile each day. She didn't know how much longer they could last. Her own head spun with hunger. At night, she lay on her futon in a sort of stupor, too hungry to sleep, too exhausted to stay awake.

It seemed that horrid winter would never leave. Finally, though, the temperatures warmed and the snow began to melt.

"Today I will go to Nishimi and buy some food. And some seeds to plant," Nobuko told the Haras after a week of warmer weather. Huddled together under several quilts, they nodded. "I'll take Kensai with me," she added.

She hoisted the little boy onto her back and set out. Because of her weakened condition and Kensai's added weight, it took much longer than normal to reach Nishimi. The village looked deserted, the streets devoid of both people and the dogs that had always run free in them. Windows were shuttered. Even the pottery factory, normally a center of activity, seemed much quieter than she remembered.

She put Kensai down and took his hand. When they entered the Abi store, Nobuko stared. The once stocked shelves were almost bare. A cold premonition filled her. She called out. Mr. Abi shuffled through the door leading from the family's living quarters.

"I've come to buy food. We need yams or sweet potatoes. Tofu if you have any. I also need to order rice seedlings. Soon it will be time to plant." Even as she said the words, she knew what Mr. Abi's answer must be.

"I'm sorry, Nobuko-san. All I can sell you is a few kilos of potatoes." He gestured to the empty shelves. "As you can see, there is little else."

Nobuko gripped Kensai's hand tighter. "But we are starving, Abi-san. Mr. and Mrs. Hara are so weak I'm not sure how much longer they can go on."

"I'm sorry." Mr. Abi's eyes reddened. "We are all suffering the same fate. We are all hungry."

Nobuko's shoulders slumped. She wanted to wail like a baby, but didn't have the strength. "What are we to do? How can we go on without food? Abi-san, when will this terrible war end?"

20
TOSHIO
Farmer-Soldier

Thoughts of Takeda Yoshida, safe on the other side of the gorge, kept Toshio's feet shuffling forward. He vowed he would one day make the man regret what he'd done. Takeda had set off the charges before everyone had crossed. Toshio didn't doubt it for a minute.

The trail narrowed and became even more slippery. The rain intensified, pelting him from above, while sporadic gunfire sounded from behind. A soldier sat with his feet dangling over the gorge's edge, wiping his glasses with a saturated scrap of blue cloth.

"You'd better come. The enemy is near," Toshio said, though his voice held indifference. The man shook his head, refusing to budge from his perch. Without further coaxing, Toshio shrugged and went on.

More days passed with no sign of another bridge or a way into the gorge. Toshio walked alone now, except for one other man; everyone else had dropped by the wayside, forged ahead or simply disappeared into the jungle. "Go on," he told the other man. "I must rest for a while."

Toshio stared at the gorge, no longer sure he even wanted to cross it. Rain dripped from the brim of his cap, a dancing curtain of despair. When he turned, his companion lay slumped against a tree. The tree wept with rain.

"We're done for anyway," the man said when Toshio collapsed beside him. "We may as well stay together."

Toshio closed his eyes.

He had no idea how long he slept—an hour, a day, a week. Nor did he know what wakened him. He elbowed his companion and whispered, "Did you hear something?" He staggered to his feet. His companion didn't move. Toshio looked down and saw the man's vacant eyes, open and staring.

A thud came from somewhere close, along with a muttered oath. Gaijins. Toshio dove into the jungle growth, spun around, and threw himself to the ground. Seconds later, five pale-skinned men appeared. They stopped and stared at the dead man. One of the men poked the body with the tip of his rifle. They spoke for several minutes in their unfathomable language. One pointed at Toshio's footprints in the mud.

When they started toward his hiding place, Toshio jumped to his feet and plunged deeper into the jungle. Crashing noises followed him into the darkness. He'd long ago discarded his rifle, rusted into uselessness by the ceaseless rain. The only weapon he had was his equally rusted bayonet. He drew it from his belt and turned to face the gaijins, Major Tamayama's words ringing in his ears: "There is no greater shame than capture by the enemy."

When Toshio first arrived in Australia, they put him in a prison meant for murderers and thieves, a fitting degradation, he thought, equal to his shame. But soon they sent him to a prisoner-of-war camp and then on to another. He finally ended up at a forestry camp, where, each day, he and his fellow prisoners cut wood for a local hospital and a nearby army camp.

Not a day passed that he didn't feel the disgrace and humiliation of his capture. The Australians offered him and the other prisoners pencil and paper to write home. Toshio refused. He would not inflict his dishonor on his wife and son or on his parents. Better they believed him dead.

A single image filled his brain every waking hour: Takeda Yoshida at the bridge. Each night after the guards turned out the lights, he lay on his cot, remembering—the explosion, the bridge unwinding, and the men spiraling to their deaths, their cries echoing off the rock walls of the gorge before being swallowed by the rain. Finally, he remembered Takeda's look of defiance, tossed at him across the empty space.

21
YOKO
The Pottery Factory

Forehead furrowed, Yoko glanced up from the letter in her hand to see Mori standing in front of her.

"We need more clay," he said. "Ishihara will be taking several apprentices for the day."

She studied the man whom she had known, sparred with, and relied upon for so many years, startled by a sudden awareness of how old and fragile he'd grown over the past two years. She held up the letter. "It's from the government. We are to begin producing ceramic hand-grenades." Her lips tightened. "My husband was right."

Mori raised his eyebrows. "I will tell Ishihara."~He moved to the chair next to her desk. "We won't be required to put the explosive powder in them, will we?"

"No, we are only to make what they call the casings."

"Do you think this means the end of the war is at hand?" Mori's voice held caution as well as curiosity.

Yoko dropped the letter onto her desk. "I suppose it means the government has run out of whatever is customarily used to build hand grenades, so maybe it does."

"We'll need to retrain the potters."

"That will be Ishihara's job, and Asai's." She sat back in her chair. "I'm thinking the time has come for you and

Ishihara to travel to Kyushu. Among other changes, we will need to find a way to get the kiln hotter."

"Does the letter state when they expect us to begin shipping the completed product?"

Yoko glanced at the letter, but didn't need to read it again. "In three months." She lifted her gaze back to Mori. "I am worried, my friend. This war has been long and neither of us has gotten younger. Do you believe you can make this trip and oversee these changes?"

Mori stood and drew back his shoulders. His chin lifted. "Do you doubt I am capable?"

"Sit down, Mori-san. I did not mean to offend. If you tell me I needn't worry about your health, I won't." She buried her relief in a cough.

Yoko stood at the top of the stairs leading to the factory floor. Four long, work-filled months had passed, months in which she had many times wished to put this hand-grenade endeavor aside and go back to what she knew best, dishware and the occasional octopus pot.

Another August. Sliding doors at the back of the barn-like room were open, but little air stirred. Ishihara worked without a shirt. His sagging skin glistened with sweat. Several women potters had removed their shirts as well. One stood next to a large bucket, ladling water over her head, shoulders, breasts.

Arms crossed in satisfaction, Yoko viewed the results of their labor, evident on plank after plank, loaded with the small round spheres, dried and ready to be fired in the kiln. She, a mere woman, had made this happen. Takeda, the dog, should he live through the war and hear of it, would scoff. Not her daughters, though. They wouldn't scoff. If only they hadn't died, they would be sharing in her success.

The euphoria she'd felt just moments before dissipated. Thoughts of her dead girls brought tears spurting to her eyes. She stumbled through the door to the office and slid it shut with a sharp click. Breathing heavily, she leaned her spinning head against the door's wooden panel. After several moments, she straightened and started toward her desk. She halted. Nobuko Ito stood next to it.

Anger welled inside Yoko's chest, making it impossible to draw a full breath. Her fingers retracted, claw-like. How dare the woman show her face here?

The gaijin's clothes hung from her slight frame, her hair fell lank and dull, and deep hollows were carved into her cheeks. A small boy peeked out from behind her.

"I need to see Mori," she said.

"What do you want with him?" Yoko lifted her chin and scowled her contempt.

"I need to speak to him."

Yoko's eyes narrowed, but the gaijin's eyes didn't waver. After a moment, Yoko moved to the door, opened it, and shouted for an apprentice to fetch Mori.

"They're dead," the gaijin said as soon as the old man entered. "They survived the winter. I didn't think they would. But without seeds to plant this spring, we've had almost nothing to eat—only what I could forage in the woods. Two days ago, Mrs. Hara fell sick. A few hours later, her husband began to fail. They were both dead by morning."

Mori drew a deep breath and let it out slowly. "Are you all right? What about the little boy?"

"Kensai is not sick. But he is hungry, and I have nothing to feed him."

Yoko reached into her desk drawer and withdrew some soybeans wrapped in a cloth. She'd been saving them for dinner. She opened the cloth and held it out to the boy. He grabbed the beans with a small, grimed hand and shoved them into his mouth.

The gaijin closed her eyes. "Thank you," she whispered.

"Nobuko-san, where are the bodies of Mr. and Mrs. Hara?"

"I didn't know what to do with them, Mori-san." Her voice trembled. "I washed them, put clean clothes on them, but I left them on their futon, because I didn't know what else to do." She wiped her eyes with the back of her arm.

"We will take care of them. In the meantime, you and the boy will stay with us."

"I can't," the gaijin said and briefly closed her eyes. "More than ever, the villagers will say I'm unlucky. Everywhere I go, death follows. I must leave Nishimi. I've brought Kensai to you, because he can't come with me and I don't know where else to leave him."

Seated at her desk, Yoko said nothing. But she wondered if the boy would be better off in Nishimi, and if he stayed, how the Moris were to care for him when no one had enough food to eat. She saw those questions in their eyes as Mori and the gaijin gazed at one another.

Mori spoke first. "Very well."

The gaijin's shoulders sagged before she straightened them and nodded. She took the boy's small hand and placed it in Mori's.

Early the next morning, Yoko attempted to dismiss how she felt seeing the gaijin, suitcase in hand, leave the Mori's house. "Good riddance," she muttered, but her heart didn't follow suit.

22
NOBUKO
The Gaijin

Nobuko trudged down the mountain, the August sun already warm. Gnats whined in the tall grass next to the road and dragonflies took flight. Her head bent, staring at the uneven dusty road, she concentrated on putting one foot in front of the other, willing herself to forget the ordeal of the Hara farm.

Haunted by her cousin's jeering prediction that she'd end up begging on the streets, she didn't know what she'd do if her aunt refused to take her in once she got to Sakayama. Her only hope was to find work, no matter how menial. Knowing Mr. and Mrs. Mori would look after little Kensai remained the one thing that brought her comfort.

She switched her suitcase to her other hand and stretched her shoulders, easing the pain growing between them. Setting down her suitcase, she looked out across the empty rice paddies and barren fields climbing the side of the mountain, to the Inland Sea glimmering in the distance. Without warning, a brilliant light appeared in the sky, nearly blinding her. It was as though the sun was rising once again, but from the north. How could such a thing be possible? Just as she started walking again, a loud CARUMPH sounded, different from anything she'd ever heard before, and a moment later, it was as though invisible hands grabbed her by the shoulders and shook her.

In the distance, a dark-looking cloud appeared to be pushing the bright light further into the sky. It lay in the direction of Hiroshima, but it looked as though it was rising out of the sea.

What was happening? Was another earthquake about to strike? With a frightened gasp, she picked up her suitcase and hurried on, expecting to see the mountain sliding toward her. Even when nothing more happened, she kept throwing nervous glances up the steep hillside and peering out over the sea until she could no longer see it.

Long before she entered Sakayama, she passed people in the fields or alongside the road, singles or in small groups, their heads down, intent on their search for food of any sort. None looked up as she passed. They seemed unaffected by whatever it was that she had seen and heard on her trek down the mountain. She gazed skyward, but all she saw was a faint layer of dust on the horizon. She hurried along the narrow streets until she came to the small house near the river where her aunt and cousins had gone to live when the army conscripted her uncle.

"It's me, Auntie. Nobuko," she called out as she slid open the door.

Footsteps shuffled toward her. Nobuko's eyes widened in shock when her aunt appeared, her eyes dull and nearly lifeless, her skin sallow. The past three years had not been kind. Instead of greeting her, her aunt looked up and down the street.

"You must come in. It's not safe outside. Someone could accost you."

Nobuko slipped off her shoes, set down her suitcase and followed her aunt's slow steps to a room at the center of the little house. She barely recognized the ancient, diminutive woman who sat on a cushion, staring at the empty table before her; her aunt's sister-in-law, a termagant who'd once brought fear to Nobuko's cousins. What had happened to make the woman little more than a shell—dementia brought on by old age? Or simply the grinding losses of the war?

"I am sorry we have little to offer you except for a place to sleep," her aunt said.

"Auntie, I am grateful for anything. I would not be a burden." Nobuko's eyes smarted with relief. At least she would have a place to stay. She swallowed. "It is good to see you. Have you been well?"

"My hips bother me," her aunt said with a shrug. "And I am constantly hungry, but so is everyone in Sakayama. I must not complain."

Nobuko thought of the past winter, of Kensai, hungry and crying himself to sleep at night, the empty shelves in the Abi's store, the gaunt faces of the villagers, the Haras' deaths. "Everyone is hungry in Nishimi, too. I fear it must be the same all over the country."

Nodding agreement, her aunt led her to a cushion and invited her to sit. "There is no tea to offer you, not even a facsimile."

Weary from her long walk down the mountain, Nobuko sank onto the cushion, waving away her aunt's apologies. "My cousins, Auntie—how do they fare?" She held her breath, waiting for the answer.

Her aunt's face turned grim. "Sadaoka and Takanori were both conscripted as soon as they finished high school.

Sadaoka fell in the Philippines. I don't know where Taka-nori is. I haven't heard from him since last spring."

Nobuko put her hand to her mouth, afraid to ask more, but needing to know. "And Mimi? What about Mimi, Auntie?"

"She is a nurse." Her aunt gestured toward her sister-in-law, whose eyes remained fixed on the empty tabletop. "In Burma, the last we heard."

"And my uncle?"

"He serves the Emperor in Manchukuo. It has been many months since I had a letter from him."

Nobuko took her aunt's hand in her own, patting the dry papery skin. "The war will be over soon, Auntie. It must be."

For two days, they remained in the house, as Nobuko's aunt was certain that if they went outside they would not be safe from scavengers. Hunger finally forced Nobuko to insist. "I will go to the market, Auntie. Something must be open."

Before she had returned to Nishimi, Sakayama's market area had teemed with people. Even when shortages had begun to grow, most people were courteous enough to bow a greeting as they passed. The few people about now were in a world of their own. Skeletally thin and furtive-looking, they passed without any sign of seeing her. The street vendors who'd once pushed their carts along the winding dirt lane, their distinctive horns or bells calling customers to buy a skewer of chicken or an ice cream in summer, a cone of roasted chestnuts or a piping hot sweet potato in winter, were no more. Most unsettling, the shops where Nobuko had hoped to find food were closed, their tin awnings pulled down and secured.

She passed the tobacconist and the shop next to it where she'd once bought barley tea for her aunt. Both were shuttered. Several people huddled against a wall, muttering or staring into space. A woman had made a bed of rags and cardboard in front of the kimono shop's barricaded door. Thinking of the maid she'd replaced, Nobuko lowered her eyes and hurried on.

After a while, her steps slowed. Sakayama appeared as barren as the Abi's store shelves. She licked her dry lips. Her aunt would be so disappointed. About to turn around and go back, a woman carrying a package emerged from a narrow alley in front of her.

Nobuko stopped her. "Excuse me. Is there a shop that is open and selling food?"

The woman shook her head then darted a look over her shoulder. "It is a special market. But you must pay extra."

Nobuko fingered the money her aunt had given her, rolled into a square of cloth, and tucked into the sleeve of her cotton yukata. She hoped it would be enough.

The alley led to a small, open square, where a cluster of people had gathered. Laid out on a blanket were limp vegetables and, on another, piles of rice and soy beans. The assemblage, though humble, made Nobuko's stomach contract in hunger. She gave a brief thought to where the food came from. Not the government; no one asked for her ration card, only money.

Her purchases in a package clutched to her side, Nobuko retraced her steps. Near the spot where she used to catch the streetcar, a circle of men had gathered, all talking and gesticulating. Curious, she pulled the threadbare sleeve of a man on crutches. "What is it? What has happened?"

The man glanced at her. "No one is sure. Something very bad has happened in Hiroshima. This man," he said, pointing to a ragged-looking fellow, "says he saw many people rushing from the city. They were frightened, and many were burned, their clothes in shreds."

Another man, speaking to the crowd, claimed to be a private in the Army. "Something terrible has happened. In Iwakuni, we heard on the radio from the Army Head-quarters in Tokyo that Hiroshima has been destroyed. No one knows for certain what is happening. I have come home to care for my family."

He started to turn away, but Nobuko put a hand on his arm, stopping him. "When did this happen?"

"Three days ago," the man said.

Three days ago. The morning she'd left Nishimi. Nobuko rubbed her fingers along the scar on her cheek. Are the Americans coming? Is it possible I may finally be able to return to my mother and father? My brother? My friends?

23
HIROTAKA
Art Student

Another year passed, another year of hiding, running, staying alive. Hirotaka stared at his protruding ribs and knew he resembled a living skeleton. Most of his uniform had rotted off his body. Several teeth had fallen out and he had large sores on the insides of his thighs. His men and those they crossed paths with fared no better—an army of living skeletons.

He couldn't remember when he'd not been hungry, even though he ate everything he could find—snails, centipedes, ants, grubs. If lucky enough to catch a lizard, he ate it whole, its tail still wiggling as it went down his throat. Occasionally, he heard of someone daring to leave the protection of the jungle during the night, going out on the beach in the hopes of catching a fish or crab. The likelihood of being shot or captured was a risk he wouldn't take, however. Nor would he order any of his men to go.

How much longer before malaria, dysentery or starvation took them all? At least fewer of the enemy pursued them, apparently satisfied to use starvation and disease as their weapons.

It had been months since he'd heard the engine of a Japanese plane, but British and American planes continually flew overhead—so often that the roar of their engines barely registered. One day, though, leaflets fluttered down from the planes, some slipping through the branches of the over-hanging canopy, sending the birds and monkeys into a screaming frenzy.

Hirotaka picked up a leaflet. Frowning, he turned it over, examining it before reading aloud the words, written in Japanese.

THE WAR IS OVER. YOUR EMPEROR HAS ACCEPTED DEFEAT. SURRENDER AND YOU WILL BE GIVEN FOOD AND MEDICAL TREATMENT. COME OUT OF THE JUNGLE. YOU WILL BE TREATED WELL.

His few remaining men stared from him to the leaflet and back again.

"It is a ruse. They are trying to trick us into coming out," one said.

"Do you think it could be true?" another asked.

"The Emperor would never admit defeat," a third said. Then added, "Would he?"

The fourth looked at Hirotaka. "What should we do, Lieutenant?"

Without answering, Hirotaka moved to a fallen log a short distance away, and lowered himself onto its smooth surface. He ignored an army of ants marching up its side, and stared at the leaflet. Could it be a ruse, a trick to lure them out of hiding only to be killed? What if it wasn't?

He glanced once more at his exhausted men. They returned his gaze, no doubt waiting for him to tell them what to do. Little could be worse than their current situation. For himself, he no longer cared. If it was an elaborate trick and death was soon to follow, he almost welcomed it; he'd long since given up any hope of returning to his old life. For his men, though, he needed to make the right decision.

He reread the message, looking for something that would tell him he could believe it. When nothing came to him, he closed his eyes and took several cleansing breaths, but his old habits of meditation failed him. Minutes passed. He stared at the words until they blurred and ran together. Finally, he drew another deep breath, stood, and called the men to him.

"I believe we should do what this says."

Without argument, the men formed a ragged line. They waded across a river, eyes searching for crocodiles, and then followed the narrow, winding path that led past the hidden trail to the village that first offered them succor. So long ago.

When Hirotaka finally led his men out of the jungle, onto the beach, he braced for the impact of a bullet, waited for it to slam into his chest. Nothing. He guided the men closer to the water's edge, halted and held his breath. Still nothing. The only sounds were the noise of the birds and monkey's in the jungle behind them, and the roar of the ocean in front of them.

The long expanse of jungle stretched as far as he could see in both directions. Surely more Japanese soldiers would pour out of it. He waited expectantly, but only a thin trickle of ragged men emerged, and gathered in small clusters on the sand.

Over a thousand men had come to New Guinea on the same ship as him, and thousands more Japanese soldiers had already been on the island. Tens of thousands. Surely so many couldn't be dead. Then he pictured all the bodies along the trails, too many to count, and the piles of bones, picked clean, devoured by the jungle.

A loud shout interrupted his thoughts. A group of foreign soldiers trotted along the beach toward them. Americans. They drew closer. Unlike the rotted and tattered remnants of clothing he and his men wore, the Americans' uniforms were whole, and above all, clean. Pointing their rifles, the Americans shouted orders. It became clear to Hirotaka that they were being told to drop their weapons and raise their hands.

He wanted to laugh. "Throw down your weapons," he said to his men.

Those who still had a knife or bayonet, corroded and useless as they were, threw them on the sand at their feet and raised their hands above their heads. The Americans circled them. Within minutes, a vehicle drove up the beach. It slammed to a stop and a Chinese man stepped out.

Before Hirotaka had time to wonder why a Chinese man was with American soldiers, wearing an American uniform, the man began to speak in slightly accented Japanese.

"On August 15, 1945, Emperor Hirohito announced Japan's surrender. You will be fed and cared for, seen and treated by a doctor, and transportation will be arranged to return you to your homes."

Hirotaka gazed in wonder at his captors, amazed at their differences. Two of the men were black-skinned, another had red hair. Yet another had nearly white hair and eyes the color of an early morning sky. We've been fighting the entire world, he thought. Winning was never a possibility.

Hirotaka and his men were taken to a compound of large tents, where other Japanese prisoners milled about. More joined them over the following days, always in small groups. They were fed, given clean trousers, and shirts with P.O.W. stenciled on the backs. The clothing hung from their frames, and the pantlegs and sleeves needed to be rolled up. A doctor checked their pulses and looked in their eyes and mouths. Best of all, though the food was strange and at times unpalatable, his stomach remained full for the first time in nearly three years.

Ten days later, launches carried them across the surf to another converted merchant ship, this one sailing under an Australian flag. It got underway as soon as all the Japanese prisoners were aboard. Larger than the ship Hirotaka had sailed on to New Guinea, the sleeping quarters cooler—but even that would have been a welcome relief, so long as it took him away from the hated jungles of New Guinea and toward home.

Lieutenant Abi gave a wry chuckle. "They want to get us off their hands before the rest of us die and they're accused of doing us in."

The two men stood at the railing, their eyes fixed on the horizon as the ship plowed through the water. The wind blew sea spray against Hirotaka's cheeks, dampened his P.O.W. shirt and pressed it against his emaciated body. He reveled in its coolness.

Finding Masato Abi at the compound had been a pleasant surprise. In the days that followed, they discovered they'd both attended the University of Tokyo and had friends and professors in common. They spoke of home. Hirotaka learned many things about Nishimi and the villagers he'd taken for granted in his youth. Seldom did they speak of their experiences on New Guinea.

Hirotaka pulled his eyes from the distant horizon, and rocked forward slightly, his shoulders hunched, before asking the question that had plagued him for so long. "Did you ever run into Corporal Hara after we left the airfield?"

Masato shook his head. "We were the last ones to leave, and the bridge across the gorge was already down when we reached it. Maybe I passed him." He shrugged. "There were many bodies along the path, both before and after the bridge."

Hirotaka stared out to sea once more. He knew Toshio Hara had probably died. But for reasons he didn't fully understand, he very much wanted the man to be alive.

They reached Yokohama the second week of September. There, they were immediately transferred to trucks and driven to a nearly unrecognizable Tokyo. Through an interpreter on the ship, Hirotaka had heard about the fire-bombing, but it would have been impossible for him to imagine the scale of destruction now before him. Buildings were reduced to piles of rubble, homes to ashes. Only the foundations remained. People dressed in rags roamed the streets, foraging for food like starved animals. As the truck rumbled past them, he saw exhaustion in the slump of their shoulders, despair on their undernourished faces. Anguish for his country felt like a physical ache in his chest—he wanted to weep for all that had been lost in a foolish and pointless war.

They were taken to a temporary barracks set up in an old school. There, it seemed to him, they spent the next several weeks in line. They lined up to receive Japanese uniforms to replace the temporary uniforms they'd been given in New Guinea. They lined up for medical examinations and inoculations. They lined up for meals, for showers, and for the latrine.

One crisp November day, after weeks of rumors and waiting, he and Masato Abi were told by a major in the Occupation Forces that they were free to go home. He felt like an errant schoolboy being dismissed by a busy headmaster.

The next morning, the two picked their way through squalor and debris, heading toward Shimbashi Station. "I'm anxious to get home and see how my parents fared," Hirotaka said. "And my brother. The last I heard from him, his squadron was heading for the Philippines."

There'd been no response to the letter he wrote from New Guinea following his and his men's capture. Nor had there been an answer to the letters he'd written his parents since he reached Tokyo. He told himself he shouldn't be surprised. The letters could have been lost. If they were received and his family wrote back, their letters may not have found him. Still…he looked around at the half-destroyed streets and bombed-out buildings of Tokyo and knew that something equally terrible could have happened to Sakayama, to his parents.

Masato didn't lift his eyes from the broken sidewalk. "I'm worried, too. My father was unwell before I left, and neither he nor my mother are young."

At the doors to the train station, street urchins clamored, begging for food and cigarettes. Hirotaka wished he had something to give them, but he had only enough money to see him home. He shook his head and brushed past, not allowing himself to dwell on the ravaged young faces with their old and haunted eyes.

Inside, he found the vast station noisy and filled with people: many, like him and Masato, vanquished soldiers, weary and eager to return home; families stood clustered together, often with only a single battered suitcase among them; old men and women stared about in frightened wonder; American military police strolled in pairs.

Hirotaka turned to Masato. "Stay here with our things. I'll go find out when our train leaves." Ten minutes later he came back to find Masato sitting cross-legged on the floor with a group of other homeward-bound soldiers. He eased himself down next to his friend. "The ticket clerk said it will be at least two hours before we can board."

Masato scowled. "What's the hold-up?"

"Who knows?"

With the others, Hirotaka fell into a brooding silence.

The two hours stretched to four before the loudspeaker squawked and announced a southbound train. He and Masato rushed to the platform, joining other passengers in a scramble for seats. They had barely left the city when the train slowed and stopped. It seemed like eons before it lurched forward, with great clanging and clashing, only to stop once again less than an hour later.

"At this rate, we won't get home until the New Year," Masato said, only half in jest.

Hirotaka shivered and blew on his hands in the unheated car. "I never thought I'd have the opportunity to complain of it, but if it gets much colder, I think we might freeze." He pulled his light jacket tighter.

The night wore on, followed by a day of starts and stops. Hirotaka stared out the window and thought of the many train trips he'd taken, both as a child and an adult. Always there'd been a sense of anticipation. At each stop, vendors had boarded the train. Fluttering flags hung from their trays of delicious snacks and treats, adding to the holiday atmosphere.

How different things were now. The towns and villages they passed through were empty of vendors and bento stands. No colorful flags or waving banners attracted his attention—they'd all been replaced by grim, bleak reminders of a lost war. He closed his eyes and thought again of Sakayama and home.

The train slowed and stopped. Hirotaka peered out the window into the early morning darkness. A tall pole with a light at its top stood next to a small building. The light harshly illuminated a narrow platform between the building and the railroad tracks. People, looking bewildered, stepped off the train, carrying their suitcases.

He nudged Masato awake. "We've stopped again."

"Is that all?" Masato hunched onto his side and closed his eyes once more.

Before Hirotaka could point out that the people appeared to be leaving the train, the door to their car opened and the conductor stepped through. "Everyone collect your things. You'll need to get off here."

Accustomed to following directions without question, most of the passengers immediately gathered their belongings.

"Why aren't we going on?" Hirotaka asked when the conductor reached their seats. "We're supposed to go to Hiroshima, to connect with the train to Sakayama."

The conductor answered with impatience. "We can't go any farther. They should have told you. No one is allowed into Hiroshima."

In Tokyo, Hirotaka had read the newspaper accounts about the black rain that fell immediately after the atomic bombs detonated in Hiroshima and Nagasaki. He knew that scores of people in both cities were dying from something they called atomic bomb disease. "What about Sakayama? Have you heard if people are getting sick there, too?"

The conductor shrugged and hurried down the aisle without answering.

By the time the train emptied, the sky had lightened. Hirotaka looked toward the mountains, where home for both he and Masato lay. "We'll need to go overland."

Masato grunted. "We've done plenty of that over the past few years."

They passed through broken fields, around empty rice paddies, over hills and across streams. That night, stomachs rumbling from hunger, they slept in a ditch, huddled together for warmth.

When they came to what should have been Hiroshima's northern edge, Hirotaka felt like they'd entered the landscape of a terrible dream, something only Salvador Dali could have imagined. The land scorched. Houses and buildings flattened. Trees blackened, their limbs twisted into

grotesque shapes. They should see the silhouettes of buildings from where they stood, but only an empty skyline
greeted their eyes.

"It is as though Hiroshima never existed," Masato said
in a voice filled with wonder.

While his friend stared at the charred and barren
landscape, a renewed sense of urgency overcame Hirotaka.
"We need to get home."

Hirotaka's apprehension grew as they neared Sakayama.
Not a strategically placed city. It didn't manufacture anything. There was no railhead, no Army headquarters nearby.
There'd been no reason to destroy it. But other possibilities
tore at him. He imagined the thing they called radiation
drifting overhead like an invisible poisonous cloud. He
agonized about his parents. All along their torturous road
home, he had seen the unproductive fields, witnessed the
signs of a starving population. He felt sure Sakayama and his
parents must be suffering similar fates. When the city at last
lay before them, he was almost afraid to enter.

Masato took his arm. "Come."

Devastation lay everywhere. The streets were littered
with garbage. Several families appeared to be living in a
streetcar rusted to its tracks. People, dressed in rags, begged
for any kind of handout. Their faces held the same hopeless
desperation as those Hirotaka had witnessed in Tokyo,
Kyoto, Osaka, and every town, big and small, their train had
passed through.

Before long, Masato halted. "I must leave you here. I
need to get to Nishimi and see if the village and my parents
have survived."

Something passed between the two as they bowed and
said goodbye. Their shared experience made them soldier-

brothers; they had served in New Guinea and survived, among the very few to do so. Hirotaka felt certain that he and Masato Abi shared a kinship that would last the rest of their lives.

Hirotaka's hands trembled, his breathing quickened as he at last approached his parents' estate. When he saw the empty space above the walls, his heart pounded. Waving bamboo and the tops of maple trees should have been visible.

He hurried to the spot where a heavy wooden gate had always stood, a servant standing ready to open it for family or visitors. But no servant waited and no gate barred his way.

Beyond the empty space, weeds and debris littered the once neatly tended gravel walkway leading to the house. Hirotaka took a tentative step, then another. His eyes darted everywhere, searching for reassurance. They found none. What little water remained in the ponds was full of algae and rubbish, his father's beautiful koi no longer swam in the ponds' green depths. Stone statues were toppled. The tea pavilion had been destroyed, its wooden platform gone, the bronze water vessel with it.

His steps quickened as he made for the entrance to the main house. He broke into a run, desperate to make sure his parents were safe and at least something remained unchanged. He slammed open the door and plunged headlong inside before coming to an abrupt halt.

Before him lay nothing but more wreckage and emptiness. He called out, but got no response.

In a daze, he moved from room to room, searching for something familiar. No ancient scrolls hung from the walls. The peacock door was gone. In his mother's quarters, there were no silk cushions on the floor, no lingering scent of her powder, no hair combs on her dressing table.

His father's office revealed the same desolation. The desk where Hirotaka had so many times imagined his father reading or writing letters, gone. The large globe with its mahogany stand was also missing, the bookshelves empty. Tatami mats, the few left, were crusted with mice droppings.

Even in the kitchen, nothing remained. No pots or pans, no cooking utensil of any sort. Dishes, drinking vessels, everything gone.

Hirotaka leaned against a wall and slowly slid to the floor. This house, where once his father imperiously enforced his will, where once his mother, slim and beautiful, glided through the elegant rooms, where once he and his brothers had played, fought, studied, and grown up, now in ruins.

His father must be dead. If he were alive, he never would have allowed the destruction of his ancestral home. He would have fought it with every fiber in his body, every ounce of strength he possessed. His mother wouldn't have stood by and watched the wanton devastation of the place she loved.

Tears slid down Hirotaka's cheeks. His head fell back against the wall. They were both dead. No one needed to tell him; he knew it in his heart. A long time passed as he stared into nothingness.

24
TOSHIO
Farmer - Soldier

Still dressed in the ill-fitting clothes he'd been given when released from the Australian prisoner-of-war camp, Toshio stood outside the open door of the Moris' house. Inside, a young boy sat on a tatami mat, playing with a yellow top. A narrow shaft of sunlight fell across his bent head. Kensai. His son. He must have made a noise, because the boy looked up, gasped, and clutched the yellow toy to his chest.

Mrs. Mori, seated next to the child, lunged to her feet, and quickly put herself between Toshio and his son. "Who are you?" she said, her voice a hoarse whisper.

"I am Toshio Hara. That is my son. I've come to take him home."

She hesitated, but then stepped aside, her hand trailing over Kensai's short hair. The boy began to cry.

"Stop sniveling," Toshio said. "You are six years-old; no longer a baby. Get your things."

The old lady had hemmed and hawed, wanting to refuse him, but she'd had no choice. With little to pack, Toshio and his son were on their way within twenty minutes.

Toshio's parents were dead. His wife, too. Mrs. Abi had told him the gaijin, the foreign American, had taken his wife's place on the farm. The gaijin, whom death followed. No doubt one of those who sucked the spirit from the living. He'd learned all about such people in Australia.

He hurried his steps, ignoring the child trailing behind him. When he stood at the bottom of the lane and looked about, he barely recognized the land where he'd grown up, working alongside his mother and father. Only weeds filled the paddy, which should have contained the residue of recently harvested rice. Many places in the dike that surrounded the paddy needed repair.

He strode up the lane to the house and barn. Weeds had completely overtaken the garden. The barn door swung drunkenly on its leather hinges. No dog barked in the yard, no ox loafed in the shed. The tools that hung on hooks were useless with rust and neglect, the leather of the ox's harness hard and dry.

Toshio narrowed his eyes and scowled. The boy sniffed.

Inside the house was no better. Toshio set his duffle bag on a work table in the kitchen. The boy dropped his top and stooped to retrieve it. "Leave it," Toshio said. "There will be no time for toys or games here. We have work to do." He handed the boy a broom. "Sweep up the mouse droppings, while I see what can be done with the tools in the barn."

BOOK THREE

Echoes from a Falling Bridge
1997-1998

1
YOKO
The Pottery Factory

Yoko opened the door wide, hoping for relief from the muggy, early-August weather. Straightening a pile of invoices on her son's desk, she heard a noise and glanced over her shoulder. The sensei stood in the doorway, an expression of horror and pity on his face. She leapt to her feet, the invoices clutched to her chest. "What? Why are you looking like that?"

"Yoko-san, something terrible has happened." For a second or two, the old man appeared unable to go on. Then he came closer, his hand extended. "It is Kazuhiro. Your son has been murdered."

Yoko shook her head, clutching the invoices closer. "No. That's not true. Whoever told you such a thing is lying. I saw him not two hours ago."

As though he'd been struck, the sensei flinched and closed his eyes. When he opened them a moment later, they were filled with unspeakable sadness. "I am sorry, Yoko-san, but it is true. I saw him myself. Kazuhiro is dead."

The invoices slipped from Yoko's hands and fluttered to the floor like dying butterflies. Her body stiffened. She couldn't breathe. The sensei's lips moved, but she heard nothing. Her legs buckled and she crashed against the desk. The sensei sprang forward and helped her into the chair.

The room darkened and spun. He pushed her head between her knees and held it there.

When her senses stopped reeling, she swallowed and searched for her voice. It came out in a whimper. "Let me up."

The sensei released his hold. She straightened, and he handed her a cup of water.

Her hand shook as she took the proffered cup. She drank several swallows. "Where is he? Where is my son?"

"In the meditation garden, by the temple."

"I will go to him." She stood, gripping the side of the desk for support.

He took her arm, his long bony fingers pressing into her flesh. "No, Yoko-san."

Uncomprehending, she stared at him. "I must go to my son."

"You don't want to see him like this. It is too terrible."

With a low moan, Yoko fell back into the chair. Her eyes filled with tears. "Why must I always be punished, sensei? Haven't I done all that has been asked of me? I put up with a monster for a husband. For the sake of the village, I kept the factory going while the men were off fighting. Even after my daughters were killed in the earthquake, I persevered. Then I let Kazuhiro run the factory after Takeda disappeared—I could have fought for control, but I didn't. And in repayment for all that, the gods have taken my only son. Why are they never satisfied?"

"I've finished cleaning that stupid pug mill," her grandson said, sauntering into the office. "Where's my father? I'm ready to go home." His gaze swung from Yoko to the sensei then back. His brows furrowed. "What's going on?"

"Your grandmother is ill," the sensei said. "You should go back outside for a while."

"Why? What's happened?"

Yoko leaned her head against the back of the chair and closed her eyes. "Tell him, sensei."

A policeman took her grandson home. After he and the sensei were gone, Yoko insisted on seeing her son's body. She walked unaided up the hill past the temple and through the tall weeds. Insects flitted around her face. She batted them away. Ahead, near a grove of trees, she spotted several uniformed policemen and a man in a white coat bending over something. Her young escort took her arm. She shook him off and hurried her steps.

When she reached the center of the grove, she cried out and clutched the arm she'd earlier rejected. In the middle of the white stones and sand, which had been raked into the patterns of the sea by the priests who tended the small garden, Kazuhiro's body sprawled. Flies swarmed above it, and on the bloody stump of his neck. Positioned on a large boulder near the garden's perimeter was her son's severed head.

Blood pulsed in Yoko's ears, drowning out the drone of the flies and the young policeman's words. Her stomach rose into her throat. "Take me away," she whispered. "Take me away from this place."

Yoko had only contempt for the police. Three weeks passed with no suspects and no arrests. The day following Kazuhiro's murder, two detectives had asked her endless questions. She'd wanted to yell at them to stop wasting time, to find out who killed her son, find out who did that terrible thing to him. But she held her temper and answered their foolish questions—questions such as who Kazuhiro had gone to see.

What idiots. If she'd known the answer to that question, she'd know who killed her son. When the two men finished with her, they wasted more time questioning all the factory workers. She could have told them the workers knew no more than she knew. The two detectives went away, but for days, uniformed police combed the woods and fields near the shrine.

They found nothing. In Yoko's opinion, the only useful thing the police had managed was to take her grandson home the day of Kazuhiro's murder. That and break the news to her daughter-in-law.

Then Eriko dropped her bombshell, calling to tell her that Kazuhiro had borrowed money from the yakuza. The moment her daughter-in-law hung up, Yoko called the police.

"This is Yoko Yoshida. I want to talk to one of the detectives handling my son's murder. Yes, yes, of course right now."

After several minutes, with Yoko growing more impatient by the second, the phone clicked and a rough voice answered. "Detective Saito speaking."

She recognized his voice as one of the detectives who'd questioned her. "I know who killed Kazuhiro Yoshida."

"Who is this?"

"This is Yoko Yoshida. Did you hear me? I know who killed my son."

"Tell me what you have discovered, Yoshida-san."

"It was the yakuza. They killed Kazuhiro. He borrowed money from them."

"How do you know that?" His gravelly voice held suspicion.

"My daughter-in-law just told me. The yakuza did it."

"Why did your son borrow money from them? Did he have gambling debts?"

"No, no, nothing like that." Yoko scowled, massaging her temple with her free hand. "It was business. He wanted to enlarge the factory and couldn't get a loan when the bank collapsed."

"Very well," Detective Saito said. "We will investigate."

It didn't surprise Yoko when no arrests were made. The police no doubt feared the yakuza, too. Or were in league with them.

The yakuza killed Kazuhiro, one of those gangsters he went to meet that fateful day. She'd seen with her own eyes the man with the ponytail. He or one of his friends was the killer. She didn't doubt it for a minute. Maybe Kazuhiro hadn't the money to pay them back. Considering her daughter-in-law's extravagance, most likely that was the case.

If only he'd had the sense to come to her. She could have given him what he needed to remodel the factory. She'd listened to him talk about his plans, and she'd patiently waited for him to come to her. It had infuriated her when he did neither, infuriated her even more that he never suspected she had the funds he needed.

Naturally she had the money. Hadn't she managed the factory for years? She hadn't been about to turn everything over to that no-good Takeda when he finally returned home—a full year after the war ended. The rotten cur didn't deserve a penny of the money she'd worked for. She'd turned over just enough to allay suspicion, then shrugged away his accusations of incompetence.

Only once had she taken the money out of its hiding place. She'd needed to take it to the bank in Sakayama and exchange it for new notes the government issued. Takeda had been away on one of his so-called business trips. She'd been terrified she'd run into him on the road or in the city, but for once luck had been on her side. Since that time, the money had remained in the secret compartment Ishihara had built in the back of the tonsu. She hadn't needed to take it out; enough to know it was there.

Her son hadn't come to her, though. He'd gone to the bank and asked for a loan. When he didn't get the money there, he went to the yakuza. Proving once again how ignorant men were, especially when they thought they knew everything.

Her lips twisted and she poured more sake into her cup, tossing it back in one gulp before pouring another. She shook her head. Life was unjust. She thought of her dead daughters and her mouth twisted again. Their deaths had nearly destroyed her.

After Takeda returned from the war, six years went by, six years of him berating her for her failure to conceive. Then the miracle had happened. Kazuhiro. Disgust filled her when she recalled her delight at her son's birth. How easily she'd allowed herself to forget that the fates would always have their way.

Her cigarette burned down to her fingers. She stubbed it out in the overflowing ashtray and reached once more for the sake bottle.

She'd been glad when Takeda disappeared all those years ago, had celebrated each day he stayed away. Despite those feelings, however, after three weeks with no word from him, she'd dutifully called the police. Just as now, they'd failed at their jobs.

Yoko's stomach was sour and her head felt stuffed with batting. The phone rang, and this time she answered.

"Honored mother-in-law, it is Eriko. I have been calling and calling." Her voice trembled as she spoke.

"I didn't feel like talking."

Eriko swallowed a sob. "I don't know who else to turn to. The yakuza has contacted me. They want their money. What should I do?"

"Have you called the police? Told them?" Yoko's opinion of her daughter-in-law, a timid woman despite her claims of modernity, had always been shaded with contempt.

Eriko's voice rose in panic. "No, no. The yakuza warned me not to. They killed Kazuhiro. What is to keep them from killing me and your grandsons? Okaasan, what am I to do?"

"Calm yourself. How long have they given you to get the money? When are they to contact you again?"

"In three days, but it might as well be tomorrow. I have no money and no way to get it. I tried, but with the stock market and the bank failures, my cousin, well…." Her voice trailed off.

Her body stiff, Yoko climbed from the cab. Only once had she been in the ridiculous structure her son and his family called home. She shuddered to see the house towering above her, casting its dark shadow across the diminutive front yard and onto the fronts of two smaller houses facing it.

"Monstrosity," she muttered, climbing the steps to the front door. She slid it open and stepped inside. "Konichiwa," she called out.

Yoshi, her youngest grandson, hurried down the stairs, a book in his hand. His eyebrows went up when he saw her. "Grandmother."

The boy had the appearance of his father at ten, but he lacked Kazuhiro's natural vigor. Yoko feared he always would. "You look tired," she said. "Are you getting your rest?"

"Yes, Grandmother. Did my mother know you were coming?"

Eriko's voice sounded weakly from the floor above. "Yoshi, who is there?"

"It's me," Yoko answered, her voice loud. "We need to talk."

"I'm not dressed."

Yoko's lips curled at her daughter-in-law's pitiful whining. "Put clothes on and come downstairs. I'll make us tea."

Eiichi sprawled in front of the television, watching a baseball game. He looked up, his eyes flickering a brief acknowledgement, before returning his attention to the game. Yoko stared at him several moments before turning to Yoshi. "Show me where the tea things are."

Eriko entered the kitchen, looking wan, her hair uncombed and the limp from her shortened left leg more pronounced than ever. "I'm not hungry."

Her pathetic-sounding voice scraped against Yoko's nerves. "Well, I am." She handed her daughter-in-law a tray set with teapot and cups and some stale wafers she'd found in a tin. "Carry this into the living room. Yoshi, you go upstairs and take your brother with you. Tell him I said to go. I need to speak with your mother."

Eiichi grumbling about not being able to see the end of the ballgame, the two boys left. Yoko lowered herself into one of the uncomfortable overstuffed chairs. Eriko poured tea and handed her a cup.

Yoko took a sip and set it down. She could wait no longer. "How much did Kazuhiro borrow? How much is the yakuza demanding?" When Eriko named a figure, Yoko drew in a sharp breath. Then she reached for the satchel she'd kept at her side since her arrival. She opened it and began counting out money.

Eriko gasped. "Where did you get it?"

Yoko glanced up from her counting. "Don't worry. I didn't borrow it from the yakuza."

"I can't believe it. Is there enough?"

"There's enough. You will pay them in full."

"How can I ever thank you?" Tears flowing down her cheeks, Eriko dropped to her knees, grasped Yoko's hands in hers and kissed them. "They killed Kazuhiro. I was sure they were going to kill me and my sons."

Yoko pulled free. The moment had arrived to tell Eriko of her plans. "Eiichi is to come and live with me. It is time he becomes a man and learns something about the making of pottery."

Eriko's eyes widened. Her tears flowed harder. "But Okaasan, he's still in high school. And he hates the pottery factory—the clay dust makes him sneeze."

In no mood to tolerate excuses, Yoko brushed her daughter-in-law's words aside. "Before the new term begins, he will enroll in the high school near Nishimi. That's still three weeks away. He will have plenty of time to come to terms with his new life." She stood, gripping the satchel with the remainder of her money. "And he will come to terms, Eriko. He has no choice. He is the oldest son. It is proper that he learn the family business."

Yoko discovered that paying the money to the yakuza somehow completed her cycle of grief. Her son was dead. She'd learned when her daughters died that she could do nothing but accept what the fates dictated. She needed to return to the business of life, and once again run the pottery factory—at least until Eiichi was grown.

Yoko squinted at the letter in her hand through a haze of smoke from the cigarette dangling at the corner of her mouth. It had come in the morning's post. She looked up when the door slid open and the sensei shuffled inside. He shoved the door closed. A wet, red-gold leaf stuck to the side of his shoe.

"Good morning," he said. "We are having a blustery day." He set his box of brushes on one of the packing platforms and shrugged out of his loose-fitting canvas jacket.

His studied movements reminded Yoko of old Mori. That and the letter. With a slight smile, she leaned back in her chair. "What do you think about resurrecting the old kiln?"

The sensei adjusted his trademark black beret and then hung his coat on a hook before answering. "You have the new kiln now. It's big enough to fire several weeks of work."

"Bah." She straightened, lifting her chin. "I could have told Kazuhiro we didn't need it. But he wouldn't listen if I had. And look what it brought him." She stubbed out her cigarette with such force, she sent the metal ashtray skittering on her desk.

"Can the old kiln be used again?" the sensei asked. "Children have been climbing over it and playing hide-and-seek in it and that pile of shards for years."

Yoko sighed. Being exasperated with Kazuhiro accomplished nothing. "You're right." She shook another cigarette out of the package and lit it. "In places, it's collapsed. Old Mori would be having fits if he could see it now." She leaned back in her chair once again. "But I don't think it will be too difficult to put back into working order. Fewer chambers, maybe. We have plenty of mature wood nearby, thanks to the government's reforestation efforts."

The sensei nodded. "They have done well."

"This younger generation considers itself modern, and yet they want some of the old things, like pottery, made the traditional way." A sardonic smile played on her lips. "Despite the current economic hardships everyone faces, they're willing to pay for it—pay more, in fact. 'Getting back to the fundamentals of living,' they call it. A few repairs here and there, that's all we need do."

"Have you talked to Sano? What are his thoughts?"

Yoko avoided a direct answer to that question. Sano was of no consequence at this point. "He may be our master potter, but he knows nothing about wood-firing. He's always worked here and we've used gas for years."

"So, if not Sano, who would manage it?" the sensei asked.

"I've been in touch with someone." She tapped the letter. "He's coming to the factory at the end of the week."

"Kazuhiro should have consulted with you," the sensei said. "Your son should have respected your wisdom and experience."

Yoko's lips tightened around her cigarette. "Yes, he should have."

Later that morning, Yoko sorted through the stack of papers on her desk. Orders had increased. She didn't know if the economy picked up or if the increase would prove to be a blip caused by the change in season. For several moments, she studied the sensei, painting chrysanthemums on a tall vase. Once again, she thought of old Mori, who'd seemed to defy aging. The sensei, too, had appeared impervious to the passing of time.

In this last year, however, he had visibly begun to flag. She wondered how much longer the two of them had on this earth. For her, all she hoped for was enough time to train Eiichi and make sure the factory continued. She wondered what the sensei most desired.

"Has your son found work yet?" she asked.

The sensei straightened and set his brush aside. "Not yet. But this morning he had a third appointment with a new credit union. We are hopeful."

"I am glad to hear it, sensei."

"It is not good when a man can't support his family," he said.

Yoko was again reminded of old Mori, who'd said something similar after his son came back from the war on crutches—from an infection that eventually led to the removal of his foot and the lower part of his leg. Yoko had given him a job in the factory, helping with the packing, but when Takeda finally showed up, he'd let the young man go—like he'd owed old Mori nothing for all his years of service.

"You are right." She sighed again, and knocked ash from her cigarette onto the concrete floor. "If Akira gets the job, will he and his family move back to Sakayama?"

Before the sensei could answer, Kotada rushed in, breathing hard, his face red. "Grandfather!"

The sensei turned at the sound of his grandson's voice. "Yes, Ko-chan, what is it?"

"The police have come to our house, Grandfather. My grandmother wants you to come home right away."

Yoko frowned and stared at the boy.

The sensei stood, his eyebrows raised in puzzlement. "The police? What are they doing at our house?"

The boy's voice quivered when he spoke. "They've come to arrest my father."

2
THE SENSEI
Hirotaka

Kotada tugged at his hand, urging him to hurry. The sensei tried to hasten his steps, but the pace and the steepness of the road soon had his lungs on fire. They reached the house just as two detectives led an ashen-faced Akira to the back of a police car.

Kotada tried to pull away and run to his father, but the sensei held onto the boy's hand, stopping him with a murmured, "Wait." He turned to the detectives. "What is going on? My son has done nothing. Why are you arresting him?"

One answered. "We've found the murder weapon. It is the Katsuragawa family sword. It has your crest on it."

"My sword? No." The sensei shook his head for emphasis. "No. My sword is inside, in a chest."

Akira stared at the ground. "It's not there, Father. We looked."

"That is not possible. It is where I keep it."

"It's not there," Akira repeated.

The sensei paused, pulling his chin in, but only for a moment. "Even so," he said to the policeman. "What makes you think it is the murder weapon and why would you think Akira is the murderer? Why not me?"

"We're not at liberty to say more," the policeman said as his partner opened the door and directed Akira into the rear seat.

"Father, no," cried Kotada, once again trying to pull away.

The sensei held tighter to his grandson's hand. "Where are you taking him?" He tried to make his voice strong, but inwardly he quaked.

"To headquarters. He is to be questioned."

Both policemen got into the car. The engine started and they drove away. Akira's pale face, staring out the car's rear window, become smaller and smaller as the police car headed down the narrow mountain road and disappeared.

Inside the house, Chieko rushed to him, sobbing. In her crib, their granddaughter whimpered. Their grandson gave way to tears as well.

The sensei brushed past his wife and hurried to the chest where he kept the few remaining family treasures he'd found the terrible winter following the war. They'd been swathed in silk and buried beneath a rock in the grounds of his family's Sakayama estate. He sank to his knees and began to pull everything from the chest. But while the cloth he kept the sword wrapped in was there, the sword, just as Akira had said, was not. He leaned back on his heels, his hands on his thighs, and stared at the emptied chest. Within a single hour, his entire world had crumbled.

The next day, a detective named Saito told the sensei his sword had been found at the edge of a rice paddy near the Shinto shrine.

"I thought the police had scoured that area. Why didn't they find my sword earlier?"

Detective Saito shrugged. "Maybe it was hidden and a dog dug it up. Who knows? But we have it now. There were traces of blood on the blade. We've already tested it—it's Kazuhiro Yoshida's blood."

The sensei remained unconvinced. "Even so. That doesn't prove my son is the guilty one. Anyone might have entered our house when we were away and taken the sword. Besides, my son had no reason to harm Kazuhiro."

"Ah, but we have a witness who swears your son harbored a hatred of the victim—stemming from something that occurred when they were teenagers," Detective Saito said.

The sensei was more stunned than indignant at the detective's words. "I'm unaware of anything happening between Akira and Kazuhiro, not in their childhoods, not ever. Nothing to generate the kind of hatred that drove whoever killed Kazuhiro."

"That is not what we were told," Detective Saito answered. But he refused to divulge any more information or say who had made the startling accusations against Akira.

When he arrived at the police station, the sensei had been confident the police would realize their error and release his son. When he left an hour later, he didn't feel certain of anything.

He returned to Nishimi just as the sun sank behind the mountains and darkness closed in. A brisk wind pulled at the lapels of his jacket. He lowered his head to it and trudged up the mountain, his steps heavy.

When he entered the house, his wife and daughter-in-law were silent, even as questions filled their worried eyes.

He pulled off his jacket, after first stuffing his beret in the pocket, and handed it to Chieko. He drew a deep breath and spoke. "I have found an attorney willing to take the case, but he warned me the evidence against Akira is strong."

It was as though a dam had broken.

"But why, husband? They were friends. Why would anyone think our son is guilty of Kazuhiro's murder?"

Although he knew Akira and Kazuhiro hadn't been enemies, he also knew they had not been friends, but he said nothing to contradict his wife's statement.

"My husband wasn't even in Nishimi that afternoon. He couldn't have killed Kazuhiro," Hiromi said.

The sensei sighed. Only when slogging through the jungles of New Guinea had he felt so helpless. "The police say the bus driver swears Akira came back to Nishimi on an earlier bus."

Hiromi shook her head. "He came home with me. We were on the bus together that evening. Don't you remember?"

"I told them, but the police are listening to the bus driver."

The bitterest of all ironies he later learned from his wife. Akira had come home the day before, eager to share with his family news that the Farmer's Credit Union had indeed offered him a position.

3
NOBUKO
The Gaijin

Nobuko fingered the scar on her cheek; time had made it nearly invisible, but a slight ridge remained.

Poor Yoko, she thought. First her daughters die in the earthquake all those years ago, now Kazuhiro. And who knew what happened to Takeda Yoshida? Dead, too, most likely, considering how long he'd been gone. Following Kazuhiro's beheading and Akira's arrest, the entire village was alive with speculation. When women came to shop each morning—despite the financial crisis people still needed to eat—they spoke of nothing else. Everyone wanted to know who could have predicted such appalling things happening in their village.

After a final glance in the mirror, Nobuko left her living quarters to open the store. She recalled Akira as a boy, often shopping with his mother. Chieko had spoiled him by giving him money to buy a toy or a treat, but he'd been a good boy, never demanding, always respectful, and he'd grown into a worthy husband and father.

Her customers told their own stories of Akira as boy and man. No one understood who told the police Akira harbored hatred for Kazuhiro Yoshida. The women said even Kazuhiro's mother swore she'd never heard such a thing;

Yoko remained convinced the yakuza had murdered her son.

Nobuko felt great sympathy for Chieko. Instead of shopping every morning, to ensure the freshness of the food, she now purchased what she needed for several days at a time, and to avoid others, came to the store late in the afternoon.

"None of us has an appetite, and my heart is not in the preparation of meals," she'd said the last time she'd come to shop. "Oh, Nobuko-san, what are we to do? My grandson still has nightmares about finding Kazuhiro's body, and he is desolate for his father. Our hearts are broken. And Akira—I shudder to think what is happening to my son."

Nobuko had laid a comforting hand on Chieko's arm. "Everyone, including Kazuhiro's mother, knows Akira is innocent. He would never do such a terrible thing."

Chieko's lips trembled. "My dear friend. I wish you were right, but I'm afraid people will say that when there is no fire, no smoke will rise. Even after the police find out who really killed Kazuhiro, for some, my son will be a marked man. The stigma of his arrest will remain."

Nobuko recognized the truth in Chieko's words. The job Akira had been promised at the credit union was already forfeited. Even if the real killer was caught, suspicion would cling to Akira. People might forget the details, but they'd remember his arrest.

Nobuko sighed, refolded a shirt and put it on a display table. The bell above the door jingled as Sachiko entered. She hurried forward, a smile parting her lips. "Welcome, welcome. It is good to see you, daughter. What brings you to Nishimi, besides paying a visit to your old mother?"

Sachiko didn't return her smile. "Hello, Mother. I'm here to make some purchases for Kensai."

Nobuko studied her daughter a moment. "Let us have a cup of tea and a chat first. You do have time?"

"I suppose."

Nobuko led the way to the stove in the center of the store where the kettle of water simmered. "How is life on the farm now that Toshio is gone?"

Sachiko shrugged and took a seat. "At least I no longer have the burden of his care and his foul temper."

Nobuko handed her daughter a cup of tea. "Something is bothering you. What is it?"

Sachiko shook her head, appearing lost in the teacup's still depths.

"I know when you are upset, daughter," Nobuko said. "Tell me what is wrong."

Sachiko set down the cup and leaned back in her chair. For several moments, she picked at a frayed spot on her trousers. "You know my father-in-law was mad, insane— had been, no doubt, since returning from that Australian prison camp."

"So many years have passed since then," Nobuko said, shaking her head in sympathy. "I remember Mrs. Mori telling me how Toshio came to their house to claim his son. He looked like a wild man, she said, and Kensai, only five or six at the time, was terrified of him. He hadn't seen his father in years."

Sachiko shifted in her chair. "Toshio grew worse over the past few years, each day more hateful and difficult to care for. I had to be around him, but sometimes I feared I would go mad, too. I'm sure his father's worsening condition placed a heavy burden on my husband. After his father died, I hoped things would get better between us."

"And they are not?"

Sachiko again retreated into long silence. "It is difficult to describe. All I can say is that Kensai is unlike himself."

Nobuko tilted her head, frowning. "In what way is he different?"

"For one thing, he's taken to disappearing, often for hours at a time. Once overnight."

Nobuko's frown deepened. "Does he not tell you where he goes?" When her daughter shook her head, Nobuko offered another thought. "Is it possible my son-in-law has taken a pillow-friend?"

"In a way, I wish it was that simple, Mother. But I don't think another woman is the reason for Kensai's disappearances. His strange moodiness is now almost constant, and he stares at Hayoto and me as if we are strangers and not his wife and son."

Nobuko opened a package of teacakes and offered one. "Maybe he blames you for something, feels you were not respectful of his father or didn't care for him as he thought you should."

Sachiko waved away the coconut-covered pink pastries. "I don't think so. But even if he did blame me for something, it doesn't explain why he is distant with Hayoto."

"How does my grandson feel about all this?"

"He hasn't said anything to me, but I know he's confused."

Nobuko had been against her daughter's marriage to Kensai Hara from the moment she announced it—aside from having career prospects, Sachiko had been full of fun and laughter, nothing like the taciturn woman she'd become. From her own experience, Nobuko knew the isolation of farm life wouldn't suit her extroverted daughter.

Her primary reason for opposing Sachiko's marriage to Kensai Hara, however, had been based on something far different. In the years following the war and after she married Masato and returned to Nishimi, Nobuko had often wondered how Kensai got along with only his father for company. Toshio seldom came to the store, and when he did, Kensai stayed behind. Then one day, the bell above the door jingled.

At the front counter with a customer, Nobuko looked up and saw a young boy of twelve or thirteen. He wasn't one of the boys from the village, if he had been, she would have recognized him. Still, something familiar about his homely face, the ears sticking out from his head, tugged at her memory. After Mrs. Murakami left with her purchases, Nobuko asked the boy if she could help him. He looked at her, unspeaking.

She asked him again, but he continued to stare. Then recognition dawned. "Kensai? Are you Kensai Hara?" A smile lit her eyes. "You are." The two years she'd spent with little Kensai and his grandparents came back in a flash. They'd shared so much pain and sorrow. She longed to draw the boy to her, hold him close as she'd once done, but his stiff posture and the accusatory scowl on his face warned her that any physical contact would be unwelcome.

"I'm glad you've come. I've thought of you often." Her smile faltered when the boy took a step back.

"My father says you are a witch. He says you killed my mother. He said you sucked her soul from her body so that you could take her place and live on our farm."

She gaped at him.

"Did you? Did you kill my mother?"

Mute, Nobuko shook her head.

Just then, Mrs. Abi emerged from the family living quarters at the back of the store. For once, Nobuko felt only relief to see her.

"What is wrong, daughter-in-law? You look pale as a chunk of tofu."

"I...I need to lie down," Nobuko managed to say before rushing past, leaving the scowling Kensai and her mother-in-law to stare after her.

For years, Nobuko did everything in her power to replace the memory of a belligerent young teenager with that of a loveable toddler chasing butterflies in a field of sweet potatoes.

"Did you hear me, Mother? What should I do?"

Sachiko's voice jerked Nobuko from her fog. "I don't know. I don't know what advice to give you. He was a strange boy. He is a strange man."

That night, perhaps brought on by memories of Kensai as a child, Nobuko went to bed thinking about the past, the war and its immediate aftermath, something she rarely allowed herself to do.

When the Emperor conceded defeat, Nobuko felt trapped between exhilaration and unbearable sadness. Ruin and desolation lay all around her. It was Japan's, but it was

America's, too. She couldn't wait to escape, go home, put the years of hardship behind her. She dreamed of the dry heat and scouring winds, the wide, clean boulevards running through all the little towns in the Central Valley, from Sacramento to Fresno. Best of all, she envisioned her parents, their arms outstretched, as she ran down the gangplank toward them.

Within two weeks of Japan's surrender, the U.S. Occupation Forces rolled into Sakayama and established offices near the center of the city. One of the first to arrive on their doorstep, Nobuko eagerly gave her information to a young sergeant.

"I'll make sure these letters you've written to your family are included with the G.I. mail sacks," he said when he'd finished questioning her. "Want to have dinner tonight? They've set up a club where we could get a decent meal, something cooked American style. A hamburger if you want it."

The image of a big juicy hamburger, with French fries and a chocolate milkshake, favorites with her and her high school girlfriends, sprang into Nobuko's mind. She wanted to say yes, yes, a thousand times, yes. But even if he could produce such a meal, which she doubted, she didn't think she could eat it. Not with so many around her starving. Besides, she didn't think a hamburger was what the sergeant had in mind.

She looked down at her clasped hands. "I'm sorry, it would not be right."

She couldn't get the vision of the hamburger out of her head. Sometimes it had a slice of cheese on it, sometimes not. Always crisp lettuce and a slice of tomato. And a pickle. The fries were lightly salted, accompanied by a dish of ketchup. She could smell it, and taste the cold sweetness of the accompanying chocolate milkshake.

The more she thought, the more she regretted her hasty refusal. The man had no doubt felt sorry for her. He couldn't have been interested in her, not the way she'd imagined. One look in the mirror at the half-starved, gaunt-faced waif she'd become assured her that no man would find her attractive.

"If he asks me again, I'll accept," she told her aunt, salving her conscience by vowing to bring half of the meal home. She scolded herself that she'd been selfish not to consider her aunt and the old woman, her aunt's sister-in-law, when the sergeant had suggested it.

Every morning she rose thinking *this will be the day I learn that I can return home.* Each night she went to bed thinking, *maybe tomorrow.* But each day proved as disappointing as the one preceding it.

Desperate, she went back to the Occupation Forces office and found that the sergeant who'd helped her earlier had gone, transferred to Tokyo. His replacement couldn't find her paperwork. She filled out the forms again and once more returned to the little house by the river to wait.

This time, the answer came quickly: her request to return to the United States was denied. Because she'd registered for rice rations, it was determined she had renounced her U.S. citizenship. At least that's the excuse they gave her.

Along with the news that her country no longer wanted her, she was handed a letter from Mrs. Peterson, a ranch owner whose property bordered her parents' farm. Her fingers shook so that she couldn't get the envelope open. Finally, she ripped it across the top.

Dear Nobuko,

The postman knew I considered your mom and dad friends, so he got in touch with me when your letter came. I'm real sorry to be the one to give you this news. When the war

*started, your parents and a bunch of other Japanese families
from around here were rounded up and sent to live in what the
government called internment camps. Your parents were sent
to one in California first, then to one in Idaho. I'm even sorrier
to tell you that your mother passed on about two years past.
I'm enclosing your father's address. He's living in eastern
Oregon now. With a relative I think. The farm got sold early in
the war to a man from Modesto.*

*I heard your brother joined the Army, but I don't have his
address. I'll try and find out and let you know where to write
him.*

*Nobuko, please understand that we were all real scared
after Pearl Harbor. I always liked your parents and I'm just real
sorry for what happened to them.*

Sincerely yours,

Jane Peterson

Nobuko's hand went to her mouth. She read the letter
again. As the full meaning sank in, a low moan escaped her lips.

She had no memory of getting back to the little house by
the river, nor of her aunt crying out at the sight of her. The
farm, her home, had been her touchstone for all the years of the
war. Knowing it was there, along with her mother and father,
waiting for her, had been all that kept her sane after the Osaka
Maru returned to Japan. Whenever some misfortune happened—when her uncle raged, when Masato left, when the villagers
turned against her, and when everyone was starving—at those
times, thoughts of her mother had brought her solace. Even
though an ocean separated them, Nobuko had felt her mother's
love enfolding her. But how could that have been if her mother
was dead?

Like refuse, she was adrift in a vast ocean. Wreckage no
one wanted. Her eyes and nose grew red from swiping away
tears. Sleep abandoned her. She refused what little nourishment

her aunt could provide. Nothing anyone could say or do brought comfort.

Why must she go on, like people claimed. She had no idea if her brother was alive or dead; her father was alone; and everything else she held dear was gone—her mother, the farm. Even her country.

Weeks dragged by, weeks in which she alternated between uncontrollable crying and wandering the house in a stupor. When she could sink no lower, her natural resiliency, that thing that had stuck with her through all the hardships, finally kicked in. Tremulous, a bit weak at first, resolution returned. She could not, would not give in to more despair.

"I have to think about the future," she told her aunt, lips trembling. "Because no matter how I might rail against it, Japan is now my home, maybe forever."

Her aunt suggested she apply for work with the Occupation Forces. "With your fluency in both Japanese and English, they are sure to hire you."

Even though resolute to find employment, Nobuko's emotions were too raw for what her aunt proposed. "I couldn't. Not after what they did." But, when it became apparent no other jobs were available, she swallowed her resentment and applied. Her aunt proved right—they hired her, almost on the spot.

It felt strange to be surrounded by American voices for the first time in six years, but she soon got used to it, and it pleased her she could give her aunt money for the black market. In the evenings, she helped her aunt with the old lady, who'd grown frailer and less cognizant of her surroundings.

"A letter came for you today," her aunt said one evening.

Although it had been years since she'd seen it, Nobuko recognized her brother's handwriting. Not the return address— what was Mako doing in Portland, Oregon, of all places? She ripped the envelope open and pulled out the single sheet of paper. Her eyebrows went up as she read. Her brother had started a landscaping business in Portland and attended school there on something called the GI Bill. That night she fell asleep wondering what Portland would be like and why her brother lived there instead of with their father.

More weeks passed and another letter came, this one from her father's cousin, telling her that her father had suffered a stroke and asked for her and Mako. Nobuko tried to obtain permission to travel to America for a brief visit. Her boss even wrote a letter on her behalf. But the government moved too slow. Her father died. At least Mako had managed to be at his side. Bitter resentment festered inside Nobuko. She declared she no longer wanted to go back, even for a visit. "If America doesn't want me, I don't want America."

On a winter morning, bundled up against the cold, Nobuko hurried along the wooden sidewalk. The war had been over nearly a year and she'd been working for the Occupation Forces for eight months.

For many, life was no better than it had been during the long years of the war. Men, women, and children begged on every street corner. Some were refugees from places harder hit than Sakayama. Hunger and desperation lined their faces, their eyes were sunken deep into their sockets, their shoulders slumped like old decrepit men.

Worse were the children…old, haunted eyes in young faces. Their hungry gazes tore at her, but she could do little for them other than share a bit of rice or piece of meat saved from lunch, or slip a coin into a pleading hand.

Among those standing alone or in groups of three or four, were veterans still wearing the remnants of uniforms. Many had returned to Japan to find their homes destroyed and their wives and children missing. Others discovered they'd been declared dead, their funerals already held. The 'living war dead,' such men were called. Avoiding the eyes of a one-armed man, Nobuko pulled her scarf tighter and hurried past.

Luckier than many, she had a place to live, in the home of a couple whose son had died in the war. They didn't welcome her, but they welcomed the rent money. She'd moved there when her cousins and her uncle returned home, her uncle now loudly vilifying the same admirals and generals he'd once lauded.

A gust of wind tore at her scarf, whipping the ends against her cheek and making her eyes sting. She quickened her pace even more.

Part of her wished she could move back to Nishimi. Mrs. Mori wrote often, passing on tidbits of gossip about Yoko Yoshida, the pottery factory, Mrs. Tanaka, and villagers. The thought of twitchy little Mrs. Tanaka, who scurried about town delivering all the latest news, made her smile. Mrs. Mori never spoke of Masato Abi, though. Never said if he'd been among those who'd made it back from New Guinea. Nobuko longed to ask, but feared what the answer might be. If Masato was dead, she didn't want to know.

At least she found her job challenging. She'd quickly been promoted to special assistant to Colonel Anderson, the commanding officer of the Sakayama Occupation Forces unit. That, and the friends she'd made, would need to be enough.

She reached the Occupation Forces' office and pushed open the door. Glad to be out of the biting wind, she hung her coat on a hook and put her handbag in her desk drawer, wishing all she'd just witnessed, what she'd seen every day since the war ended, could be put aside so easily.

One of the things the Occupation Forces in Sakayama had been charged with was oversight of the transfer of lands from the hands of the noble classes, who'd held it for centuries, to those of the peasants and farmers who lived and worked on them.

The duty corporal brought her the day's schedule. She ran down the list of people she and Colonel Anderson were to meet that morning. Her eyes stopped on a name she recognized: Hirotaka Katsuragawa.

Her brows knitted together and she fingered the scar on her cheek. Her mind flashed back to that hot summer day and the old man, Haiashi. They'd sat on a bench next to the koi pond, and he'd enthralled her with stories of the Katsuragawa family.

Nobuko wondered how Hirotaka Katsuragawa would react to his changed circumstances. Like the man who had pounded on the table, demanding to keep his family's property? Or the one who had tearfully begged to retain what he considered his heritage? She didn't blame either of the men for thinking the world had gone crazy. The old order, the authoritarian, top-down structure of old Japan, the one they'd grown up with, was gone. It had been replaced with something that, to them, was unrecognizable, something called democracy.

Hirotaka Katsuragawa arrived twenty minutes early for his meeting. He was like neither of those men, nor like any of the others she and Colonel Anderson had met. She served him tea while they waited for the colonel to join them in the small room set aside for such discussions.

Hirotaka set down his cup and cleared his throat. "I will be happy to make legal the transfer of Katsuragawa lands to those who live and work on them."

Nobuko remained silent while she considered the man who sat before her, trying to judge if he meant what he said. Short in build, and broad through the chest and shoulders, his square face had a deep frown line separating eyebrows that slanted upward above piercing black eyes. Those eyes told her nothing.

"That is unusual, Hirotaka-san. Most who come here are angry with these new rules, angry they are being forced to give up what they consider is theirs."

"In New Guinea, I vowed that if fate allowed me to return to Japan, I would do so not as part of the noble class, but as plain Hirotaka Katsuragawa."

They both understood he had little choice in the matter. His family's great wealth was gone, his parents and both of his brothers, dead. The manufacturing and electrical companies the family owned were nationalized during the war, most now bankrupt, fire-bombed, or otherwise destroyed. Their grand estate in Sakayama lay in ruins. Whatever remained would be sold for little.

"All I ask is to keep the property in Nishimi," Hirotaka said. "I would like to live in Haiashi's house—he was the caretaker—and become part of the village."

When Colonel Anderson came into the room with his aide and a stenographer, Nobuko translated Hirotaka's request. After Hirotaka left them, the colonel told her that Hirotaka's willingness to transfer his other properties surprised him so much, he hadn't hesitated to grant the appeal for the Nishimi property. "I just hope I won't regret it."

Nobuko didn't see Hirotaka again, though she often wondered how he fared in Nishimi, if the villagers accepted him as plain Hirotaka Katsuragawa, or if they bowed and deferred whenever they met him on the street. She suspected the latter.

One evening, after another grueling day of meetings, she came back to her lodgings wanting only to warm her chilled body in a hot bath, drink a cup of tea and crawl into bed.

Her landlord, however, entertained a guest. At sight of him, Nobuko halted in midstride, unable to breathe or say a word. Masato. Though older and thinner, he had the same warm and humorous eyes, the same smile, the same dear face. How often she had dreamed of it.

Masato rose from his chair and walked toward her.

Nobuko's heart jumped, her lips trembled. She held her breath.

He stopped a few feet away and bowed deep, from the waist. "Nobuko-san, please forgive me for not coming to you sooner. My mother said you had returned to America. I just found out that you were here, in Sakayama."

Nobuko blinked away tears. Warmth crept over her skin. Her voice came out whisper-soft. "I was here, waiting for you."

Only as she said the words did she realize that waiting for him was exactly what she'd been doing. They married three months later.

When Nobuko woke, late the following morning, her cheeks were damp with tears. Her life with Masato had been all she could have wished. They'd worried when no child arrived the first year or even the next, but the waiting had made Sachiko's eventual birth all the sweeter. A joyful man. He always found a way to make her laugh. His health had been the only thing that posed a threat to their happiness. She had him for over fifteen years, though, and for that she was thankful.

Nobuko had known from the beginning that Sachiko's marriage wasn't a happy one, not in the sense her own had been. And yet, her daughter had never sought her advice. Until yesterday. And then she'd had none to give.

4
YOKO
The Pottery Factory

Yoko inwardly smiled at Eiichi's obvious tactics. Her grandson arrived in Nishimi on the bus, a small knapsack on his shoulder, face sullen and uncompromising. He refused to speak to her, making it clear he'd come under duress and intended using silence to register his protest. His defiance amused her. I've dealt with tougher nuts than you, my boy, she thought.

She showed him where he would sleep. He put his knapsack down and looked around the tiny room, disdain written on the curl of his lip.

"I'm going back to the factory for another hour or two." She waved her hand around the room. "In the meantime, settle in, find yourself something to eat, stroll around the village—it's been several years since you've spent much time in Nishimi. Tomorrow, you'll begin your work."

He looked around the room once more, making no effort to hide his contempt, but said nothing. She left, once again hiding her amusement at his blatant attempts to alter what she had set in motion.

The next morning, she woke him early. Over breakfast, she spelled out how his days would go. "Follow Sano and observe everything he does. But for the first few days, do not ask questions—in other words, keep your eyes open and your mouth closed." She paused, waiting for him to protest. Instead, he shoveled more rice into his mouth. She narrowed her gaze. "School resumes in ten days. Until then, you will work the same hours as the apprentices. When school begins, you will work in the factory after school and on Saturdays, just as your father did at your age."

The boy could remain silent no longer. "You have no television."

"That is true," Yoko said, glad to get a response, even though not one she'd expected. "I've never cared for television myself, but there is a set at the factory. You are free to watch it while you eat your noon meal and at morning and afternoon breaks. Be forewarned, however, the others like certain programs and only during serious competitions do they watch sports."

Eiichi scowled and returned to his breakfast.

She considered him. Not altogether hopeless. Rude and insolent, yes. Lazy, too. But who could blame him, saddled with a mother claiming to be a modern woman, yet spineless, allowing him to do whatever he wished. And judging by the way the boy behaved, her son hadn't been much of a father. At least Kazuhiro hadn't been the barbarian his own father had been. He may have ignored his wife and sons, but she doubted he'd ever abused them.

She glanced at the clock on the wall and stood. "If you're finished, rinse your dishes and put them on the counter. It's time for us to leave."

For the most part, the boy maintained his sullen silence. At breaks, when an apprentice near his own age tried to draw him out, he answered questions in a dull monotone, betraying nothing, keeping his responses as short as possible. The apprentice soon gave up.

He's tough, Yoko thought with a touch of admiration—tougher than she'd figured him to be.

By the end of the third week, she wondered if she'd underestimated his determination to remain as unyielding as possible.

Sano laughed. "I think you may have met your match, Yoko-san."

She glanced at Eiichi, sitting alone at the end of the room during their afternoon break, engrossed in a sports magazine. "At least he's been showing up after school. I thought he might not. Do you think we'll ever make a potter of him?"

"I'm not sure, Yoko-san. His heart is very far from this place. Whether that will ever change, who knows?"

She frowned. "I thought it was in his blood. I believed we had only to prick his skin to find it." Even Takeda, her whore-mongering husband, had been an excellent potter when he made the effort. And Kazuhiro had been nearly as good as Sano. But after Takeda's disappearance, Kazuhiro needed to devote his time to managing the factory. Until the bank failure, he did the job well. Then the yakuza got their hooks into him.

She sighed. Nothing she did or said would bring her son back—she'd learned that lesson well. The more you railed, the more the fates took delight in your pain. "Well, time will tell about Eiichi," she said. "But if he continues this obstinate path, I may need to think of something else."

Sano looked thoughtful. He put his cup on the tray. She thought him about to say something, the issue of needing more money, perhaps, a subject he'd brought up more than once. "Time to return to work," he muttered instead.

After their evening meal, Eiichi withdrew to his tiny room to study. Yoko lingered at the table. They were moving ahead with her plan to refurbish the old kiln. Before they'd vanished, the yakuza's Vietnamese workers had completed their projects to a point the factory workers could finish them, including the outside patio and garden. The waterfall might not be quite as grand as Kazuhiro had envisioned, but impressive enough to draw favorable comments from their visitors.

Yoko did expect visitors. Because of the financial crisis and unemployment problems, this year there would be fewer than Kazuhiro had hoped for. Some would come, however. And when things improved, as they inevitably would, they'd have even more visitors. Like her son, she envisioned them drinking tea and admiring the garden. And when they got back in their cars or on a bus, they would carry bags containing their purchases. Which reminded her, she needed to place an order for bags with Nishimi Pottery Factory printed in bright red letters on their sides.

Yes, Kazuhiro's plan had been a good one. If only the bank hadn't failed. She momentarily turned her thoughts to the bankers who'd caused so much heartache. "Greedy devils," she muttered. Still, when the bank closed, what had possessed her son to go to the yakuza to borrow the money for his vision? He should have known such a move would end in disaster.

5
THE SENSEI
Hirotaka

The guard's heavy footsteps on the bare concrete floor thudded like heartbeats in the sensei's ears as he followed the guard down a row of cells, their top-to-bottom vertical bars making them appear like cages in a zoo. Each cage held a silent prisoner. A blistering stench of urine, feces and disinfectant stung his nose and eyes and mixed with the miasma of hopelessness and fear hanging in the air. His stomach churned. Which of these bleak, near lifeless creatures was his son?

The guard stopped, took a key from the ring on his belt and unlocked a cell door. Like the other prisoners, Akira sat cross-legged on the concrete floor, his eyes cast down, his shoulders slumped. The sensei straightened his own shoulders and entered the ten-by-eight-foot space. Behind him, the click of the lock sounded, followed by the guard's retreating footsteps. Akira didn't look up.

The sensei's eyes slid over the metal sink hanging from one wall and the open toilet, a slit trench in the floor, then swung back to the figure of his son. "Akira." There was no response. "Akira," he said again.

At last Akira lifted his head. "I hoped you wouldn't come."

The sensei laid a trembling hand on his son's shoulder. His throat tightened. Images flashed through his mind of a chubby toddler in the garden, chasing after a hummingbird, and later a young boy stretched out on the floor, engrossed in a book about samurai. He remembered a teenaged Akira in his school uniform, one shoulder dragged down by a heavy bookbag. With an effort, he forced all those images from his mind.

"Akira, we must talk."

His son remained on the floor, his head once again lowered.

"Did you hear me, Akira? We need to speak of this."

"I know." His son's voice was empty of feeling.

"I've retained an attorney. Has he contacted you?"

"He was here this morning."

"And? What did he tell you?"

"Nothing good," Akira replied in the same listless voice.

The sensei's patience frayed. "Did he tell you about the bus driver saying you were on an earlier bus? Did he tell you that?"

Akira mumbled something.

The sensei frowned and leaned closer. "What did you say?"

Akira finally looked up. "It's true," he said, a touch of defiance in his voice. "I did take an earlier bus."

The sensei reached a hand to the cell door to keep from staggering. "I don't understand. You didn't come home until that evening. Where were you?"

Akira hung his head once more. "I went back to Sakayama."

"Why? Did you leave something?" When his son failed to answer, the sensei went on. "Well, if not the driver, someone on the return bus will remember you."

"I didn't take the bus. I was waiting for it, outside the Abi store, but a truck driver stopped for cigarettes. He offered me a ride."

"Was anyone else waiting? Did anyone see you?"

"I don't remember."

The sensei squeezed his son's shoulder, resisting the urge to shake it. "Akira, you've got to think. Someone must have been there and seen you."

Akira threw off the hand and sprang to his feet. "Don't you think I've tried to remember? Do you think I want to be here? Do you think I like my wife and son knowing what I'm accused of?" His son's voice shook. "And my daughter—will I see her first steps, hear her first words? Will she start off to school one day with no word of encouragement from her father? Worse, will she be so shamed, she never speaks of me?"

The sensei started to reply, but couldn't trust his voice.

Akira paced the confined space, his face clenched tight as a fist. "Anyone who knows me, knows I could never do that terrible thing. But when I think of my son witnessing that nightmare scene, I feel such outrage I really do want to kill someone." He stopped pacing and the anger drained from his face, replaced by despair. "What can I do, Father? I am helpless."

The sensei reached a trembling hand for his son's shoulder once again, hesitated then pulled it back. His eyes pleaded for forgiveness. "Akira, I am sorry. I wasn't thinking. Naturally you've tried to remember." He clasped his hands together to still their shaking. "I know you are frustrated and humiliated by all this, but you must participate in your own defense. We need to prove you were nowhere near when Kazuhiro was killed, that you had nothing to do with it. The truck driver will help us."

If possible, his son's shoulders fell even more. "How can we find him? I don't know his name. And I wasn't paying attention to the name on the truck. My mind was elsewhere."

"Do you remember its color?"

"Blue. Maybe green. I don't know. I told you. I don't remember."

The sensei drew a breath, searching for forbearance. "What did the police say when you told them?"

"They didn't laugh outright, but they may as well have done." Akira gave a harsh sound. "I don't think they'll spend very much time looking for him. They have me. They will busy themselves proving my guilt, not my innocence."

"Then we will need to find him ourselves. Perhaps Abi's store is part of his regular route." The sensei did his best to instill confidence in his voice, something he was very far from feeling; he knew nothing about locating anyone. He'd proved that long ago on New Guinea, searching for Toshio Hara after the bridge went down. He squared his shoulders. He wouldn't let that failure repeat itself. "I ask again, why did you return to Sakayama that day?"

Akira renewed his pacing. "It was a silly reason," he said. "I'd spent the morning at the credit union. The interview went well. I knew they were going to offer me the position, and they did. Not that it matters now—I'm sure they'll have nothing to do with me after this." He drew a breath, exhaling heavily. "Anyway, I was nearly home when I remembered I'd promised Hiromi to check and see if our old apartment was still available. I could have waited and gone back another day—even with me working again, we both knew it would be a while before we had the money to move back." He stopped, a rueful smile on his lips. "I was just so excited, you see."

Hearing his son's words, seeing the bleakness in his eyes, a lump formed in the sensei's throat. He wished he knew what to say to give Akira hope.

They both turned at the sound of keys rattling. The cell door swung open, its hinges squeaking in protest.

"Time's up." The guard's face showed not an ounce of warmth.

The sensei looked back at his son. "I will try to find the truck driver. Did you talk to your old landlord?"

Akira dropped his head. "He wasn't in."

The sensei stepped down from the bus in front of Nobuko Abi's store. Just as the last time, exhausted, his body aching. Several times on his way up the mountain he needed to pause and catch his breath. He neared the door to his house, the gravel in the path crunching beneath his feet, and halted. Several moments passed before he could bring himself to move forward. As soon as he entered, his wife and daughter-in-law bombarded him with questions.

"Is he well? Is he eating?" Chieko asked.

Hiromi gazed at him, her eyes pleading. "Are they investigating the yakuza? It is crazy to believe my husband would harm anyone. What proof do they have besides gossip and an old sword? It must have been the yakuza that killed Kazuhiro—one of them crept into this house and stole your sword to kill him." She looked to Chieko, who nodded agreement.

The sensei held up his hand. It shook and he lowered it. "Wait. I need to sit." His wife plumped a cushion and helped him ease onto it. He'd never felt so old and useless. He looked around the room for his grandson. "Where is Kotada?"

"In the loft, studying," Hiromi said.

"Good." He sighed then began to answer their questions. "Our son looks well enough. I suppose he's eating, though I doubt he's very hungry." His eyes lingered on the familiar features of his wife's face. The last year had been hard on her, making room in their small house for their son and his family once more, taking care of their grandchildren…now, with Akira's arrest, the strain showed even more. He hated adding to her burden, but he had no choice. "I believe he'll be there for a while longer."

Chieko tightened her lips and nodded.

He turned to his daughter-in-law. "I don't know if the police are investigating the yakuza at all. They seem convinced Akira is guilty."

Hiromi's hand went to her mouth. She gave a little moan.

"Were you aware that Akira came home on an earlier bus, then returned to Sakayama that same day?"

Hiromi dropped her hand. A furrow formed between her brows. "No. Why would he do that?"

"He said you wanted him to check on your old apartment. He said he'd forgotten, but didn't want to wait another day to find out."

"I did ask him to talk with Mr. Chikata," Hiromi said through trembling lips.

He sighed again. "Unfortunately, Mr. Chikata wasn't in that afternoon and no one else remembers Akira being there."

"But the bus driver knows us. He would remember, wouldn't he?" Hiromi's voice held both hope and fear.

Recalling the look on his son's face that morning, the sensei felt a fresh wave of disappointment. "He got a ride back to Sakayama with a truck driver. I spent the afternoon looking for a detective to track the driver down."

The sensei stared into the darkness. Although she hadn't spoken, he knew Chieko was also awake. It had been two weeks since their son's arrest. Every day of those two weeks, he'd walked down the track to the pottery factory and called the private detective's office. Each day, he expected to hear the man announce he'd located the truck driver. Each day, disappointment.

Hiromi wanted to take time off from work.

"There is nothing you can do," he'd told her. "And your work at the telephone company will help keep your mind off Akira's troubles."

He wished he, too, could lose himself in work, but the economy still struggled and he had little to do at the factory, just a few pieces each week. Seldom could he escape his mounting fears in his studio.

He felt Chieko turn toward him. "Husband? Are you awake?"

"Yes."

"Husband, what will we do if the real killer isn't found and our Akira is convicted?"

6
SACHIKO
The Farmer's Wife

A cool breeze rattled the tall rice stalks, and muddy water rippled at Sachiko's knees. Next to her, Kensai held a withered leaf between his callused fingers. His mouth a grim line, he examined the yellowish, rod-shaped lesions on the leaf's desiccated surface. He thrust the leaf aside and waded farther into the paddy. He examined another plant and then another before returning to where Sachiko stood.

"They are all the same? Every plant is infected?"

Without looking at her, he nodded. "Leaf blight."

She drew a sharp breath. "What did we do wrong?"

Kensai, ignoring her question, waded out of the paddy.

She followed. "Husband?"

His face buried in his hands, he finally spoke. "Many things are possible. Too many weeds in the paddy; damage to the seedlings during shipping; the weather. It could be any or all those things, but it's none of them. The real reason is that I am cursed. I have always been cursed." He dropped his hands to his side, threw back his head and glared up the mountain to the back of the pottery factory. "I thought things would be different with both gone, but their evil spirits continue to bring me ill luck."

Sachiko stared, a sick feeling in her stomach. He must be going mad. In the years of their marriage, she'd grown accustomed to his long, brooding silences sometimes followed by irrational talk. She'd assumed this behavior came from growing up with crazy old Toshio as his only company. But, as she'd told her mother, since his father's death, everything about her husband was different now, even his silences.

Too often she found his eyes on her, assessing, measuring. She might be hoeing weeds in the garden, feeding the dog or preparing a meal. Tensing, she'd look up and see him, his eyes boring into her. She had no idea what his thoughts were, what he looked for. If not at her, he gaped at Hayoto, as if he'd never seen the boy.

After old Toshio died, she'd hoped they could put the past behind them, forget the war and the Australian prison camp Toshio blamed as the root of all his troubles. Hoped they could make the farm the happy place she'd once envisioned. To start, she'd decided to put to good use the room Toshio had commandeered as his own, the biggest and nicest one in the house. After scrubbing and cleaning it, she brought in a few things to make it more comfortable, more homelike. At first, they did gather there in the evenings, reading, repairing equipment or mending clothes. Without Toshio's glowering presence, Sachiko found it companionable.

Then Kensai demanded the room be returned to the way his father had left it. He insisted Sachiko and Hayoto stay out unless given permission to enter. Like Toshio, he expected his meals served to him on a tray. Her husband now sat in his father's chair and slept on his father's futon, while she and Hayoto ate and slept in the smaller room near the kitchen, the room the three of them had once shared.

Hayoto had been devastated when Kensai yelled at him to "get out and stay out." He'd rushed from the room, his head lowered, but not enough to hide the stricken look on his face. She'd started after him, wanting to assure him everything would be all right, his father loved him. But she couldn't tell him that; she was no longer sure it was true.

Now she feared the loss of their rice crop would send her husband over the edge.

Sachiko put the clean dishes on the shelf and wiped the kitchen counter. Hayoto, seated at the cleared table, worked on his geometry homework. She glanced out the window. As the day faded, the mountains cast lengthening shadows across the failed rice paddy. If she hadn't known it to be diseased, she would be looking forward to the coming harvest. Instead, they needed to destroy it. There'd be no tractor again this year, and nothing to put aside for Hayoto's future. Her son had two more years of high school. She'd always hoped he would enter the University of Tokyo one day, following in her own and her father's footsteps.

Well, at least there'd be plenty to eat in the months ahead, thanks to her large garden. The sow had produced a bumper crop of piglets to sell. Money would be tight. Hayoto, still growing, would need new winter boots and a jacket. She hated the thought of going to her mother. She knew Nobuko would lend them a hand. Still, asking for her help was something Sachiko would avoid if she could.

The sun disappeared behind large billowing clouds building on the western horizon. More shadows formed.

She tensed, and a chill ran along her spine. Kensai stood

in the doorway with a newly-mended hoe in one hand, his eyes wide and unfocused.

She made her voice tentative, cautious. "Husband? Do you need something?"

Kensai gazed at her with a look so strange she took a step backward.

"Why did you put a spell on me, enticing me to marry you?"

She took another step back, bumping against the counter. "What do you mean?"

"You are a witch. You killed my seed. Like your mother, you've brought a curse to this farm, to my life." With each word, Kensai grew more agitated, his voice hoarser. "My father warned me, but I wouldn't listen."

"Husband, what are you saying? I'm not a witch." He was mad. She'd been right to worry.

"You are a witch. I will cast you out." He raised the hoe and struck.

Sachiko screamed and ducked as the hoe sliced the air only inches from her head. Kensai prepared to strike again. She darted to the door as the hoe came down, digging itself into the wooden countertop. He jerked it free and swung as she ran out the door into the dirt yard. She threw a look over her shoulder to see him crash against the doorjamb in his rush to follow.

Hayoto yelled from the open doorway. "Father! Stop!"

Kensai ignored the boy. He stood in the hard-packed dirt with his feet spread, grasping the hoe with both hands, and swinging it up and down in front of him like a kendōka preparing for a joust.

Sachiko's gaze fixed on her husband. From the corner of her eye she spotted the dog, chained to his post. The dog stopped its routine pacing and cocked its large black head at them.

Kensai lunged at her. She shrieked and darted away, stopping feet from the barn. Panting, she spun and faced him, her mind whirling. This couldn't be happening.

Hayoto sprinted across the yard and grasped his father's arm. Kensai shook him off and lunged at Sachiko.

"Father, stop!" Hayoto grabbed once more for his father's arm. This time, Kensai whirled and swung, just missing Hayoto's head as the boy jumped aside.

The dog yanked its chain taut and barked furiously. The thick hair on its neck bristled.

"Kensai! No!" Sachiko rushed forward, her voice shrill. Kensai spun back to her, slashing. This time he struck a glancing blow to her shoulder and she cried out.

The dog thrashed and barked.

Hayoto dashed to her side yelling. "Father! No! Stop!"

Kensai, paying no heed to Hayoto's pleading, circled them, waving the hoe in front of him. His eyes, wild, darted between mother and son. He squeezed them shut and roared. "You are witches. I will kill you both." He began circling them once again, jabbing the hoe this way and that.

The dog went silent. It took several steps backward before dropping to its haunches. Crouched and tense, it kept its eyes on Kensai, whose ever-tightening circle brought him nearer.

The dog sprang. Its bared teeth inches from Kensai's throat, the chain jerked tight and the dog fell to the ground, momentarily stunned. It scrambled to its feet, crouched, and prepared to spring again.

Kensai turned his fury on the animal, slashing at it with his weapon. The dog let out a scream and fell to the ground. Another blow and it lay silent. Kensai continued to hack the dog's inert body, yelling with each downward thrust.

Sachiko's only thought was for her son. She grabbed his arm and pulled him after her. "Come!"

They ran down the lane, the sounds of Kensai's howls following.

"Quick, into the rice paddy."

They darted over the dike and splashed into the water. The mud sucked at the house slippers Sachiko still wore as she half-pulled and half-pushed Hayoto.

"Over there," she whispered. "Duck down."

Moments later, Kensai splashed in. She lifted her head and peered around a diseased rice plant. The setting sun cast an orange glow on the surreal scene. Kensai moved along a row of rice at the far side of the paddy, flailing with the hoe, knocking over or uprooting the diseased plants, spraying muddy water in every direction.

Sachiko clutched her son's arm as Kensai worked his way down the row. The sound of the hoe grew fainter. With careful steps, hunched over and making as little noise as possible, she and Hayoto retraced their steps, drawing closer to the paddy's edge.

They ducked down, only their heads above the water, when Kensai reached the far end of the paddy and turned toward them again, still slashing to the right and left. When he reached the end of yet another row, he turned and stood motionless. Sachiko dared a quick look. Because of the waning sunlight, she could no longer make out her husband's features, but his head tilted to one side, as though he listened for something. She slipped back into the water, but sensed his eyes, like a poisonous weight, boring into her. Heart pounding, she resisted the urge to jump and run, pulling Hayoto after her. She breathed an audible sigh at the sounds of Kensai's renewed thrashing through the plants.

"We must wait a little longer, until full dark," she whispered. Hayoto looked at her with terror-filled eyes and nodded. Shivering, they remained in the cold water as Kensai moved up and down the rows of rice.

When darkness fell, sudden and complete, Sachiko nudged Hayoto. "Now."They crept to the edge of the paddy, clambered up the side of the dike and rolled over the top, into the lane.

Still hunched over, they scurried down the lane. When they reached the mountain track, the three-quarter moon had broken free of the clouds and cast its pale light over the landscape. Sachiko stopped and straightened. Looking back, she could just make out the dim figure of Kensai, still hacking at rice plants.

Her shoulders sagged in brief relief. "Come, we must hurry before he follows," she said, grasping Hayoto's arm and pulling him up the track, toward Nishimi.

Soon, trees towered above them, their branches swaying. In the shadows, she imagined glowing eyes and feared a wild boar, or even a wolf. People claimed there were no more wolves in Japan. They were supposed to be extinct. But, Sachiko had heard stories since childhood of a lone wolf, spotted in these very woods.

Several times, certain she heard Kensai's stealthy footsteps behind them, she pulled Hayoto off the road to hide behind a tree or a rock. She didn't trust that Kensai would allow them to escape. But when he didn't appear after ten or fifteen minutes, they crept back onto the road and continued making their way upward, until another sound frightened them into hiding.

As the night wore on, the air became colder. Their clothes were still wet from the rice paddy. Chilled through, Sachiko ached to her very core. The wound to her shoulder throbbed. She touched it and she drew her hand away. Blood shone black in the moonlight.

Hayoto's voice shook when he spoke. "Mother, why? Why did my father try to harm us?"

"I don't know, but do not worry. I will keep you safe." She prayed it would be so.

With every step, her shoulder pulsed. They'd stopped to hide so many times, it was nearly sun-up by the time they reached Nishimi and her mother's store. After a moment's hesitation, Sachiko lifted her hand and pounded on the door.

7
NOBUKO
The Gaijin

The neighbor's rooster crowed, and a pinkish glow seeped through the window, shredding the remains of the night. For several minutes, Nobuko lay on her futon thinking of the day ahead. Finally, she rose, reached for her robe, and padded into the store to light the fire in the stove; the approach of fall had brought colder nights.

After returning to her living quarters and lighting the small kerosene space heater there, she pulled on her customary brown mompei, the pants she'd once so hated, a yellow cotton blouse, and a sweater the color of sun-ripened apricots. She screwed her thinning hair into its normal bun and secured it with her favorite tortoise-shell comb.

A loud pounding interrupted her thoughts. She hurried through the store, turned the lock, and, frowning, opened the door.

Her eyes widened. "What in the world?" Before her stood Sachiko and Hayoto, blue-lipped and shivering. She pulled off her sweater and threw it around her grandson's shoulders. "Get over by the stove, both of you."

Eyes cast down, her daughter and grandson followed her directions. Huddled close, they soaked up the stove's warmth.

"You're wet. Has it been raining?" Nobuko peered at Sachiko's shoulder. "And you've been injured. What has happened?"

Sachiko shook her head and reached for Hayoto's hand.

Her daughter's drawn face and Hayoto's mute shivering told Nobuko that whatever their story, it would need to wait. She pulled clothes from the store shelves, and as soon as the two had stopped trembling, ushered them to her living quarters.

When her daughter finally woke up, well past noon, Nobuko took a deep breath, easing the tension that had been building in her all morning. Her grandson slept on, his head buried beneath his blanket.

Sachiko's face softened as she bent to adjust Hayoto's bedding. When she straightened and surveyed the blanket's gentle rise and fall, her eyes filled with pain.

Nobuko touched her daughter's arm and nodded toward the door. "Come," she said in a low voice, and led the way from her living quarters to the store.

Earlier, she had placed a sign in the window announcing the store closed for the day. The blinds still down, soft shadows fell across shelves and tables of goods. She waved Sachiko to one of the chairs next to the stove and took the other. "Now you must speak. You must tell me everything that has happened." She glanced at her daughter's bandaged shoulder. "Everything."

Sachiko stared down at her clasped hands. "It's Kensai. He tried to kill us."

Nobuko gasped.

"Mother, I think his father's death deranged him. With the rice crop failing…it must have been too much."

"But…." Nobuko shook her head. "I can't believe he actually meant to harm you."

"I tried to tell you." Despite the hint of accusation in Sachiko's voice, her red-rimmed eyes held only confusion. "He accused me…he said I put a curse on his seed so our babies wouldn't live. He was in such a wild rage…I had to take Hayoto and flee."

Her daughter's unspoken allegation held truth—some of this was Nobuko's fault. "I should have told you long ago the real reason I didn't favor your marriage to Kensai. I worried even then that Toshio's oddness might become his son's. You were so insistent, though." With her eyes, she pleaded for her daughter's understanding and forgiveness.

Sachiko remained silent for some moments, her gaze once again fixed on her clasped hands. "What is so dreadful is that Hayoto has been forced to become part of all this, of everything that has happened."

Nobuko longed to tell her daughter Hayoto would soon forget what had happened. Instead, she tried to lace her words with hope. "You are right to worry about him, but he is bright and healthy and perhaps, as time passes and he becomes older, the memory will fade." She spoke the words along with a silent prayer they might, at least in part, be true.

Sachiko stared at her. "You think he could forget his father tried to murder us both?" Her voice dropped to a whisper. "Mother, he saw…he saw Kensai kill our dog, hacking the poor creature into pieces."

Nobuko grimaced.

Noises came from the living quarters behind them. Sachiko glanced toward the door. "He is awake. Mother, I don't know what to do. Where can we go so that my son will be safe?"

"You will stay here."

"But will we be safe?"

Nobuko took Sachiko's clenched hand. "Daughter, I learned long ago there is always danger. You'll be as safe in Nishimi as anywhere."

Nobuko pushed a tree branch aside as she followed her usual path through the woods. Three days had passed since the morning she discovered her daughter and grandson, cold, wet and shivering, on her doorstep.

If only she could turn the clock back to a time before the banks collapsed and the whole country went into a tailspin. To a time before a foolish Kazuhiro Yoshida decided to seek help from the yakuza and Akira Katsuragawa was accused of his murder. A time before Toshio Hara died and Kensai went mad. Nishimi had been a peaceful place then, or so she had allowed herself to believe.

In truth, there had always been strife in the village. Even when she'd first come to Nishimi, all those years ago. Most of the village men were gone, conscripted, and sent to fight a war in China that later spread to war with the United States and Great Britain. The earthquake that took the lives of so many village children. She had only to close her eyes to see the small, still bodies lying in the dirt.

After the war, everyone suffered. Toshio wasn't the only one affected by what he experienced—few young men returned unchanged. The Moris' son came home with an infection that eventually caused him to lose his foot and part of his leg. Mrs. Nito's husband and the Ishis' son didn't come home at all. Yoko Yoshida's husband returned even meaner than he'd been before he left, terrorizing the village children right up to the day of his mysterious disappearance. Years passed before the village and the country recovered from those bad times.

She stopped to rest on a fallen tree, drifts of dried leaves piled beneath it. At least she'd had Masato. A smile played over her lips. Her husband's good humor and loving ways had soothed away the hurt she'd felt when many of the villagers continued to rebuff her, continued to claim she brought bad luck. He'd stood between her and his mother, who grew more difficult as she aged. Few husbands would have been so loyal and protective.

A twig snapped and her daughter appeared before her on the path, a sliver of sunlight dappling her face.

"Mother, here you are."

Nobuko shifted slightly and patted the place beside her on the log.

Sachiko eased down. "You've been gone so long, I thought you might have fallen or something."

"I like coming here, especially in the mornings. I find it peaceful to sit and contemplate the world." Nobuko pointed to the maple trees. "Look, the leaves are turning as red as scalded lobsters. And the oak trees—they wear their golden crowns well."

Sachiko looked up, nodding. "Very pretty."

"You used to spend hours in the woods, you and Kazuhiro."

"Yes," said Sachiko.

"What happened, daughter? What happened between the two of you? You were such good friends. Your father and I thought one day you would marry."

Sachiko frowned. "For one thing, I went away to university. Then I had a job I liked in Sakayama. Besides, you know his mother wouldn't have allowed it."

"You gave up your job readily enough when you married Kensai. And if she'd been given enough money, Yoko would have agreed to anything. We both know that. No, it was something else."

Sachiko rose. "Let's go back. It's chilly this morning and I don't like leaving Hayoto by himself."

Nobuko rose, instantly contrite. "I shouldn't have tarried so long."

Sachiko took her arm. With hastened steps, they climbed the path, passing the pottery factory, where apprentices were loading the old earthen kiln for its first firing in two decades. They continued their hurried progress along the road to the store.

As they stepped onto the porch, Nobuko paused, a little out of breath. She waved her hand in the direction of the store. "One day this will be yours and Hayoto's."

Sachiko nodded.

The bell above the door jangled as Nobuko pushed it open. She froze. In the middle of the room Kensai stood, one arm around Hayoto, pinning the boy's body to him. With his other hand, he held a long knife to her grandson's throat.

Behind her, Sachiko screamed. Released from her spellbound state, Nobuko grabbed at her daughter, using her body to block Sachiko from rushing forward.

Kensai tightened his hold on Hayoto. "Stand back! Stand back or I'll kill him."

"Let him go! Take me, my husband, take me instead!" Sachiko said, again trying to push past Nobuko.

Hayoto struggled against Kensai's hold. "Keep still," Kensai said and jerked the boy backward. Hayoto stopped struggling, but his eyes remained wild and fearful.

Sachiko continued to plead. "Please, husband. Take me. I beg of you."

"No. Stay where you are. Go get the old lady from the pottery factory," he said to Nobuko. "Bring me Kazuhiro Yoshida's mother."

Nobuko stared at him. "Why? Why do you want Yoko?"

"Go get her. Now."

Sachiko took a hesitant step forward, her hand outstretched. "Hayoto!"

Kensai's eyes glittered. "One step closer and I will kill him." Sachiko stiffened and stopped.

Nobuko hurried out the door, throwing a fearful glance over her shoulder.

It took less than a minute to reach the pottery factory. Heart racing, she ran inside to find Yoko talking to the sensei.

Yoko scowled at her. "What do you want? Can't you see I'm busy? Why do you burst in this way?"

Nobuko ignored the coldness in Yoko's voice. "You must come. It's Kensai Hara. My son-in-law has gone crazy. He's holding a knife to my grandson's throat. He ordered me to get you. I don't know why, but you must come, quickly."

"What are you talking about?" Yoko gaped at her. "What sort of trick is this? I'm not going anywhere with you."

Nobuko filled with even more panic. "You must. Sensei, tell her."

"We will both come." The sensei straightened his shoulders and took Yoko's arm. "Let us find out what has happened." Despite his age, the sensei's grip remained strong enough to force Yoko to walk with him.

No one spoke as Nobuko led the way back up the hill to the store. The door stood ajar. For an instant, she hesitated, terrified of what they might find inside. But everyone stood just as she'd left them, Kensai and Hayoto in the middle of the room, near the stove, Sachiko just inside the door. Her daughter wheeled when they entered, her eyes pleading and desperate. Hayoto, though several inches taller than his father, was limp and unresisting. Kensai held the boy upright.

"I have brought her, Kensai."

"And the sensei as well. Perfect. It is fitting that he is here to witness. Lock the door. Leave the shade down."

With shaking hands, Nobuko followed her son-in-law's instructions.

"What are you doing, Kensai?" The sensei spoke in a calming voice. "Why do you want us here? Why are you threatening to harm your own child?"

"He's not mine. He's the spawn of her devil son." Kensai nodded to Yoko, whose mouth fell open in shock.

"No!" Sachiko shouted. "Kensai, that is not true. I swear it."

Kensai gave her a scornful look. "I don't believe you. But it makes no difference. It is just one of the reasons he had to die."

"Who had to die?" The sensei's voice remained calm.

Nobuko's questioning gaze flew from the sensei to Kensai.

"Kazuhiro, of course," Kensai said.

"You?" Yoko hissed. "You did that awful thing to my son?" Her hands reached out like talons as she lunged at Kensai. Once more the sensei grasped her arm, tightening his hold as she fought to break free.

Nobuko edged closer to Sachiko and took her daughter's hand, icy and trembling, into her own.

In a flat voice, Kensai answered. "For retribution."

"Retribution?" Yoko spat. "Retribution for what?"

"The bridge, and what his father did to my father."

The sensei paled and closed his eyes. "The bridge—of course."

Nobuko stared at her son-in-law. Her heart beat so fast, she could scarcely breathe. "What are you both talking about? This is all craziness. Kensai please let Hayoto go. He's done nothing. He loves you."

Kensai ignored her, his eyes on Yoko. "Takeda Yoshida, your husband, ruined my father's life. He was the cause of my father's great shame—capture by the enemy. For two years, the Australians held him prisoner, forced him to labor among spirit people, their black faces painted white. All my father's problems after the war, his sickness, our struggles on the farm—everything that happened is because of Takeda Yoshida and what he did. His evil spirit even ruined our rice crop. It is fitting that his son should die by my hand."

Yoko glared. "Whatever Takeda did is nothing to do with me and had nothing to do with Kazuhiro." Her mouth twisted as though she'd tasted something bitter, making clear she hated her missing husband more than ever.

As if she hadn't spoken, Kensai stared at the sensei. "You were there. My father saw you from across the gorge. You did nothing to stop Takeda from blowing up the bridge."

The sensei, still gripping Yoko's arm, reached his other hand toward Kensai. "I'm sorry. I was as shocked as your father when the bridge fell. I didn't know what Takeda planned."

Kensai shook his head. "That is no excuse. You were the leader, the lieutenant. You should have stopped him. That's why I used your sword to kill Kazuhiro—it was easy to enter your house and steal it. I'd hoped the police would think you'd done it, but when they accused your son, hauled a noble Katsuragawa off to jail, it was almost as satisfying. They were quick to believe my story of Akira's hatred for Kazuhiro." Kensai's lips curled into a lop-sided grin. "Now it has come full circle."

Nobuko had heard enough. "What do you want of Sachiko, Hayoto and me? We weren't there. We had nothing to do with what happened to Toshio in the war."

"That's right," Kensai said, finally turning his attention to her. "You weren't there. You were on our farm, taking my mother's place. I remember you very clearly. My father explained how you used your witch's tricks to suck the life from my mother. I didn't believe him. Not then. Now, I do. She's one, too," he said, nodding to Sachiko. "So, don't you agree this is perfect? Except for the sensei's jailed son, we're all together now. Only the dead are missing."

The sensei dropped Yoko's arm. "So now that you have us here, Kensai, what do you plan to do?"

"This," Kensai said. He shoved Hayoto aside, and in a single motion, brought the knife down and plunged it into his own belly, wrenching it upward as it entered.

Yoko reared backward. Her mouth opened, but no sound came out.

Eyes wide with horror, Nobuko clutched her arms over her stomach as her son-in-law slowly dropped to his knees. He fell forward, onto the knife's hilt, driving it deeper into his body.

Sachiko darted forward. "Kensai!" She dropped to her knees beside her husband's prone figure.

"Father!" Nobuko grabbed for Hayoto, but her grandson threw her off, rushed forward and fell to his knees beside his mother. "Father," he said again, this time in a whisper.

The sensei knelt and held a trembling finger to Kensai's throat. He shook his head and rose wearily to his feet.

Unable to move, Nobuko stared at the widening pool of blood seeping into the narrow cracks in the wood-planked floor.

Kensai's body was taken away, leaving only the blood-soaked floor as evidence of what had transpired. The police questioned everyone. When they finally left, the sensei went with them, to fetch his son from jail. The doctor Nobuko called arrived from Sakayama. He examined Hayoto and gave the boy a sedative, telling Sachiko it would likely cause him to sleep for the next twelve hours or more.

For some reason, even though the police had finished questioning her, Yoko lingered. Now she stood near the door, her arms crossed in front of her, her expression odd. "He was right about Kazuhiro being the boy's father."

Sachiko wearily lowered herself onto a chair before answering. "No."

Yoko scoffed. "Nonsense. You have but to look at the boy—his height, his looks—they are all Kazuhiro's. With those splayed teeth and jug ears, it is inconceivable Kensai Hara produced the seed that led to that boy's birth."

Silent, Sachiko shook her head.

Nobuko gazed from one to the other, her brows knitted in a frown. Could such a thing be possible?

Yoko, like a dog with its teeth around a rabbit's neck, wouldn't let go. "I have no doubt he is my grandson. Eiichi isn't working out and I'm sure his brother will be just as worthless to me. Hayoto still has some growing to do, but with those wide shoulders, he will become a great potter."

"No." Sachiko surged to her feet. She shook her head with sudden force, and her voice filled with suppressed anger. "I promise you, Yoko. He is not your grandson."

Yoko reached for the door, opened it, and turned once more to Sachiko. "I don't believe you."

Sachiko glared back. "Believe me or not, it's true."

"Bah!" Yoko said and stalked out. The door slammed behind her.

Nobuko hesitated before she spoke. "I don't mean to doubt your word, daughter. Especially not now, after all that has happened this day. But Yoko is right—Hayoto does have Kazuhiro's look about him."

Sachiko dropped back into the chair. Her shoulders fell. The flush of anger faded from her cheeks. "He is not Kazuhiro's son. He is Kazuhiro's brother."

Nobuko stared, not wanting to believe her ears. "Sachiko! What are you saying?"

Sachiko's lips tightened. She answered in a dull voice. "I'm saying that seventeen years ago, Takeda Yoshida raped me."

The blood drained from Nobuko's cheeks. She thought of Mrs. Mori's long ago warnings about Takeda, how she should take extra precautions around him. She cursed herself for not protecting her daughter. "Why didn't you tell me?"

Sachiko closed her eyes. "I was too ashamed."

"Oh, Sachiko. My dear child." She sank down on the chair next to her daughter's and reached for her hand. "Tell me now. Tell me how this terrible thing happened."

Sachiko drew a trembling breath, remembering.

The bus wound its way up the mountain to Nishimi. Sachiko gazed out the window. Instead of seeing rice paddies or fields of millet, she pictured herself in a bridal kimono, like the one she'd seen in a shop window in Sakayama. Kazuhiro stood tall and handsome at her side, a black kimono over his formal, wide-legged black and white-striped hakima. She drew a deep breath and let it out slowly. She could hardly wait for their wedding day, followed by their wedding night. At that thought, her cheeks reddened. She glanced around to see if another passenger watched and could read her thoughts.

Maybe this weekend Kazuhiro would think the time had come for them to make their announcement. She hoped Nobuko would greet the news with happiness. Surely her mother already knew—she and Kazuhiro had been soulmates since childhood.

Surprised not to see him waiting for her when she got off the bus, she spent the evening telling Nobuko of her job, the movies she'd seen with friends, how Mimi was faring— her mother's cousin, a nurse, was divorced and worked in a hospital, raising her two children on her own. "I'm sure the little I pay in rent is useful to her, but she always tries to return it, saying it isn't necessary."

Nobuko chuckled. "Mimi has always had a mind of her own. Just like you and your friends, she and I used to go to the movies together. Merle Oberon and Cary Grant...they were our favorites. We tried never to miss a movie one of them starred in." She laughed again and patted the back of her head. "I once tried to style my hair like Merle Oberon's, but it refused to wave and curl. Alas, it is no longer black and shiny like hers, either."

Sachiko admonished her. "Your hair is beautiful, all silver and gray. I like the way you coil it into a figure-eight at the back of your head. Like a geisha's."

Nobuko preened a moment and smiled, appearing pleased with her daughter's compliment.

The following morning, Sachiko helped in the store— rearranging displays of cosmetics, refolding and restacking linens, towels, and other soft goods, restocking shelves—the same things she'd done as a teenager. She also kept glancing toward the door. But each time it opened and the bell above it jingled, instead of the one she longed to see, one of her mother's customers entered, market basket in hand. *Why doesn't he come? He knew I would be home this weekend.* When they saw her, the women stopped and chatted endlessly, then took forever to make their selections, pay for them and leave.

Finally, after she'd all but given up, Kazuhiro arrived, looking harried. "We have a large order from a new department store. I must see to it. Everyone is working hard to complete it in record time, hoping for the store's continued business."

After only a few minutes, he said he needed to return to the factory. Sachiko lowered her head, not wanting him to see the tears pooling in her eyes. Work came first and always would, even after they were married. "I understand." She looked up in time to see him hurry out the door, the bell jingling in his wake.

Had something happened since her last visit to Nishimi? Had Kazuhiro met someone else? She tried to force away the tension coiling in her neck and shoulders, not wanting to believe his distraction was anything but what he said—a big order from a new customer.

Outside, the sun shone. It was a fine spring day. She would go for a walk—she couldn't be sad in the woods. Especially in spring, with the dogwood in bloom, the maple trees shooting out nubs of young leaves.

"I'll be back in an hour or two," she called to her mother. Nobuko nodded without looking up from her ledger.

The path she followed was one she and Kazuhiro had often taken as children, pretending to be Indians, searching through the moldering leaves and pine needles for deer tracks or rabbit holes or signs of other woodland creatures.

Remembering those carefree days, her spirits lifted. She broke off a dogwood blossom, less fragile than it looked, and tucked it behind her ear. It had been months since she'd been completely alone. Though not as crowded as Tokyo, plenty of people filled Sakayama's sidewalks and stores. When she wasn't at work, she was generally with one of her friends or on a bus. She drew a deep breath. Unlike the clean mountain air in Nishimi, the air in the city was filled with the fumes of trucks, buses, and cars.

A sparrow lit on a nearby tree branch, its head cocked. Something rustled in the brush, followed by what sounded like furtive footsteps. Sachiko grinned. Kazuhiro. He must have decided to forsake work after all. They'd often played this game—him jumping out from behind a tree to frighten her, followed by a laughing game of hide and seek. She chuckled and ran down the path.

She rounded a large granite outcropping and skidded to a stop. Takeda Yoshida. His eyes glinted and his mouth twisted in an evil grin. Heart beating wildly, Sachiko turned and scrambled back the way she'd come.

Takeda was old, but he was big, his legs and arms long. She'd gotten no more than a few yards when he grabbed her shoulder and spun her around. She screamed.

Takeda clapped his hand across her mouth. He threw her to the spongy ground and ripped at the waistband of her slacks, one hand still covering her mouth. Her panties came down. Frantic, she tried to pull them back up, but he batted her hand away then grabbed her arm and twisted it above her head.

It felt as though she was being split in two. She reared and bucked. Her frenzied movements seemed to excite him further. Instinct stilled her. When he finished thrusting, he climbed off her.

She rolled to her side and vomited, then moaned and curled into a fetal position. She had no idea how much time passed. When she finally pushed herself into a sitting position, Takeda was gone. The crushed dogwood blossom lay on the ground.

The buttons of her trousers were gone, but she did the best she could, tucking the waistband into the elastic of her panties. She pulled her blouse down, straightening it to cover the bite marks. She stumbled farther down the path, finally coming out of the woods near the elementary school.

Which way should she go? Down the track, to where, she didn't know, or back up the mountain to Nishimi? But then what would she say to her mother? She couldn't tell Nobuko what Takeda had done. She couldn't tell anyone.

Still undecided, she looked down the track once more and spotted Kensai Hara walking toward her.

Nobuko didn't want to hear more. "Daughter, I—"

"I told Kensai I'd fallen. He escorted me home. You were talking with a customer and didn't see me. I tried to wash everything Takeda had done off me, scrubbing until my skin turned raw. Then I burned my clothes. The next day, I went back to Sakayama. I just wanted to forget. Only later did I worry I could be pregnant. It wasn't long before I knew."

Nobuko's throat filled with pain, her eyes with unshed tears. How could she not have known, never suspected? "Did you tell Kazuhiro?"

Sachiko nodded, twisting the wedding band on her finger. "I thought if Yoko believed the child Kazuhiro's, she wouldn't object to our marriage."

"What did he say?" Blood pounded in Nobuko's ears.

"He was furious." Sachiko straightened her shoulders and lifted her chin, her eyes gone cold. "He said we could never marry, that he could never bring himself to touch me. He said I was 'used goods.'"

The blood pounded even harder in Nobuko's ears, at her temples, as rage filled her. "How dared he? And Takeda—Takeda was simply allowed to get away with what he did to you?"

Sachiko bent her head. "Takeda disappeared soon after," she whispered.

Nobuko sank back in her chair, the fury of a moment before replaced by a cold premonition. Was there another body yet to be discovered? She took a shaky breath. For a while, neither woman spoke.

"I feared Kensai would kill Hayoto," Sachiko finally said. "Maybe at the last minute he remembered the infant who fell asleep in his arms, or the young boy who shadowed his every move. He was a good father once, and not a bad husband." She paused. "Although he never said so, he had to know I was pregnant when we married. I wanted to give him another child, a child truly his. I felt I owed it to him."

Nobuko didn't think her daughter had owed Kensai Hara anything, but she kept that thought to herself. "Will you tell Hayoto?"

"One day. It's only right that he knows."

"What about Yoko?"

"Maybe. If I do, it will be Hayoto's decision."

Nobuko had another thought. "Perhaps my grandson would like to become a potter."

"Or a shopkeeper or a farmer. Or maybe none of those things. Maybe he will want to go away to university. I hope so."

For the first time since entering the store that morning to find Kensai holding her grandson hostage, Nobuko smiled. "It's good to have choices."

Sachiko nodded.

"But, what of you, daughter? What will you do now?"

Sachiko sighed and rose from her chair. "Hayoto and I must return to the farm and drain the rice paddy. We'll have to burn the rice to keep the blight from spreading. And we need to see to the ox—I hope Kensai turned it out, though who knows."

"And then?"

"I don't know, Mother. I can't think that far ahead right now. Stay at the farm, I suppose, at least until winter sets in. It can be a peaceful place. Maybe Hayoto and I can make it so again."

Nobuko nodded, remembering a little boy chasing butterflies.

8
THE SENSEI
Hirotaka

It took longer than the sensei expected to arrange for his son's release; no one wanted to take responsibility, even for a man proven innocent. Finally, the papers were signed. A short time later, he and Akira sat in the back of the last Nishimi-bound bus, surrounded by empty seats.

In a quiet voice, he told his son what occurred that morning. Then he tried to explain what happened all those years ago on New Guinea. Once again, he pictured the gorge and the bridge, the long line of men trailing across it. He could almost feel the unrelenting rain against his skin, smell the rotting vegetation and see the churning river far below. In dreams, he still heard the screams echoing off the sides of the gorge as men spiraled like starfish to their deaths.

Eyes intent, Akira listened until the sensei had finished. "You're telling me Kazuhiro died because of something his father did more than fifty years ago to Kensai's father?"

The sensei nodded. "The noise from that falling bridge still echoes."

The bus engine labored and the driver downshifted.

Akira looked out the window for a few minutes before responding. "How could Toshio have been so sure Takeda set off the charges?"

"The gorge was narrow enough at that point to easily see across. I have no doubt he saw Takeda push the plunger that set off the explosive charge."

Just as, moments later, he had clearly seen Toshio Hara's face and the looks of dismay on the faces of the other men staring across the gap separating them. In his heart, he knew Kensai Hara had been right. He should have stopped Takeda at the bridge. He should have been a better leader to his men. For all the years since that long-ago day, he'd felt the burden of his failure.

He put his hand on his son's arm. "I wanted to explain to Toshio that I hadn't know what Takeda was about to do. Since he avoided the village, I journeyed to his farm, but Toshio wouldn't hear me. Every year I made the journey, hoping he would relent."

He fell silent, recalling the long descent into the valley and partway up the other side to the Hara's isolated farm. The first few years, he'd been filled with hope and determination, only to be turned away by Kensai, no doubt at his father's orders. Over the years, it became little more than an annual ritual, a hopeless pilgrimage.

"After he died, I wrote a letter, apologizing for my weakness. I put it in his casket, hoping in the afterlife he would be more willing to forgive."

"Father, you were young, hardly more than a boy. And sick. You can't blame yourself for what Takeda Yoshida did. He was an evil man."

"You are right," the sensei said with a sigh. "Takeda was evil. Now he is gone, as is Kazuhiro, his son."

"So too are his victims—Kensai as much a victim as Toshio."

The sensei nodded.

"And we are here," his son said.

"Yes. We are here."

The sensei leaned back in his seat. He was the last of Nishimi's New Guinea survivors. First Masato died of liver failure and then Takeda had disappeared. Next it was Toshio. They were all gone. Soon it would be his turn. Kensai had been right. There was a kind of symmetry to it.

The two men sat in silence as the bus wound the rest of the way up the mountain to Nishimi, each lost in his own thoughts. When the bus came to a stop, Akira stepped down first and then held out his hand.

Happy to accept assistance, the sensei took the proffered hand and climbed down. After the bus rumbled away, his eyes were drawn to the light glowing from a window near the back of Nobuko Abi's store. They were still awake. His gaze then slid past the darkened bulk of the pottery factory to find Yoko's small house. A light glowed there, too.

Akira tugged at his arm. "Come, Father."

Too weary to protest, the sensei followed his son up the steep track. Several times he had to stop and regain his breath. He waved Akira to go on, but each time, Akira waited. They finally passed beneath the vine-covered remnants of the old gate, their footsteps sounding in the gravel path leading to the house.

"Go on." the sensei said when they came to the door.

Akira slid it open. He took one step inside and halted.

Over his son's shoulder, the sensei spotted Hiromi, her eyes wide and bright. Beside her stood Chieko, holding their grandson's hand. Not a breath or a hair stirred.

Then Akira, his face flushed, made a deep, formal bow to his wife.

Their small daughter in her arms, Hiromi silently returned the bow.

Next, Akira bowed to his mother. When he straightened, Kotada pulled loose from his grandmother's hand and propelled himself at his father.

Akira sank to his knees and embraced his son.

The restraint that had held them all back broke, and the small house filled with joyous noise.

On a brilliant fall morning two weeks later, the sensei watched Akira and Hiromi bustle out the door, in a hurry to catch the bus to Sakayama. Although Akira's suit hung from his shoulders, he had lost the terrible pallor he'd brought home from jail. The night before, a defiant gleam in his eye, his son had announced he would go to the Farmers' Credit Union.

"If they haven't filled the position, I will convince them they must take me on," he'd said. "If they refuse or have already hired someone, I will find a position elsewhere." The new-found confidence in his son's posture and in his voice pleased the sensei.

Kotada, dressed in his gray school uniform and carrying his book bag, rushed out of the house moments after his parents left, trailing goodbyes over his shoulder just as Akira had once done.

The sensei smiled in remembrance while allowing his wife to help him with his jacket. He pulled his beret from the jacket's pocket, set it on his head and wound a scarf around his neck. He glanced toward his granddaughter, asleep in her crib, then back at his wife. "I will see you this evening," he said, and stepped onto the sunlit gravel path.

As he passed through the gate and made his way down the track to Nishimi and the pottery factory, his thoughts went once again to Nobuko and her family. Sachiko and Hayoto had gone back to the farm. He wondered if they planned to stay there or if they would return to live with Nobuko. The village would help them recover, but it would take time.

He smiled, remembering Yoko's look of consternation several days earlier. She'd been forced to admit defeat and send her grandson, Eiichi, home to his mother in Sakayama. The boy had been cut from a different cloth than his father; he would never be happy as a potter. Poor Kazuhiro. Perhaps it was as well he hadn't lived to know that sad truth.

The sensei put worrisome thoughts aside and looked about.

Leaves had fallen from most of the trees—only a few still clung to twigs. A small brown warbler flitted from one bared branch to another.

Farther on, he passed a rice paddy. The tall stocks waved in the gentle breeze, their beads of grain rattling together, glowing golden in the sun. It would soon be time to harvest. A lone black-tailed kite circled overhead in the crystal blue sky.

The sensei quickened his pace. What waited in the drying room for him to paint?

About the Author
TONI MORGAN

Toni came home to Oregon from a summer as an exchange student in Denmark knowing two things: she loved history, and she loved traveling and meeting new people. Her parents collected early-American antiques. By their measure, anything over 75 years of age qualified. The house of Toni's host family in Denmark was 400-years-old, and the church where her host-father preached was 800-years-old. She saw where battles had been fought and where Danes had lived ten centuries before she was born. It was a revelation. Her writing career began with that trip, keeping the editor of her hometown paper apprised of all she saw. A former NYT editor, he convinced her that she should continue writing. Although a west-coaster by birth, marriage, and preference, Toni has lived in many places, including nearly four years in Japan. That rich experience led her to write *Echoes from a Falling Bridge*, *Harvest the Wind* and *Lotus Blossom Unfurling*.
(http://authortonimorgan.com)

www.ingramcontent.com/pod-product-compliance
Lightning Source LLC
Chambersburg PA
CBHW051212120726
47905CB00004B/1089